ON THE J

GREAT THINKERS

ON THE JOHN UNIVERSITY™

GREAT THINKERS

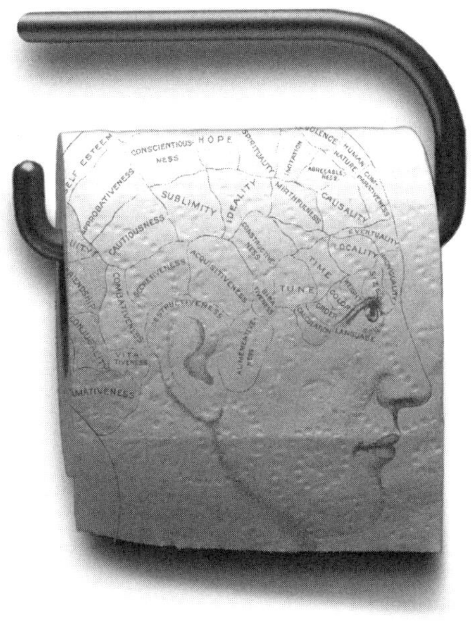

SWEETWATER
PRESS

SWEETWATER
PRESS

On the John University: Great Thinkers

Copyright © 2008 Sweetwater Press

Produced by arrangement with Cliff Road Books

ISBN-13: 978-1-58173-740-0

Book design by Miles G. Parsons
Cover design by Ford Wiles
Contributors: Locke Peterseim, Megan Roth, Russ Mitchell, Stephanie Doyle, Matt Ray, and Adeline Black

Printed in the U.S.

HERODOTUS: FATHER OF HISTORY

Herodotus liked to find out what happened in the past so that what people did would be remembered later. This so-called "father of history" was himself historic, born around 485 BC in Turkey, in a Greek town called Halicarnassus.

Herodotus was skilled at writing detailed, lengthy accounts of his encounters with peoples and places as he traveled the lands around the Eastern Mediterranean. But the historian is most well-known for writing *The Histories,* a record of his examinations into what started the war between the Persians and the Greeks—a war that began when he was a child. The actual original title of the book, *Historie,* means "inquiry" in Latin. The book traces the growth of the Persian empire and highlights the pivotal event of the Battle of Marathon, where the Persians were defeated by the Greeks. Herodotus grew up reading the works of Homer as a boy, and in many ways, *The Histories* has a Homeric epic feel (in other words, it was a really long book). Editors eventually divided *The Histories* into nine books (named after the Muses).

How accurate his recordings were, however, has often been debated. His other nickname: "father of lies" or perhaps more researcher and storyteller than historian. But give him credit for traveling the world in search of new information. Herodotus always thought the Greeks could learn more from others, and he often wrote about the other cultures he visited, such as the Egyptians and Scythians. But he did also write about places he'd never been, including Africa.

A Tenth-Century Reading List

Beowulf (circa 1100)
Shahnama by Ferdowsi
Waltharius (circa 920)

Marie Curie

- Her Prizes: Nobel Prize in Physics (1903); Davy Medal (1903); Matteucci Medal (1904); and Nobel Prize in Chemistry (1911).

- In 1995, she was the first and only woman laid to rest under the famous dome of the Pantheon in Paris, on her own merits, next to her husband.

- Greer Garson and Walter Pidgeon starred in the 1943 U.S. Oscar-nominated film, *Madame Curie*, based on her life. "Marie Curie" also is the name of a character in a 1988 comedy, *Young Einstein*, by Yahoo Serious.

- Three radioactive minerals are named after Marie and her husband Pierre Curie: curite, sklodowskite, and cuprosklodowskite.

- Pierre and Marie Curie University, the largest science, technology and medicine university in France (and also the successor institution to the faculty of science at the University of Paris) is the school where Marie Curie taught and is named in honor of her and Pierre. The university is home to the laboratory where the couple discovered radium.

- Marie Curie M.S. 158 is another school named for her. The school is located in Bayside, New York, and like Curie Metropolitan High School, located in the community area of Archer Heights on Chicago's Southwest Side, it also specializes in science and technology.

- In 2007, the Pierre Curie Paris MÈtro station was renamed the "Pierre et Marie Curie" station.

- When Marie was young, her sister Zofia died from typhus and, two years later, her mother passed away from tuberculosis. These tragedies caused her to part from her Roman Catholic religion and become an agnostic.

- At the University of Paris, she studied mathematics, physics and chemistry. In early 1893 she graduated first in her class. A year later, she earned her master's degree in mathematics. In 1903, she received her DSc, also from the University of Paris, becoming the first woman in France to complete a doctorate. Later, in 1909, Marie became that school's first female professor.

THE OTHER CURIES

Pierre Curie

French-born Pierre Curie received his licenciateship in physics in 1878 and his Ph.D. in 1895 at the Sorbonne. He worked as faculty at the Sorbonne for his entire career.

His early interest was in crystallography. Together with his brother Jacques, Pierre discovered piezoelectric effects. Later, he turned his attention to magnetism, where he showed that the magnetic properties of a given substance change at a certain temperature—this temperature is now known as the Curie point.

After marrying Marie, Pierre began helping with her study of radioactive substances. Their work formed the basis for research in nuclear physics and chemistry. Pierre Curie was killed in a carriage accident in Paris in 1906.

Irène Joliot-Curie

Irène Curie, the oldest daughter of Pierre and Marie Curie, was born in Paris in 1897. She studied at the Faculty of Science in Paris and served as a nurse radiographer during World War I. She received her Ph.D. in science in 1925. A year later, she married fellow scientist Frédéric Joliot.

Throughout her career, Irène researched natural and artificial radioactivity, transmutation of elements, and nuclear physics.

Together, she and Frédéric were awarded the Nobel Prize in chemistry in 1935 for their work with the synthesis of new radioactive elements. The next year, Irène was appointed Undersecretary of State for Scientific Research.

In 1946, Irène became director of the Radium Institute. She took part in the creation and construction of the first French atomic pile in 1948. She was also instrumental in the establishment of the center for nuclear physics at Orsay.

In addition to science, Irène promoted the social and intellectual advancement of women. She was a member of the Comité National de l'Union des Femmes Françaises and of the World Peace Council.

Frédéric and Irène had two children. Irène Joliot-Curie died in Paris in 1956.

Jean-Frédéric Joliot

As assistant to Marie Curie, Jean Frédéric Joliot not only studied science but also found his wife, Marie's daughter Irène. Frédéric was born in 1900, in Paris, where he attended the Ecole de Physique et Chimie. In 1925, he joined the Radium Institute as assistant to Marie Curie. He received his Ph.D. in 1930.

While serving as a lecturer in the Paris Faculty of Science, Frédéric joined Irène in studying the structure of the atom. Together, they also discovered artificial radioactivity, perhaps their most important work. They produced the isotope 13 of nitrogen, the isotope 30 of phosphorus, and, simultaneously, the isotopes 27 of silicon and 28 of aluminum. For this significant work, the couple received the Nobel Prize for chemistry in 1935.

In 1937, he became a professor at the Collège de France and left the Radium Institute. For his new laboratory, he commissioned the construction of the first cyclotron in Western Europe.

Frédéric also took an active part in political affairs and served as president of the World Peace Council for a time. When Irène died in 1956, he assumed her position as Chair of Nuclear Physics at the Sorbonne, while retaining his professorship at the Collège de France. He died two years later.

EXTRA CREDIT: On a humanitarian note, Pierre and Marie's second daughter, Eve, married American diplomat H. R. Labouisse who became director of the United Children's Fund and received on its behalf the Nobel Peace Prize in 1965.

PHILIP JOHNSON: ARCHITECT

You've heard the proverb that "people who live in glass houses shouldn't throw stones." Well, it was made famous for generations in many languages, but it was Philip Johnson who actually lived it. His house was made of glass, and he was known to throw a stone or two.

Johnson is credited for bringing the art of architecture to the American public. A Harvard-educated historian with roots in Greek culture, Johnson fell in love with architecture during a visit to the Parthenon and other historical monuments.

He studied the art form and produced shows of great work for the Museum of Modern Art (MoMA) in New York. Even his presentations—and his writings about those shows—became controversial. Not everyone agreed with what he had to say, and some, such as Frank Lloyd Wright, even boycotted his shows. But following World War II, which he endured as a war correspondent of some measure, Johnson returned to Harvard and actually studied his beloved art.

He is credited with designing dozens of renowned buildings, but it was his own home in New Cannan, Connecticut, that brings the irony. It is a house of glass and steel, built with nature as its walls. It drew great praise for its unique and minimalist style.

Johnson died in 2005, but his glass home remains open to the public as a historical treasure, and a model of it is on display at MoMA.

Five of Johnson's Most Famous Works

1. The Seagram Building, New York
2. Four Seasons Restaurant, New York
3. Amon Carter Museum, Fort Worth, Texas
4. John F. Kennedy Plaza, Dallas, Texas
5. IDS Center, Minneapolis, Minnesota

AMERICAN LITERATURE
WILLIAM FAULKNER

William Faulkner (1897–1962) was one of the greatest and most influential American writers of all time. He is primarily known for his novels, although he also wrote short stories and screenplays. He is considered a "Southern writer" with the tone of his work often being dark or Gothic.

Faulkner was born and raised in Mississippi. Most of his novels are set in the fictional Mississippi county of Yoknapatawpha. Faulkner created the county, including drawing maps of its geography, and often had the characters of different novels interact in Yoknapatawpha. For instance, in his novel *Absalom! Absalom!* (1936) one of the characters references the flood that shapes the story of his earlier novel *As I Lay Dying* (1930).

Faulkner's writing is convoluted and complicated. His stories generally come in pieces that the reader must gain one at a time throughout the entirety of the novel, such that the story is often incoherent and not understood until the book is completely finished. His writing is also dense and full of heavy description; many words are modified with four or five adjectives. Despite its difficulty, the brilliance of his writing continues to draw readers.

- Faulkner suffered with a drinking problem throughout his life.
- He was an obsessive liar and well known for it in his hometown of Oxford, Mississippi.
- He wore a soldier's uniform and walked around downtown Oxford after World War II, claiming to have fought in the war, even though everyone knew this was untrue.
- He won the Nobel Prize for Literature, two Pulitzer Prizes, and two National Book Awards.
- He was always in economic straits despite some commercial success.
- His novels include *The Sound and the Fury* (1929) and *Light in August* (1932).

William Faulkner and Clark Gable Go Hunting

During his later years as a writer, the southern novelist William Faulkner worked in Hollywood as a screenwriter of motion pictures. Faulkner, the author of As I Lay Dying and The Sound and the Fury, who struggled with alcoholic dependency throughout his life, sought to improve his financial standing by writing for the pictures.

Because of his alcoholism, he had limited success in the movie industry, although he did have a few successes worthy of mentioning, including a wrestling picture with Wallace Beery. The time in Hollywood did, however, produce numerous friendships with prominent members of the business, including Humphrey Bogart and Howard Hawkes, the director of Scarface (1932) and Bringing Up Baby (1938). According to biographer M. Thomas Inge, he also became a companion of one of Hollywood's current leading men, Clark Gable. In his biography, Inge recounts a humorous tale about a hunting expedition during which Gable solicited Faulkner's opinion on the greatest living writers. The writer responded with various living authors and included himself. Gable then asked him if he wrote, and Faulkner responded by asking Gable what he did.

In the 1991 film *Barton Fink*, Joel and Ethan Coen fictionalize both William Faulkner and his peer F. Scott Fitzgerald with the character W. P. Mayhew, an alcoholic writer troubled by writer's block and heartache. Mayhew, like Faulkner, had written wrestling pictures.

GEORGES BIZET: MUSICIAN

Georges Bizet was born in Paris, and before he was ten, he was such an accomplished pianist that he was accepted into the Paris Conservatory of Music.

By his sixteenth birthday, Bizet had written his first major work, *Symphony in C Major*, as part of a class assignment. The piece was viewed as a tremendous critical success, and his career was launched. Two years later, he had won a scholarship in composition to the Prix de Rome in, of course, Rome, and from there the momentum of his work changed beat much like the concertos that were his hallmark.

He moved into opera and wrote one of the most famous and enduring pieces, *Carmen*. Performed for generations and in many languages, *Carmen*, based on a novella, became widely acclaimed by some of classical music's most renowned composers. Much like his career began in a burst, it ended. Before his fortieth birthday, Bizet died. But his legacy lives on as the foundation of many great classical works of the twentieth century.

Famous Words of William Faulkner

- Clocks slay time... time is dead as long as it is being clicked off by little wheels; only when the clock stops does time come to life.
- It's a shame that the only thing a man can do for eight hours a day is work. He can't eat for eight hours; he can't drink for eight hours; he can't make love for eight hours. The only thing a man can do for eight hours is work.
- Facts and truth really don't have much to do with each other.
- I would say that music is the easiest means in which to express, but since words are my talent, I must try to express clumsily in words what the pure music would have done better.
- My own experience has been that the tools I need for my trade are paper, tobacco, food, and a little whisky.

WORLD LITERATURE
OCTAVIO PAZ LOZANO

Octavio Paz Lozano, typically referred to as Paz, did not limit himself to one career or one outlet for his writings.

You may have read some of the hundreds of books, essays, and poems he wrote during the 1900s. He was known for his powerful words on important subjects, and his work was translated from his native Spanish into many languages. He won the Nobel Prize in literature in 1990.

But Paz's life may be more closely defined with both his experiences and his writings about the political turmoil involving his native Mexico. As a child, Paz's family was exiled from Mexico, and he grew up in the United States. Perhaps because his formative years were spent under such political influence, disorder was never far from him. He gave up law school and returned to Mexico to teach and to write.

His work became renowned and won him invitations to influential conferences around the world. He studied in the U.S. and abroad before finally returning to Mexico City, which opened an entirely new career.

Because Paz's work had so much influence in Marxism, he also became sort of a political critic whose writings had a popular following. Mexico named him in 1962 as its ambassador to India. Even while serving in the diplomatic world, he continued to produce powerful poetry and to lecture all over the world, culminating with the Nobel. He was a man of influence.

SAMUEL COLERIDGE

If you've heard the expression "not a drop to drink" then in a roundabout way, you know Samuel Taylor Coleridge. The English poet, critic, and philosopher is probably best known for his long poems *The Rime of the Ancient Mariner* and *Christabel.* In the first poem, the quote "water, water everywhere, ne any drop to drink" became "but not a drop to drink."

Coleridge is considered one of the founders of the Romantic Movement in England, along with his buddy William Wordsworth. The youngest of ten children, Coleridge was picked on by his older brother Frank. He often hid in a local library, where he discovered his passion for poetry.

In 1792, while studying at Jesus College in Cambridge, Coleridge won the Browne Gold Medal for an ode that he wrote on the slave trade—just the beginning of his literary accomplishments.

At the end of 1799, he fell in love with Sara Hutchinson, the sister of Wordsworth's future wife and the focus of his 1802 work *Dejection: An Ode.* During 1809–10, he and Sara wrote and edited the political magazine *The Friend,* and from 1808-1819 Coleridge lectured often in London and was considered the greatest Shakespearean critic of the time.

Coleridge's life began to crumble, however, due to neuralgic and rheumatic pains and an addiction to opium. He lived on the verge of suicide, eventually living with a surgeon for treatment and writing more poetry, including *Kubla Khan,* based on a dream and published before it was completed, as well as several theological works. He died in 1834, still living with the same physician from whom he had sought treatment for his opium addiction. An autopsy revealed he had an enlarged heart. Coleridge write his own epitaph in the last year of his life.

Chuang Tzu: A Taoist Who Didn't Know He Was

Chuang Tzu, also known as Zhuangzi, was an incredibly significant Chinese philosopher in the fourth century BCE. during the period known as the Warring States Period. The period corresponded to the Hundred Schools of Thought, a time of incredible expansion in Chinese culture and intellect. Chuang Tzu's most significant contribution to the period includes *Zhuangzi*, the Taoist book with which he was involved. It contains his sometimes-skeptical philosophies and places him with Lao Tzu as the most vital of philosophers of Taoism.

Ironically, some scholars suggest that Chuang Tzu never identified himself as a Taoist. The philosopher has been placed among the Taoists in Chinese tradition, yet he mentions Tao infrequently in *Zhuangzi*. School of Oriental and African Studies Professor A. C. Graham, acknowledging the absence of Taoism in the ancient text, was prompted to observe, "Zhuangzi never knew he was a Taoist." Particularly striking are the text's inner chapters, which have been translated numerous times by various philosophers. In these inner chapters much of the focus of Chuang Tzu's writings reflects the Hellenistic philosophy of "skepticism." Like the works attributed to the Hellenistic skeptics such as Arcesilaus, Chuang Tzu's inner chapters suggest an examination of meaning systems of his time, and these usually result in doubt.

Nonetheless, the manuscript survives as a cornerstone of the Taoist belief system and urges people to welcome spontaneity in their lives. With the impulsiveness, the *Zhuangzi* explains, men and women will find the ability to embrace the adjustments in their lives, even the transformation from life to death: "Life and death are one thread, the same line viewed from different sides."

CRASH COURSE
MOLIÈRE

He may have been known for his comic theatre, but his death was anything but humorous. In 1673, during a showing of his final play, *La malade imaginaire* (*The Imaginary Invalid*), Molière, who suffered from pulmonary tuberculosis, began coughing and hemorrhaging while acting the part of the hypochondriac Argan. He was able to wrap up his performance, but collapsed again, and died a few hours later.

During his lifetime, Molière had completely transformed French comedy. Born Jean Baptiste Poquelin, he suffered the death of his mother when he was ten, and he wasn't particularly close to his father. He seemed destined to follow his father's intentions for him to have a career in office, but at age twenty-one, Molière decided he had his own plans—theatre. Together with a friend and 630 livres they founded L'Illustre Thètre. He changed his name to Molière, possibly after a small village in Southern France.

Eventually Molière made his way to Paris and performed in front of the King at the Louvre. He became famous for his farces. While controversial, he was careful not to make fun of the monarchy or the authority of the church—and became one of the king's favorites. During his time in Paris, Molière wrote thirty-one of the eighty-five plays performed on his stage, while also directing his company.

The laws of the time would not allow actors to be buried in the sacred ground of a cemetery. But Molière's wife asked King Louis XIV to allow a "normal" funeral held in the evening. The king allowed it, and Molière was buried in the part of the cemetery reserved for unbaptized babies. Some say more than eight hundred people attended Molière's secret funeral.

ALEXANDER GRAHAM BELL

- Bell was one of the cofounders of the National Geographic Society, and he served as its president from 1896 to 1904. He also founded the *Journal of Science* in 1883.
- When Bell passed away on August 4, 1922, millions of phones served by the Bell System in the USA and Canada—in his honor—went completely quiet for one minute.
- Long before Bell filed a patent application in 1875, Daniel Drawbaugh claimed to have invented the telephone. But he did not have a journal or record of it, so the Supreme Court rejected his claims (four votes to three). Bell had kept excellent records and therefore was awarded the patent for the telephone.
- Bell was granted eighteen patents in his name, and twelve others he shared with collaborators.
- As a child, Bell was curious about his world, collecting botanical specimens and "experimenting." His best friend was Ben Herdman, a neighbor whose family operated a flour mill. John Herdman admonished the two boys one day, telling them to do something useful. Young Bell asked what needed to be done at the mill. He was told wheat had to be dehusked through a laborious process. Well, by age twelve, Bell built a homemade device that combined rotating paddles with sets of nail brushes, creating a simple dehusking machine. It was used at the mill for many years.

Alexander Graham Bell Milestones

1872: Founded a school for deaf-mutes in Boston, Massachusetts.

1874: Developed the basic ideas for the telephone while working on a multiple telegraph.

1875: Filed the first patent for telegraphy.

1876: Transmitted the first complete sentence.

1877: Formed Bell Telephone Company to operate local telephone exchange operation.

1880: Invented the photophone, transmitting speech by light rays.

1882: Acquired a controlling interest in the Western Electric Company, Elisha Gray's company.

1885: Formed American Telephone and Telegraph Company to operate the long distance network.

1886: Introduced the first wax recording cylinder, forming the basis for the modern phonograph.

1896: Elected the first President of National Geographic Society.

1907: Devised a kite capable of carrying a person.

1917: Developed "hydrodrome," at 70 mph the fastest boat in the world for many years.

Famous Words of Alexander Graham Bell

- What this power is I cannot say; all I know is that it exists and it becomes available only when a man is in that state of mind in which he knows exactly what he wants and is fully determined not to quit until he finds it.
- Before anything else, preparation is the key to success.
- Great discoveries and improvements invariably involve the cooperation of many minds. I may be given credit for having blazed the trail, but when I look at the subsequent developments I feel the credit is due to others rather than to myself.
- Sometimes we stare so long at a door that is closing that we see too late the one that is open.
- The most successful men in the end are those whose success is the result of steady accretion. It is the man who carefully advances step by step, with his mind becoming wider and wider—and progressively better able to grasp any theme or situation.
- A man, as a general rule, owes very little to what he is born with—a man is what he makes of himself.
- The nation that secures control of the air will ultimately control the world.

MICHEL DE MONTAIGNE: THE ESSAY MAKER

If you just dreaded writing those essays in high school or college, say hello to Michel de Montaigne, known for "popularizing" the essay as a literary genre. His time came during the French Renaissance but to this day his massive volume *Essais* contains some of the most widely influential essays ever written.

Of course, he had to be pretty smart to "invent" the essay, and boy was he. In about 1539 he began his studies at a top-notch boarding school in Bordeaux called the College of Guyenne, where he mastered the entire curriculum by the age of 13. After that he studied law and began his law career. By 1557 he was appointed a counselor of the high court, and from 1561 to 1563 he was at the court of Charles IX. He was awarded the collar of the order of St. Michael—the highest honor of the French nobility. During this time he made friends with a poet, and soon began his literary works.

In 1571, Montaigne retired from public life and holed up in his library (for about 10 years). Thus began his focus on Essays, first published in 1580. So what is *Essays* all about? In a nutshell, it's a collection of subjective essays on various topics. Montaigne writes about religious conflicts, marriage, child-raising, education, human nature, death, and much more. Often, Montaigne goes off on tangents about his own personal experiences, which critics often note. But he became known for his ability to merge his intellectual side with his casual anecdotes. And many of his quotes became famous.

EXTRA CREDIT: One of Montaigne's most famous quotes: "Life itself is neither good nor evil, it is the place of good and evil, according to what you make it."

FRANK LLOYD WRIGHT

Believe it or not, one of the most influential American architects got his start playing with blocks as a kid.

You've probably heard of Frank Lloyd Wright, designer of more than four hundred structures across the United States, but what you probably don't know is that Wright first started studying "architecture" with some geometric blocks good ol' Mom purchased when he was in kindergarten. A teacher herself, she'd seen the blocks during a visit to the 1876 Centennial Celebration in Philadelphia.

The geometric shapes allowed the blocks to be assembled in many different forms, and Wright spent hours playing with them. He later wrote that they were the foundation of his building, if you will.

Wright—originally named Frank "Lincoln" Wright—in fact sort of toyed with architecture from the beginning. There's no evidence he ever graduated high school, but the University of Wisconsin admitted him as a special exception. He only took a few classes on a part-time schedule, but worked closely with engineers before leaving school.

He moved to Chicago, which was rebuilding following the great fire, and went to work at architectural firms. His talent grew, and he started to prove he could design unique houses, leading him to start his own firm. Born two years after the end of the Civil War, Wright didn't see his career gain a foothold in greatness until the turn of the century when he developed the "Prairie House," sort of the creation of what commonly is called the ranch-style houses, low with sloping roofs and minimal chimneys.

His career blossomed from unique bungalows and stunning mansions into great projects such as the Guggenheim Museum in New York and many of the buildings on the campus of Florida Southern College, but then he returned to his blocks. Between 1917 and 1924, Wright developed the "textile block system," which used precast concrete blocks in unusual patterns. Five houses in California remain in that design.

And, to think, he probably got the idea in grade school.

FRANK'S FIERY FORT

While Frank Lloyd Wright was known for his buildings that were constructed from the ground up, he also was known for one that came down more than once. The bad karma behind the home called the "Taliesin" all started with a scandalous love affair with one of the wives of Wright's clients, Edwin Cheney. Wright ended up leaving his first wife, Catherine Tobin, after the affair with Mamah Borthwick Cheney, and began building his new summer home in Spring Green, Wisconsin.

The year was 1911 and the valley where the home was built originally was settled by Wright's maternal family, the Lloyd Joneses, during the Civil War. The home—dubbed *Taliesin*, meaning "shining brow" because the home sat on the brow of a hill—had three wings that included his living quarters, an office, and farm buildings.

Wright and Mamah Borthwick (she changed her name, having left her husband) moved in just after Christmas. Three years later the house gave *shining brow* new meaning when one of the servants set fire to the home, murdering seven people with an axe as the fire burned. Among the dead were Mamah and her two children.

Wright decided to rebuild, naming the new quarters "Taliesin II." But the living quarters erupted in fire again, this time in 1925. This time, the fire apparently sparked near a telephone in Wright's bedroom.

Yes, thus began Taliesin III. Eventually, Wright purchased additional surrounding land, turning Taliesin into a 2.4-kilometer estate and using the home as an experiment of sorts—continuously evolving it.

Frank's fiery fort finally withstood time and was designated a National Historic Landmark in 1976.

CRASH COURSE
ALBERT CAMUS

Albert Camus was one brainy guy, and stuck by his guns when it came to his beliefs—even when it disenchanted the ladies. See, he didn't really believe in marriage. But he got married anyway, in 1943 to Simone Hie. She was a morphine addict, so perhaps that didn't bode the marriage well to begin with, but eventually the union ended due to infidelity on both sides.

Seven years later, he gave the institution of marriage another go—even though he continued to argue vehemently against it—this time wedding Francine Faure. She seemed like a good match intellectual-wise, being a pianist and mathematician. But despite fathering twins, Camus had several affairs, including a very open one with a Spanish actress.

His busy love lives aside, Camus had plenty of time for other, more productive activities. The French-Algerian author, philosopher, and journalist won the Nobel prize in 1957, the second-youngest to receive the Nobel Prize for Literature.

After working as a newspaper editor and supporter of the French resistance during World War II, Camus began tackling novels, among them the controversial *The Rebel,* which was published in 1951. In the book, which analyzed rebellion and revolution, Camus rejects communism, offending many of his friends, including close pal Jean-Paul Sartre. The unwelcome reception saddened him, and he shifted his literary focus to translating plays and becoming more philosophical.

Eventually he devoted his life to human rights; in fact, his Nobel prize was not for a novel but for an essay against capital punishment. Camus's literary career likely would have spanned many more years if it weren't for the car crash that ended his life at age 47. His publisher and friend, Michael Gallimard, also died in the crash.

At the time of his death, Camus was planning to head a theater company and write a novel about his life growing up in Algeria. The latter, although unfinished, was published posthumously as The First Man in 1995.

Interesting Facts About Nikola Tesla

Regarded as one of the most important inventors and physicists of the late 1800s to early twentieth century, Nikola Tesla is mostly remembered for his revolutionary contributions in the field of electricity and magnetism. Tesla laid the foundation of modern alternating current electric power (AC) systems with his various patents and theories, therefore playing an essential role in the genesis of the Second Industrial Revolution. Here are some other facts worth noting.

- Tesla introduced the first commercial fluorescent light bulbs at the New York World's Fair in 1939.
- He arrived in America in 1884 with very little money and immediately began working for Thomas Edison. Within a year he left Edison's shop for new employment, because Edison reneged on an offer of $50,000 in exchange for redesigning Edison's inefficient generators.
- It was rumored in 1915 that Tesla would win the Nobel Prize for physics. Unfortunately for Tesla the rumor proved false, and the prize was awarded to William Henry Bragg for his use of X-rays in studying the structure of crystals.
- He created the largest man-made lightning bolt ever recorded, proving that the earth acted as a conductor of electricity. His bolt was 135 feet long.
- Tesla told reporters in 1899 that he was capable of transmitting wireless signals from Pikes Peak to Paris using wireless telegraphy.
- Late in life, he was often observed feeding pigeons and collecting wounded ones to take home for rehabilitation.

PHILOSOPHY 101

MOSES MAIMONIDES

Jewish philosopher Moses Maimonides was undoubtedly the most influential figure in Jewish philosophy of the middle ages, serving as a cornerstone of Jewish thought. His writings included several texts concerning Jewish philosophy, as well as several others on medicine and law. He created the thirteen principles of Jewish faith.

Born in Spain in 1135, Maimonides became an exiled settler in Egypt after an invasion from the Almohad, a Muslim dynasty that left the Jews with little choice but to flee their homeland. His travels abroad exposed him to various ideas viewed as secular by the traditional Jew, and the contrasting beliefs significantly affected his philosophies. Islamic thinkers Ibn Rushd and Al-Ghazali influenced the young philosopher, as did the classics of Greeks such as Aristotle and Plato. The Greek perspective particularly played a role in shaping the Maimonides idea of "negative" or "apophatic theology," in which the only statements toward a description of God that may be considered accurate are negative. In other words, mankind is incapable of describing the greatness of God, but rather must satisfy himself by describing what God is not.

Maimonides explained the required convictions of Judaism in his thirteen principles. The outline describes what one must believe in order to be a good Jew. According to Maimonides, several acknowledgments are necessary, including the existence of God, God's unity, God's incorporeity, God's eternity, that God alone should be the object of worship, revelation through God's prophets, the preeminence of Moses among the prophets, God's law given on Mount Sinai, the immutability of the Torah, God's knowledge of human actions, reward of good and retribution of evil, the coming of the Jewish Messiah, and the resurrection of the dead. The thirteen principles were later narrowed by Jewish scholars to include only three core beliefs: in God; in Creation; and in retribution.

OVID

Poor guy, this Ovid. He spent his days writing about love, only to be banished to an island in the Black Sea.

Born Publius Ovidius Naso, it's no wonder the world called him Ovid for short. He was up there with Virgil and Horace as one of the three great canonical poets (poems that tell a short story). In 16 BC, his *Amores* were published. Book I consisted of fifteen somewhat whimsical love poems. He touched on adultery—a taboo subject of the times—and in future poems explored seduction.

His most famous work, however, had to do with Greek mythology. *Metamorphoses*, an epic poem, tells the tales of humans being transformed into trees, constellations, and other beings. But the same year that masterpiece was revealed, Augustus banished him to the Black Sea, to an island called Tomis. No one is certain why, but Ovid speculated that it had to do with something political. Some said perhaps he knew of a conspiracy against Augustus, others that he was somehow involved in Augustus's granddaughter's alleged affair with Decimus Silanus—she, too, was banished around the same time as Ovid. Still others said it was much simpler than that. Ovid wrote about adultery in his poems, which held severe consequences, including banishment.

During his exile Ovid wrote two more poems, not about love but about sadness and desolation. Ovid died ten years after being exiled.

Master of Meter

Ovid was a master of the elegiac couplet but he made use of a wide range of meters, including the elegiac couplets in the *Amores* and his two long didactic poems, the *Ars Amatoria* and *Remedia Amoris*; iambic trimester and anapests in the two fragments of the lost tragedy *Medea*; and dactylic hexameter in *Metamorphoses*.

ANDRÉ-MARIE AMPÈRE

A physicist and mathematician born in east-central France during the late eighteenth century, André-Marie Ampère was one of the primary scientists involved in the knowledge of electromagnetism. Acknowledged for a scientific law which shares his name, Ampère discovered the relationship between the integrated magnetic field around a closed loop and the electric current passing through it. His discovery laid the foundation of electrodynamics, the investigation into the physics of electromagnetism.

Ampère began studying mathematics early in life and rapidly demonstrated an impressive comprehension of the science. Also considered a polymath of history, poetry, philosophy, and the natural sciences, he studied relentlessly as a child and was appointed by the Lycèe of Lyon as a professor of mathematics. He later received an appointment to a polytechnic school at Paris, a position he gained on recommendation by fellow mathematician and astronomer Jean Baptiste Joseph Delambre, the Permanent Secretary for the Mathematical Sciences at the French Academy of Sciences.

His time at the polytechnic allowed Ampère to pursue his scientific research, and in September of 1820 he became aware of a great new discovery. A Danish physicist and chemist by the name of H. C. Orsted found that a magnetic needle is acted on by a voltaic current. A week later the French Academy of Sciences received a demonstration of the phenomenon, using parallel wires. When carrying currents, he explained, the wires either attracted or repelled each other. His exhibition gave birth to the study of electromagnetism and paved the way for theorists of physics such as James Clerk Maxwell and Albert Einstein.

CRASH COURSE
AVICENNA

The foremost physician and Islamic philosopher of his time, Avicenna wrote almost 450 treatises on a variety of subjects, most of them concentrating on medicine and philosophy. Of his works, *The Book of Healing* and *The Canon of Medicine* are the most famous. These philosophical and scientific texts remained standard medical texts at universities throughout Europe and the Middle East for centuries.

Deemed by historians to be a father of early modern medicine, Avicenna introduced systematic experimentation and quantification into physiology, introduced the concept of quarantining infectious patients to limit the spread of diseases, and created the idea of a syndrome. He was the first to acknowledge the influence of climate and environment on health, and in his *Canon of Medicine* he created rules and principles for testing the effectiveness of new drugs and medications. The guidelines form the basis of clinical pharmacology today, and include the now controversial concepts of human testing.

EXTRA CREDIT: Avicenna was considered a polymath of several subjects other than philosophy and medicine. These included astronomy, poetry, mathematics politics, and warfare.

GIACOMO PUCCINI

This Italian composer would be quite proud to find out that his *La Bohème* and *Madama Butterfly* are among the most frequently performed operas to this day. Puccini was destined really—he was born in Lucca, Italy, into a family with five generations of musicians. He eventually worked as a church organist and choir organist in town, but when he saw a performance of *Aida*—a show he walked nearly twenty miles to see—he was stirred to opera composition.

In 1880, he enrolled in the Milan conservatory and composed his first opera. But it was years later, while living at Torre del Lago not far from Lucca, that he hit the height of his success with *La Bohème* and *Madama Butterfly*. *La Bohème* is considered one of the most romantic operas ever composed—and the most popular opera ever—and while *Madama Butterfly* initially was not well received, it was reworked and became a sensation.

- In *La Bohème* the spotlight shines on the love of Mimi and the poet Rodolfo in the Latin Quarter of Paris. It's a story of innocent love, betrayal, and the final death of the heroine.
- *Madama Butterfly* is a story of love betrayed, the innocent Japanese heroine of the title deserted by her faithless American husband and finally compelled to suicide.

Turandot, Puccini's final opera, was left uncompleted when he died. Franco Alfano finished the last two scenes based on the composer's sketches. But some said Alfano did not follow the sketches at all—the sketches were apparently undecipherable anyway. When Arturp Toscanini conducted the opening sold-out performance in 1926, he opted to leave out Alfano's part of the score. At the point where Puccini's opera ended, Toscanini stopped the orchestra and the conductor turned to the audience and explained why it was ending so abruptly.

Interesting Facts About Puccini

- In 1903, having become obsessed with driving fast cars, Puccini nearly died after a major car crash. He slowed down on the opera front after that.
- In 1909, Puccini's wife, Elvira, falsely accused their maid Doria Manfredi of having an affair with Puccini. After the maid committed suicide, the Manfredi family sued Elvira and won. Puccini was ordered to pay damages.
- Puccini was a cigar chain smoker who near the end of 1923 was diagnosed with throat cancer. Puccini died a year later in Brussels, where he was undergoing experimental radiation therapy. News of his death reached Rome during a performance of *La Bohème*. The opera stopped playing and the orchestra strummed up Chopin's *Funeral March* for an astonished audience.
- Although Puccini is most well-known for his operas, he also wrote some orchestral pieces, chamber music, sacred music, and songs for voice and piano.
- The Puccini Festival is held each summer in Torre del Lago and presents several operatic performances, attracting approximately forty thousand visitors to the Teatro dei Quattromila open-air theater.
- Puccini's works have been used extensively in more modern times in a variety of movies, including music in *Rocky Balboa* (2006), *Bend It Like Beckham* (2003), *Under the Tuscan Sun* (2003), *The Life of David Gale* (2003), *40 Days and 40 Nights* (2002), *G.I. Jane* (1997), *One Fine Day* (1996), *Natural Born Killers* (1994), *Weekend at Bernie's* (1989), The *Witches of Eastwick* (1987), *Fatal Attraction* (1987), *A Room With a View* (1986), and *The Killing Fields* (1984).

MESTRIUS PLUTARCHUS

Better known in English as Plutarch, this Greek historian, biographer, essayist, and Middle Platonist was born back in AD 46 in a little Greek town called Chaeronea. His writings strongly influenced English and French literature. Admirers included Ralph Waldo Emerson, Michel de Montaigne, Alexander Hamilton, John Milton, and Sir Francis Bacon.

Plutarch for many years was a priest at a temple near his home, and eventually his writings and lectures made him somewhat of a celebrity in the Roman empire. He was mayor of his town and was known to welcome guests from throughout the empire at his estate for conversation. The dialogues—Plutarch moderated from his marble chair—often were recorded and published, eventually becoming seventy-eight essays known collectively as the *Moralia*.

- In the *Moralia*, Plutarch shares his belief in reincarnation, writing a consolation letter to his wife about the death of their two-year-old daughter.
- Plutarch's *Parallel Lives* was a whopping 800,000 words—at least; more may have been written, but what survived was 1,300 pages of fine print. It is a series of biographies of famous Romans compared to famous Greeks, sort of lessons for living.
- At the birth of the Italian Renaissance, the rediscovery of *Parallel Lives* stimulated popular interest in the classics. *Lives* did more than survive—it became a literary success across Europe.
- In his plays, Shakespeare paraphrased parts of Thomas North's translation of Plutarch's *Lives*, sometimes quoting from them verbatim.
- Emerson called *Lives* "a bible for heroes" and said reading Plutarch caused a "tingling" in the blood.

ZARATHUSHTRA

Knowledge about Zarathushtra, a prophet and religious icon also known as Zoroaster, proves exceptionally difficult to obtain. Modern scholars of theology and religious history argue over many aspects of his life and work, yet they tend to agree upon one fact: he changed religious thought forever. Seen as a prophet by his followers, Zarathushtra created the world's first monotheistic religion, which aptly became known as Zoroastrianism.

Zarathushtra, believed by many to have lived roughly 300 years before King Alexander III of Macedon, demonstrated originality and potency in his innovative message. Most scholars agree that it is logical to associate him with ancient lands now known as Iran, and all recognize his legacy of spreading teachings of dualistic monotheism and the expectation of an afterlife through a transfiguration of life and existence. Before the teachings of Zarathushtra, the Indo-Iranian religious traditions were ritualistic in nature, and did little to afford mankind with passable answers for the problem of good and evil. Zarathushtra discovered that these concepts existed as the underlying force which motivated everything in life.

Early Christians recognized Zarathushtra as the premiere forerunner of their faith. The acknowledgement stemmed from his prophecies that a Messiah would come to earth, a doctrine known as the Saoshyant, or Savior of the Future. When struggles began to develop between the Christian nations of the West and the Sasanid Empire in Persia, however, the Christian acceptance of Zarathushtra as a prophet began to wane. He became regarded as a teacher of witchcraft and heresy, and followers of Zoroastrianism began to be perceived as sacrilegious infidels.

Christians were, of course, not the first to view him as a false prophet. Many in his own land of Persia viewed his teachings as deviant. According to legend, Zarathushtra's death resulted from such sentiment. His life came to an end when the leader, who had aged to around seventy, was murdered by a priest.

JANE GOODALL AND THE FAR SIDE CONTROVERSY

An English zoologist, Jane Goodall is known throughout the world for her study of chimpanzees. Beginning her work in the Gombe Stream National Park in Tanzania, she discovered habits that significantly transformed the scientific world's awareness of the species. She assumed the enormous task of ensuring the survival of the species in their natural habitats at that time, and has since received international extolment for those endeavors. To the world she's a scientific hero; but to at least one chary cartoon chimp, she's little more than a tramp.

Here's the story. Cartoonist Gary Larson's *The Far Side* once included a comic strip illustrating two grooming chimpanzees. When the grooming chimp discovers a human hair on the other she inquires, "Conducting a little more 'research' with that Jane Goodall tramp?" That is pretty funny stuff, but to the Jane Goodall Institute it seemed downright insulting. Finding Larson's caricature of the zoologist to be in bad taste, the Institute took action. Lawyers for the nonprofit drafted a letter to Larson, but to their dismay Goodall herself blocked any legal action. The zoologist found the clever jab hilarious.

Some time after the incident, Larson has donated the proceeds from the strip itself as well as merchandise such as t-shirts and coffee mugs which feature the cartoon. Also, Goodall composed the preface for a collection of *Far Side* comics titled *The Far Side Gallery 5*. In the scientist's introduction she recounted the controversy and praised Larson for his creativity and vision in his work, which often demonstrates the similarities between animals and humans. In the end, the tasteless cartoonist and the wanton scientist remained friends, but no grooming has ever been reported between the two icons.

John Maynard Keynes

John Maynard Keynes was an English economist born in 1883, the year Karl Marx died. He *isn't* remembered as an editor, Cambridge lecturer, or director of the Bank of England, though he did all those things. Instead, it was his book, *The General Theory of Employment, Interest, and Money* (1936), that led Richard Nixon to say "We are all Keynesians now."

Besides being a dull economist, he

- Married a Russian ballerina after numerous romantic relationships with men.
- Was a member of the Bloomsbury Group: a posh, London-based intellectual group led by Virginia Woolf.
- Dated Bloomsbury members: artist Duncan Grant and writer Lytton Strachey.
- Called President Woodrow Wilson a "blind, deaf Don Quixote."

Keynes's personal investments made him wealthy, but the Great Depression hit him hard. For much of the Depression, he (literally) stayed in bed and wrote his most famous work, *The General Theory*. In it, he argues that when an economy is slow, government should increase its spending because private markets can't. When private markets can't spend any more money, people get laid off and unemployment goes up. The government, Keynes argued, should step in at that stage. The concept of *intentionally* running a high deficit was groundbreaking. Some economists never accepted it, but President Franklin D. Roosevelt finally did and used it to help get the U.S. out of the Depression. With his ideas, Keynes revolutionized economics and single-handedly formed macroeconomics as a study.

Famous Words of Keynes

- I can't remember my telephone number, but I know it was in the high numbers.
- The avoidance of taxes is the only intellectual pursuit that still carries any reward.

CHRISTOPHER WREN

Christopher Wren may be noted for his contributions to architecture. After all, he helped design the rebuilding of London after the Great Fire of the early 1600s. And he also is credited for his architectural efforts in designing St. Paul's Cathedral, which replaced the one destroyed by the fire. That building, with its high dome, has been the influence on many subsequent buildings, including the United States capitol in Washington D.C.

But truth be known, in his day and age the profession of "architect" really didn't exist. There were no college courses, no professional requirements and no specialized training. You simply had to be a whiz at math and study its advanced applications. And that sort of explains Wren's evolution. Because the guy was a math whiz long before *Good Will Hunting* made it sort of cool.

For instance, Wren was so good that he helped improve telescopes and microscopes built during his day—the 1600s. He used those devices and his knowledge to help sailors navigate their ships. He helped the King of England understand what the moon was like by creating a map of it. He even studied the planet Saturn. Primitive telescopes could tell only so much. The rest was built on analysis and theory.

So Wren studied Saturn and wrote a paper about it. Nice paper full of nice theories. But another scientist at the time, Huygens, also wrote a paper on Saturn, which was published first, and Wren read it. That paper discussed how Saturn was not a strangely shaped orb but was a ball surrounded by rings that orbited it.

Wren liked that concept so much that he never even published his own theories. They lay dormant until his death, which, by the way, came at age 90. In himself, he was a pretty strong structure.

EXTRA CREDIT: Christopher Wren actually was one of three people with that name. He had an older brother who was named Christopher, but he died on the day he was born. So when Christopher was born, his parents used the name again. Christopher's second son also was named Christopher, and this son wrote about his father's work.

JACKSON POLLOCK

Maybe you've heard of Jackson Pollock. He was an artist whose style of painting tended to make people a bit vehement in stating their opinions. After all, some of his most powerful and recognized works might look like the drop cloth you took off the floor the last time you painted your bedroom.

His was a paint splatter style—with him putting his "canvas" on the floor—and proceeding to spray, splatter, and pour paints onto that canvas. As you can imagine, some critics thought it was powerful and creative. Others thought it was a mess. Whatever you want to call it, it worked.

Pollock's work that he called *No. 5, 1948*, became the world's most expensive painting. In November 2006 it was sold at auction by film producer David Geffen for $140 million.

That was such a grand statement of validity for his work. But then there was the documentary about Pollock—its name includes an expletive—from 2006 that features a truck driver who bought a Pollock original at a thrift store for $5. You get the idea: Art is in the eye of the beholder, especially if said art was nontraditional and abstract.

As if such stories weren't legacy enough, there was Pollock's "Andy Warhol moment." He was immortalized in a movie in 2000 called *Pollock*. This was a project of actor Ed Harris, who directed the movie and was nominated for an Academy Award for playing Pollock. Marcia Gay Harden played Pollock's wife, artist Lee Krasner, and she won an Oscar for Best Supporting Actress.

That movie was, unlike some of Pollock's work, a critical success because Pollock's life made for the perfect movie script. He painted successfully in an unconventional and controversial style that challenged his fragile psyche.

Like many artists, Pollock chased those demons with alcohol. And in 1956, when he was forty-four, Pollock was driving to his home on Long Island with his current girlfriend and other friends. A mile from home, he wrecked his convertible in a one-car crash, killing himself and one of his passengers.

Jackson Pollock's Art

- You might have a difficult time naming a painter whose style was more diametrically opposite of Jackson Pollock's than Norman Rockwell. The man who made scenes from America a staple on the *Saturday Evening Post*, actually took time to make a commentary on Pollock's style in his work called "Connoisseur." In that painting, a man drawn in the typical Rockwell style seems to be studying a painting that might have been done by Pollock.

- Here are the contrasts in commentaries that Pollock's style evoked: Artist/satirist Craig Brown said that he was astonished that "decorative 'wallpaper,' essentially brainless, could gain such a position in art history." And the *Reynolds News* in 1959 included a headline that said, "This is not art—it's a joke in bad taste."

- There continues a debate about whether twenty-four paintings and drawings found in a locker in New York in 2003 were original works by Pollock. Physicists have analyzed this work, but the results are inconclusive.

- So what did Jackson Pollock think of his own style of work? He was asked many times, but here's one answer: "When I am in my painting, I'm not aware of what I'm doing. It is only after a sort of 'get acquainted' period that I see what I have been about. I have no fear of making changes, destroying the image, etc., because the painting has a life of its own. I try to let it come through. It is only when I lose contact with the painting that the result is a mess. Otherwise, it's pure harmony, an easy give and take, and the painting comes out well."

Wee Little Inventors

Thomas Edison: At the ripe age of six, Edison burned down his father's barn while experimenting with fire. Other mischevious events included convincing another young tike to swallow large amounts of powders to fill himself with gas. (Edison wanted to launch the first human balloon.) By his early teenage years, Edison had created his first real, practical invention—none other than the electrical cockroach trap. Using strips of tinfoil, wires, and a battery, the contraption was designed to shock an insect upon its arrival into the trap. It's no surprise that Edison became one of the most prolific inventors of history.

Alexander Graham Bell: Most widely known for the inventions he crafted as an adult, it's a fact that Bell was quite the innovative thinker as a schoolboy as well. At age fourteen, he created a rotary brush that would remove the husks from wheat. He created the device for a friend's father who owned a flour mill.

Charles Hall: Known for his aluminum refining system which he patented at age twenty-two, Hall began working on the electrolytic machine at age sixteen. He saved loose change and allowance to buy chemistry materials and experimented for years as a teen. The result: a commercial aluminum refining system that proved quite effective later on!

Extra Credit:

- Robert Fulton created the paddlewheel at age thirteen.
- Philo Farnsworth created the notion of optical scanning at fourteen.
- At just nineteen, Igor Sikorsky designed the first helicopter.

MARCEL PROUST

Born in Auteli near Paris, Proust began writing at an early age and is considered a pioneer of the modern novel. In 1896, he began working on his first novel—it wasn't published until 1954 and was titled Jean Santeuil posthumously by editors. It was 1908 when Proust really began to grow as a writer. By 1909, he had begun working on *¿ la recherche du temps perdu*, a seven-volume masterpiece consisting of more than 2,000 literary characters. Marcel is the narrator—Marcel is not Proust but does resemble him in many ways.

Proust passed away before he could finish the last revision of the final volumes but his brother, Robert, completed the last three volumes. The book was translated into English, published between 1922 and 1931 *as Remembrance of Things Past*. As late as 1995, new translations in three countries became *In Search of Lost Time*.

Interesting Facts About Proust

- Throughout his life Proust suffered from asthma. For many years he lived in a soundproof flat, often sleeping during the day and writing at night.
- The first four volumes of *In Search of Lost Time* have been published in the United States under Viking imprint and in paperback under the Penguin Classics imprint.
- Proust was one of the first openly homosexual European novelists. Although details of his homosexual life—including an affair with a married man who was killed in an air accident and alleged visits to a male brothel—have long fascinated biographers, they have shed little light on his literary successes.

CRASH COURSE

REMEMBRANCE OF THINGS PAST

Writer Alain De Botton published a book called *How Proust Can Change Your Life*, which gives you some indication of the respect with which the author of *Remembrance of Things Past* is treated. This seven-volume meganovel is difficult to describe because so much of it is "in search of lost time." Proust relies heavily on memory and flashbacks to show how consciousness changes over the course of a lifetime. Volume 1, *Swann's Way*, recalls the narrator's childhood and his love for Swann's daughter, Gilberte, and for Odette. In *Within a Budding Grove*, the narrator falls out of love with Gilberte and in love with Albertine. Volume 3, *The Guermantes Way*, finds the narrator climbing the social ladder. In *Cities of the Plain*, he discovers that one of the upper crust, Baron Charlus, is gay. The homosexual theme doesn't stop there, however. As it turns out, the narrator learns that Albertine may be a lesbian. He was about to break up with her, but this discovery makes her suddenly cool again. By volume 5, *The Captive*, Albertine is living with the narrator, but she runs away amid various scandals. As one can tell from the title of the next volume, *The Sweet Cheat Gone*, Albertine dies. Gilberte has risen in the social ranks to become Mlle de Forcheville. In the final volume, *The Past Recaptured*, World War I wages as the narrator realizes that his fellow socialites are much less interesting than his own personal memories.

TYCHO BRAHE

Although born long before NASA's time (1546), the Danish nobleman and astrologer Tycho Brahe is credited with the most precise astronomical and planetary observations of his time. His findings were used by his assistant Johannes Kepler to come up with the laws of planetary motion.

Tycho—he rarely is referred to by his surname—was given an estate on the island of Hven and money to establish a research institute, where he built large astronomical instruments and took precise astronomical measurements. He worked to originate his own model of the universe, calling it the Tychonic system. No one before Tycho persisted in making so many repeated observations, cataloging planets and stars.

Tycho lost part of his nose during a fight with a classmate. Alcohol was involved, of course. Tycho was twenty-two then and studying at the University of Rostock in Germany. The fight—in which Tycho lost the bridge of his nose—took place at a dance at a professor's house. Supposedly this is where Tycho found his love for medicine and alchemy. For years people thought he wore a nose bridge replacement made of silver and gold blended into a flesh tone, and used glue to keep it there. But in 1901 medical experts opened his tomb and checked out his remains. The nasal opening of his skull was lined with green, a sign of copper exposure.

Tycho loved to party—with lots of people—at his castle. His dwarf Jepp—no kidding—acted as a court jester. During dinner Jepp sat under the table.

Tycho died in October 1601. Recent investigations found high levels of mercury in his hair, suggesting he died of mercury poisoning. The plot thickens thanks to a 2005 book that claims Kepler, Tycho's assistant, had plenty of reasons for murdering his boss. Authors Joshua Gilder and Anne-Lee Gilder argue that Kepler had the opportunity, AND stole Tycho's data.

KONRAD "CONNY" PLANK

When it came to postwar European popular music, Konrad "Conny" Plank covered the gamut, from progressive to avant-garde to electronic music. Born in 1940 in Germany, this record producer and musician was known for his creativity and ability to shape some of the most important and innovative recordings of his time.

Plank helped characterize the musical genre known as Krautrock and had an impact on studio production and engineering techniques worldwide. He also had a brilliant career as a keyboardist and guitarist, playing on albums by Guru Guru, Cluster, and Os Mundi. Between 1979 and 1986 he joined forces with Dieter Moebius on five Moebius & Plank studio albums. The Moebius & Plank sound influenced techno and electronica as well as future musicians.

- Plank was one of the first European producers to fully explore the potential of multi-track recording facilities for creating spectacular production effects that were more than just gimmicks. His best work is the complete opposite of the smooth sound that prevailed in most commercial pop and rock music during the time.
- Plank favored a very "live" production sound, especially on drums. His open, sometimes clangorous drum and percussion sounds undoubtedly had a significant influence on producers and engineers such as Steve Lillywhite, Hugh Padgham, and Nick Launay.
- As late as the 1980s Plank remained in high demand with the new trend of electronic pop and New Wave artists, including Devo, Ultravox!, Freur, and The Tourists. He also worked on pop and rock productions with artists such as The Scorpions, Clannad, Killing Joke, Play Dead, and Gianna Nannini.

While touring with Dieter Moebius in South America, Plank became sick. Before dying of cancer in 1987, some of Plank's last work included the recording of concerts on The Eurythmics' *Revenge* tour, and samples used on the NED Synclavier on their Savage album.

American Literature
Henry David Thoreau

Henry David Thoreau actually was born flip-flopped—David Henry Thoreau. His classic book, *Walden*, contains reflections of simple living in nature's surroundings. Thoreau also thrust himself into the spotlight when he wrote the essay, "Civil Disobedience," arguing for individuals to resist civil government. And he didn't stop there—his works include more than twenty volumes of books, articles, essays, journals, and poetry. Thoreau also was a longtime abolitionist. He spoke often—casually and in formal lectures—against the Fugitive Slave Law and in support of Wendell Phillips' writings and abolitionist John Brown. His own nonviolent resistance beliefs later influenced men such as Mahatma Gandhi and Martin Luther King Jr.

Thoreau's Milestones

1837: Graduated from Harvard University.

1838: Established a school in Concord, where he taught until 1841, when it closed.

Early 1840s: Contributed nature essays and poems to the transcendentalist journal *The Dial*.

1841–1843: Lived in Ralph Waldo Emerson's home. Worked as a tutor on Staten Island.

1845–1847: Built a small cabin on the shores of Walden Pond outside Concord. Lived a simple lifestyle studying nature and writing.

1849: Published the book of observations *A Week on the Concord and Merrimack Rivers* and the essay "Civil Disobedience."

1854: Published *Walden*, a collection of essays on his experiences living on Walden Pond.

1863: *Excursions*, a collection of essays, was published after his death.

1864: *The Maine Woods*, a collection of three essays describing trips he had taken to Maine, was published after his death.

1865: *Cape Cod*, a collection of travel essays, was published after his death.

1895: Poems of Nature was published after his death.

Johann Wolfgang von Goethe

Goethe's literary works covered the spectrum: poetry, drama, literature, theology, humanism, and science. His masterwork is *Faust*, a two-part drama about a scholar who is offered knowledge by the devil. It took him twenty-six years to complete. The second part of *Faust* was finished in the year of his death (1832) and was published posthumously.

Goethe generally is considered the most significant writer in the German language. Early on, however, Goethe—who took lessons in everything from fencing to dancing—thought painting might be his true calling. One thing he knew for certain: law school, which he did for three years, was not for him—he despised it, much preferring poetry classes and writing poems about his new love. In 1770, he anonymously published *Annette*, his first collection of poems.

The rest, as they say, is history.

One of his most important works was a tragedy, *Gˆtz von Berlichingen* (1773) (his first real recognition). *The Sorrows of Young Werther* (1774), which some call the world's first best-seller, recounts an unhappy romantic infatuation that ends in suicide, a writing process Goethe admittedly used to quell his own issues involving obsession. The book itself, which appeared to glorify suicide, was quite controversial at the time, when Christian doctrine denied burial of those who committed suicide.

In the science arena, Goethe wrote about plant morphology and color theory, even influencing none other than the great Darwin.

- Goethe was fascinated by minerals. In fact, the mineral goethite, an iron-bearing oxide mineral found mostly in soil, is named after him.
- Goethe's poetry was set to music by countless composers, including Mozart.

Enrico Fermi: Nuclear Physicist

Born in 1901 in Rome, Italy, Enrico Fermi was very close to his brother Giulio, so when his brother died at a young age, Enrico found solace in studying physics and mathematics. He made gyroscopes, measured the magnetic field of the earth, and studied science and mathematic books given to him by a friend of the family.

At age seventeen, he enrolled in Scuola Normale Superiore in Pisa. There he earned bachelor and doctoral degrees. In 1925, he began teaching at the Institute of Physics in Rome and there formed a notable team of scientists to help with his research. This team made important contributions to practical and theoretical aspects of physics, including Fermi-Dirac statistics, the theory of beta decay, and the discovery of slow neutrons.

Although Fermi was certainly able to complete the most complicated mathematical equations, he often opted for the simpler route in order to receive quicker results. He also kept meticulous notes on his research and referred to his earlier findings to help him solve new problems.

Fun Fermi Facts

- Fermi's lecture notes, especially those for quantum mechanics, nuclear physics, and thermodynamics, were transcribed into books that are still in print.

- Time magazine listed Fermi among the top 20 scientists of the 20th century.

- The Fermilab particle accelerator and physics lab in Batavia, Illinois, is named after him.

- Fermi 1 & Fermi 2 nuclear power plants in Newport, Michigan, are named after him.

Fermi's Large Feats

Fermi won the Nobel Prize in physics in 1938, the same year he moved his family to the US and began working at New York's Columbia University. He then moved to the University of Chicago where he began research that led to the construction of the first nuclear reactor—Chicago Pile-1. This massive pile of graphite bricks and uranium fuel was constructed under the football stadium at the University of Chicago.

After World War II, Fermi served on the General Advisory Committee of the Atomic Energy Commission, which advised the commission on nuclear matters and policy. It was during this time that he wrote opposition to the development of a hydrogen bomb, stating moral and technical rationales.

In his later years, Fermi experimented with particle physics and concentrated on teaching at the University of Chicago. He died in 1954, at age 53.

EXTRA CREDIT: Fermi's son Giulio worked with Nobel laureate Max Perutz on the structure of hemoglobin.

THE FERMI PROBLEM

Physicists often puzzle themselves with Fermi problems—a way of making informed estimations about quantities that seem otherwise impossible to compute. Reportedly, Enrico Fermi came up with what people now call a classic Fermi problem: How many are there in ? To answer the question, you would multiply a series of estimated numbers that would theoretically yield the correct answer. For example:

1. Take the approximate number of people living in Chicago. (estimate: 5,000,000.)

2. Assume that there are approximately two people living in each household, approximately one household in twenty has a piano and they have it tuned once a year. So,
    5,000,000 divided by 2 = 2,500,000
    1 (piano) divided by 20 (households) = .05
    2,500,000 multiplied by .05 = 125,000 (pianos in Chicago)
    125,000 multiplied by 1 (tuning per year) = 125,000

3. Now, it probably takes a piano tuner about two hours to tune a piano, including travel time, and each piano tuner works eight hours in a day, five days in a week, and fifty weeks in a year. So,
    50 multiplied by 5 = 250
    250 multiplied by 8 = 2,000
    1 (piano tuning) divided by 2 (hours) = .5 (tunings per hour)
    2,000 multiplied by .5 = 1,000 piano tunings per year per piano tuner

4. And, finally,
    125,000 divided by 1,000 = 125 piano tuners in Chicago

Obviously, this equation has many assumptions, but this is the way Fermi would have gone about calculating his research. He would first find the rough answer (getting a quick, ballpark result) then move on to the more accurate conclusion.

Galen of Pergamum

Reading about one of Galen's operations is like reading something out of a horror novel. But that was Galen for ya. Born around AD 129, Galen performed many daring brain, eye, and other surgeries that were not attempted again for almost two millennia. When performing cataract surgery, he would insert a long needle-like instrument into the eye behind the lens and then pull the device back slightly to remove the cataract. The slightest blip and his patient would have been blind for life. But Galen, who was born in the ancient Greek city Pergamum, Mysia, (now Bergama, Turkey) became known as a leading Greek physician of his time—his theories led Western medical science for decades.

By the age of twenty, he had spent four years serving as an attending in a local temple. Galen studied the human body, but dissecting of human corpses was against Roman law. No problem for Galen; he simply opted for pigs and apes. After his father died, Galen left Pergamum to study in Smyrna, Corinth, and Alexandria for the next decade or so before returning home, where he worked for a few years as a physician in a gladiator school. Talk about a place to gain some experience! Gladiator school provided excellent opportunities to treat many types of trauma.

In 162 Galen moved to Rome, where he lectured and wrote extensively about his anatomical knowledge. He quickly became known as a top-notch doc and had quite the clientele base. One of his patients, the consul Flavius Boethius, introduced him to the imperial court. Not a bad connection—he then became the physician for the Emperor himself (Emperor Marcus Aurelius). In 166, though, Galen returned to his native city, where he lived until he went back to Rome permanently in 169.

Galen spent his remaining years at the Roman imperial court, where he was given time to write and experiment. He studied the function of the kidneys and the spinal cord on various animals and identified veins and arteries.

Galen's death is thought to have been around 200, but some scholars argue that textual evidence shows he lived as long as 216. Of the six hundred books he wrote, only twenty survive.

CRASH COURSE
TACITUS

Publius (or Gaius depending on who you ask) Cornelius Tacitus was a big muckity-muck back in the Roman Empire, serving as a senator and a historian. His two major works, the Annals and the Histories, examine the reigns of the Roman Emperors you may have heard of—Tiberius, Claudius, and Nero.

Tacitus wrote about his world, in a bold and witty manner, but little is known of his personal life, other than that he studied rhetoric in Rome—who knew such a thing could be studied?—and planned for a career in politics and law. He lived through Domitian's reign of terror, which began in 89 AD and included heavy taxes on the provinces. The times did not sit well with Tacitus and left him despising tyranny.

In 97 he advanced from Senator to consul. Later he was proconsul of Asia. During his time as a politician, he reached all-time popularity as an orator when he delivered the funeral speech for Lucius Verginius Rufus, a famous veteran soldier.

The first of his works, *Dialogus*, a discussion of oratory, welcomed him into the world of authorship. He then wrote *Agricola*, an upbeat biography of his father-in-law, followed by a long absence from politics and law, which gave him time to write the *Histories* and the *Annals*.

EXTRA CREDIT: Some say his work is the most reliable source of history for the era, but Tacitus's facts occasionally are questioned. The *Histories*, written from primary documents and his own knowledge of the period, is thought to be more accurate than the *Annals*.

WILLIAM BUTLER YEATS

Like many great poets, William Yeats's life and work was affected
profoundly by a frustrating failure to woo the woman he loved. In
1889, three years after he had published his first significant poem, *The
Isle of Statues*, Yeats met Maud Gonne, a rich heiress and art student,
who was a devotee of Irish Nationalism. And those politics were Yeats's
undoing.

Yeats was smitten with this young beauty from the start, and
though she was friendly with him, Gonne was staunchly entrenched in
a political lifestyle that Yeats did not or would not share. He tried to
get over her and was involved in a relationship that lasted a year, but
when it was over, he returned to Gonne and asked her to marry him.
She refused.

Three more times—every year for three years—Yeats again
proposed. Every time she rejected him. And in 1903 she really rejected
him—she married another man.

He didn't give up, and five years later, she finally succumbed to his
charms for a night of wild passion. But that didn't work either. She
told him he had to get over her. He tried. He wrote to her of his
prayers for both their abstinence. She wrote him about how abstinence
could be good for poets. So enflamed he was with Gonne that twenty
years later he wrote a poem about their one night. It was called *A Man
Young and Old*. And he didn't give up, proposing one last time, in
1916. He was fifty-one, and he didn't really put his heart into this
proposal. And, again, she said no.

Yeats, however, wanted to wed and have a family, and if Maud was
going to reject him, he knew exactly what to do. He courted and
proposed to her twenty-one-year-old daughter, Iseult, a rough-and-
tumble young woman who had once chased him. She, too refused.
Saddened but undaunted by rejection, he later that year married
Georgie Hyde-Lees, age twenty-four, and they had two children and
twenty-three years of marriage before Yeats died.

Confucius

No belief system in history has influenced the Chinese as much as those of Confucianism. The centuries-old values of China originate directly from the philosophical teachings of a man referred to as Confucius. Unlike most Western religions, and many Eastern ones as well, Confucianism included neither deities nor priests. Instead, the teachings of Confucius focused on the attainment of harmony achieved principally through a strict social order.

It is believed that Confucius was born K'ung Fu-tzu in 551 BC during the Spring and Autumn Period. If the speculation is accurate, his birth would have corresponded with the beginning of the Hundred Schools of Thought philosophical movement. Historians are certain that Confucius was born in an area now known as Shandong Province, probably near the ancient city of Qufu, in the Chinese State of Lu. The Records of the Grand Historian indicate that Confucius was the product of an illicit marriage, as his father was very old and his mother quite young.

Dying when Confucius was barely old enough to walk, his aristocratic father left the boy to be raised by his mother. Although his parents had been of noble blood, the scandalous marriage left the woman and child in poverty, and his rise in society linked him to the shǏ, men whose positions were gained through skills as opposed to heredity. Confucius stressed the love of parents and children, explaining that those who show respect and reverence to their parents will follow suit when engaged with neighbors and friends. Confucius also believed that man would view his ruler as a parental figure, and would therefore remain loyal to him as well.

Students of kung-chiao will find the teachings of Confucius in several texts, the most prominent of which is known as Lun Y, or the Analects. The text, for centuries the fundamental course of study for a Chinese scholar, stresses propriety, righteousness, loyalty, and filial piety. Emphasizing the importance of ritual, the text's transcription of Confucian wisdom demonstrates how such ritual implies order. By following the rituals which inevitably become duties, the followers develop structure and self discipline. The teacher apparently did as he suggested others to do, and it is believed that as a child he enjoyed placing ritual vases on the sacrifice table.

Records indicate that at nineteen Confucius married Qi Quan and had a child the next year. For several years he worked various jobs including cowherd and bookkeeper, until at fifty-three he gained the position of Justice Minister of Lu. He dedicated himself to the Ministry until he found himself greatly disappointed by the Duke of Lu, whose careless debauchery began to lead the state into shambles. Resigning from the position at age sixty-eight, Confucius returned home and began spreading his philosophy to whoever would listen. The teacher immediately gained several disciples.

Confucius employed the *Five Classics* in his instruction, and it was from his interpretation of these texts that Confucianism was born. The texts, made up of *Yi Jing* (*The Classic of Changes*), *Shi Jing* (*The Book of Odes*), *Liki* (*The Classic of Rites*), *Shu Jing* (*The Classic of History*), and *Lin Jing* (*Spring and Autumn Annals*), were of utmost importance to Confucius and his pupils. Referring to himself as a "transmitter who invented nothing," he stressed that the texts be studied as well as venerated for their meaning.

The life of Confucius came to an end around 479 BC, and within a few hundred years his values spread throughout the many states now constituting the nation of China. Thanks to his grandson and disciples, his name became one of great honor. For centuries government officials held his descendants in high esteem, and his teaching continues to thrive in China today.

Confucius Says…

- When it is obvious that the goals cannot be reached, don't adjust the goals, adjust the action steps.
- He who learns but does not think, is lost! He who thinks but does not learn is in great danger.
- If you think in terms of a year, plant a seed; if in terms of ten years, plant trees; if in terms of 100 years, teach the people.
- We should feel sorrow, but not sink under its oppression.
- The superior man acts before he speaks, and afterwards speaks according to his action.

POP QUIZ

1) How many radioactive elements are named after female scientist Marie Curie and her husband Pierre?
   a) 1
   b) 3
   c) 5
   d) 10

2) What are the two most famous works of Islamic physician and philosopher Avicenna?
   a) *The Book of Healthcare* and *The Canons of Navarone*
   b) *Medicinal Theory* and *Medicinal Practice*
   c) *The Book of Healing* and *The Canon of Medicine*

3) Jane Goodall is famous for her study of what animals in their natural habitat?
   a) Koalas
   b) Platypus
   c) Giraffes
   d) Chimpanzees

4) There are more than 2,000 literary characters in the seven-volume masterpiece written by Marcel Proust. What is the narrator's name?
   a) Casey Kasem
   b) Oliver
   c) Marcel

5) Chinese philosopher Confucius influenced a belief system that stressed what?
    a) Confusing thought
    b) Hand-to-hand combat
    c) Selfishness, debauchery, thievery, and drunkenness
    d) Propriety, righteousness, loyalty, and filial piety

ANSWERS:

1) b (curite, sklodowskite, and cuprosklodowskite)
2) c
3) d
4) c
5) d

CONTEMPORARY PHILOSOPHY 101

Ordinary language philosophy—A meta-philosophy employed by conjecturing cerebrals in custody of the ostentatious inclination toward the attainment of a quixotic appointment with a being of the converse gender

Analytic philosophy—Nothing is absolutely true. If one uses logic to find out what is true, they may find some truth. Actually, that's incorrect.

Continental philosophy—Science does not have a monopoly on truth. History makes man who he is, even if he fell asleep in third period.

Critical theory—It is easier to understand literature if you criticize it. "Jane Austen sucks" does not count as criticism. The same goes for understanding society, and social critical theory purports to make changes in society. Paris Hilton, however, has yet to respond favorably to any criticism.

Marxism—This section pending due to governmental backlog.

Personalism—Only persons are real. Unfortunately that includes the person in the next stall who just peed on your shoe. But no worries, because the pee isn't real. For that matter, neither are your shoes.

New Confucianism—Confucius say, "Man who lives in glass house should change underwear in basement."

An Eleventh-Century Reading List

Dream Pool Essays by Shen Kuo (1088)
Le Chanson de Roland (Between 1140 and 1170)
The Tale of Genji by Murasaki Shikibu (Early 11th Century)

Aeschylus: Father of Tragedy

One day he was watching grapes grow, the next his career in tragedy writing was spawned. That's the tale of how playwright Aeschylus became the "Father of Tragedy." As child, Aeschylus was shown to worship the Mother and Earth goddess Demeter, and was sent one day to the countryside to watch grapes ripen. By his own account he took a snooze; in his dream Dionysus appeared (he's the god of wine who inspires madness) and ordered Aeschylus to begin writing tragedies. Well, that he did, beginning the very next morning, and with much success, eventually writing nearly ninety plays.

Many of Aeschylus' works were influenced by the Persian invasion of Greece, which took place during his lifetime. When he died in approximately 456 BC, his epitaph didn't even mention his success as a playwright, but did note his participation in the Greek victory at Marathon.

Check out his play *The Persians* to learn about this period of Greek history. His other surviving tragedies include *Seven Against Thebes*, *The Suppliants*, the trilogy known as *The Oresteia* (consisting of the three tragedies *Agamemnon*, *The Libation Bearers*, and *The Eumenides*), and *Prometheus Bound*. Nearly all of Aeschylus's plays won first prize at the City Dionysia, an annual spring dramatic festival. Together with Sophocles and Euripides, Aeschylus is one of the earliest Greek tragedians whose plays survive.

Legend has it that Aeschylus died when an eagle accidentally mistook his bald head for a rock and dropped a turtle on it. Whether that's true or not, Aeschylus left behind two sons, one who carried on his gift for drama. Euphorion even took first place at the City Dionysia, defeating both Sophocles and Euripides in 431 BC.

Sergei Prokofiev: Musical Genius

Considered one of the most influential composers of the twentieth century, Sergei Prokofiev (pronounced PRO KO fee ehv) was always closely linked to his native Russia. Like the work of Igor Stravinsky, he was famed internationally for his symphonies and operas, but his influences were all Soviet—for better or for worse.

He studied music as a boy in Saint Petersburg and began writing in Russia, though he later lived for a few years in the United States, Paris, and the Bavarian Alps. While spending a year composing in the Alps, Prokofiev met and fell in love with Spanish singer Lina Llubera. They married and moved to Paris, but he longed to return to Russia.

His fan base in his native Ukraine and the other Soviet states was growing, his symphonies and other works gaining in popularity. He went home in 1935. But this was not the same Russia he had left. With Hitler's regime threatening the Soviet Union, the country became increasingly strict about every aspect of activities, including music.

Prokofiev quickly found that he had to play to someone else's tune. The Soviets created a "Composers' Union," which maintained control of all artists and their comings and goings, meaning Prokofiev and his peers were estranged from the musical world. He adapted to the new policy and created a series of songs and compositions, but one of his operas was postponed because its producer was imprisoned and executed.

In 1941, after Prokofiev had his first of several heart attacks, World War II broke out. He and other artists were evacuated to the south, but he had to leave his family behind. Some think the separation was forced.

There, isolated from Lina, he took up with Mira Mendelson, a twenty-five-year-old. Though he and Lina remained married for seven more years, their marriage increasingly fell from favor with the government, which had banned marriages to foreigners. He and Mira married, and Lina was arrested and charged with espionage for trying to send money to her mother in Spain. She received twenty years in prison but later was released and left the country.

Prokofiev's music fared less well than his marriage. He spent two years writing an opera based on *War and Peace*, but government-required revisions stymied its public debut and later decided his music was a dangerous influence for the Soviet people.

He died in 1953, the same day as Josef Stalin passed. Because of the crowds of mourners in Red Square, Prokofiev's body was left sitting for three days after a funeral service at the nearby Composers' Union. His funeral featured paper flowers and taped music, because all the real stuff was used for Stalin's.

And the following day's newspapers wrote of his passing on page 116. The first 115 pages were all about Stalin.

Child Prodigy

Prokofiev was a prodigy. He displayed musical abilities by age five. His mother wrote down his first piece, called Indian Gallop. It was intricate. He learned to play chess at seven and composed his first opera, *The Giant*, at nine. At eleven he started formal training, but already was doing his own pieces. At thirteen, he enrolled at the Saint Petersburg Conservatory. His classmates found him arrogant.

IGOR STRAVINSKY

When *Time* magazine recognizes you, then you've probably done well. That's exactly what the publication did for Stravinsky, naming him one of the one hundred most influential people of the century—not only for his composing but also for this renowned Russian's great work as a pianist and conductor.

It seemed Stravinsky was fated for music infamy from the beginning. His father was a well-known bass singer in a Saint Petersburg theater and Stravinsky, who studied music theory as a child, was already at age eight mesmerized by a performance of the ballet *The Sleeping Beauty*. And at fourteen, he was playing Mendelssohn's Piano Concerto in G Minor—not an easy task for a young teenager.

But his parents had other plans: law. And so law school it was. But he attended only a few classes before the death of his father opened up the doors to more music classes. Then, the aftermath of Bloody Sunday got him out of having to take his law finals. In 1906, he received a "half-course" diploma. After that, it was music all the way.

That's when he met Nikolai Rimsky-Korsakov, a leading Russian composer, who became like a second father to Stravinsky, as well as a mentor. Stravinsky took weekly classes from his new mentor, instead of the more traditional route of entering a conservatory. It was during this time that Stravinsky also got married—to his cousin, Katerina Nossenko. Together they had four children.

Stravinsky first achieved notoriety with three ballets performed by the Russian Ballets, while he was living in Switzerland. The premiere of the third, called *The Rite of Spring* (first performed in 1913), provoked a riot with its series of episodes depicting a wild pagan spring ritual.

In the 1920s he focused on neoclassicism, using mostly traditional musical forms such as the symphony. But, as the decades progressed, so did Stravinsky's style, becoming briefer but more rhythmic and complex.

ASTRONOMY 101
NICOLAUS COPERNICUS

Everyone knows that the sun is the center of the solar system. Some even remember that the Catholic Church convicted an Italian astronomer named Galileo Galilei of heresy in 1633 for saying so. Unfortunately, many fail to remember that the suggestion originated in the head of a fellow from Poland named Nicolaus Copernicus. In actuality, Galileo's conviction resulted from publicizing Copernicus's theory. The idea first appeared in his book *De Revolutionibus Orbium Coelestium* which, when translated, means "on the revolutions of the celestial spheres." The text, printed in Nuremberg in 1543, is considered the seminal work on heliocentrism, the theory that the sun is both stationary and the center of the solar system. Listed below are some other out-of-this-world details about him:

- Copernicus viewed his studies in astronomy as a hobby, and not a serious obligation.
- He was known to his contemporaries as a doctor and, like his guardian uncle, the Canon of Frauenburg Cathedral.
- Copernicus worked as a military leader conducting defense against an invasion of the Knights of the Teutonic Order.
- Legend says that he held the first copy of *De Revolutionibus Orbium Coelestium* in his hands before he died.
- Copernicus is referred to as a polymath, which is defined as a genius in many subjects. Historians recognize him as being proficient as a mathematician, astronomer, physician, classical scholar, translator, Catholic cleric, jurist, governor, military leader and diplomat, and as an economist.

AYN RAND

Born into an agnostic family of non-observing Jews, Alisa Zinov'yevna Rosenbaum entered the world through early twentieth-century Russia. She later became known as Ayn Rand and eventually developed into an internationally-celebrated novelist, as well as the creator of the philosophy of "objectivism." A believer of rational individualism and laissez-faire capitalism, Rand rejected the communist belief system of her native Russia, as well as all religious beliefs. These contrasting philosophies often play large roles in her novels.

The best-selling of her novels include *The Fountainhead* and *Atlas Shrugged.* Both were published mid-century, several years after the writer immigrated to the United States, where she got a job writing in Hollywood. With the intention of making her own success through the enactment of her own beliefs, Rand set out to prove the morality of rational self-interest. She succeeded in her goals, and *The Fountainhead* brought her both fame and financial security.

After years of writing fiction, Rand began devoting her writing to the subjects of philosophy, art, and economic theory. Of particular interest to her were the concepts of individualism and capitalism. She developed her concepts into a structure she called Objectivism, a philosophy proclaiming that reality and consciousness exist independently of one another. As a result, the sole purpose of human life is to pursue one's own happiness and the only way to achieve this happiness is through a social system that displays full respect for individual rights: namely, laissez-faire capitalism.

The reactions to Rand's philosophies vary greatly. As a result, they have been highly controversial since their conception, as have her novels. Nonetheless, her texts continue to be widely purchased. As of 2007, approximately 800,000 were being sold each year.

EXTRA CREDIT: *BioShock,* an award-winning video game released by Microsoft in 2007, centers around a story influenced by *Atlas Shrugged* and Objectivism. Playing the game makes many people find their own happiness. Others wish for increased independence from the Internet for installation of the game.

WALT WHITMAN

Walt Whitman had to fork over his own dollars to get his writing career going, but it was money well spent. It was his first major work—*Leaves of Grass*—and it was published in 1855. The work, an endeavor to reach out to the common folk with an American epic, was a collection of poems that was expanded and revised all the way up until his death in 1892.

This Long Island native was a key part of the shift between Transcendentalism and realism—and preferred to use both notions in his writings. As a poet, "the father of free verse" was not afraid to stir things up, as he did with *Leaves of Grass*, often described as obscene for its unconcealed sexuality. Whitman often wrote freely about sexuality, including prostitution.

Speaking of sexuality, Whitman's own sexuality is often discussed along with his poetry. He's often labeled either homosexual or bisexual. Truth be told, no one even knows if he ever had a sexual relationship with another man.

Along with publishing poetry, during the American Civil War Whitman worked as a journalist, teacher and government clerk, and volunteered as a nurse. Early in his career, he also wrote a temperance novel, *Franklin Evans* (1842).

Whitman was interested in politics during his lifetime. He supported the Wilmot Proviso and opposed the extension of slavery generally, but did not believe in the abolitionist movement.

Whitman's poems, generally prose-like, went way out of the poetic box. For one thing, he used some pretty bizarre images and symbols, from rotting leaves to debris.

Whitman suffered a stroke in his later years, and then moved to Camden, New Jersey, but he got sicker and died at age seventy-two. More than one thousand people attended his public viewing—in just three hours. You could barely see his coffin because so many people had left flowers and wreaths.

J. Robert Oppenheimer

J. Robert Oppenheimer was born to wealthy parents in 1904. He was a bright youth, graduating from high school with straight As. He had a feel for languages and learned Dutch in six weeks so he could deliver a speech in the Netherlands. After graduating *summa cum laude* from Harvard, he completed his doctorate in Germany. He took professorships in theoretical physics at the California Institute of Technology and University of California, Berkeley.

Entrenched in work, he remained isolated from social issues, admitting that he only learned of the 1929 stock market crash after it happened. The Nazi-led invasion that sparked World War II, however, caught his attention. When President Roosevelt created the Manhattan Project—an effort to gain atomic weapons knowledge before Hitler could—Oppenheimer accepted the nomination to act as director.

His intense labor paid off in the creation of the atom bomb. After seeing the explosion of the first test bomb, Oppenheimer recalled a verse from a Hindu epic:

If the radiance of a thousand suns
Were to burst into the sky
That would be like
The splendor of the Mighty One.
I am become Death, the destroyer of worlds.

Because of his instrumental work in its creation and introduction into the world, Oppenheimer became known as the "father of the atomic bomb."

After the war, Oppenheimer chaired the United States Atomic Energy Commission. He argued against developing the hydrogen bomb, stating that he had moral dilemmas and thought the research too costly. Eventually the political climate turned against Oppenheimer. His security clearance was revoked, and he came under investigation.

Oppenheimer left Berkeley in 1947 to accept the directorship of the Institute for Advanced Study in Princeton, New Jersey, where he filled Albert Einstein's former position. He died of throat cancer in his Princeton home in 1967.

Famous Lovers:
Anaïs Nin and Henry Miller

Enter the young and naïve heroine…

"Do not seek the because—in love there is no because, no reason, no explanation, no solutions." —Nin

AnaÔs Nin (1903–1977) was a French-Cuban writer. She kept a journal from the time she was eleven years old. When the journal was published, it drew a lot of attention for its quality writing and intensely personal, often sexual, and provocative subject matter. She called her journal her "kief, hashish, and opium pipe," her "drug and [her] vice." Though a married woman, love and intimate relationships were always important to Nin.

Enter the experienced and passionate hero…

"The one thing we can never get enough of is love. And the one thing we never give enough is love." —Miller

Henry Miller (1891–1980) was a prolific American novelist, with books including *Tropic of Cancer* (1934), *Black Spring* (1936), and *Tropic of Capricorn* (1939). His writing style was influenced by surrealism—the artistic and cultural movement that expresses ideas through unexpected comparisons and associations often in a dream-like manner. Most of his novels involve factual representations of Miller himself while simultaneously being fictional. Miller's life and writing were rich and Bohemian.

The meeting…

When a mutual friend introduced Nin and Miller at a luncheon at her Parisian home, it was not love at first sight. She did find great interest in his writing, though, and financed his work, paying for his living expenses and the first publishing of *Tropic of Cancer*. They were both married at the time, but eventually their friendship grew into a passionate love affair that left Nin writing "I only love the kitchen because Henry is there." Nin's journal and Miller's letters chronicle the happenings of their affair and ardor of their furious infatuation.

THOMAS PAINE

"O! ye that love mankind! Ye that dare oppose not only tyranny but the tyrant, stand forth!"

With those words, Thomas Paine gave his greatest contribution to the revolution of enlightenment thought. Paine was a radical lover of liberty, an inventor, a revolutionary, a deist, abolitionist, and, most importantly, a writer. *Common Sense*, his most famous work, was published in 1776 after he left his homeland of England to join the American Revolution. The book was a revelation. Not only did *Common Sense* call for a revolution against tyranny, it called on every person to make revolution their responsibility- their duty! He said, "I offer nothing more than simple facts, plain arguments, and common sense. . . ." Paine succeeded in winning the hearts and minds of the American colonies, selling five hundred thousand copies the first year alone. To further both the revolution and the man he admired most, he donated all the royalties from his pamphlets to George Washington's Continental Army.

Paine went on to write another important book that would inspire another revolution, *Rights of Man*. Written in 1791, it caused such an uproar in England, that he was put on trail while absent, and convicted of provoking rebellion and libel against the Crown. The book was mainly a defense of the French Revolution from critics and in it he argues for freedom from government and complete human equality. In *Rights of Man*, he dismissed rule by the aristocracy, nobility, monarchy, and all other governments who fail to protect the dignity of mankind.

EXTRA CREDIT: In Greenwich Village, in New York City, there hangs a plaque dedicated to Thomas Paine that reads: "The world is my country. All mankind are my brethren. To do good is my religion. I believe in one God and no more."

Louis Althusser: A Sad Ending

Louis Althusser (1918–1990) was an Algerian philosopher. After studying in Paris, his work was heavily influenced by Marxism and Structuralism. He is most widely known for his work on the concept of ideology in his essay *Ideology and Ideological State Apparatuses: Notes Toward an Investigation.*

In that essay, he uses the metaphors of Sigmund Freud and Jacques Lacan to explain the theory that individuals' identities are created for them by institutions like religion, government, education, family, and so on. Althusser claimed that these institutions interrupt a person's life and tell them who they are supposed to be. People believe the message they receive and become this other identity, this "subject" before they even realize what has happened. Althusser called this the working of "ideology," and since it happens before an individual is even aware of it, he said people are forced into becoming subjects by ideology before they are even born. His work inspired the likes of Jacques Derrida, Michel Foucault, and Judith Butler.

Althusser's life took a turn for the worse when he fought for France in World War II. He was captured and held in a German POW camp for some time. After the war, he suffered from mental and emotional trauma for which he underwent electroshock therapy, a common treatment of the day. From that time on, Althusser suffered from mental illness. In 1980 during a bout of mental instability, he strangled his wife to death. He claimed to have no clear memory of what happened but recognized that he had killed her. He was committed to the Sainte-Anne psychiatric hospital until 1983. He lived the end of his life alone in Paris, until he died of a heart attack in 1990.

Franz Kafka

He may be known as one of the great novelists of his time, certainly one of the greatest German writers, but Franz Kafka lived his life knowing only one claim to fame: He invented the hard hat worn by factory and construction workers.

Most know Kafka for his novels and short stories that have been translated into several different languages. Scholars have studied his work for the better part of a century. But his life was a tragic story borne from a difficult childhood and filled with the ironies, struggles, and tragedies that populate the greatest literary works.

Kafka grew up in a family of nine in Prague—though two of his brothers died as children—and under the rule of a robust and engaged father, Hermann. Franz's father wanted his eldest child to make something of himself that was substantive and reflected success.

Though Kafka became exposed to literature when he studied the classics in high school, when he went to college, he pursued first chemistry and, when that didn't satisfy his yearning to study the arts, the law.

That course work allowed him time to pursue his favored courses, and he made two friends who ultimately would be responsible for his literary career, fellow student Max Brod and journalist Felix Weltsch. Oh, and he did earn a doctorate in law.

Still, after a year as a law clerk, Kafka had to follow his father's direction and pay his bills, so he went to work in the insurance business. Though his job gave him time to dabble with writing, he worked the long, boring hours as best he could for more than six years, serving a couple of different companies, earning promotions along the way.

And in that role in 1912 he created the civilian hard hat, an invention that won a national medal because it significantly reduced deaths among steel-mill workers in Bohemian factories.

Had he penned his autobiography, Kafka probably would have made that the centerpiece accomplishment of the story. For Kafka never knew he could write, much less knew he could make a living at it.

In 1917, at the age of 34, he contracted tuberculosis, which caused a slow and painful deterioration of his body. He endured clinical depression, migraines, insomnia, and many other ailments. He tried many natural treatments, but nothing seemed to work.

He had been living for a year in Berlin, trying to develop some quality of life, but in 1924 he returned to Prague and entered a sanatorium near Vienna. There he died at age forty, reportedly of starvation. His TB-ravaged body simply could not ingest anything to eat.

He had written and published a few short stories, but there was really nothing to show of his literary genius. None of his novels were completed, and he left behind largely unfinished manuscripts, which he had instructed his good friend Brod to destroy upon his death.

Luckily for literature, that didn't happen.

Dora Diamant, a young woman with whom he had lived in Berlin during his last years—he never married—kept twenty of his notebooks and thirty-five letters he had written to her until the Gestapo seized them a decade later.

Brod, seeing the work, overruled Kafka's instructions and developed his unfinished novels—one of them, The Castle, stopped in mid-sentence—into publishable works. All were different from his original German, but they were embraced by literary scholars as masterpieces.

And those letters to Diamant that the Gestapo seized? They've never been recovered. Scholars across the world have tried to find them among the Germans' remnant archives from World War II. Though pieces of them have been located, they largely have vanished. All that remains of the work of Franz Kafka were three novels, some short stories—and the safety helmets worn in factories.

Kafka's Stories

- "A Hunger Artist"—The title of this short story refers to a man whose craft is starving himself to the brink of death. In the good old days, crowds used to gather around him as he wasted away in a cage. As the years go by and people lose interest in his art form, he has to come to terms with suffering, art, and what it means to sell out to the public. (Ironically, Kafka himself died from starvation as he was being treated for tuberculosis. His throat was so sore he could no longer eat).

- "A Country Doctor"—This surreal tale describes the events of one night as a rural doctor tries to find a horse to make a house call. Mysterious horses appear, but as he rides off, his maid is placed in danger. He arrives to discover a patient who may or may not be dying. Can he rescue the patient and his maid, or are forces working against him?

- "The Metamorphosis"—Gregor Samsa wakes up one morning to the surprise of his life: he has turned into a giant insect! Will he be squashed underfoot by his family? Will he ever return to normal?

- "In the Penal Colony"—A condemned prisoner is subjected to a unique torture device, a machine that carves the victim's punishment in words deep into his flesh. He is literally "sentenced" to death.

MUSIC APPRECIATION

JOHANN SEBASTIAN BACH

Everyone knows Bach has something to do with music—if you don't at least know that much, you've got a lot more reading to do. He is, after all, one of the greatest composers ever. But there's a lot more to Bach you might not know.

First, this German composer and organist, born in 1685, wrote more than two hundred cantatas and more than one thousand works altogether. Among his most famous pieces: the *Art of Fugue*, the *Brandenburg Concertos*, the *Cello Suites*, the *English Suites*, the *French Suites*, *Goldberg Variations*, *Mass in B Minor*, *The Musical Offering*, and *Partitas*.

In 1703, tension mounted during one of his first jobs as church organist at St. Boniface's Church in the old town of Arnstadt. The problems were twofold. First, Bach thought choir should consist of higher caliber singers and second, Bach often missed work due to visits to stay and learn from Dieterich Buxtehude, a highly regarded organist of the time.

Three years, later, however, Bach was offered a new job, in a bigger city, with more pay and a better choir. The church was so gung-ho about Bach's arrival it agreed to his proposal to renovate the organ and paid for publishing a cantata he wrote for the inauguration of the new council. Only a year had passed, though, and Bach was climbing the next rung of the career ladder—a better job in Weimar, in the private orchestra of the ducal court.

HENRY FORD – OVER THE YEARS

1863: Born July 30 in what is today Dearborn, Michigan.

1879: Leaves home to go work in Detroit machine shops.

1888: Marries Clara Bryant and goes back home to live on a farm.

1891: Goes back to Detroit again, this time as an engineer with Edison Illuminating Company.

1893: The Ford's only child is born.

1896: Finishes first automobile—called the Quadricycle—and tootles around Detroit.

1899: Leaves Edison to make cars full-time.

1899: Becomes partner in new Detroit Automobile Company.

1901: Becomes engineer in new Henry Ford Company. Disputes with bankers and resigns.

1903: America meets the Model.

1908: Famous Model T in the works.

1910: Highland Park, Michigan, factory opens.

1913: First moving automobile assembly line opens.

1919: Henry Ford's son, Edsel B. Ford, becomes president of Ford Motor Company.

1941: Ford Motor Company and UAW sign contract.

1943: Edsel B. Ford dies at age forty-nine.

1947: Henry Ford dies at age eighty-three.

Famous Last Words

Pope Alexander VI	Wait a minute...
Sigmund Freud	This is absurd! This is absurd!
George Bernard Shaw	Dying is easy, comedy is hard.
Winston Churchill	I'm bored with it all.
James Joyce	Does nobody understand? (Joyce was famous for some of the most difficult books in literature, including *Ulysses*)
Mozart	The taste of death is upon my lipsÖ I feel something that is not of this earth.
Gertrude Stein	What is the answer? [no response] In that case, what is the question? (said to Alice B. Toklas)
Aldous Huxley	LSD, 100 micrograms I.M. (in a request to his wife that she obliged before he died)
Voltaire	Now, now, my good man, this is no time for making enemies (to a priest when asked to renounce Satan)
Karl Marx	Go on, get out! Last words are for fools who haven't said enough! (in response to his housekeeper who asked what his last words were to be)
Ludwig van Beethoven	Friends applaud, the Comedy is over.

CLOSED FOR REMODELING

Humor has long been a staple of storytelling, and literature has always had its share of pranksters. Writer and social activist George Bernard Shaw was no exception. The author of Pygmalion, Shaw often vented his anger at social injustice through sardonic novels and stage plays. The name alone of one such play, *Closed for Remodeling*, nearly ruined the Savoy Theatre in the London city of Westminster.

A vocal opponent of Britain's involvement in World War I, Shaw received great disapproval for his dissent and was nearly tried for treason by the British government. He responded angrily through his best outlet: his position as a celebrated playwright. From this point forward his plays would be consistently more critical of society and government. He created a scathing piece that condemned the so-called "Great War."

Throughout World War I, London's theaters had been closed, and crowds eagerly awaited the reemergence of their favorite pastime. In a mischievous reaction to his recent public criticism, the playwright donned his new play with the title *Closed for Remodeling* and waited. Everyone in the business was excited about the triumphant return of the theater, and the Savoy eagerly booked Shaw's newest piece. The show opened and, night after night, the turnout was atrocious. After three weeks of terrible box office receipts the stage manager of the Savoy Theatre discovered the culprit. The name *Closed for Remodeling*, posted all over London, was leading would-be patrons to believe that the house was indeed in a state of renovation and therefore closed to the public.

When approached by the producers of the show, Shaw denied any malevolence on his part. He agreed to change the name of the show to Heartbreak House, and the Savoy opened to a fervent audience. The show continues to be billed by that name.

The Sarcasm of George Bernard Shaw

- "Beauty is all very well at first sight, but whoever looks at it when it has been in the house three days?"

- "The fact that a believer is happier than a skeptic is no more to the point than the fact that a drunken man is happier than a sober one."

- "Martyrdom… is the only way in which a man can become famous without ability." – from *The Devil's Disciple*

- "It is dangerous to be sincere unless you are also stupid."

- "The reasonable man adapts himself to the world; the unreasonable one persists in trying to adapt the world to himself. Therefore all progress depends on the unreasonable man." – from *Maxims for Revolutionists*

- "A government that robs Peter to pay Paul can always depend on the support of Paul." – from *Everybody's Political What's What*

George Bernard Shaw was vexed his whole life at how difficult spelling was. In his will, he set aside a large amount of his wealth to fund a new alphabet with phonetic spelling. He also wanted someone to estimate the cost in man-hours of how much money was wasted writing and printing in English with an alphabet of only 26 letters instead of the 40 letters he would prefer to see used. Ultimately, £8,300 from Shaw's estate was given towards the development of the new alphabet, though the idea still hasn't caught on.

BRITISH LITERATURE
WILLIAM SHAKESPEARE

Shakespeare is perhaps *the* greatest writer in the English language. Students around the world are required to read his works, from *Hamlet* and *Macbeth* to *King Lear* and *Romeo and Juliet*. And those are just some of his famous tragedies—let's not forget the other end of the spectrum, comedies such as *Much Ado About Nothing*, *A Midsummer Night's Dream* and *The Taming of the Shrew*.

Shakespeare was born and raised in Stratford-upon-Avon. When he was eighteen he married Anne Hathaway, who was twenty-six and pregnant, and together they had three children: Susanna and twins Hamnet and Judith. Between 1585 and 1592 he began a successful career in London as an actor, writer, and part owner of the playing company the Lord Chamberlain's Men, later known as the King's Men.

He appears to have retired to Stratford around 1613, where he died three years later. Shakespeare produced most of his known works between 1590 and 1613. His early plays were mainly comedies and histories, genres he perfected by the end of the sixteenth century. Next he wrote mainly his tragedies until about 1608, considered some of the finest in the English language.

Shakespeare's work has made a lasting impression on later theatre and literature. He expanded the dramatic potential of characterization, plot, language, and genre. Until *Romeo and Juliet*, for example, romance had not been viewed as a worthy topic for tragedy. Soliloquies had been used mainly to convey information about characters or events; but Shakespeare used them to explore characters' minds.

Shakespeare influenced novelists, including William Faulkner and Charles Dickens, and scholars have identified 20,000 pieces of music linked to Shakespeare's works.

EXTRA CREDIT: Shakespeare was buried in the chancel of the Holy Trinity Church two days after his death. A stone slab covering his grave is inscribed with a curse against moving his bones.

The Shakespeare Controversy

William Shakespeare is widely regarded as the most important figure in all of English Literature. There is, however, a growing body of evidence that suggest that Shakespeare was not the author of the works traditionally attributed to him.

Anyone who wrote what is attributed to him would have needed an extensive background in literature, language, writing, and culture. The town that he grew up, Stratford, had no school capable of teaching the higher forms of learning contained in the works bearing his name. His parents were not literate, and early in his life he showed an open disregard for study. There are only six known examples of Shakespeare's handwriting in existence; all of them are signatures, and three of them are in his will. The hand that penned them is unsure, and the scrawling way they were written suggests that Shakespeare is unfamiliar with the use of a pen. It seems obvious to many that either he copied a signature that was prepared for him or that someone guided his hand while he wrote.

A well-stocked library would be an absolute requirement for any author whose works demonstrate a familiarity with the literature of all ages, and yet, there's no evidence that Shakespeare ever owned a library, nor does he mention any books in his will. His own daughter, Judith, was illiterate and at age twenty-seven could only sign her name. What person, who was made famous by writing, would allow their children to grow up unable to read?

These are just a few of the many unanswered questions that remain after Shakespeare's death. Many have suggested that it was in fact Sir Francis Bacon who penned most of the works attributed to Mr. Shakespeare. He had the intelligence, education, and means. We may never know.

THE MANY PLAYS OF SHAKESPEARE'S CONTEMPORARIES

What about Shakespeare's competition? Here are some examples of pieces written by some of the well-known playwrights of his period.

Christopher "Kit" Marlowe (1564–1593)
- *Dido, Queen of Carthage*
- *Tamburlaine*
- *The Jew of Malta*
- *Doctor Faustus*
- *Edward II*
- *The Massacre at Paris*

Thomas Middleton (1580–1627)
- *The Phoenix*
- *The Honest Whore*
- *Michaelmas Term*
- *A Trick to Catch the Old One*
- *A Mad World, My Masters*
- *A Yorkshire Tragedy*
- *The Puritan*
- *Your Five Gallants*
- *The Bloody Banquet*

Robert Greene (1558–1592)
- *The Scottish History of James IV*
- *Alphonsus*
- *Friar Bacon and Friar Bungay*
- *Orlando Furioso*

George Chapman (1559–1634)
- *The Blind Beggar of Alexandria*
- *An Humorous Day's Mirth*
- *All Fools*
- *Monsieur D'Olive*

QUICK & EASY SHAKESPEARE

Here is a simple breakdown of William Shakespeare's three most famous tragedies.

- *Romeo and Juliet* – Two families are in the midst of a terrible feud. Children of each family, Romeo and Juliet, fall in love. They marry in secret and violence breaks out amongst the youth of the clans. After a threat of forced marriage, Juliet fakes her own death. She wakes hours later to find that her love has committed suicide in despair over her death. She responds by planting a dagger into her own body.

- *Hamlet* – Prince Hamlet returns home and receives a visit from the ghost of his late father. The spirit informs him that the prince's uncle, Claudius, poisoned his father to marry his mother and take the throne. Determined to avenge his father but uncertain of the truth of the spirit's message, Hamlet feigns insanity and spurns Ophelia, who kills herself in despair. Hamlet finds enough evidence for revenge, but Claudius suspects the prince and plans to poison him. Ophelia's brother, Laertes, challenges Hamlet. With swords and poison everyone dies: Hamlet's mother drinks the poison intended for Hamlet, who stabs Laertes, who stabs Hamlet, who stabs Claudius.

- *Macbeth* – King Duncan is informed that Macbeth defeats an invasion of the rebel Macdonald. The king praises his kinsman for his bravery. Three witches appear before Macbeth and inform him that he will become king. Macbeth tells his wife and the two begin to plot Duncan's murder. The deed is done and Macbeth blames two servants, leading Macduff to suspect him of foul play. Macbeth and his wife fall into madness of guilt. Viewing Macbeth as a tyrant, Macduff plans a rebellion and eventually beheads the murderous king.

THE SAVIOR OF BOOZE: LOUIS PASTEUR

Because gallons of milk are known to get smelly when spoiled, and because the labels on them generally proclaim "pasteurized," grocery store shoppers may tend to believe that Pasteur's work related only to moo-juice. In fact, the method originally had nothing to do with milkÖ it was all about the booze.

Considered one of the greatest scientists of the nineteenth century for his contributions with new information about microorganisms, Louis Pasteur changed the world. He discovered that life forms existed that were so minute that they could be seen only under a microscope. Armed with that knowledge, Pasteur advanced the sterilization of liquids through a process now known as pasteurization. He also accomplished monumental achievements with curing and preventing diseases that harm and kill humans, cattle, and plants.

Before beginning his studies in the biological and chemical sciences, Pasteur showed extraordinary talent as a painter, creating portraits of his family and friends. Had young Louis decided to pursue his artistic career rather than a scholarly one, the modern world might be a remarkably different place. Luckily, he decided that he wanted to be an educated man, and enrolled in classes at …cole Normale SupÈreure in Paris.

After completing his studies, Pasteur began employment as the head of the science department at the University of Lille. An industrial city that produced wine and beer, Lille offered Pasteur an incredible opportunity on which to focus his vigor and imagination. The townspeople recognized fermentation as a delicate process, but had little cognizance as to why some batches of booze went bad.

Armed with a microscope, the chemist ascertained that little life forms known as bacteria were the culprit. More specifically, the lactic acids created by the bacteria caused the wine and beer to spoil. To remedy the situation, Pasteur created a process which gently heated potable liquids to 140º F. Winemakers were initially horrified at the idea, but soon came around after the taste was proven to be improved by the method. Shortly thereafter beer brewers adopted the technique, improving both the taste and shelf life of the product.

It is probably a rare sight to see a barroom filled with drinkers tipping their glasses to science. If, however, there ever was a chemist who deserved a drink to his health, it is Pasteur. Cheers, Louis.

Mysophobe

Louis Pasteur's work with bacteria made him a bit of a mysophobe, a term referred to in slang as "germaphobe." According to many reports, he refused to shake hands with anyone he met, including royalty. Thank goodness he never had to use a keyboard.

JOHANNES BRAHMS

Johannes Brahms spent much of his life composing in Austria and spending time with composer and pianist Clara Schumann. He is most remembered for *Lullaby and Goodnight,* and his first symphony, which conductor Hans von Bulow referred to as *Beethoven's Tenth.* Here are a few more tidbits on the composer:

- Brahms once fell asleep while composer Franz Liszt was playing piano for him.
- He played with tin soldiers until he was almost thirty years old, and carried candy in his pocket to give out to neighborhood children.
- Schumann was his best friend, and he spent two years of his life helping her raise her children.
- The Third Symphony supposedly came to him during a meal in which he was enjoying fresh asparagus and champagne.
- Brahms was known for the red and white checkered underwear that was almost always visible underneath his baggy pants. He often forgot to cinch his pants when conducting, and audiences regularly witnessed him tugging at his pants when they began to fall down during performances.

James Watt

James Watt, Scottish inventor, was responsible for magnificent improvements to the steam engine in the late eighteenth century. These developments greatly affected changes brought on by the Industrial Revolution by moving the engine from the remote coal fields into the factories of urban centers where many mechanics and engineers were exposed to them. Listed below are more remarkable details of the inventor's life.

- His mother home-schooled him for most of his childhood.
- Watt married his cousin, Margaret Miller.
- He was a member of the Lunar Society, a dinner club and informal learned society of philosophers and industrialists in Britain, as well as the Royal Society of Edinburgh and the Royal Society of London.
- The "watt," a unit of electrical power equal to the power developed in a circuit by a current of one ampere flowing through a potential difference of one volt, is named after him. The naming is in honor of his contributions to steam engine development.
- In the book *Human Accomplishments* by Charles Murray, Watt ties Thomas Edison for first among 229 of the history of technology's most significant figures.

Inventors of Time

"To us, the moment 8:17 a.m. means something—something very important, if it happens to be the starting time of our daily train. To our ancestors, such an odd eccentric instant was without significance—did not even exist. In inventing the locomotive, Watt and Stephenson were part inventors of time."

—Aldous Huxley

FOOD FOR THOUGHT—
GREAT THINKING VEGETARIANS

"Nothing will benefit human health and increase chances for survival of life on Earth as much as the evolution to a vegetarian diet."
—*Albert Einstein*

"Answer me, machinist, has nature arranged all the means of feeling in this animal, so that it may not feel?..." —*Voltaire*

"To become vegetarian is to step into the stream which leads to nirvana." —*Buddha*

"Now I can look at you in peace; I don't eat you anymore."
—*Franz Kafka*

"You have just dined, and however scrupulously the slaughterhouse is concealed in the graceful distance of miles, there is complicity."
—*Ralph Waldo Emerson*

"I do feel that spiritual progress does demand, at some stage, that we should cease to kill our fellow creatures for the satisfaction of our bodily wants." —*Mahatma Gandhi*

"The animals of the world exist for their own reasons. They were not made for humans any more than black people were made for whites or women for men." —*Alice Walker*

"So convenient a thing it is to be a reasonable creature, since it enables one to find or make a reason for everything one has a mind to do."
—*Benjamin Franklin*

"A man can live and be healthy without killing animals for food; therefore, if he eats meat, he participates in taking animal life merely for the sake of his appetite." —*Henry David Thoreau*

Paul Cézanne

The term "struggling artist" is a cliché often applied to writers, painters, and even actors who can't find enough work to pay their bills. It's a cousin to the term "starving artist." Such a person works odd jobs and lives a plebian life to ensure he can devote himself to the passion for his work.

Paul Cézanne was a struggling artist like so many, but let us not leave you with the wrong impression, if you pardon the pun. Cézanne is one of the most beloved French artists from what is called the post-impressionistic era. He had a strong command of color, design, and form that set apart his portraits, landscapes, still-life paintings, and watercolors. He was both prolific and inventive.

But, yes, he struggled. Just not like most artists.

Cézanne was born and resided in southern France, the son of a rich banker. He lived a comfortable life and inherited both money and property. He generally didn't worry about his next paycheck, his next meal, or having a roof over his head.

At age thirteen he attended College Bourbon, where he learned about real art for the first time. One of his classmates was writer Emile Zola—remember that name; it, too, will come up later—though Zola was not in as advanced classes as was Cézanne.

When he graduated, he wanted to pursue art, but his father, the banker, would not hear of it. It was law school for Paul. That was the way it was to be. But that didn't keep Cézanne from taking drawing lessons on the side.

Law school completed, he had it out with his father. He was going to pursue his art. His father finally relented, and later he even embraced his son's career choice. At his death, he left him about 400,000 francs, which was an enormous amount in those days. No, Paul Cézanne did not want for anything more than opportunity. But that, too, proved elusive.

In 1863, when he was twenty-four, his work was part of a show in Paris for artists who had been rejected by the jury from the famous Paris Salon. It was Cézanne's first big opportunity, but he struggled to gain attention and favor.

Every year for the next eighteen, Paris Salon rejected Cézanne's entries for its shows. Finally, another artist intervened on Cézanne's behalf, getting him into a show at the Salon in 1882. But that was the only time the Salon included Cézanne. And it was another thirty years before Cézanne even had his first solo show.

It was hard for him to expose his work to the public. He even struggled to find nude models for his portraits. They were scarce, so he used his wife, family members, and neighbors as his subjects.

In 1870, at the outset of the Franco-Prussian War, Cézanne had a mistress, a woman named Hortense, and they left Paris for Marseille, where Cézanne started to paint mostly landscapes. A few months later, the government declared him a draft dodger. He managed to dodge that charge, however, when the war ended a month later. But that wasn't nearly as big an issue as was Hortense.

Cézanne knew his father wouldn't approve of her, and he just kept the secret from him, remembering how hard it had been to establish his career path with his father's blessing. Even after he and Hortense had a son, Paul, he kept the secret. He was afraid his father would cut off his 100-franc allowance. Later, Dad learned all about it and accepted Hortense. He gave Paul 400 francs for his family, and at his death left him their family's estate. But this is not a happy ending.

Remember his friend Zola? Well, in 1886, about the same time Cézanne was trying to win favor for Hortense, it seems Zola used his childhood friend as the basis for a fictitious artist in the novel *L'CEuvre.* Cézanne didn't like that, considered it a breach of faith, and cut ties to his old buddy.

Soon, many more of his relationships began to sour. In 1890 he contracted diabetes, which changed his personality and caused him to struggle with his family and friends. He went to Switzerland with Hortense and Paul in an effort to resolve their issues, but that didn't work. He returned home to Provence to live, and they to Paris. She later ran out of money and moved back to Provence, but they lived separately, with Cézanne moving in with his mother.

He and Hortense reconciled for a time after his mother died, but the relationship continued to be stormy. He even rewrote his will leaving her out of it. She burned items left to him by his mother.

Cézanne needed to get away from it all, and built himself an isolated studio, becoming another clichÈ, the "reclusive artist." He stayed there virtually until the day he died, in 1906. Cézanne was out working on a landscape in a field. A storm blew up, but he sat there for two hours in the downpour before he thought better of it.

On the way home he collapsed. A driver took him home, and his housekeeper helped to revive him. The next day, after trying to work again, he fainted. His model called for help, and he was put in bed, where a few days later he died of pneumonia, his struggles finally over.

Ironically, in death, unlike not always in life, he was embraced for his great and powerful work. The year after he died, his paintings became parts of large-scale exhibits in Paris, and many now hang in the most famous galleries all over the world. His life has come full circle: He is the inspiration for struggling artists everywhere.

Artistic Advice

Cézanne's advice to a fellow artist just two years before his death: "May I repeat what I told you here: Treat nature by means of the cylinder, the sphere, the cone, everything brought into proper perspective so that each side of an object or a plane is directed towards the central point. Lines parallel to the horizon give depth. But nature for us men is more depth than surface, whence the need to introduce into our light vibrations, represented by the reds and yellows, a sufficient amount of blueness to give the feel of air."

HUNTER S. THOMPSON: GONZO JOURNALIST

"I hate to advocate drugs, alcohol, violence or insanity to anyone, but they've always worked for me."

Hunter Stockton Thompson was well known for his passions for journalism, writing, drugs, alcohol, and firearms. He invented and made famous a style of reporting called "Gonzo journalism," where the reporter imbeds themselves in the action to the point that they become the central figure of their stories.

Thompson created a persona in his writings he called Raoul Duke ("the Duke"). He would use a blend of fact and fiction when portraying himself in his writings and would use Raoul Duke as a surrogate for himself when he needed or desired to be self-destructive, violent, or callous. At one point in the late 1970s, Thompson admitted in a BBC interview that he sometimes didn't know where he ended and the Duke began. When invited to speak at any event, he commonly wondered who it was that they wanted to see. Did they want him, the quirky author, or "the Duke"—the angry, drug-obsessed iconoclast?

He commonly wrote in the first person and let his emotions and past experiences color whatever he was writing about. His main goal was to break away from the cold, objective style of reporting that was the dominant form of writing at the time.

Thompson was a passionate supporter of the right to bear arms and was a longtime member of the National Rifle Association, owning a vast a collection of guns and explosives. He was a cofounder of "The Fourth Amendment Foundation," an organization devoted to the protection of privacy rights, and aided victims of unwarranted search and seizures. He was also a member of the U.S. Air Force (honorably discharged) and, afterward, the Hell's Angels, an experience he later wrote about.

NICCOLO MACHIAVELLI

Niccolo Machiavelli began his political career more than five hundred years ago in the independent city-state of Florence. He did pretty well, bringing his leadership to the public for more than a decade and traveling throughout Europe as a diplomat.

So how did Machiavelli wind up with such a ruthless reputation?

Well, first came the collapse of the republic. Then he lost his job. Not that those are very good excuses. But then he tried repeatedly to suck up to the new regime, and they brushed him off over and over again. Machiavelli took his bruised ego and went, unwillingly, into early retirement.

Since he couldn't actively participate in the political process, he did the next best thing and wrote about it. Still, that couldn't feed his ego because the books he was remembered for were all published after he died.

So Machiavelli wrote , trying to win over the reigning Medici family, but used rather confrontational tactics. Machiavelli argued that a leader's character and/or skill determines a state's success—quite a bold statement at that time. The book explores all the ways the prince's glory can be boosted while serving the public interest. This focus on practical success by *any* means—even at the expense of traditional moral values—earned his "Machiavellian" reputation.

In his *The Art of War* Machiavelli wrote in similar tones. And in *Discourses on Livy*, which focuses on the Roman republic's history, Machiavelli makes it clear that only success and glory truly matter.

Famous Words of Niccolo Machiavelli

- Entrepreneurs are simply those who understand that there is little difference between obstacle and opportunity and are able to turn both to their advantage.
- I'm not interested in preserving the status quo; I want to overthrow it.
- Princes and governments are far more dangerous than other elements within society.

EUCLID OF ALEXANDRIA

Euclid was a reclusive Greek man who lived in Egypt three centuries before the birth of Jesus Christ. His life was important, his impact on the world everlasting.

You want proof? Euclid provided it—geometric proofs. Euclid is known as the "Father of Geometry." Many of the axioms and proofs you tried to master in high school can be traced to this mathematician who studied at Plato's Academy. The work he did remains the basis for the math we know and love—twenty-three centuries later. Six of his works survive to this day:

- *Elements*: Called the most successful textbook in the history of mathematics, it introduced geometry to the world and includes theories about factoring numbers.
- *Data*: A sequel to *Elements*, it discusses the given information in mathematical problems.
- *Catoptrics*: This analyzes the shapes of images in mirrors.
- *Divisions of Figures*: This discusses the division of geometric figures into equal parts or ratio-sized parts.
- *Phaenomena*: Theories about geometric shapes in astronomy.
- *Optics*: Obviously about vision, this discusses the relative size of items and shapes when viewed from different angles and distances.

For all we know about Euclid's work and theories, we know next to nothing about the man. He lived in Alexandria, Egypt, but there are no records of when he died. Except for artists' impressions, there are no likenesses of him.

St. Paul

The curious story of St. Paul, the man most credited with spreading Christianity to the world in the years after Jesus's death, is well chronicled in the New Testament. But even accounts by Luke in The Acts of the Apostles seem in slight contradiction with the way Paul described some of the details in his own thirteen epistles.

There are two versions to many facets of Paul's life, but here are the most pertinent elements:

- Paul was first named Saul and hailed for Tarsus, which is modern-day Turkey. By some accounts he was a tentmaker, but not even Paul has acknowledged that. He changed his name to Paul as he began to tour other countries. He was a Jew and a Roman citizen.
- He persecuted Christians until one day on the road to Damascus he had a conversion. A bright light struck Paul down, and the face and voice of Jesus appeared and asked, "Saul, Saul, why doest thou persecute me?"
- Paul immediately went to Jerusalem and began to tell everyone of his conversion.
- He embarked on a journey, traveling at times with students and other believers, such as Barnabas and Timothy, to spread the word of Christ.
- He traveled to dozens of locations in Asia Minor and to Rome. He taught the message to Gentiles and at his home in Antioch converted Jews who were fleeing Jerusalem. He advised churches and led thousands to the doctrines of Christ.
- He was imprisoned and beaten many times. He would spend years at a time behind bars. He escaped death, even when he was stoned, and he was undaunted in his passion to preach.

But the most questioned aspect of his life surrounds his death. Paul had been arrested in Jerusalem and charged with bringing a Gentile into the temple. He was about to be put to death when Roman soldiers intervened. The Roman commander imprisoned him and had him beaten and, when Paul insisted, sent him off to Rome for trial. Paul wanted to go to Spain, but no one really knows if he got his wish. Some say he spent two years in Rome under arrest.

Many believe he was martyred in Rome—some say on the same day as Saint Peter—and one account says he was beheaded during the reign of Nero.

Clouding the facts is his great mission to Malta. Apparently Paul was sent to Rome via boat and became shipwrecked on Malta, where he preached the gospel and converted the people. So powerful was his work there that the Roman Catholic Church has named him the patron saint of Malta.

His final days in Rome—whether he was martyred there or not— were spent preaching the gospel of Jesus.

Primary Tenets Taught by Paul

- Love one another.
- Pray and invite others to pray.
- Pray at all times.
- Rebuke/correct and forgive.
- Forgive and be compassionate.
- Practice and expect high ethical and moral standards of church members.
- Receive each other as we would receive Christ Jesus.
- Seek humble righteousness.
- Share with those in need those things that God has entrusted to you.
- Support the conscience of fellow Christians.
- Support the right of those involved in Christian ministry to be fairly paid for such ministry.
- Support the sanctity and fullness of fellow-members' marriage relationships.
- Understand that God is one and that we are directly God's children.
- Understand that we are one in Christ.
- Do not sue fellow church members.

American Colonial Poets

Listed below are some of America's first poets and their more well-known poems. The poets are considered colonial, as they all began writing prior to American Independence in 1776. Also recorded are the colonies or cities in which they presided while composing their gifts to American culture.

Anne Bradstreet, Salem (1612–1672)

- "Contemplations"
- "The Tenth Muse Lately Sprung Up into America, by a Gentlewoman in such Parts"
- "To My Dear and Loving Husband"
- "To Her Father with Some Verses"
- "The Flesh and the Spirit"
- "The Author to Her Book"

Edward Taylor—Massachusetts Bay Colony (1642–1729)

- "Huswifery"
- "Upon a Spider Catching a Fly"

Phillis Wheatley—Boston (1753–1784)

- "On Being Brought from Africa to America"
- "To the King's Most Excellent Majesty"
- "An Address to the Atheist"
- "Thoughts on the Works of Providence"
- "To His Excellency General Washington"
- "To S.M., a Young African Painter, on Seeing His Works"
  Philip Morin Freneau—New Jersey (1752–1832)
- "The Wild Honey Suckle"
- "On Mr. Paine's Rights of Man"
- "On the Religion of Nature"
- "On the Emigration to America and Peopling the Western Country"

Evil Genius: The Peculiar Habits of Adolf Hitler

Few would deny that Adolph Hitler impacted the world more than any other leader of the twentieth century. As a fascist dictator and the leader of the Nazi party, Hitler invaded most of mainland Europe, during which time he orchestrated the methodical genocide of approximately six million Jews. Many have blamed his martial conquest of Europe, as well as the deliberate attempt to eliminate what he called "Europe's undesirables," on syphilitic infection. If his many eccentricities, including those reported by the U.S. Office of Strategic Services are any indication, the syphilis theory may hold water.

According to reports, Hitler's twisted interests included his enjoyment of watching "snuff films," which depict the actual killing of a human being. In Hitler's collection of such productions, political prisoners were cruelly tortured and executed: all for the pleasure of the Führer. The films were made specifically for Hitler by his personal staff.

Hitler, like many people, loved attending the circus. According to some, however, his obsession stemmed from the belief that the performers were risking their lives specifically for his pleasure. Although the performers were surely hoping to please their leader, the idea that they risked death in the erotic sense demonstrates the delusional thinking of the megalomaniac.

Finally, there is the issue of Hitler's unusual humility in contrast with the hubris characteristic of such a man. Apparently incredibly shy about his body, he refused to undress in front of others. Regardless of the temperature, Hitler was neurotic about being completely covered in public. As a result, he never removed his overcoat while outdoors.

POP QUIZ #2

1) How did astrologer Tycho Brahe lose part of his nose?
   a) In an astrology accident
   b) In a fire
   c) In a fight with a classmate

2) The unit of electrical power known as the "watt" is named in honor
   of which contribution made by Scottish inventor James Watt?
   a) Contributions to steam engine development
   b) First to use the phrase "Watt's up?"
   c) Continually asked his wife "Watt's for dinner?"

3) Which two of Bach's many themes have been particularly used in
   rock songs?
   a) Foccacia and Feud in D minor
   b) Stocatto and Lewd in A minor
   c) Toccata and Fugue in D minor

4) Euclid of Alexandria is known as the father of what?
   a) Alexander the Great
   b) Literature
   c) Nicholas and Alexandra
   d) Geometry

5) Who is the main character in Kafka's "The Metamorphosis"?
   a) Oliver
   b) Gregor
   c) Marcel

6) Who is the Father of Tragedy?
    a) Hippocrates
    b) Socrates
    c) Euclid
    d) Aeschylus

7) What was Stravinsky's third ballet?
    a) *The Rite of Spring*
    b) *The Nutcracker*
    c) *The Sleeping Beauty*

8) Which is NOT an Ayn Rand novel?
    a) *Atlas Shrugged*
    b) *Leaves of Grass*
    c) *The Fountainhead*

9) How did Anaïs Nin and Henry Miller meet?
    a) At a bar
    b) In the park
    c) Through a friend

10) How many times did poet William Yeats propose to Maud Gonne?
    a) 3
    b) 4
    c) 5

Bonus: How many times did she refuse his proposal?

ANSWERS:

1) c
2) a
3) c
4) d
5) b
6) d
7) a
8) b
9) c
10) c
Bonus: 5

Hernán Cortés

Hernán Cortés, a Spanish conquistador of the sixteenth century is famous for initiating the conquest of the Aztec Empire on behalf of Charles V, King of Castile. Most people are aware of his involvement in the conquering of the New World, but here are some facts often forgotten:

- Friend Francisco López de Gómara described Cortés as impatient, arrogant, and roguish.
- Cortés dropped out of law school at the University of Salamanca in 1501 to join the military.
- He was nearly killed by the owner of a house after falling off of an estate's wall while trying to visit his girlfriend.
- Diego Velasquez, an important settler in Hispaniola, hired Cortés as an officer in a group hired to overpower Cuba. Together they conquered the island, and Cortés became a respected leader in the Caribbean.
- Aztecs first mistook him for Quetzalcoatl, a light-skinned, bearded God-King of the Aztecs. Quetzalcoatl means "feathered snake."
- When Cortez arrived in the ancient city of Tenochtitlan he burned it to the ground, killing all who lived there. He then built Mexico City on the ruins.
- In 1527, Cortés brought cocoa beans combined with sugar to Spain, giving birth to the civilized world's obsession with chocolate.

Queen Elizabeth II

Known throughout the world as the Queen regent of the United Kingdom, Elizabeth II has lived through one of the most extraordinary times in history for the British royal family. Because of the evolution of politics within the Queen's realm, namely the development of democracy in the U.K., a transition has occurred changing the role of royal nobility from an authoritative one to that of figurehead. Listed below are some remarkable facts about the Queen.

- Elizabeth II is also Queen of Canada, Australia, New Zealand, Jamaica, Barbados, the Bahamas, Grenada, Papua New Guinea, the Solomon Islands, Tuvalu, Saint Lucia, Saint Vincent and the Grenadines, Belize, Antigua and Barbuda, and Saint Kitts and Nevis.

- The Queen has sent more than 280,000 telegrams to couples who are celebrating their diamond wedding anniversary.

- In 1953 and 1954, Queen Elizabeth II became the first monarch to circumnavigate the globe on a six-month tour around the world.

- Queen Elizabeth II is the only female member of the royal family to serve in the armed forces. While serving she learned to drive a car.

- The Queen has presented her staff with approximately 78,000 Christmas puddings, continuing the custom of King George V and King George VI.

- In 1986, the Queen became the first British Monarch in history to visit the nation of China.

- In 2003, Queen Elizabeth II posed for the first and only hologram portrait of a member of royalty.

PSYCHOLOGY 101
CARL JUNG

Carl Jung was a Swiss psychologist and the founder of analytical psychology, a branch of psychology that believes dreams, mythology, and folklore are the best tools for unlocking the secrets of the unconscious mind. Carl Jung, in opposition to many modern psychologists, believed that modern science was ill-equipped to deal with the complex nature of the human psyche. He believed that the universal models for all people, or archetypes, could be found in similar stories that exist in all cultures.

As in evolution, where modern humans share physical similarities, Jung thought that we also shared a common psychological heritage, which he called "the collective unconscious." The idea is that there is a "personal consciousness," which are your thoughts and feelings that make up your personality. Deeper, beneath that, like a piece of fruit, there is a core that all people share that makes them distinctly "human."

Like many anthropologists, Jung took note that all cultures had creation stories, a higher power they respected, demons, and stories that explained all manner of phenomena. He said, "As far as we can discern, the sole purpose of human existence is to kindle a light in the darkness of mere being."

Carl Jung studied under Sigmund Freud and before their split, many felt he was set to inherit Freud's throne as the figurehead of the psychiatric field. Jung's work was also unique in the fact that he employed the long-forgotten field of alchemy to explain the psyche. He felt the purpose of alchemy ("turning lead into gold") and the field of psychology ("to know thyself") shared a common purpose and that the allegories and symbols of both could be interchangeable. To turn the emotional, animal self (lead) into an enlightened being (gold) was the goal of all psychology—to have ultimate knowledge of the self.

Jung's work has been influential to psychologists, counterculture, and people around the world. The C.G. Jung Institute, founded by student and peer Marie-Louise Von Franz, still exists today in Zurich.

THOMAS AQUINAS

Thomas Aquinas was headed on the road to the ministry when something seemed to go wrong. Growing up in Sicily, he was planning as early as age five to follow in his uncle's footsteps into a Benedictine monastery. And in fact that's the age when he began his studies with the monks.

At sixteen he went to study at the University of Naples and came under the influence of the Dominicans, a religious sect counter to the Benedictines. He started having second thoughts about the traditional Catholic structure.

Because of the deep traditions of Italy, Thomas's family didn't take those changes of heart too well, and his brothers seized him when he was traveling to Rome and took him home. He was held captive there for a year, and some biographers wrote that his brothers even tried to tempt him from his commitment with a prostitute. Legend has it that angels descended from Heaven and girded him for chastity.

Finally, Pope Innocent intervened and allowed him to study under St. Dominic. He was 17. Miracles and legends seemed to follow Aquinas. Monks claim to have seen him levitating, and when one of his essays was laid at the bottom of the cross, friars claimed that the image of Jesus descended upon it and that a voice said, "Thomas, thou hast written well concerning the sacrament of My Body."

He spent most of his career in Paris educating himself and others. When he fell in disfavor with traditionalists there, he returned to Rome and later died on the road while traveling to try to mend divides between the Greek and Roman churches.

Fifty years after Aquinas's passing, Pope John XXII made him a saint and gave his teachings great prestige. Festivals were held in his honor, and his doctrines were cited as among the most definitive of the Catholic Church. His preaching and teaching became iconic examples for all who followed, and he became the patron saint of all Catholic education. Many schools to this day bear his name. Ever heard of any school called St. Thomas Aquinas?

EXTRA CREDIT: James Joyce rated Aquinas second among the great Western philosophers. Joyce's No. 1? Aristotle.

HIPPOCRATES: CONTRIBUTIONS TO MEDICINE

Hippocrates first described clubbing of the fingers—clubbed fingers are sometimes called "Hippocratic fingers." Clubbed fingers are an important diagnostic sign in chronic suppurative lung disease, lung cancer, and cyanotic heart disease.

Hippocrates first classified illnesses as acute, chronic, endemic, and epidemic.

Hippocrates also described the symptomatology, physical findings, surgical treatment, and prognosis of thoracic empyema.

The Hippocratic school of medicine described the ailments of the human rectum as well as their treatments. Hemorrhoids, though believed to be caused by an excess of bile and phlegm, were treated by Hippocratic physicians in relatively advanced ways.

Famous Words of Hippocrates

- Walking is a man's best medicine.
- The chief virtue that language can have is clearness, and nothing detracts from it so much as the use of unfamiliar words.
- Science is the father of knowledge, but opinion breeds ignorance.
- Life is short, art long, opportunity fleeting, experience treacherous, judgment difficult.
- A wise man should consider that health is the greatest of human blessings, and learn how by his own thought to derive benefit from his illnesses.
- If we could give every individual the right amount of nourishment and exercise, not too little and not too much, we would have found the safest way to health.
- Prayer indeed is good, but while calling on the gods, a man should himself lend a hand.

CRASH COURSE
THE HIPPOCRATIC OATH

The Hippocratic Oath is an oath traditionally taken by physicians pertaining to the ethical practice of medicine. It is widely believed that the oath was written by Hippocrates, the father of medicine, in the fourth century BC, or by one of his students.

I swear by Apollo Physician and Asclepios and Hygeia and Panacea and all the gods and goddesses, making them my witnesses, that I will fulfill according to my ability and judgment this oath and this covenant:

To hold him who has taught me this art as equal to my parents and to live my life in partnership with him, and if he is in need of money to give him a share of mine, and to regard his offspring as equal to my brothers in male lineage and to teach them this art—if they desire to learn it—without fee and covenant; to give a share of precepts and oral instruction and all the other learning to my sons and to the sons of him who has instructed me and to pupils who have signed the covenant and have taken an oath according to the medical law, but no one else.

I will apply dietetic measures for the benefit of the sick according to my ability and judgment; I will keep them from harm and injustice.

I will neither give a deadly drug to anybody who asked for it, nor will I make a suggestion to this effect. Similarly I will not give to a woman an abortive remedy. In purity and holiness I will guard my life and my art.

I will not use the knife, not even on sufferers from stone, but will withdraw in favor of such men as are engaged in this work.

Whatever houses I may visit, I will come for the benefit of the sick, remaining free of all intentional injustice, of all mischief and in particular of sexual relations with both female and male persons, be they free or slaves.

What I may see or hear in the course of the treatment or even outside of the treatment in regard to the life of men, which on no account one must spread abroad, I will keep to myself, holding such things shameful to be spoken about.

If I fulfill this oath and do not violate it, may it be granted to me to enjoy life and art, being honored with fame among all men for all time to come; if I transgress it and swear falsely, may the opposite of all this be my lot.

David Hume

David Hume was a controversial Scottish writer from the eighteenth century whose philosophies on life, religion, and science were an inspiration to many. Albert Einstein, Charles Darwin, and future U.S. President James Madison were said to have been influenced by Hume's views. Einstein even said Hume inspired his famous Theory of Relativity.

So controversial were Hume's views he carefully disguised his personal opinions in dialogue and examples that sometimes could be contradictory. Further, many of his most famous works were published either anonymously, posthumously, or so late in his life that he could not be affected by their impact.

He was a prodigy—his parents sent him to the University of Edinburgh at ten or twelve years old—and by twenty-six he had written perhaps his most famous book, *A Treatise of Human Nature*, which was four years in the making. The book was widely banned at its release, and Hume didn't acknowledge having written it until just before his death in 1776.

He ignored the criticism and had a prolific career. *The History of Great Britain* took him fifteen years and a million words, and the book covered eleven volumes. For decades it was considered the definitive historical reference.

However, it was the subject of religion in which Hume became a polarizing figure. He was known to be an atheist—though some of his writings cleverly cast doubt on that fact—and this kept him from many appointments he sought. But there was one time, Hume told friends, he was converted to Christianity—at least for a moment. While walking in Edinburgh to supervise the building of his new home, he had to cross a loch that recently had been drained. He slipped and fell into the mud. Now Hume was a rather corpulent fellow, and he became, well, stuck there. Some women of Edinburgh saw him but refused his request for help. They told him he was an atheist and that he had to convert before they would help. So Hume followed their requests and recited The Lord's Prayer and the Apostle's Creed. Then the women hoisted him out of the mud. He called these women "the most acute theologians he ever met."

MICHELANGELO

Michelangelo di Lodovico Buonarroti Simoni, more commonly known simply as Michelangelo, sculpted two of his most famous works, the *Pieta* and the *David*, before he turned thirty. And another interesting fact—he did not hold painting in high regard, yet created two of the most influential works in fresco in the history of Western art: the scenes from Genesis on the ceiling and *The Last Judgment* on the altar wall of the Sistine Chapel in Rome.

Later in life he designed the dome of St. Peter's Basilica in the same city and revolutionized classical architecture.

Michelangelo's father sent him to study grammar in Florence as a young boy, but his son showed zero interest in school. Instead, he spent his time copying paintings from churches and hanging out with painters.

So Michelangelo was apprenticed in painting when he was thirteen and later in sculpture—he must have paid better attention to those teachers.

In 1505 Michelangelo was invited to Rome—he'd been invited before—by the newly elected Pope Julius II. He was commissioned to build the Pope's tomb. That job took forty years, in part because he also was commissioned to paint the ceiling of the Sistine Chapel, which took approximately four years to complete (1508–1512).

Michelangelo originally was commissioned to paint the Twelve Apostles, but lobbied for a different and more complex scheme. The composition eventually contained more than three hundred figures and had at its center nine episodes from the Book of Genesis, divided into three groups: God's Creation of the Earth; God's Creation of Humankind and their fall from God's grace; and lastly, the state of Humanity as represented by Noah and his family. Among the most famous paintings on the ceiling are the Creation of Adam, Adam and Eve in the Garden of Eden, the Great Flood, the Prophet Isaiah, and the Cumaean Sibyl.

The fresco of *The Last Judgment* on the altar wall of the Sistine Chapel was commissioned by Pope Clement VII. Michelangelo worked on the project from 1534 to October 1541. *The Last Judgment* spans the entire wall behind the altar of the Sistine Chapel.

CRASH COURSE

VIRGINIA WOOLF

Virginia Woolf was a prominent British novelist, essayist, and lecturer. She wrote such canonical Modernist novels as *Mrs. Dalloway* (1925), and *To the Lighthouse* (1927) as well as nonfiction, feminist texts like *A Room of One's Own* (1929) and *Three Guineas* (1938). Her fiction tends to focus on the shift in culture and society at the turn of the century from Victorian to Modernist tendencies. She highlights the changing role of women and growing materialism, and laments the effects of war. Her nonfiction has claimed her spot as one of the most pivotal feminist writers.

She married Leonard Woolf, her self-titled "penniless Jew," and they formed the Hogarth Press in their London home. The press printed such important works as T.S. Eliot's masterpiece poem "The Wasteland," pieces by Freud, both of the Woolfs, H.G. Wells, and Katherine Mansfield, among many others. The press continues to operate to this day.

From their London home, Virginia and Leonard participated in the Bloomsbury Group: a loose association of thinkers in the early twentieth century that met regularly to discuss literature, art, and politics. Other members included Clive and Vanessa Bell, John Maynard Keynes, and E.M. Forster. Virginia acted as an informal leader of the group. The group helped shape her ideas and writing.

Virginia had several extramarital, usually lesbian, love affairs. One of the most famous, with fellow Bloomsbury group member and poet Vita Sackville West, inspired Woolf's novel *Orlando*, a lesbian love-letter of sorts.

For most of her life, Woolf suffered from depression. She had a nervous breakdown in 1941 from which she never recovered. She drowned herself on March 28, 1941, by weighing her pockets with stones and walking into the River Ouse.

What Will They Think of Next? Common Products and the Great Thinkers Behind Them

Adhesive Tape: The first adhesive tape, known as Scotch Tape, was invented by Richard Drew, a 3M employee and banjo player, in 1930.

Aluminum Foil: Initially, foil was fashioned from tin, and wasn't replaced by aluminum until 1910. A man by the name of Charles Martin Hall created the electrolytic process that turns aluminum into foil in an efficient way for mass production.

Aspirin: Believe it or not, Hippocrates was the one to first discover the properties of the willow plant that relieved pain in the fifth century BC Later, in the nineteenth century, scientists labeled the compound as salicin and created Aspirin.

Band-Aids: The Band-Aid, a trademarked bandage, was created in 1920 by a man named Earle Dickinson. Dickinson's wife was always injuring her fingers with kitchen knives while cooking. He created Band-Aids after discovering that adhesive tape and gauze would fall off quickly while one was using his or her hands.

Chapstick: A doctor by the name of C.D. Fleet created Chapstick in the 1880s. His first tube looked like a small candle wrapped in foil. His wife then began selling pink Chapstick, which proved to be a hit among the ladies of Lynchburg.

Compact Disc: An inventor named James Russell created the compact disk in 1965 and was granted twenty-two patents for his system of compact disk creation, recording, and playing. The disc wasn't manufactured on a large scale until the 1980s when Philips began to sell the CD.

HENRIK IBSEN

Henrik Ibsen was a little out there for his time, but today he's often referred to as the father of modern drama. In his home country, Norway, he's especially revered in big ways.

This Norwegian playwright's works were considered quite scandalous at the time. Take *Ghosts,* for example. In this 1881 play, a widow fesses up to her pastor that she had been hiding the troubles of her marriage. The pastor's earlier advice (back when he was her fiancé) had been to marry him despite his having fun with the ladies. She took his advice, thinking she could change her future hubby.

Of course, things didn't work out that way. Her husband continued his fun way—right up 'til he died—and their son turned out to have syphilis. Venereal diseases were a big hush-hush thing back then.

In *An Enemy of the People,* which came out in 1882, Ibsen challenged a main Victorian concept. See, the community back then was looked at as a dignified society that could be trusted. *An Enemy of the People* featured a physician as the play's protagonist. He was quite an upstanding guy in the community. The town was a hot vacation spot because of its awesome public bath.

In the play, Doc discovers that the bath's water is nasty—contaminated. He rightly expects to earn praises for letting the town folk know about the cooties but instead is labeled an "enemy of the people" by his former friends. Some even toss rocks at his windows. Nice.

Ibsen's folks were Knud Ibsen and Marichen Altenburg, who lived in a small Norwegian town. He came from a line of some of the oldest and most prominent Norwegian families but soon after he was born, his family had financial issues.

His parents handled their money problems in different ways—his mom turned to God, his father just went sad. The characters in Ibsen's plays often seem like his folks, while the plays' themes tend to focus on financial troubles and dark secrets.

At a mere fifteen, Ibsen fled home and started to learn the pharmacist biz while writing plays. Soon after, he fathered an illegitimate child with a servant maid he wanted to have nothing to do with (after he got her pregnant). While Ibsen did fork over some child support bucks for a few years, he never met his son.

He spent the next several years working at the Norwegian Theater in Bergen, where he helped produce, write, and act in a whopping 145-plus plays.

In 1858 Ibsen married Suzannah Thoresen and they had their only child, Sigurd. They lived pretty poor, and Ibsen grew depressed with Norwegian life. Six years after stepping up to the alter he fled to Sorrento, Italy, alone. He would not go home for nearly three decades.

The Wild Duck (1884) is considered by many to be Ibsen's greatest play. The story centers on the young Gregers Werle, who goes home after a prolonged exile—sound familiar?—and is reunited with his boyhood pal Hjalmar Ekdal. His old buddy had an unhappy homelife, and he spills the beans to Gregers after Gregers persists on learning the truth. Gregers learns more than he bargained for. For one, Gregers' father got their servant pregnant and then married her off to Hjalmar to legitimize the child. Gregers also discovers that another man was locked up for a crime Gregers' daddy actually committed. Phew.

Ibsen died in what is now Oslo in May 1906 after suffering a bunch of strokes. In 2006, the 100th anniversary of Ibsen's death was commemorated in Norway—other countries, too—and dubbed the "Ibsen year" by Norwegian officials. Also on this date the Ibsen Museum reopened a completely restored writer's home, and a biographical puppet production of his was performed in New York City.

EXTRA CREDIT: *An Enemy of the People* was turned into a hit film, *Ganashatru* by Satyajit Ray, an Oscar-winning movie-maker from India. In 1978, Steve McQueen of the U.S. also made a movie out the play—and gave himself the lead role.

CRASH COURSE
A DOLL'S HOUSE

If this 1879 Henrik Ibsen play were written in the 1970s, it could have been called "I Am Woman, Hear Me Roar." A Doll's House tells the story of Nora, the pampered, sheltered wife of the patronizing Torvald. His pet names for her include "songbird" and "little squirrel," which tells you all you need to know about him. He fell ill early in their marriage, and in order to get the money to pay for his medical bills, Nora forged some papers. His pride would have been wounded if he had known that she had squirreled away the cash necessary to save him, so Nora never tells. Unfortunately, her secret is discovered by Krogstad, a disgruntled employee of Torvald's bank. He threatens to blackmail Nora. Eventually Torvald discovers the truth about her "crime." Never mind the fact she saved his life. He berates her so harshly that by the time he tries to apologize for his cruel words, she is outta there. The play ends with her slamming the door, leaving Torvald in the dust.

Henrik Ibsen's Crazy Habits

- Henrik Ibsen began writing everyday at 4:00 a.m.
- He wrote with a pet scorpion on his desk.
- He had an affair with a 27-year-old when he was 63.

THE PARABLES OF JESUS CHRIST

Jesus's style of using stories to illustrate the points he wanted to convey to the public was a cornerstone of his ministry. Called "parables," these stories appear through the Gospels to present lessons for all. He told these stories to small groups and great masses. They were the backbone of his most famous teachings, enduring today in many Sunday School lessons.

There are at least fifty parables in Matthew, Mark, Luke, and John, and eleven of the parables appeared in three of the four books. Luke has thirty-four of these stories, and Matthew twenty-nine. John included only two. Some of these were only a verse or two—two of them share being the longest with sixteen verses—they vary in length among the authors. The story of The Sower even was two parts in Matthew.

But one thing is clear: These parables introduced phrases, characters, and messages that remain common today in both Biblical teachings and nonsecular conversation:

- The Good Samaritan: Help others, no matter the circumstance.
- The Prodigal Son: Love conquers all sins.
- Lost sheep: We all become strays in life.
- Unclean spirit: Your soul may not live up to your actions.
- Budding fig tree: Labor bears fruit.
- Good Shepherd: A man must lead his flock.
- Great Physician: God can heal all things.
- Rich Man, Poor Man: Earthly possessions don't guarantee Heaven.
- Pharisee and the Tax Collector: Don't brag about what you do in comparison to others.

Jesus' Miracles

The Gospels list at least three dozen miracles that Jesus performed. Most of them were general healings, though some were directed at nature and a few more were about casting out demons.

There were three resurrections: a little girl, a boy, and his friend Lazarus.

Some of his most famous were:

- Turning water into wine (his first)
- Curing a man of demons
- The cleansing of the leper
- The cure at Bethsaida
- The man with the withered hand
- The tempest stilled
- Expulsion of devils
- Five thousand fed with five loaves and two fishes
- Jesus walks on the water
- The blind man sees
- A possessed boy
- The man born blind
- The raising of Lazarus from the dead
- The servant's ear healed

The feeding of the five thousand with the loaves and fishes—symbols to this day of efforts to feed the hungry—was written in all four gospels, one of only two miracles accounted for by all four writers.

Guess the other one. Yes, perhaps his most famous miracle of all: Jesus walks on water. It was the enduring message of showing Peter that faith will allow anything to happen.

Peter didn't have enough faith, and when he tried to walk out on the sea to meet Jesus, he sank.

Jesus' Time

Jesus's life is the divider of the history as we know it. All years before his birth are listed as BC, meaning "Before Christ." Some think AD means "After Death." Actually AD is for *anno domini*, which in Latin means "in the year of our Lord."

Logic would say that Jesus, then, was born in AD 0 and died in about AD 33, because we known he lived to be thirty-three. But no one really knows the exact date of His birth or death. The Gospels that chronicle his life in the New Testament of the Bible were given great historical credence because they were written soon after his death, but even their accounts are not specific.

Scholars have used the names and events they described and traced them against other historical information. Their findings suggest that Jesus was born sometime between 6 BC and AD 4. Why?

Matthew and Luke wrote that Jesus was born during the reign of Herod the Great, who died in 4 BC And Luke said it occurred during the first census of the Roman province of Judea, which was in AD 6

And then there's the matter of Christmas itself. We celebrate Jesus's birthday every December 25, but there is no evidence that he was born on or near that date.

Jesus's death on the cross at Calvary also is a question mark on timing. Pontius Pilate was the Roman officer who was said to have crucified Jesus. Pilate served as the "prefect" of Judea between AD 26 and 36 And the events such as the Last Supper and his trial in Jerusalem were said to be during Passover, a Jewish holiday celebrated in early Spring. Good Friday, the day Jesus was crucified, and Easter Sunday may be arbitrary celebrations based on these facts.

So even if no one knows exactly the span of Jesus's life, that calendar drawn up in Medieval times, which attempted to count backward to Jesus's birth and set that as its starting point, doesn't seem to be far off.

Who Was Jesus?

The entire belief system in Christianity is based on one simple tenet: Jesus is the son of God, born to the virgin Mary and her husband Joseph, and who died on the cross as a sacrifice for the sins of mankind. All those who believe this will be forgiven and spend eternity in Heaven.

Though most other religions acknowledge the life of Jesus and the story of his ministry and miracles, many do not accept his Divine heritage.

Here are some examples of how Jesus is recorded in the histories of several religions:

Islam: Jesus was a messenger of God sent to lead the children of Israel through scripture. Muslims believe he was born to the virgin Mary but that he was not crucified by the Jews. Rather, they believe he ascended into Heaven when he was alive. He is believed to have been a Muslim.

Judaism: Jews think the idea that Jesus was God, part of a Holy Trinity or even the Messiah, to be heresy. He wasn't even considered to be a prophet. They believe Malachi, who wrote the last book of prophecy in the Old Testament to be the last prophet. Jesus didn't fulfill the requirements specified in the Torah to be a prophet. In fact, some Jews think to believe anything else means you no longer are a Jew.

Hinduism: Jesus is believed to be the son of God born to a virgin, but he also is believed to be a Brahman with two births. Various sects have differing views, ranging from Jesus as a messenger of God, to being the epitome of perfection, to being a reincarnation of Elisha who studied under John the Baptist.

Buddhism: There are varying views, but most think Jesus was a person who dedicated His life to the welfare of human beings.

New Age: There are a wide variety of views, but generally the churches believe that all humans can attain Christhood. Some think Jesus had various incarnations. Most think he was a preacher and leader who protected women and children.

Indira Gandhi

The Prime Minister of India from 1966 to 1977 and then again from 1980 until her assassination in 1984, Indira Gandhi was India's first and only female prime minister. The daughter of Jawaharlal Nehru, a central proponent of India's independence movement, and the granddaughter of nationalist leader Motilal Nehru, Gandhi was raised in a powerfully political environment. When India gained independence from the British crown in 1950, Nehru became India's first prime minister. At this time Gandhi, educated at Oxford, began serving as her father's unofficial personal assistant. For the next several years she climbed India's political ladder until she received the nomination of Prime Minister in 1966.

Gandhi's initial popularity with the Indian voter resulted in leftist policies and her involvement with the "Green Revolution," known officially as the Intense Agricultural District Programme (IADP). The IADP attempted to ensure copious amounts of grain for those citizens living in India's urban centers. As a result of her support for the green agenda, as well as other populist platforms which included the nationalizing of India's financial institutions, Gandhi received support from the country's largely popular Socialist Parties.

Increasing instability entered India during the mid-seventies, which resulted in Gandhi's support of a "State of Emergency," which included, among other things, the arrest of all political opposition. The period included "President's Rule," forced curfews, and suffocating censorship in the press. As a result, Gandhi's opposition grew rapidly. In 1977, overestimating the party's popularity, Gandhi and President Ahmed called forth an election, which they lost to the Janata Party. Within months, the Janata Party had her arrested. The arrest had an unexpected influence, however, and her support among the people quickly began to grow again. Because infighting plagued the current administration, voters reelected her in 1980. Her term would last four years, until October 31, 1984. On that day, two of Gandhi's bodyguards—secretly members of a separatist Sikh militant group— gunned her down only moments before she was to be interviewed by a documentary crew from Ireland.

SALADIN

Anyone born inside a grand castle is probably destined to do great things. Such was the case for Saladin. His castle was in Tikrit, where he was born sometime in 1137 to 1138. The Kurd's destiny was to become Sultan of Egypt and Syria, and a major Muslim political and military leader.

The Ayyubid dynasty, which Saladin founded, eventually would rule over Egypt, Syria, Iraq, Hejaz, and Yemen. But Saladin is most well known for joining and leading the Muslim armies during the Crusades and recapturing Jerusalem in 1187. During this time, Saladin established a solid reputation throughout Europe as a gallant knight.

During the conquering of Jerusalem, many people were slaughtered. But afterward Saladin granted amnesty to all common Catholics—even to the defeated Christian army—as long as they could pay the set ransom.

The Ayyubid dynasty only continued for fifty-seven years beyond Saladin's death, but his legacy lives on within the Arab world today. With the escalation of Arab nationalism in the twentieth century, Saladin's valor and leadership brought new importance.

Saladin died in Damascus, Syria, just after dawn on March 4, 1193. His treasury did not have enough money to pay for his funeral because he had given most of his money away to charity. He is buried in a mausoleum outside the Umayyad Mosque in Damascus.

Several movies about Saladin have been released, including the 1963 Egyptian film *Al Nasser Salah Ad-Din.* Two years later in the *Doctor Who* serial *The Crusade,* he was played by Bernard Kay. The 2005 Ridley Scott movie *Kingdom of Heaven* starred Syrian actor Ghassan Massoud as Saladin. The 2007 Swedish movie *Arn—The Knight Templar* has Saladin portrayed by Indian actor and supermodel Milind Soman.

The Saladin, built by Alvis, was a six-wheeled armored car named after Saladin and used by the British Army and others.
Saladin is an animated television series inspired by the life of Saladin and produced by the Multimedia Development Corporation (MDeC) in Malaysia. Production began in May 2004 and the first episode will air in late 2009.

ELI WHITNEY AND THE COTTON GIN

Eli Whitney envisioned a device that could clean seed from cotton and make the South flourish—and make himself, of course, incredibly rich. He began working on it right away and within just a few weeks of his idea, he had a rough model of his cotton gin—a machine that was separating fiber from seed. After making his model perfect, he filed for a patent in June 1793. It wasn't until nine months later that he got his wish—a patent for the cotton gin.

Whitney's gin did in fact bring the South richness, but planters weren't too thrilled about paying to use the new machine. Whitney was out of business by 1797. Congress turned down another patent—his first one expired in 1807—and Whitney gave up trying to patent future inventions, including his milling machine.

Whitney is, of course, still best remembered for his extraordinary cotton gin invention, but he also was the father of the mass production system. In 1798 he started the method by mass manufacturing muskets. He used a machine so the parts could become interchangeable. Although the cotton gin business failed, the musket manufacturing business brought much wealth to the Whitneys.

Famous Words of Eli Whitney

- I have now taken a serious task upon myself and I fear a greater one that is in the power of any man to perform in the given time—but it is too late to go back.
- One of my primary objects is to form the tools so the tools themselves shall fashion the work and give to every part its just proportion.
- I have always believed that I should have had no difficulty in causing my rights to be respected.

CRASH COURSE
JOHN LOCKE

John Locke was a philosopher and writer of the late seventeenth century who was known for his views on liberalism and self, but he also was a writer of great influence on matters of government and economic forces. The son of a Puritan couple, he started a career in medicine, mainly because he saw the need. But he quickly developed a passion for philosophical essays. Politics became his primary interest, and his writings became both controversial and influential.

- **Slavery:** He wrote the Constitution of the Carolinas, which defined how man had perpetual ownership over his own slaves as property.
- **Property:** He uses this term broadly to cover human interests and hopes and, of course, material goods.
- **Labor creates property:** Man limits his ability to produce by his capacity to consume. He introduced "durable goods," in which man can exchange perishable goods for those that last longer and create wealth.
- **Supply and demand:** He defined supply as quantity and demand as rent. The price is always set by the number of people who want to buy something. Money masters all things, he believed, and there was always plenty of rent of money.
- **Currency:** He didn't like the paper stuff, saying gold and silver were the proper currency to create value for an object and to create a promise for a consumer.
- **Trade:** His theories might be lost on America. He believed countries should encourage balanced trade and not carry national debt.

But all of that seemed very basic when you heard him write about "self." Locke believed people were born without preconceived concepts and learned everything they needed to know. He called self "that conscious thing," and he believed the self was more than capable of self preservation.

JANE AUSTEN

Born in 1775, Jane Austen is one of the most widely read British writers ever. The plots of her novels, including best-selling *Sense and Sensibility* and *Pride and Prejudice,* focus on moral issues.

But her books did not thrust her into the spotlight during her own lifetime. *A Memoir of the Life of Jane Austen,* written by her nephew and published in 1870, helped bring her more notoriety. However, it wasn't until the 1940s that Austen was labeled a truly great writer.

In the 1780s—educated by her father and brothers—Austen began writing poems, stories and plays to entertain her family. She put at least two dozen of these into notebooks, now called the *Juvenilia.* Austen continued to live at her parents' home into adulthood, and eventually decided to become a professional writer.

Austen had six brothers and an older sister, Cassandra, who was her dearest friend throughout her life. Her brother Henry was her literary agent and also lil' sis' connection to a large social circle in London.

In 1802, Austen received her only marriage proposal while visiting two sisters (the sisters' younger brother proposed and Austen accepted). By the next morning, however, fickle Austen had changed her mind and told him so. She was more careful after that—she never married.

In 1808, Austen's brother Edward provided his mother and sisters a large cottage in the village of Chawton, which was part of his estate— they previously had been living in Bath. It was during her time there that Jane published her four most successful novels, *Sense and Sensibility, Pride and Prejudice, Mansfield Park,* and *Emma.* Today, the Chawton Cottage is a museum. The house and garden are open to the public.

In 1816, Austen fell ill, and the following the year she died. She has been described as dying from a degenerative disease widely believed to have been Addison's disease.

JANE AUSTEN'S MOST FAMOUS NOVELS

Sense and Sensibility (1811)
Pride and Prejudice (1813)
Mansfield Park (1814)
Emma (1815)
Persuasion (1817) (posthumous)
Northanger Abby (1817) (posthumous)

All six were made into films, including the following:
In the 1995 movie *Sense and Sensibility*, directed by Ang Lee, Emma Thompson played Elinor Dashwood, Kate Winslet played Marianne Dashwood, Hugh Grant starred as Edward Ferrars, and Alan Rickman played Colonel Brandon.

Persuasion was a made-for-TV film (1995) that starred Amanda Root as Anne and Ciarán Hinds as Captain Wentworth.

Mansfield Park was a 1999 movie directed by Canadian Patricia Rozema and starred Embeth Davidtz, Sheila Gish, Harold Pinter, and Frances O'Connor.

Northanger Abby, directed by Giles Foster, was released in 1986. Peter Firth played Henry Tilney.

Famous Words of Jane Austen

- They are much to be pitied who have not been given a taste for nature early in life.
- Good-humoured, unaffected girls, will not do for a man who has been used to sensible women. They are two distinct orders of being.
- A woman, especially, if she has the misfortune of knowing anything, should conceal it as well as she can.
- Friendship is certainly the finest balm for the pangs of disappointed love.
- A large income is the best recipe for happiness I ever heard of.

CRASH COURSE
SENSE AND SENSIBILITY

In this Jane Austen masterpiece, Elinor is all sense (reason) and Marianne is all sensibility (feeling), or at least for most of the book they are. However, once each feels the pain of desertion from the man they love, they begin to see the wisdom in the other sister's point of view. Older sister Elinor loves Edward Ferrars, but she is too dignified and, well, sensible, to show it. He shares her restraint, which keeps him from telling her one tiny, important fact—he has been secretly engaged to Lucy Steele for, oh, about four years now. Oops. Meanwhile, Marianne meets the love of her life, John Willoughby, while running through a field in a storm. She twists her ankle, and, like a knight in shining armor, he comes to the rescue. Turns out, though, that this knight is a bit rusty. He harbors a few secrets of his own, which make his competitor for Marianne's affections, Colonel Brandon, all the more attractive as Marianne wises up and gets a little more sensible. Eventually everyone lives happily ever after, once they learn to balance out their reason with their emotions.

Jane Austen was so humble and shy about her writing that no one ever caught her with a pen in hand. "No matter how suddenly one arrives, she has heard the door close … and hidden the white sheets," writes biographer Virginia Moore.

ROBERT GODDARD

If you've heard of the Goddard Space Flight Center, then perhaps you're familiar with this American professor and scientist who launched the world's first liquid-fueled rocket. (The day was March 16, 1926; the place was Auburn, Massachusetts.)

Goddard continued launching rockets through 1935, reaching speeds of up to 550 mph. Despite ground-breaking work in his field, Goddard's theories often were made fun of. Goddard received more than two hundred patents for his work, but only eighty-three came during his lifetime. Although he received little recognition while he was living, Goddard would become known as one of the fathers of modern rocketry.

Goddard's Legacy

A crater on the moon is named after Goddard, as is the Goddard Space Flight Center—built in 1959. Then there's the Goddard School of Science and Technology elementary school in Worcester, built in 1992 in his hometown.

Also named after Goddard are the Dr. Robert H. Goddard Collection and the Robert Goddard Exhibition Room (both can be found in the Archives and Special Collections area of Clark University's Robert H. Goddard Library). Step outside the library, and you'll find a structure of the flight path of Goddard's first liquid fuel rocket.

In 1967 Robert H. Goddard High School was built in Roswell, New Mexico. Their mascot? The "Rockets," of course. Robert H. Goddard Middle School is located in Glendora, California. That school's mascot is a little more specific: the Titan IIIC missile. Goddard Middle School is also located in Littleton, Colorado (mascot = the Vikings).

In Auburn, Massachusetts, the Pakachoag golf course has a small memorial with a statue in his name. No, it has nothing to do with golf—it's the site where he launched the first liquid-propelled rocket.

Art 101

Pierre-Auguste Renoir

As a boy, Pierre-Auguste Renoir often visited the Louvre to study the French master painters. Little did he know that his own works would someday hang in the famous museum. But in 1919, he was able to visit the Louvre—and see his paintings hanging next to the old masters.

Renoir was a French artist and leading painter in the development of the Impressionist style. His paintings are noted for their vibrant light and saturated color, most often focusing on people in intimate and candid compositions. The female nude was one of his primary subjects. In characteristic Impressionist style, Renoir suggested the details of a scene through freely brushed touches of color, so that his figures softly fused with one another and their surroundings.

Renoir was born in France, the child of a working class family. As a boy, he worked in a porcelain factory. His drawings were so good that he was chosen to paint designs on fine china. Before enrolling in art school, he also painted hangings for overseas missionaries, and decorations on fans.

In his later years, after developing rheumatoid arthritis, Renoir moved to a warmer climate, close to the Mediterranean coast. He painted during the last twenty years of his life, even when arthritis severely limited his movement and he became wheelchair-bound. Renoir began developing deformities in his hands and ankylosis of his right shoulder, requiring him to adapt his painting technique. In the advanced stages of his arthritis, he painted with a brush strapped to his paralyzed fingers.

During this period he created sculptures by directing an assistant who worked the clay. Renoir also used a moving canvas, or picture roll, so he could paint large works with his limited joint mobility.

Extra Credit: Two of Renoir's paintings have sold for more than $70 million. *Bal au moulin de la Galette, Montmartre* sold for $78.1 million in 1990.

Aldous Leonard Huxley

Aldous Huxley's claim to fame is *Brave New World*, the novel that foresees developments in reproductive technology, biological engineering, and sleep-learning that combine to alter society. The controversial book, which dehumanizes aspects of scientific progress, has been removed from classroom and library shelves over the years. The American Library Association ranks *Brave New World* Number 52 on their list of The 100 Most Frequently Challenged Books of 1990–2000.

Aldous Leonard Huxley, born in 1894, was an English writer who lived the latter part of his life in Los Angeles. Although it went unpublished, he had completed his first novel at the age of seventeen. Most well known for his novels and essays, he also wrote numerous short stories, poems, travel pieces, and scripts.

Huxley, a known big fan of mescaline and LSD, received in 1959 the American Academy of Arts and Letters Award of Merit for *Brave New World*. Two decades earlier he received the James Tait Black Memorial Prize for *After Many a Summer Dies the Swan*.

Notable film works include the original screenplay for Disney's animated *Alice in Wonderland*—although it was rejected for being overly literary—two productions of *Brave New World*, and one each of *Point Counter Point*, *Eyeless in Gaza*, and *Ape and Essence*. He was a credited screenwriter for *Pride and Prejudice* (1940), coauthored the screenplay for *Jane Eyre* (1944), and worked on the screenplay of *Madame Curie* (1943).

Famous Words of Aldous Huxley

- An intellectual is a person who has discovered something more interesting than sex.
- A bad book is as much of a labor to write as a good one, it comes as sincerely from the author's soul.
- A man may be a pessimistic determinist before lunch and an optimistic believer in the will's freedom after it.
- After silence, that which comes nearest to expressing the inexpressible is music.

AURELIUS

Marcus Aurelius Antoninus Augustus—some called him simply "the wise"—was Roman Emperor from 161 until he died in 180. He ended the reign of the "Five Good Emperors," and also is remembered as one of the most important Stoic philosophers.

Marcus Aurelius's best-known *Meditations* is still thought of as a literary testament to a government of service and duty. John Steinbeck, by the way, has the character Lee in his book *East of Eden* read often from *Meditations* as a sage-like being. And in *The World According to Garp*, John Irving has the character Garp ponder over a quote of Marcus Aurelius from *Meditations*.

On the more personal side of things, Aurelius wed Faustina the Younger in 145. They were married thirty years and together had thirteen children:

- Annia Aurelia Galeria Faustina (147–sometime after 165)
- Gemellus Lucillae (died around 150), twin brother of Lucilla
- Annia Aurelia Galeria Lucilla (148/50–182), twin sister of Gemellus, married her father's coruler Lucius Verus
- Titus Aelius Antoninus (born after 150–161)
- Titus Aelius Aurelius (born after 150–161)
- Hadrianus (152–157)
- Domitia Faustina (born after 150–161)
- Fadilla (159–after 211)
- Annia Cornificia Faustina Minor (160–after 211)
- Titus Aurelius Fulvus Antoninus (161–165), twin brother of Commodus
- Lucius Aurelius Commodus Antoninus (Commodus) (161–192), twin brother of Titus Aurelius Fulvus Antoninus, later emperor
- Marcus Annius Verus Caesar (162–169)
- Vibia Aurelia Sabina (170–217)

MUHAMMAD

Muhammad is the most important human figure of the religion of Islam—and is looked upon by Muslims as the messenger and prophet of God, or Allah, the final and the most supreme in a series of prophets of Islam.

Muhammad was born in AD 570 in the Arabian city of Mecca but was orphaned in his youth and raised by his uncle. When he reached working age he was employed as a merchant, and at age twenty-six he married. He grew unhappy, though, with life in Mecca, and fled for a mountain cave for meditation and reflection. According to Islamic beliefs it was here, in the month of Ramadan, where he obtained his first revelation from God. He would have been forty years old. Three years later Muhammad began preaching these revelations to the public, declaring that "God is One" and that the people must "surrender" to him completely. He told the people that he was a prophet and messenger of God.

Few people listened—some even treated him rather harshly, so much so that Muhammad and his followers had to flee to Yathrib (now Medina) to evade persecution. This time of escaping actually was a historically significant event—the Hijra—and begins the Islamic calendar. In Medina after eight years of fighting with the Meccan tribes, Muhammad's followers—now in the thousands—occupied Mecca. In 632 Muhammad returned from Medina. There, he became sick and died. But by then, most of the Arabian Peninsula had converted to Islam.

During his lifetime, Muhammad reported receiving many revelations. Those revelations form the verses of the Qur'an—the "word of God" for Muslims. Along with the Qur'an, Muslims uphold Muhammad's life and traditions.

EXTRA CREDIT: Muhammad translates to "praiseworthy" and is mentioned four times in the Qur'an.

GEOMETRY 101

PYTHAGORAS

$a^2 + b^2 = c^2$ —You knew *someone* had to have come up with this famous little math equation. Pythagoras is your guy, or Pythagoras of Samos. Born between 580 and 572 BC—yes, the good ol' Pythagorean theorem is *that* old—Pythagoras hails from a Greek island called Samos.

Deserving, he is given the nickname "father of numbers," but Pythagoreanism (and it was called that even way back then) actually was more a religious movement than a math class movement. Herodotus called Pythagoras "the most able philosopher among the Greeks."

The Pythagorean theorem is a geometry rule that states that in a right-angled triangle the square of the hypotenuse (the side opposite the right angle), c, is equal to the sum of the squares of the other two sides, b and a—that is, $a^2 + b^2 = c^2$.

Famous Words of Pythagoras

- Concern should drive us into action and not into a depression. No man is free who cannot control himself.
- A thought is an idea in transit.
- As long as man continues to be the ruthless destroyer of lower living beings he will never know health or peace. For as long as men massacre animals, they will kill each other.
- Do not say a little in many words but a great deal in a few.

WILLIAM BLAKE: ROMANTIC POET

Though his work earned him the legacy of being one of the most influential poets and artists of the Romantic Era, William Blake was not exactly a warm and sensitive guy until the very end. In fact, for the first few decades of his life, some would say he was an out-and-out troublemaker.

Blake, like many artists, was a bit of a prodigy. He never had a formal education, being home schooled by his mother. Though his artistic talents were apparent, his parents knew better than to send him to art school. They knew he was a handful. Instead he was enrolled in drawing classes.

And when Blake was unleashed upon the world at the ripe age of fourteen, he began to show the artists and teachers of London that he was a force that had to be reckoned with—and not just in the artistic or literary sense.

Blake began his career as an engraver, creating metallic images of other people's work, and he was quite good at it. He pioneered several new approaches to this art form, including the use of color. After he had served a seven-year apprenticeship, at age twenty-one, Blake became a professional engraver.

Throughout that internship, Blake was often at odds with his teacher—James Basire—and his fellow students. And he later even listed Basire as a lifelong artistic rival.

He was sent off on a work detail to Westminster Abbey to separate him from a classmate with whom he quarreled. And while sketching works in the Abbey, he was pestered by students from a nearby school. One of them tormented Blake so frequently that, in frustration, Blake knocked that student off a scaffold to the floor below.

At twenty-one he enrolled as a student of the Royal Academy, where he argued with his instructors about the quality of the art the academy featured. For all six years he studied there, Blake constantly criticized the school's president for his views.

During that time he also participated in a prison riot. Citizens stormed the gates of Newgate Prison in London to free the prisoners in protest of some new laws that had been passed. History books differ on Blake's role in these riots. Some writers say he was an innocent bystander caught up in the surge of people. Others say he was right at the front of the pack, leading its anarchy. Either way, he was there during the uprising.

He even rebelled against the conventional attitudes toward sexuality, writing in his poems about what he felt was the absurdity of forced chastity, about marriage without love, and for the rights of women to be self-fulfilled.

Blake married Catherine Boucher, who was nineteen at the time and took pity on Blake for being jilted by another woman. She was six years younger than he, and she was illiterate. She signed their marriage license with an "X." Though the couple never had any children and their marriage wasn't always the best of times, Blake loved Catherine, and she loved him. He taught her to write, and she helped him color his illustrated poems.

But Blake's biggest problem with authority came in 1803, when he was forty-six. Blake got into a fight with a soldier; he was charged with assault and—worse—saying nasty things about the King. He was acquitted at trial, but Blake later took his revenge by including the image of the soldier, John Scofield, in manacles in one of his illustrations.

Perhaps that run-in mellowed Blake, or perhaps he simply decided to put his frustrations into his poems and artwork, but the final days of his life tell us that he had found a measure of inner peace for which he was not quite so well known as he was his recalcitrance.

In his last days, at age seventy, Blake was struggling to finish his illustrations for *Dante's Inferno,* which would become his most renowned work. Catherine was said to have watched him struggle with that difficult assignment as he battled his failing health. As she sat by his side and watched, Blake was moved by her tears and quickly drew her portrait. Then he put down his tools for the last time and began to sing hymns.

He turned to Catherine and told her that he would be with her forever, then closed his eyes and died. A woman staying in the same house watched this last day and later was quoted as saying, "I have been at the death, not of a man, but of a blessed angel." Blake was buried a few days later in an unmarked grave, on the eve of his and Catherine's forty-fifth anniversary. She said in later years that she believed she was visited regularly by Blake's spirit, and she would not sell any of his works without consulting with "him." On the day she died, it was written that she was very happy and called out to Blake as if he were in the next room, saying "I'm coming to join you."

Interesting Facts About William Blake

Blake's most famous and powerful works were based on Biblical times and stories. *Jerusalem*, *The Bible*, and *Dante's Inferno* all were in both words and images his translation of the events and characters described in the Bible. He never completed *Dante's Inferno*, but it still became his most famous work for its inventive images of Hell. Some of the sexual images in his work were removed by one of his colleagues after his death.

Blake claimed he had visions of God and angels. As early as age four, he told his parents about what he had seen. Even as an adult, he said he saw religious images, which became central to his writings.

Blake was a great influence on popular songwriters. His own songs have been adapted by such artists as U2, Van Morrison, Bob Dylan, and Allen Ginsberg.

RICHARD WAGNER

If you've ever tried to solve a crossword puzzle, you may have a clue about this man. Richard Wagner was a renowned German operatic composer, and many historians consider Wagner's most famous and influential opera to have been *Tristan und Isolde.*

Those two lovers' names are often the solution to 34 Across or 28 Down. They are as much a staple of the puzzles as the "goddess of dawn" (Eos, if you care). But such mundane fame—and the real historical kind—for this opera almost eluded Wagner, because he endured great difficulty and a tumultuous lifestyle to compose and present Tristan and Isolde's story.

Though known as a composer, Wagner was always drawn to the story, which was the lure of opera for him. He had been influenced greatly at an early age by exposure to theater, and he studied Shakespeare as a teenager, thinking of a career as a playwright.

And when he turned to composing, he showed a penchant for a good story. He even wrote the libretto to accompany his music, which was not and is not routine among composers.

After getting married, moving to Russia, losing his wife to a soldier and taking her back, Wagner found himself living in Dresden in 1849. Embroiled in political turmoil among leftists, he played a key role in the movement for unification of the German states into one democratic nation.

The king had rejected the call for change, and there was an uprising in which Wagner played a marginal role. The revolution quickly was quashed, but arrest orders for the revolutionaries forced Wagner to flee first to Paris and then Zurich.

He spent twelve years in exile, and thus was isolated from the German musical scene in which he had become entrenched. That left him with no significant means of income. He persuaded a friend back in Germany to stage operas he had written, just so he could earn a living.

Wagner's love life didn't help him, either. He had this penchant for getting involved with other men's wives, which often disrupted his work, not to mention his residences. Or perhaps his habit inspired him. Nevertheless, he had two wives, a few mistresses, and some illegitimate children, all of whom he had to finance.

During his exile, he fell in love with a woman named Mathilde Wesendonck, who was, of course, married. He was friends with the woman's husband, a silk merchant, who set up Wagner in a house near Zurich. Mathilde, however, never returned Wagner's love. Or at least she said she didn't. They wrote letters and saw each other, but Mathilde told her husband that there was nothing romantic about the relationship. Still, Mr. Wesendonck thought they maybe shouldn't live so near each other.

Jilted and evicted from the house, Wagner yet was inspired by Mathilde, and it was then that he began to write the story of Tristan and Isolde. The process took most of three years.

In 1861, the political ban in Germany ended. Wagner, by then forty-eight years old, returned, moving to Prussia, and started to launch *Tristan und Isolde*. For three years he tried to have that opera produced in Vienna, but despite dozens of attempts, no one could stage the show. Many thought it was unplayable, and that didn't help Wagner's difficult financial status.

His big break came when, in 1864, King Ludwig II took over Bavaria. Ludwig was only eighteen, but already he was an admirer of Wagner's operas. He had Wagner brought to Munich and paid all his debts. That allowed, after several more arduous rehearsals, for *Tristan und Isolde* to premier in 1865 at the National Theater in Munich, his first such debut in fifteen years.

One final sidebar: The conductor of that performance was Hans von Bülow, whose wife, Cosima, became embroiled in an affair with Wagner and gave birth to his illegitimate child. That daughter's name? Isolde. Their affair was such a scandal, King Ludwig moved Wagner to Switzerland. Cosima convinced her husband to give her a divorce and moved there, where she married Wagner. They had two more kids, but there is no record if one of them was Tristan. They were married until Wagner's death, thirteen years later.

So the next time you see a crossword clue about a famous character in Wagner's operas, you will know the story behind that answer.

YUKIO MISHIMA

Writers often end their novels and short stories—even their plays—with dramatic and grisly scenes that shock their readers and viewers. Yukio Mishima did that to his own life, virtually writing an ending that was as unexpected, horrific, and upsetting as anything his pen could conceive.

A bit of history on Mishima: He was a Japanese prodigy who wrote forty novels, poetry, twenty books of short stories, at least twenty books of essays, eighteen plays, and even an operatic libretto, before embroiling himself in a political life that was his undoing.

Actually, he was born in 1925 as Hiraoka Kimitake to a family of governmental and educational leaders. He basically was removed from the household for several years by his grandmother, who took over his guardianship. She was a pretentious sort, given to an aristocracy to which she was neither born nor married. She also was sometimes violent, morbid, and extremely controlling. She wouldn't let Mishima play any sport, play with other boys, or even to go outside, requiring him to spend most of his time with his female cousins and their dolls.

With that foundation, he was returned at age twelve to his father's rule, which meant he was subjected to corporal punishment, invasions of his privacy, and other frightening tactics that today would be deemed abusive. But it was at that time that he began to write his first stories. He read Oscar Wilde and many other classic writers voraciously and attended for six years one of Tokyo's elite schools, where he was accepted to write for the literary magazine.

His first short story was so acclaimed by his instructors for its techniques and insights that they created his pseudonym, Mishima, to protect him from classmates who often bullied him.

When he apparently purposefully failed his physical for being drafted into the army during World War II, Mishima was prohibited by his father from writing and directed to finish his education and take a government job. But Mishima, of course, continued to write secretly, and at last his father relented. He quit the government job and dove into his craft.

132

He spent the next two decades writing novels—several of which became movies, such as *The Sailor Who Fell from Grace with the Sea* and *Way of the Samurai*—short stories, and plays. He traveled extensively, became an avid weightlifter, married, and had two children. A hint of normalcy after all the turmoil—it was short-lived.

In 1967 Mishima, never a fan of the post-war government, formed a private army of young martial arts students who were sworn to protect the emperor. He trained them himself. His goal was to return the power of Japan to the emperor, though not necessarily the current token monarch.

In 1970, he and four cohorts took over the Japan Defense League headquarters. They had a manifesto and a list of demands. They took hostages and prepared to affect change. In a scene right from a script, he moved to a balcony to address assembled soldiers, intending to rouse them to take over the government and restore the emperor's power. But he failed. Angered, they mocked and jeered him. The cause was lost.

Mishima retreated to the office and ordered the implementation of his own ritualistic suicide, in which a predetermined lieutenant would cut off his head. The assigned person failed, and a second person had to take over the beheading.

Unbeknownst to many, Mishima had spent hours writing this scene in his "death poems," which explained his detailed plans for this suicide. His biographers later suggested that the coup was not really his goal but simply the means to end his own life.

Yasunari Kawabata

The writer many say is responsible for getting Japanese literature translated into Western languages, Yasunari Kawabata, built that reputation on a long career of novels and short stories that left his readers grasping at the end. That's because Kawabata's trademark was to leave many of his works unfinished, or at least without clear resolution.

Yes, this penchant earned him criticism from some reviewers and cries of frustration from his loyal readers. Maybe that was why Kawabata wrote the ending to his own life in much the same way: He committed suicide at the age of seventy-two. Some family members have disputed that version of his death and said he had succumbed only to illness, but many sources concur that he took his own life. Their reasons are varied, but none of them is clear.

Kawabata was an accomplished star of literature, Japanese or otherwise, rising from a debut short story he published shortly after completing Japan's version of college (they called it Upper School). His breakthrough came at age twenty-six or twenty-seven with the short story "The Dancing Girl of Izu," a romantic tale of a college student and a young dancer.

Romance and even eroticism were the themes of many of his stories, but those weren't what Kawabata told his colleagues were his greatest influences.

Kawabata was born into a well-to-do family, but his parents died when he was a toddler. He was sent to live with his grandparents, and his sister was sent to an aunt. They saw each other just one time, when he was ten.

His grandparents had both died by the time he was fifteen, and he was forced to move in with his mother's family to finish his education. He did so quickly, pursuing a humanities degree in Tokyo, where he first started writing in a literary magazine.

Kawabata's career had blossomed fully by the outbreak of World War II, but he was not active in the military, or the new government that the war's end left behind. He simply withdrew into his writing, also working as reporter for a local newspaper. Still, he said the war and his own sad childhood were what most influenced his writing.

To be sure, the influences were positive. Kawabata wrote numerous stories, at least a dozen of which were translated into English. His most acclaimed, perhaps, was *Snow Country*, which, along with *Thousand Cranes* and *The Old Capital*, earned him the distinction in 1968 of being the first Japanese winner of the Nobel Prize for Literature.

Seemingly at the top of his world, four years later Kawabata gassed himself. Some, including his widow, think it was an accident. He was in poor health, having been diagnosed with Parkinson's Disease. And there were other personal factors, such as a failed love affair. But there remained another twist to the story that may have provided the issue that compelled his choice.

One was the suicide of fellow Japanese writer and political activist Yukio Mishima, who at forty-five had arranged his own death by having his fellow political militants behead him in a ritual. Kawabata was said to be obsessed with Mishima's death. One biographer wrote that he confided that he had had nightmares about Mishima's suicide for two hundred to three hundred nights in a row.

This haunting led to deep depression, and Kawabata was said to have told friends he often wished his plane would crash when he was on journeys. His true motives went to the grave with him, leaving his life's story unfinished, just as he left many others.

A Pragmatic Thinker: John Dewey

John Dewey is famous for his philosophical ideas rooted in the theory of pragmatism. Born in Burlington, Vermont, in 1859, he attended the University of Vermont in Burlington and then taught school for two years before enrolling in graduate studies at Johns Hopkins University in Baltimore. He received his Ph.D. in 1884 and taught at the University of Michigan, the University of Chicago, and New York's Columbia University.

Beliefs

He believed knowledge comes from adaptation to environment.

Along with Charles Sanders Peirce and William James, Dewey founded the theory of *pragmatism*. The theory considers important the actual consequences of action in the determination of meaning or truth.

Pragmatism focuses on the ends of an action as a vital component of truth, rather than the means.

Accomplishments

By way of his outgoing personality and strong opinions, Dewey became one of the leading social commentators of the time. He wrote frequently for scholarship and for popular publications such as the *New Republic* and *Nation*.

While at the University of Chicago, Dewey founded and directed a laboratory school at Chicago, where he applied his developing ideas on teaching.

While in New York at Columbia University, Dewey wrote articles about the theory of knowledge and metaphysics, many of which were published in two important books: *The Influence of Darwin on Philosophy and Other Essays in Contemporary Thought* (1910) and *Essays in Experimental Logic* (1916).

During this time, he also wrote *How We Think* and what has been called his most important work in the field, *Democracy and Education*.

TIME PERSON OF THE YEAR

It was *TIME* Magazine's tenet from the very beginning that history is shaped by the great minds that influence society during their time. This theory, most commonly attributed to writer Thomas Carlyle, is part of what spun off the annual "*TIME* Person of the Year" tradition.

However, it wasn't purely philosophical reasons that urged editors at *TIME* to begin the hunt each year for the most memorable and newsworthy figure. It was actually an approaching deadline and a very slow week in news that began the annually awaited and highly revered tradition.

In 1927, the last week of December, editors at *TIME* were struggling to find a cover subject for the magazine. It was holiday season, and the world seemed to be trickling to a halt for the last few weeks of the year—or, in other words, not a creature was stirring. In a frantic brainstorm, however, they realized that though Charles Lindbergh had been a hot topic that year with his famous flight from New York to Paris that May, they had never actually put Lindbergh on the cover.

Lindbergh's May flight wasn't exactly fresh news in the very last week of December, so the editors put their heads together and came up with a brand new concept: they decided that from that point forward, the cover of the January edition would feature not a personality of the week, but someone who had made a great influence over the past twelve months. The January 1928 cover featured Charles Lindbergh on the cover, along with the words "Man of the Year."

The following year, Walter P. Chrysler was featured on the January cover, chosen as Man of the Year, and it was clear that the annual tradition was set to continue. The magazine editors eventually switched the title of the tradition to "Person of the Year," after several instances of highlighting a "Woman of the Year."

POP QUIZ

1) What was one of the primary subjects of French artist Renoir's paintings?

   a) The female nude
   b) Flowers and trees
   c) Architecture

2) The revelations of Muhammad form the verses of what book?
   a) *Muhammad's Revelations*
   b) *Webster's Dictionary*
   c) *The Qur'an*

3) How did Japanese writer Yukio Mishima's life end?
   a) Prolonged illness
   b) Ritualistic suicide
   c) Car accident

4) John Dewey helped develop what theory?
   a) Theory of relativity
   b) Pragmatism
   c) Efficiency

5) What monarch was the first to circumnavigate the globe?
   a) Queen Elizabeth II
   b) King Richard III
   c) Mary, Queen of Scots

ANSWERS:

1) a
2) c
3) b
4) b
5) a

LEONARDO DA VINCI: GREAT THINKER, PAINTER, SCULPTOR, INVENTOR, AND ALL-AROUND AWESOME GUY

The *Mona Lisa* and *The Last Supper*, need we say more? So obviously Leonardo da Vinci has some talent. But let's dig a little deeper. Da Vinci was more than an artist—the Italian genius also had other talents on his resume, just a few: scientist, mathematician, engineer, inventor, anatomist, sculptor, architect, botanist, musician, and writer. Phew.

Born on April 15, 1452, as the illegitimate son of a notary and a peasant girl in a Tuscan hill town near Vinci, Italy, da Vinci was educated in the studio of a renowned Florentine painter named Verrocchio—aka Andrea di Cione in 1466. His earliest known work is a pen-and-ink drawing of the Arno valley drawn in 1473. Between 1476 and 1478, da Vinci did several commissioned pieces including an altarpiece for the Chapel of Saint Bernard and *The Adoration of the Magi* at Scopeto, which was never completed.

Much of his earlier working life was spent in Milan, while later he worked in Rome, Bologna, and Venice, spending his final years in France at the home given to him by King François I.

He and the King had become close friends (obviously: the King gave him a house). Legend has it that on May 2, 1519, the King even held Leonardo's head in his arms as he died.

But back to da Vinci's two most famous works. His most notorious painting of the 1490s, *The Last Supper*, was painted in Milan. The painting represents the last meal shared by Jesus with his disciples before his capture and death. A novelist observed Leonardo at work and wrote that some days he would paint from dawn till dusk without stopping to eat, and then not paint for three or four days at a time. Apparently Da Vinci was troubled over his ability to adequately depict the faces of Christ and the traitor Judas.

Among the works created by da Vinci in the 1500s is the small portrait known as the *Mona Lisa,* the laughing one. The painting is famous, in particular, for the elusive smile on the woman's face, its mysterious quality brought about perhaps by the fact that the artist has subtly shadowed the corners of the mouth and eyes so that the exact nature of the smile cannot be determined. The shadowy quality for which the work is renowned came to be called *sfumato*, or "Leonardo's smoke."

Interesting Facts About Leonardo da Vinci

Da Vinci had a brilliant sense of observation and perception evident in his painting and in the pages of his notebooks. He wrote about and drew detailed designs of machinery five hundred years ahead of his time. Along with drawings of a bicycle, airplane, helicopter, and a parachute, he also recorded observations on subjects including geology, anatomy, flight, and gravity.

Many of the thirteen thousand pages of his notebooks are written in mirror image. Many scholars believe that da Vinci used this means of writing to ensure privacy; however, another school of thought says that since da Vinci was left-handed, he probably found it quicker to write from right to left.

Da Vinci's notebooks are kept in various locations including the Louvre, the national library of Spain, the British library in London, and others. There is one privately owned notebook, the Codex Leicester, owned by Bill Gates.

Da Vinci was a master of anatomy. He made detailed drawings of muscles and tendons as a part of his study under Verrocchio. He was so good at what he did that he was allowed to dissect human corpses at several hospitals, drawing the human skeleton, the heart and vascular system, as well as other organs. Several of his drawings show comparisons of human organs with the corresponding organs of birds, frogs, bears, and other animals.

Just a Few of Leonardo's Inventions

Parachutes
Flying Machines
Submarines
Underwater Rebreathing Devices
Self-Flotation/Ocean Rescue Devices
Swimming Fins
Pumping Mechanisms
Dredging Systems
Steam Calorimeters
Water-well Drill
Swing Bridges
Canals
Leveling/Surveying Instruments
Pulley Systems
Cranes
Street-lighting Systems
Treadle-operated Lathe
Compasses
Contact Lenses

EXTRA CREDIT: Several people have used the specifications found in da Vinci's notebooks to construct working machinery. In 2000, Katarina Ollikainen built da Vinci's parachute, and skydiver Adrian Nicholas demonstrated that the device actually worked. (Brave!) Two years later, Judy Leden, a British hang-gliding champion, successfully flew a fixed-wing glider that was built using da Vinci's specifications!

CRASH COURSE
GENGHIS KHAN

Considering the lack of factual information about his early life, it is quite amazing how many movies and television shows have been produced depicting the life of the fearsome Mongolian ruler—many bearing his same name. Among the many was *Genghis Khan*, released in 1965 and starring Omar Sharif; *Genghis Khan*, a Chinese film released in 1998; *Cheng Sing Gong*, a Hong Kong television series released in 1987; and *Genghis Khan*, released in 1950 from Philippines. He even was played by John Wayne in the film *The Conquerer*, released in 1956.

The long-bearded Khan earned his status by bringing together many of the nomadic tribes of northeast Asia and founding the Mongol Empire. He then invaded East and Central Asia, eventually occupying most of those lands.

Genghis Khan passed away in 1227. The cause is unknown, but legends vary from falling off his horse, to pneumonia, to injuries sustained in battle with the Tanguts. He was buried in an unmarked grave somewhere in Mongolia, which also was where he was born. His family lived on to conquer all of modern-day China, as well as most of modern Russia, southern Asia, Eastern Europe, and the Middle East.

The Genghis Khan Mausoleum, located in Inner Mongolia, China, was built many years after his death (in the 1950s) as a memorial to the famous leader.

Also in more recent times, Khan was named by *National Geographic* as one of the 50 Most Important Political Leaders of All Time. A *Washington Post* article (December 31, 1995) selected Khan as the "Man of the Millennium."

EXTRA CREDIT: Khan actually was born with the name Temüjin. At about age forty (the year 1206), after uniting several tribes under his own rule, he was acknowledged as "Khan," a title for Turkic and Mongolian rulers. He was not referred to as Genghis until after his death.

Vasco Da Gama

Dom Vasco da Gama is the famous Portuguese explorer who commanded the first ships that sailed from Europe to India. He took three famous journeys.

Vasco Da Gama's Voyages

First voyage: In July 1497, four ships left Lisbon carrying 170 men. The caravan included the 178-ton *São Gabriel*, headed by Vasco da Gama; the *São Rafael*, led by da Gama's brother Paulo da Gama; the caravel *Berrio*, led by Nicolau Coelho; and a storage ship—its name is not known—sailed by Gonçalo Nunes.

People thought the trip would be impossible because no one believed the Indian Ocean was connected to any other sea. Da Gama cruised around the Cape of Good Hope and after many stops in Africa, they reached Calicut on May 20, 1498. Zamorin, the Hindu ruler of Calicut, welcomed da Gama but failed to arrange a trade treaty. Tension eventually grew between da Gama's crew and the Zamorin, and in August they decided to leave.

In September 1499, da Gama returned to Portugal, sharing with the King his stories of trade prospects with India. Thirteen ships were immediately sent to establish trade with India. They returned with everything from silks and spices to precious gems and shawls, making the King very happy.

Second voyage: In February 1502 da Gama and twenty ships left for India. They did not reach East Africa until June 14. After stopping briefly at Mozambique, they sailed to Kilwa (now Tanzania) and then cruised along southern Arabia before proceeding to Cannanore, a southwest Indian port. There they waited for some Arabian ships to attack. Several days had passed when they finally spotted an Arabian ship to loot, which they did. They not only took all the merchandise, they killed all passengers and set the boat on fire.

They then shoved off for Calicut, further north in India, attacking the town there, too. Unable to control the Zamorin's army there, da Gama then sailed south to Cochin. The King of Cochin also was an enemy of the Zamorin and da Gama was smart and played that to his side, building an alliance. In February 1503 the fleet left for Mozambique, landing on the shores of Portugal months later, in October, with a million dollars in gold.

Third voyage: Da Gama now had a reputation for being able to fix any and all problems that came up in India. So he was shipped off there one last time in 1524. The goal: to replace the unskilled Eduardo de Menezes as representative of the Portuguese possessions. Da Gama's luck ran out, however. He was plagued with malaria not long after arriving in Goa. He died in Cochin on Christmas Eve. His body initially was buried at St. Francis Church in Kochi, but his remains were sent back to Portugal in 1539. His body was re-interred in Vidigueira in a casket ornamented with gold and jewels.

Interesting Facts About Charlemagne

- Charlemagne wed four times and had numerous concubines, resulting in abundant children. He was close with his family and often brought his sons on campaigns. Only one legitimate son, Louis, survived him to inherit the empire.
- Charlemagne's methods often were extreme. The result: the largest territory to be governed under one ruler in Europe in the Middle Ages.
- Charlemagne's support of learning resulted in a "Carolingian Renaissance" in which art and literature thrived, as well as the preservation of many Latin manuscripts that would otherwise have been lost.
- The offices created or adapted by Charlemagne lasted for centuries in the variations of counts, dukes, and marquises across Europe.
- Charlemagne restructured the monetary system, creating the system of pounds, shillings, and pence used across Europe in the middle ages and in Britain until the 1970s.

CRASH COURSE

CHARLEMAGNE

751: Charlemagne's father Pippin was declared king, beginning the Carolingian dynasty.

768: Pippin died and the kingdom of Francia was divided between Charles and his brother Carloman.

771: Carloman died; Charles became sole ruler.

772: Charlemagne raided the Saxons—his first raid. It was successful but was just the beginning of a lasting struggle against the decentralized pagan tribes.

774: Charlemagne conquered Lombardy and became King of the Lombards.

778: After an unsuccessful siege at Saragossa, Spain, Charlemagne's retreating army suffered ambush by the Basques at Roncesvalles.

781: Charles made a pilgrimage to Rome and had his son Pippin proclaimed King of Italy; here he met Alcuin, who agreed to come to Charlemagne's court.

782: In response to recent attacks by Saxon leader Widukind, Charlemagne reportedly had 4,500 Saxon prisoners executed.

787: Charles launched his educational plan, ordering bishops and abbots to open schools near their churches and monasteries.

788: Charlemagne seized control of Bavaria, bringing all the territory of the Germanic tribes into one political unit.

791–796: Charles conducted a series of campaigns against the Avars in present-day Austria and Hungary.

799: Pope Leo III was attacked in the streets of Rome and fled to Charlemagne for protection. The King had him taken safely back to Rome.

800: Charlemagne came to Rome to oversee a synod where Leo cleared himself of the charges laid on him by his enemies. At Christmas mass, Leo crowned Charlemagne Emperor.

804: The Saxon wars finally came to an end.

813: Charles delegated imperial power to Louis, his last surviving legitimate son.

814: Charlemagne died in Aachen.

SOCRATES

Along with Plato and Aristotle, Socrates is known as the first of the three great Athenian philosophers. Born a long time ago in Athens (469 BC), he lived through the time of Pericles and the Athenian Empire. He was not from a wealthy family—his father was probably a stone carver, and Socrates' mother was a midwife. When the Peloponnesian War began, Socrates fought for Athens. Pretty typical stuff. But Socrates' mind was anything but typical.

When he reached middle adulthood, Socrates began to contemplate the world around him, and began to try to answer some difficult questions: What is wisdom? What is beauty? What is the right thing to do? He knew these questions were difficult to answer, and thought it would be better to have a lot of people discuss the answers together, to come up with a plethora of ideas. So he began to stroll around Athens asking people he met questions such as "What is piety?" Sometimes people wouldn't give him the time of day. Others would try their best to answer him. Then Socrates would try to teach them to think better by asking them more questions—showing them the problems in their logic.

That didn't sit well with some. While some ignored him, others argued back. But Socrates soon had a group of young men who listened to him and wanted to learn from him how to think. Plato was one of these young men. Socrates never charged them any money. But in 399 BC, some Athenians got mad at Socrates for what he was teaching them. They charged him in court with impiety—disrespecting the gods—as well as corrupting the youth.

People thought Socrates was against democracy, and he probably was—he believed the most intelligent people should make the decisions for everyone. But the Athenians couldn't charge him with being against democracy, because they had promised not to take revenge on anyone after the Peloponnesian War. So they used the vague religious charges instead. A trial in front of an Athenian jury resulted in a conviction and a death sentence. Soon after, prison guards gave him a cup of hemlock to drink. And the poisonous plant killed him.

WORLD LITERATURE
ALEXIS DE TOCQUEVILLE

Tocqueville was born Alexis-Charles-Henri Clérel de Tocqueville on July 29, 1805. A French "political thinker" and historian, he is best known for *The Old Regime and the Revolution* (1856) and *Democracy in America*, which appeared in two volumes, one in 1835 and the other in 1840, and was published after extensive travels in the United States. Both of these works explored the effects of the rising equality of social conditions on the individual and the state in western societies.

The Tocqueville family roots were in the landed nobility of Normandy (several places there are named after his family). Before writing his main literary successes, Tocqueville earned his law degree and was named auditor-magistrate at the court of Versailles. There, he met Gustave de Beaumont, a prosecutor substitute, who partnered with him on various literary works. Both later were sent to the United States to study the penitentiary system.

Tocqueville was an active participant in French politics, first under the July Monarchy, which lasted from 1830 to 1848, and then during the Second Republic from 1849 to 1851, which succeeded the February 1848 Revolution. Tocqueville retired from politics after Louis Napoléon Bonaparte's December 2, 1851, coup, and then began his work on the first volume of *The Old Regime and the Revolution*, which was completed by the time he died of tuberculosis.

EXTRA CREDIT: In *Democracy in America,* Tocqueville wrote of the New World and its emerging democracy. He saw democracy as the answer to balanced liberty and equality. A critic of individualism, Tocqueville thought that the coming together of people for a common purpose would bind Americans to an idea of nation larger than selfish desires—making a civil society that wasn't exclusively dependent on the state.

Martin Luther

Despite being born into a time of tension and conflict—the transitional period between the Middle Ages and the Modern Ages—Martin Luther helped mold many of the changes which took place during the time. As an "Augustinian monk" he rebelled against Papal indulgences and though it was not his intention, he started a chain reaction through all of Europe. Luther's influence went beyond the religious sphere. His translation of the Bible contributed greatly to a uniform written German language. Although he was very innovative, he sometimes held onto old prejudices—against the Jews, for example. The Reformation was unstoppable, and continued even after Luther's death.

Luther's wife Katharina—she was sixteen years younger than him, by the way—wore the pants in the family, so to speak, at least in terms of the household expenses. But she also was a good housewife and liked to garden. And running the Luther household was a monumental task. She managed their own six kids, one of her relatives, and eventually six of Luther's sister's children, too. As if that wasn't enough of a crowd, Luther also housed students in his home.

Toward the end of his life Luther was sick with many ailments. The death of his daughter Magdelena in 1542 also was difficult for him. Luther's attitude toward people who held different beliefs, especially the Jews, worsened during his last years. His 1523 work *Jesus Was Born a Jew* showed a conciliatory attitude; however, in later years the aging reformer sentenced all who did not want to convert to his beliefs. His 1545 work *Against the Papacy at Rome Founded by the Devil!* was his last blow against the Roman Church. Luther continued to teach at Wittenberg University until the end of his life; his last lecture ended with the words: *"I am weak, I cannot go on."*

"Change does not roll in on the wheels of inevitability, but comes through continuous struggle. And so we must straighten our backs and work for our freedom. A man can't ride you unless your back is bent." —Martin Luther

A TWENTIETH-CENTURY READING LIST

The Way of All Flesh by Samuel Butler (1903)
The Call of the Wild by Jack London (1903)
Howards End by E. M. Forster (1910)
The Rainbow by D. H. Lawrence (1915)
A Portrait of the Artist as a Young Man by James Joyce (1916)
Ulysses by James Joyce (1922)
The Great Gatsby by F. Scott Fitzgerald (1925)
The Sound and the Fury by William Faulkner (1929)
Brave New World by Aldous Huxley (1932)
The Grapes of Wrath by John Steinbeck (1939)
Native Son by Richard Wright (1940)
The Sheltering Sky by Paul Bowles (1949)
1984 by George Orwell (1949)
Invisible Man by Ralph Ellison (1952)
Lord of the Flies by William Golding (1954)
Lolita by Vladimir Nabokov (1955)
Catch-22 by Joseph Heller (1961)
A Clockwork Orange by Anthony Burgess (1962)
One-Hundred Years of Solitude by Gabriel Garcia Marquez (1967)
Slaughterhouse-Five by Kurt Vonnegut (1969)
Deliverance by James Dickey (1970)
Ragtime by E. L. Doctorow (1975)
Roots: The Saga of an American Family by Alex Haley (1976)
The Final Days by Carl Bernstein and Robert Woodward (1976)
Sophie's Choice by William Styron (1979)
The Color Purple by Alice Walker (1982)
Midnight's Children by Salman Rushdie (1980)
Ironweed by William Kennedy (1983)
Beloved by Toni Morrison (1987)
Hard-Boiled Wonderland and the End of the World by Haruki
    Murakami (1991)
A Fine Balance by Rohinton Mistry (1995)
Angela's Ashes by Frank McCourt (1996)

Crash Course
The Great Gatsby

They don't call this book great for nothin'. F. Scott Fitzgerald paints a memorable portrait of the Jazz Age in this uncompromising examination of the American Dream. Handsome man of mystery Jay Gatsby lives in a splendid mansion on the north shore of Long Island. Despite his lavish parties and the free-flowing champagne, he is largely reclusive and unhappy. He has achieved fame and fortune, but has not won the heart of his lady love, Daisy. The book begins with Daisy's cousin, Nick, telling the story. He has moved into a small house next door to Gatsby, and he is instantly intrigued by the man. Gatsby begins to open up to Nick, telling him that years ago he and Daisy had an affair, but he was too poor to marry her. She married the philandering, boorish Tom Buchanan instead, and, like Gatsby, she is rich and unhappy. Gatsby persuades Nick to help reunite him with Daisy now that he's wealthy enough for her. They rekindle their romance, but soon Daisy accidentally runs over her husband's mistress, Myrtle. Myrtle's husband blames Gatsby for his wife's death and shoots him. Daisy, shallow to the end, stays with her husband, Tom, and their comfy lifestyle.

F. Scott Fitzgerald coined the term "The Jazz Age" to describe the period from 1918 to 1929. The beginning of the Jazz Age coincides with the close of World War I, and its ending came when the stock market crashed, sending the US into the Great Depression.

TITUS LUCRETIUS

Titus Lucretius, a Roman epic poet who was born about 99 BC, was a one-hit wonder of lasting importance. His reputation has endured for 2,100 years.

Lucretius wrote only one poem. *De Rerum Natura*—or "On the Nature of Things"—was about the Epicurean philosophy of life. Followers of Epicurus believed that knowledge was the key to a successful life and that the body really didn't need a lot of other sensations. Romantic entanglements were a waste of time.

Learn, be temperate, and avoid sex, drugs and, well, rock 'n roll. Lucretius probably wouldn't have been dancing to "Achy Breaky Heart." But he certainly expounded on those theories in this six-book poem. He wanted to help rid the world of superstition and fear of death. He didn't think there was anything to fear.

Life to him was but a state of being. You existed. You were. When you died, you simply became devoid of sensation and thought. Thus, you really couldn't miss being alive. He felt people feared death because of what happened when they were alive, such as pain, but that those things wouldn't be relative when they died. So why bother?

Oh, and he discarded any concept of divinity or an after-death world. When you were gone, you were gone. He thought religion to be a bad thing, writing: "So potent was religion in persuading to evil deeds."

His arguments gained him stardom. Writes Cicero: "The poems of Lucretius ... exhibit many flashes of genius, and yet show great mastership."

How did Lucretius develop all these dark philosophies? Well, he not is alive to tell us, of course, but historians say that he was driven mad by a love potion, which seems strange given his views of romance. He wrote his poem during sane moments and killed himself when he was forty-four.

Maybe he was the inspiration for "Love Potion Number Nine?"

SULEIMAN

In the West they called him Suleiman the Magnificent—he simply was one of the most powerful rulers of all sixteenth-century Europe. In the East they referred to him as "the Lawgiver" because he had completely transformed the Ottoman legal system, setting up a fair set of laws throughout the empire. No matter what they called him, Sulleiman was the longest-ruling Sultan of the Ottoman Empire. His reign lasted nearly fifty years, from 1520 to 1566, the year he died and the year his son, Selim II took over.

Suleiman was born along the coast of the Black Sea, sometime in 1494. By the age of seven, along with the usual subjects of science and history, he already was studying military tactics in the schools of the Topkap› Palace in Istanbul. Years later, Suleiman would single-handedly guide Ottoman armies to conquer the Christian areas of Belgrade, Rhodes, and most of Hungary. He seized most of the Middle East in his battles with the Persians and large regions of North Africa as far west as Algeria. Under his command, the Ottoman fleet controlled the seas from the Mediterranean to the Red Sea and the Persian Gulf.

His empire ever expanding, Suleiman established legislative changes related to all corners of civilization—education, taxation, and criminal law. *Kanuns*, his canonical law, repaired the form of the empire— changes that lasted for centuries after his death.

Suleiman was more than a powerful ruler, he also was a distinguished poet, goldsmith, and patron of culture. He oversaw the golden age of the Ottoman Empire's artistic, literary, and architectural development. When it came to his love life, Suleiman did not follow tradition. Instead, he married a harem girl, who as queen became as famous as Suleiman himself.

Suleiman was seventy-one when he died on September 5, 1566, while conducting the siege of Szigetvar in Hungary.

Perhaps a Venetian ambassador summed up Suleiman best, saying in 1525, "I know of no state which is happier than this one. It is furnished with all of God's gifts. It controls war and peace with all; it is rich in gold, in people, in ships, and in obedience; no state can be compared with it. May God long preserve the most just of all Emperors."

JANE ADDAMS

Laura Jane Addams founded the U.S. Settlement House movement and was the first American woman to win the Nobel Peace Prize.

Born in Cedarville, Illinois, the eighth of nine children, Jane learned from her father to care for people. While visiting London in her twenties, Addams was impacted by an essay that described slum conditions.

In 1889 she and a friend founded Hull House in Chicago, one of the first U.S. settlement houses. At its peak, Hull House received two thousand visitors weekly. The "house" had an adult night school, kindergarten classes, a public kitchen, an art gallery, a coffeehouse, a gymnasium, a swimming pool, a music school, and more. The night school was sort of the beginning of today's community college continuing education classes.

In 1901 Addams founded the Juvenile Court Committee, a private nonprofit organization in Chicago that protects children from abuse and neglect. Addams became a member of the NAACP and in 1911 the first vice president of the National American Woman Suffrage Association.

Addams also helped organize the Women's Peace Party and the International Congress of Women in hopes of averting World War I. In 1917, after the war began, she was expelled from the Daughters of the American Revolution. In 1920 she was elected first president of the Women's International League for Peace and Freedom, the successor organization to the Women's Peace Party. She continued in the presidency until her death.

EXTRA CREDIT: In 1998 the Women's International League for Peace and Freedom (British Columbia Branch) had Canadian artist Christian Cardell Corbet custom design a bronze medallion of Addams to celebrate her lifetime of achievements.

Dr. Wernher von Braun

Dr. Wernher von Braun, a German rocket physicist and astronautics engineer who lived up until 1977, was one of the leading developers of rocket technology in Germany and the United States. Some say he's *the* preeminent rocket scientist of the twentieth century.

In his young adult life, von Braun was the key figure in Germany's prewar rocket development program, designing the deadly V-2 combat rocket during World War II. Postwar, he and others were brought to the United States as part of what was then the secret Operation Overcast. A decade later, von Braun became a naturalized U.S. citizen.

Von Braun worked on the American intercontinental ballistic missile (ICBM) program before joining NASA, where he directed NASA's Marshall Space Flight Center and served as chief architect of the Saturn V launch vehicle, the superbooster that propelled the Apollo spacecraft to the Moon. His supporters deem him the father of the United States space program. He received the 1975 National Medal of Science.

Wernher von Braun's Published Works

- *First Men to the Moon* (1958). Portions of work first appeared in This Week magazine.
- *Project Mars: A Technical Tale* (2006). A previously unpublished science fiction story by von Braun.
- *The Voice of Dr. Wernher von Braun* (2007). A collection of speeches delivered by von Braun during his career.

CRASH COURSE

JONATHAN SWIFT

You've surely heard of Jonathan Swift's masterpiece—*Gulliver's Travels,* first published in 1726. As with his other writings, the book was published under a pseudonym—the fictional Lemuel Gulliver. But the true man behind the masterpiece was Jonathan Swift, a prolific writer famous for his satires.

Some of the correspondence between the book's printer and Gulliver's also-fictional cousin who negotiated the book's publication are actually intact today. *Gulliver's Travels* is often thought of—mistakenly so—as a children's book. In fact, it is a sophisticated satire of human nature based on Swift's own experiences. Each of the four sections—recounting four voyages to mostly fictional exotic lands—has a different theme, but each attempts to crush human pride.

Swift was born in Dublin, seven months after his father's death—a theme that eventually became a central focus in Swift's life. In 1731 he wrote *Verses on the Death of Dr. Swift,* his own obituary published in 1739. In 1732, his good friend and collaborator John Gay died. In 1735, John Arbuthnot, another friend from his days in London, died. In 1738 Swift began to show his own signs of illness and in 1742 suffered a stroke. Swift could no longer speak and began to fear he would become mentally disabled.

In 1744, his dear friend Alexander Pope died. Then, on October 19, 1745, Swift passed away. After being laid out in public view for the people of Dublin to pay their last respects, Swift was buried by Esther Johnson's side, in accordance with his wishes. Esther was someone Swift had a long and mysterious relationship with—and was the intrigue of many biographers.

The bulk of Swift's fortune was left to found a hospital for the mentally ill, originally known as St. Patrick's Hospital for Imbeciles, which opened in 1757, and which still exists as a psychiatric hospital.

CHRISTIAAN HUYGENS

Christiaan Huygens, born in 1629, was a Dutch mathematician, astronomer, and physicist commonly associated with the scientific revolution.

The list of his discoveries and achievements is lengthy: light consisting of waves (to become instrumental in the understanding of wave-particle duality); modern calculus; Saturn's moon Titan (discovered in 1655); Saturn's planetary rings, and the fact they are made of rocks; observations and sketches of the Orion Nebula; wrote the first book on probability theory; and invented the pendulum clock.

The oldest known Huygens-style pendulum clock, dated 1657, is displayed at the Museum Boerhaave in Leiden, The Netherlands, which also has an important astronomical clock owned and used by Huygens.

Huygens also devised what is now known as the second law of motion of Isaac Newton in a quadratic form.

Things Named After Christiaan Huygens

- The Huygens probe
- Asteroid 2801 Huygens
- A crater on Mars
- Huygens Region, the brighter interior of the Orion Nebula
- Mons Huygens, a mountain on the Moon
- Huygens Software, a microscope image processing package
- Achromatic two-element eyepiece designed by Huygens
- W.I.S.V. Christiaan Huygens: Dutch study guild for the studies of mathemathics and computer science at the Delft University of Technology
- Huygens Laboratory: Home of the Physics department at Leiden University, The Netherlands
- Huygens Supercomputer: National Supercomputer facility of The Netherlands at SARA in Amsterdam
- The *Christiaan Huygens*, a ship of the Nederland Line

REMBRANDT HARMENSZOON VAN RIJN

It originally was thought that Rembrandt Harmenszoon van Rijn had produced more than six hundred paintings, four hundred etchings, and two thousand drawings. However, research in recent decades, led by the Rembrandt Research Project, have narrowed his work down to approximately three hundred paintings, just under three hundred prints, or etchings—and many more than two thousand drawings in his lifetime.

Rembrandt, a Dutch painter born in 1606, generally is considered one of the greatest painters and printmakers in all of European art history and certainly the most important in Dutch history.

His greatest creative successes are thought to be his portraits of his contemporaries, self-portraits, and illustrations of scenes from the Bible.

But his success as a portrait painter was followed by years marked by personal tragedy and financial hardship. His son Rumbartus died two months after birth in 1635 and his daughter Cornelia died at just three weeks in 1638. Two years later, Rembrandt and his wife had their second daughter, also named Cornelia, and she died after living just a month. Only their fourth child, Titus, who was born in 1641, survived into adulthood. Rembrandt's wife died in 1642 soon after Titus's birth—his drawings of her sick on her deathbed are among his most moving works.

Rembrandt lived beyond his means, buying art and rarities, which probably caused a court arrangement to avoid his bankruptcy in 1656. He had to sell most of his paintings and large collection of antiquities. He also had to sell his house and his printing press and move to more modest accommodation in 1660.

Rembrandt outlived his son, passing on October 4, 1669, in Amsterdam. He was buried in an unmarked grave in the Westerkerk.

A Short List of Great Thinking Freemasons

The Freemasons are a fraternal organization created during the Enlightenment era. It is a hierarchical organization that uses symbols and allegories to pass on knowledge of a moral or metaphysical nature to its initiates. Open only to men of good standing in the community, the organization requires a belief in a Supreme Being, which, reflecting its Enlightenment roots, is open to interpretation among its members.

Wolfgang Mozart: Austrian composer of more than 600 compositions.

Rudyard Kipling: English author, poet, and winner of the Nobel Prize in Literature.

Winston Churchill: Hero of World War II, served two separate terms as Prime Minister of Britain.

Booker T. Washington: Educator, author, and founder of countless schools throughout his life.

Henry Ford: Revolutionized industrial production with invention of assembly lines.

Voltaire (Francois-Marie Arouet): French Enlightenment thinker, writer, and social-reformer. He joined the Masons when he was eighty-four and died two months later.

W. E. B. DuBois: Educator, civil rights activist, sociologist, writer, and historian.

"Buzz" Aldrin: American Astronaut, the second man to walk on the moon.

Douglas MacArthur: One of only five men ever to rise to the rank of Five-Star General in the US Army.

Jack Dempsey: American heavyweight boxing champion who held the title for seven years.

Clark Gable: American actor, most famous for his work in *Gone with the Wind.*

Jesse Jackson: Baptist minister, politician, and civil-rights leader.

"Buffalo Bill" (William Cody): Iconic American soldier, hunter, and showman.

Gene Autry: Known for his acting and music career as "the cowboy singer".

Charles Lindbergh: American aviator who flew the first solo flight across the Atlantic Ocean.

Will Rogers: Cherokee-American actor, cowboy, comedian, writer, and humorist.

John Wayne: Actor, life-long conservative, and symbol of idealized rugged masculinity.

"Duke" Ellington: Jazz artist, pianist, composer, and bandleader.

Harry Houdini (Ehrich Weiss): Hungarian-American magician, escapologist, actor, and investigator.

"Davy" Crockett: American frontiersman, US Representative from Tennessee, and Alamo martyr.

CHARLES DICKENS

Many of his works are well-known … *Oliver Twist, Great Expectations, A Tale of Two Cities, David Copperfield, A Christmas Story* … but there's a lot about this great English writer you may not know:

Charles Dickens was born in Hampshire, the second of eight children to John Dickens, a clerk in the Navy Pay Office at Portsmouth, and his wife Elizabeth Dickens. When he was ten, the family relocated to London.

At just twelve years old, Dickens began working ten-hour days in a boot-blacking factory, earning six shillings a week pasting labels on jars of polish. His earnings helped support his family. The shocking conditions of the factory had a lasting impression on Dickens.

David Copperfield was Dickens's favorite of his books, and his most autobiographical.

In 1834, Dickens became a political journalist, reporting on parliamentary debate and traveling across Britain via stagecoach to cover election campaigns for the *Morning Chronicle.*

His journalism, in the form of sketches appearing in periodicals, formed his first collection of pieces, *Sketches by Boz,* published in 1836. This also led to the serialization of his first novel, *The Pickwick Papers,* that same year.

On April 2, 1836, he married Catherine Thompson Hogarth, the daughter of George Hogarth, editor of the *Evening Chronicle.*

Dickens and Catherine had ten children. They separated in 1858.

On June 9, 1865, while returning from France, Dickens was involved in a rail crash. The first seven carriages of the train plunged off a cast iron bridge that was being repaired. The only first-class carriage to remain on the track was the one in which Dickens was traveling. Dickens spent some time tending the wounded and the dying before rescuers arrived. Before leaving, he remembered the unfinished manuscript for *Our Mutual Friend,* and he returned to his carriage to retrieve it. Typically, Dickens later used this experience as material for his short ghost story *The Signal-Man,* in which the central character has a premonition of his own death in a rail crash.

Contrary to his wish to be laid to rest in Rochester Cathedral, he was buried in the Poets' Corner of Westminster Abbey. The inscription on his tomb reads: "He was a sympathiser to the poor, the suffering, and the oppressed; and by his death, one of England's greatest writers is lost to the world."

EXTRA CREDIT: Dickens's will stipulated that no memorial be erected to honor him. The only life-size bronze statue of Dickens, cast in 1891 by Francis Edwin Elwell, is located in Clark Park in the Spruce Hill neighborhood of Philadelphia, Pennsylvania.

The Charles Dickens Museum in Holborn is the only one of Dickens's London homes to survive. He lived there only two years, but it was during that time that he wrote *The Pickwick Papers, Oliver Twist,* and *Nicholas Nickleby.* The museum contains a major collection of manuscripts, original furniture, and memorabilia.

The Dickens World themed attraction, covering 71,500 square feet and including a cinema and restaurants, opened in Chatham in 2007. It stands on a small part of the site of the former naval dockyard where Dickens's father had once worked in the Navy Pay Office.

Famous Words of Charles Dickens

- Electric communication will never be a substitute for the face of someone who with their soul encourages another person to be brave and true.
- A boy's story is the best that is ever told.
- The pain of parting is nothing to the joy of meeting again.
- The whole difference between construction and creation is exactly this: that a thing constructed can only be loved after it is constructed; but a thing created is loved before it exists.
- An idea, like a ghost, must be spoken to a little before it will explain itself.
- I never could have done what I have done without the habits of punctuality, order, and diligence, without the determination to concentrate myself on one subject at a time."

CRASH COURSE
A TALE OF TWO CITIES

In this oppositional plot line, Charles Dickens contrasts Paris and London during the French Revolution. The story begins when Dr. Alexander Manette is released from eighteen years in the Bastille for having knowledge about the Marquis de St. Evrémonde assaulting a peasant girl. M. and Mdm. Defarge take Manette back to London to his daughter, Lucie. Years later they are asked to testify that they saw Charles Darnay, the nephew of Evrémonde, flee to England to escape trumped up charges of treason. Through a twin plot device, Darnay is saved by Sydney Carton who happens to look a lot like him. The two young men become buddies, and while both love Lucie, Darnay wins her hand. More years pass and once again false charges affect Darnay. He learns that a beloved old servant has been imprisoned in Paris, so he goes to the war-torn city to help. He is imprisoned and sentenced to die. Only his "twin," Carton, can save him, if he is willing to take his place on the guillotine. Do Darnay and Lucie live happily ever after, or does Darnay lose his head and Carton win Lucie's hand? You'll have to read the book to find out.

Useless Trivia

Charles Dickens was nearly caught vacationing with his mistress. Desperately trying to hide the fact that he was traveling with actress Ellen Ternan, who was rumored to have broken up his marriage, he told few people that he was involved in a serious train wreck on June 9, 1865. At first he rushed to aid the wounded, but when he realized press would soon arrive and discover him with Ellen, he grabbed the manuscript he was working on (the novel *Our Mutual Friend*) and left the scene of the accident.

Timeline
Albert Einsten's Life

1879: Albert Einstein entered the world in Germany, born to a man who sold feather beds.

1884: Einstein was given his first compass, and his curiosity to explore the natural world kicked in.

1889: At age ten, Einstein began to obsess about science, reading book after book.

1894: The Einsteins moved to Italy.

1895: Einstein attempted to skip high school by enrolling in a top technical university, but he failed part of the entrance exam—not the science portion, of course, but the arts section.

1896: Einstein graduated from high school and started at the ETH (the Federal Polytechnic) in Zurich.

1898: Einstein met his sweetheart, Mileva Maric, a classmate from Hungary.

1900: Einstein graduated from the ETH.

1901: Einstein became a Swiss citizen and began tutoring. A pregnant Mileva moved to Hungary to give birth at her parents' home. Einstein moved to Bern.

1902: In January, Mileva had a daughter—the couple eventually put her up for adoption. Einstein began working at the Swiss Patent Office.

1903: Einstein and Mileva wed.

1904: Mileva had their first son, Hans Albert.

1905: Einstein "invented" his Special Theory of Relativity and submitted *On the Electrodynamics of Moving Bodies* to a top physics journal. He applied his theory to mass and energy and formulates the equation $e=mc2$. He was just twenty-six years old.

1907: Einstein began applying the laws of gravity to his Special Theory of Relativity.

1910: Son Eduard was born.

1911: Albert began teaching at the German University in Prague. He was the youngest to attend the first world physics conference, held in Brussels.

1912: Albert began teaching theoretical physics at the ETH in Zurich.

1913: Einstein began working on his new Theory of Gravity.

1914: Einstein began heading the Kaiser Wilhelm Institute in Berlin and teaching theoretical physics at the University of Berlin. The family moved to Berlin but the family—all but Albert—returned to Zurich soon after, and a divorce followed.

1915: Einstein's General Theory of Relativity was unveiled.

1917: Einstein collapsed and became gravely ill. His cousin Elsa nursed him back to health.

1919: Einstein married Elsa. A solar eclipse proved Einstein's General Theory of Relativity was right on.

1921: Einstein was awarded the Nobel Prize in physics.

1932: Identified as a Jew, Albert began to feel the pressure of Nazi Germany.

1933: Einstein and Elsa made their home in Princeton, New Jersey, where Albert began working at the Institute for Advanced Study.

1936: Elsa died after a short sickness.

1939: World War II began. Einstein wrote a famous letter to President Franklin D. Roosevelt warning that Germany could construct an atomic bomb.

1940: Einstein became an American citizen.

1955: Einstein died of heart failure.

THAT'S WHAT HE SAID:
ALBERT EINSTEIN

- Everyone should be respected as an individual, but no one idolized.

- A man should look for what is, and not for what he thinks should be.

- A table, a chair, a bowl of fruit, and a violin; what else does a man need to be happy?

- Do not worry about your difficulties in Mathematics. I can assure you mine are still greater.

- All religions, arts, and sciences are branches of the same tree.

- Few are those who see with their own eyes and feel with their own hearts.

- Everything should be made as simple as possible, but not simpler.

- Everything that can be counted does not necessarily count; everything that counts cannot necessarily be counted.

- As far as I'm concerned, I prefer silent vice to ostentatious virtue.

- Common sense is the collection of prejudices acquired by age eighteen.

- An empty stomach is not a good political adviser.

- Anger dwells only in the bosom of fools.

- A perfection of means, and confusion of aims, seems to be our main problem.

- A person who never made a mistake never tried anything new.

SALON AT 27 RUE DE FLEURUS, PARIS: GERTRUDE STEIN'S LIVING ROOM

Gertrude Stein was an expatriate American writer living in Paris, France, at the turn of the twentieth century. In her Parisian home, she fostered an environment of art and literature by hosting weekly, Saturday evening meetings where thinkers, artists, and writers would come together and discuss each other's work. If you could've been there, you would have run into some of the most famous faces of the day. People like:

Pablo Picasso (1881–1973) was a Spanish painter and sculptor. He helped found the Cubist school of painting—painting that attempts to break up the subject, assess it, and reform it in an abstracted version. His paintings are among some of the most expensive in the world. His pieces include *Les Demoiselles d'Avignon* and *Guernica.*

Georges Braque (1882–1963), the French painter, who helped Picasso form cubism. Much of his painting tried to explore different perspectives of the same object at the same time, such as his piece *Violin and Pitcher.*

Ernest Hemingway (1899–1961) was an American journalist and novelist. He won the Pulitzer Prize for *The Old Man and the Sea* and the Nobel Prize for literature in 1954. His writing uses short, concise sentences with no frills. His other works include *The Sun Also Rises, A Farewell to Arms,* and *For Whom the Bell Tolls.*

F. Scott Fitzgerald (1896–1940) was an American writer best known for his novel *The Great Gatsby* which portrays life after WWI with its newly found wealth and materialism. The novel was ranked second in the Modern Library's "100 Best Novels of the Twentieth Century."

Gertrude Stein herself wrote many radically experimental works including *Tender Buttons.* She was painted by Picasso, edited Hemingway, collected Braque's paintings, and brought Hemingway and Fitzgerald together into their longtime friendship.

Francis Bacon

Francis Bacon's legacy is that of philosopher and essayist. His powerful, elegant words shaped thoughts, opinions, and even nations in the early seventeenth century.

Perhaps you remember the name from history class. Bacon was the guy who wrote *The New Atlantis*, a book about Utopian society that many think laid the foundation for the founding principles of the United States. In that novel he envisioned a land where women had greater rights, there was no slavery, debtors—he was one, but more on that later—didn't go to prison, there was separation of church and state, and everyone enjoyed freedom of religion. Sound familiar?

Bacon played a leading role in creating British colonies in Newfoundland and, yes, Virginia and the Carolinas. In 1609 he wrote the government's report on the Virginia Colony that helped shape its future.

But Bacon was not always or nearly so revered. What he was: controversial and of questionable lineage. The history books insist that he was the youngest of five sons of Sir Nicholas Bacon, the Lord Keeper of the Great Seal for Queen Elizabeth I. But perhaps he was more than that.

Many historians say he was actually Elizabeth's son. She never acknowledged his birth, if that were the case, but she sure paid him a lot of attention along the way. As a child, he often played in her court, and she called him "the little Lord Keeper."

Some authors say that when he was fifteen, he learned that he was the Queen's son during an incident in her court. The Queen overheard one of her ladies repeating this story, and she seized and beat the woman. Francis intervened and was said to have been told by the Queen herself why the beating occurred and that he was in fact her son.

If that were true, Bacon didn't reap any great benefits. Upon gaining this knowledge, he was sent to France, starting a twisting and unusual course for his life.

As a teenager, Bacon said he wanted desperately to serve truth, country, and church, but he had trouble achieving a position that allowed him the right toehold for those goals, even with help from an influential uncle. He studied and practiced law, but he ran into dead ends at every opportunity for a court appointment until his uncle talked the bar into making him a barrister.

In 1591 he became friends with Robert Devereux, the Earl of Essex. Devereux was the Queen's favorite, and Bacon became the man's confidential advisor. He seemed on the road to greatness, even if his mother wouldn't acknowledge him publicly or allow him a path to the throne.

Bacon, though, was in debt. His father died before he had built an inheritance, and Francis borrowed more than he could afford. Even as a lawyer and later seated in Parliament, he struggled.

Devereux tried to help, giving Bacon a property that he promptly sold for 1800 pounds, but he that was not a solution. He was the Queen's Counsel, but he couldn't get a public office. His friends even tried to marry him to a rich widow, but she chose another man who had money. Eventually, in 1598 Bacon was arrested for his debts.

For some reason, the Queen began to show more favor for him. He became one of her learned counsels, though he drew no salary, and he severed ties with Essex. The Queen then appointed him to investigate treason charges against his old friend and benefactor. Bacon aggressively pursued Devereux, who was executed in 1601.

Sir Francis Bacon's political career—he was knighted in 1603—took many twists and favorable turns after James I ascended to the throne, but that career ended twenty years later when Bacon was—you guessed it—arrested for being a debtor.

He was charged with twenty-three counts of corruption, and he admitted guilt and asked for leniency. Some said he wasn't really guilty, but Bacon said he wanted to save James from scandal. He was fined forty thousand pounds, jailed a few days, and declared no longer suitable for public office. His life became his essays and opinions on a myriad of subjects.

Bacon died five years later. But one little footnote must be added to his curious life: The former friend whom he prosecuted and executed, Robert Devereux, a political foe of the Queen, actually was her other secret son. These two friends-turned-combatants were really bastard brothers of the Queen of England.

VIRGIL

If you caught the movie *Troy* and realized there was more to the plot than just seeing Brad Pitt show off his buff body and try to sound ancient, you may know something of the work of the Roman epic poet Virgil.

The story of the battle of Troy, and the use of the Trojan horse, was the focal point of that movie and one of the most memorable aspects of Virgil's most famous work, the *Aeneid*. Back in those BC days, the Greeks wrote their stories of history and mythology, and the Romans came along and translated them into their own versions or simply created a differing history.

The Greeks' favorite epic poet, Homer, gained fame for his writing about Odysseus in *The Odyssey*, but the Romans had to do a version about a character named Ulysses. You get the picture. So it was that Virgil took on the story of the Trojan hero Aeneas and other aspects of Greek history.

He spent the last ten years of his life penning the poems into a twelve-book set. The first six were seen as Virgil's version of *The Odyssey*, and the last six were his counterpart to *The Iliad*. But before his work was completed, Virgil died. He was traveling to Greece—on-site reporting, perhaps—and took ill with a fever. Virgil had wanted the book burned, but Emperor Augustus ordered that his work be finished. His students took up the task and published the final chapters with very little editing. The version you may have read is not without its flaws.

Still, it was regarded as one of the great literary works of the Roman Empire, because the Romans loved how it revealed their superiority and pitied their victims. Ironically, Virgil himself was a victim of the Romans.

During the strife that led to the assassination of Julius Caesar and the defeat of his killers, Brutus and Cassius, by his loyalists led by Mark Antony, the victors paid off their soldiers by giving them land they had captured in northern Italy. Among the parcels given away was the estate belonging to Virgil, an experience that influenced his writing and led to a conflicted book called the *Bucolics*.

POP QUIZ #2

1) The shadowy quality of Leonardo da Vinci's *Mona Lisa* is known
   as __________.
   a) Stuffed tomato
   b) Leonardo's shadow
   c) sfumato

2) What was one of Socrates' famous pupils?
   a) Plato
   b) Michelangelo
   c) Jesus

3) Seventeenth-century philosopher Francis Bacon wrote a book that
   many think laid the foundation for the founding principle of
   __________.
   a) Reaping what you sow
   b) Communism
   c) The United States

4) What was Charles Dickens' most autobiographical book (as well as
   one of his favorites)?
   a) *A Tale of Two Cities*
   b) *David Copperfield*
   c) *The Great Pickwick*

5) Sulieman the Magnificent was a powerful ruler and also a(n)
   __________.
   a) Goldsmith
   b) Electrician
   c) Renowned chef

6) Gertrude Stein hosted weekly meetings so that thinkers, artists, and writers would come together and _________.
   a) Promote their pyramid marketing businesses
   b) Share new recipes and gardening tips
   c) Discuss each other's work

7) Who was born with the name Temüjin?
   a) Genghis Khan
   b) Sun Tzu
   c) Alexander the Great

8) Where did Vasco de Gama's second voyage go?
   a) America
   b) India
   c) Egypt

9) Martin Luther started what movement?
   a) Surrealism
   b) Communism
   c) Protestant Reformation

10) Who wrote *The Great Gatsby*?
    a) William Faulkner
    b) F. Scott Fitzgerald
    c) Marcel Proust

ANSWERS:

1) c	6) c
2) a	7) a
3) c	8) b
4) b	9) c
5) a	10) b

Robert Boyle

If you've ever sat in a high school chemistry class and cursed your instructor for putting you through the memorization of all those elements, laws, and experimental efforts, you were misdirecting your ire. Your frustration definitely should have been focused on a guy from Ireland: Robert Boyle, a sort of child genius in the mid-fifteenth century. He was a natural philosopher, physicist, inventor, and all-around scientist. But what he was mostly was a chemist. Robert Boyle is credited with founding modern chemistry.

He didn't invent the Periodic Table, but he can be held responsible for a lot of your other pain. And there would be no surprise if he were to get a chuckle from that, because Robert Boyle was a bit of a prodigy. The seventh son and fourteenth child of the first Earl of Cork, Robert learned to speak Latin, Greek, and French as a child. Before he was age nine, he was sent to Eton College. Three years there, and he was off to travel with a French tutor.

At age fourteen, he spent the winter in Florence, Italy, studying with the aging scientist Galileo. You get the picture. Three years later, his father died, and he inherited enough holdings that he didn't need to work. He declared himself a scientist and dived into studying, learning, and experimenting. His approach was a bit unusual. He didn't like to read too much about the work of other scientists. Once he learned a principle to apply or developed a theory, he didn't want his objective mind sullied by what another person thought.

At age thirty-two, Boyle developed the pneumatical engine and followed that by proving a law about gases and how they vary under pressure. This law was named Boyle's Law, which you most likely studied and tested. But he didn't stop there. Before his death in 1691, at age sixty-four, Boyle had experimented, postulated, and written about such issues as the expansion of sound, the force of freezing water, various gravities, crystals, electricity, and even color.

So if you ever again find yourself contemplating those subjects, just remember the Irish scientist from four centuries earlier who developed the idea.

GOTTFRIED LEIBNIZ

Gottfried Wilhelm Leibniz was a German polymath—a what, you might ask? Well, that just meant he was *really* smart. How smart?

Let's start with his writing: Leibniz wrote primarily in Latin and French (remember, he was German). And moving on to math: he invented calculus and discovered the binary system—the foundation for virtually all modern computer plans. Don't forget philosophy: Leibniz is mostly known for optimism—he believed our universe is the best possible one God could have made. He was, along with René Descartes and Baruch Spinoza, one of the three greatest seventeenth-century rationalists.

As if that wasn't enough, Leibniz also made major contributions to physics and technology and anticipated ideas that surfaced much later in biology, medicine, geology, probability theory, psychology, linguistics, and library science. His writing subjects were endless: politics, law, ethics, theology, history, and philology.

Famous Words of Gottfried Leibniz

- Indeed every monad must be different from every other.
- For there are never in nature two beings, which are precisely alike, and in which it is not possible to find some difference which is internal, or based on some intrinsic quality.
- But in simple substances the influence of one monad over another is ideal only.
- I also take it as granted that every created thing, and consequently the created monad also, is subject to change, and indeed that this change is continual in each one.
- I do not conceive of any reality at all as without genuine unity.
- And as every state of a simple substance is a natural consequence of its preceding state, so that the present state of it is big with the future.

CRASH COURSE
FYODOR DOSTOEVSKY

Many are familiar with the pages of *Crime and Punishment*, one of the most famous novels of all time. But many might not know that its author, the Russian novelist Dostoevsky, himself spent five years imprisoned.

Dostoevsky was jailed on April 23, 1849, for being a part of a liberal intellectual group called the Petrashevsky Circle. Czar Nicholas I—after seeing the Revolutions of 1848 in Europe—buckled down on any sort of underground organization he felt could jeopardize autocracy. On November 16, Dostoevsky and others in the Petrashevsky Circle were sentenced to death. After a mock execution—the "circle members" stood outside in freezing weather waiting to be shot by a firing squad—Dostoevsky's sentence was lessened to four years of exile with hard labor at a prison camp in Siberia.

After years of brutal suffering, Dostoevsky was released from prison in 1854, but was still required to serve in the Siberian Regiment. Dostoevsky spent five years as a private and then as a lieutenant, stationed in what is now Kazakhstan.

Dostoevsky's experiences in prison and the army had a huge impact on him, changing his political and religious views. He rejected contemporary Western European philosophical thoughts, and followed in his writing traditional, rural-based, rustic Russian values. But even more significantly, his Christianity was strengthened—specifically his Orthodox faith—which he wrote about in *The Peasant Marey* (1876).

His writings became darker and more complex. His characters began to agonize over themes of spiritual torment, religious awakening, and the psychological confusion caused by the conflict between traditional Russian culture and the influx of modern, Western philosophy.

EXTRA CREDIT: While in Kazakhstan, Dostoevsky began a relationship with Maria Dmitrievna Isaeva, the wife of an acquaintance in Siberia. They married in February 1857—after her husband's death, of course.

Vincent van Gogh

You'd heard Vincent van Gogh cut off his left ear, right? Not sure if it was really true? Well it is—his lobe, anyway. This famous Dutch-Post Impressionist artist produced more than two thousand works, including approximately nine hundred paintings and more than one thousand drawings and sketches. Most of his best-known works were produced in the final two years of his life, during which time he cut off part of his left ear following a breakdown in one of his close friendships.

Thankfully, he's also remembered for his brilliant work—his paintings and drawings include some of the world's best known, most popular, and most expensive pieces.

Van Gogh was given the same name as his grandfather—and a first brother stillborn exactly one year before. It has been suggested that being given the same name as his dead older brother might have had a deep psychological impact on van Gogh from the beginning, and that elements of his art, such as the portrayal of pairs of male figures, can be traced back to this.

Van Gogh spent his early adult life working for a firm of art dealers. After a brief time teaching, he became a missionary worker in a very poor mining region. He did not embark upon a career as an artist until 1880.

Van Gogh met fellow painter Paul Gauguin in November 1887 when Gauguin arrived in Paris. They became fast friends, traveling and painting together. Quickly, though, their relationship deteriorated. They quarreled about art, and van Gogh feared Gauguin was going to abandon him.

The tension peaked on December 23, 1888. Van Gogh stalked Gauguin with a razor—that's when the ear lobe incident happened. Gauguin left and did not see Van Gogh again. Van Gogh was in critical care for several days before beginning to suffer from hallucinations and paranoia that he was being poisoned.

Augustine of Hippo

Saint Augustine played a tremendous role in the development of Western Christianity. Born in 354 in Algeria, the Bishop Augustine himself was drastically influenced by Platonic principles. When the Roman Empire in the West was starting to crumble, he created the concept of the Church as a spiritual City of God—separate from the material City of Man. His thought deeply influenced the medieval people.

Augustine was born in present-day Souk Ahras, Algeria, to a Christian mother, who pleaded with him not to become Christian. Augustine was educated in North Africa, lived as a pagan intellectual, took a concubine, and became a Manichean, a Gnostic religion. Later he converted to Christianity and became a bishop.

Augustine was one of the most productive Latin authors, and his works consist of more than one hundred titles, including *The Confessions*—often called the first Western autobiography. Many of his writings are still read around the world.

In Roman Catholicism and the Anglican Communion, Augustine is a saint and preeminent Doctor of the Church, as well as the patron of the Augustinian religious order. Many Protestants, especially Calvinists, consider him to be one of the theological fathers of Reformation teaching on salvation and grace. In the Eastern Orthodox Church he is a saint, and his feast day is celebrated annually on June 15. Among the Orthodox he is called Blessed Augustine, or Saint Augustine the Blessed.

Famous Words of Augustine of Hippo

- Habit, if not resisted, soon becomes necessity.
- Since you cannot do good to all, you are to pay special attention to those who, by the accidents of time, or place, or circumstances, are brought into closer connection with you.

Benedict de Spinoza

Baruch or Benedict de Spinoza spent most of his life grinding lenses—truly, that was his job: a lens grinder. In fact, that may have been what killed him—yet a magnum opus published after his death made him famous.

Born in 1632, the Dutch philosopher (he actually was of Portuguese Jewish origin) was not considered one of the great rationalists of seventeenth-century philosophy until years after his death. He actually laid the foundation for eighteenth-century Enlightenment and modern biblical criticism. His magnum opus, titled *Ethics*, also brought Spinoza the fame of being considered one of Western philosophy's definitive ethicists.

While working as a lens grinder, Spinoza rejected rewards and honors such as prominent teaching jobs, and handed over his entire family inheritance to his sister. His moral character and philosophical achievements prompted twentieth-century philosopher Gilles Deleuze to dub him "the absolute philosopher."

Spinoza died in February 1677 of a lung illness, possibly tuberculosis due to years of breathing in fine glass dust while grinding lenses.

Recent philosophers have called Spinoza the "prince of philosophers," and in the Netherlands, Spinoza's portrait was featured on the Dutch 1,000-guilder banknote— legal tender there until 2002, when the euro came onto the market. Also in the Netherlands, the highest and most prestigious scientific award is dubbed the *Spinoza prijs* (Spinoza prize).

Famous Words of Spinoza

- Do not weep; do not wax indignant. Understand.
- For peace is not mere absence of war, but is a virtue that springs from a state of mind, a disposition for benevolence, confidence, justice.
- All things excellent are as difficult as they are rare.
- Fame has also this great drawback, that if we pursue it, we must direct our lives so as to please the fancy of men.

DRAMA 101
SOPHOCLES

Sophocles was the second of the three ancient Greek tragedians, born twenty-eight years after Aeschylus, the "father of tragedy." Sophocles wrote an astounding 120 plays, possibly more, during his lifetime. Seven have survived—*Ajax, Antigone, Electra, Oedipus at Colonus, Oedipus the King, Philoctetes*, and *Trachinian Women.*

Born to a wealthy merchant, Sophocles was able to study all of the arts—music, dancing, and gymnastics—and as a teenager he already was chosen to lead a boys' choir at a celebration of the victory of the Salamis (a decisive naval battle between the Greeks and the Persians).

Sophocles was quite the high achiever—for nearly half a century he won the most awards at ancient Athens dramatic competitions, never receiving lower than second place. An accomplished actor, he even performed in some of his own plays. In two plays in particular, he performed juggling acts that spectators talked about for years.

He was known for character development, and was the first to add a third actor to the stage. In *Oedipus the King*—generally considered his greatest accomplishment—Oedipus kills his father and marries his mother. Tragic stuff, and often called the "perfectly structured" play with its masterful plot and artful suspense.

Sophocles died in 406 BC, more than ninety years old. Some accounts say he choked while eating grapes sent to him by an actor. Others say that he tried to read a section of *Antigone* aloud without taking a breath, and passed out. He was buried in the family tomb about a mile outside of Athens.

PABLO PICASSO

Think Picasso, think Cubism. That was his art form. While you may not be able to rattle off any of his works—*Les Demoiselles d'Avignon* from 1907 is among the most famous—you might recognize his daring and expressive style.

But before we explore his artistic prowess, check out his real name, it might be a record of sorts: Pablo Diego José Francisco de Paula Juan Nepomuceno María de los Remedios Cipriano de la Santísima Trinidad Martyr Patricio Clito Ruiz y Picasso. It's a series of names honoring various saints and relatives. Added to these were Ruiz and Picasso, for his father and mother, respectively, as per Spanish custom.

Picasso was born in Malaga, Spain, to a middle-class family. His father was also a painter, specializing in birds and other game. According to his mom, Picasso's first word was *pencil* (in Spanish, of course—*lápiz*—and at that age he hadn't exactly ventured into sculpting yet but loved to draw).

When Picasso had entered his teenage years, Daddy Picasso one day found his son painting over an unfinished sketch of a pigeon—and was awestruck at the teen's precision and technique. Convinced his son had surpassed him, Picasso's father vowed to give up painting.

In 1895, Picasso's seven-year old sister died of diphtheria, a traumatic event in his life that led to a family move to Barcelona. Picasso's father persuaded the officials at a top-notch arts academy there to allow his son to take an entrance exam for the advanced class. The process often took students a month, but Picasso completed it in a week, and the impressed jury admitted Picasso, who was still thirteen. At sixteen, Picasso then went to the most prestigious art school in the country, Madrid's Royal Academy of San Fernando.

And the rest, as they say, is history.

GEORGE GERSHWIN

If George Gershwin hadn't died at such an early age, who knows how many more songs he would have composed, or how many more Oscars would have adorned his shelves?

Early in 1937, Gershwin began to complain of blinding headaches and the smell of burned rubber. He had developed a cystic malignant brain tumor. In June, he performed in a special concert of his music with the San Francisco Symphony Orchestra. Later, while working on the score of *The Goldwyn Follies* in Hollywood, he collapsed and, on July 11, 1937, following surgery for the tumor, he died at the mere age of thirty-eight.

Gershwin, who wrote most of his works with his older brother, Ira Gershwin, composed songs for Broadway, for the classical concert hall, and for the popular mainstream. He was victorious at all three. Many of his compositions have been used on television, and countless singers and musicians have recorded Gershwin songs.

Gershwin was born to Russian-Jewish immigrant parents in Brooklyn, New York. His parents had bought a piano for brother Ira, but to their surprise—and Ira's relief—George was the one who liked to play it. When he was fifteen, Gershwin quit school and found his first job: a "song plugger" for a publishing firm in New York City's Tin Pan Alley. His "salary:" $15 a week.

In 1916, he started working for Aeolian Company and Standard Music Rolls in New York, recording and arranging piano rolls. He produced likely hundreds of rolls under his own and fictional names. And then came 1919, his breakthrough year—he scored his first big national hit with his song *Swanee*. Major work after major work soon followed.

George Gershwin is buried in the Westchester Hills Cemetery in Hastings-on-Hudson, New York. He was inducted into the Long Island Music Hall of Fame in 2006. The George Gershwin Theatre on Broadway is named after him.

Ben Franklin's Inventions

- **Bifocals:** Franklin could barely see and needed glasses to read. But he'd have to put them on to read, then take them off when he was done. He got tired of that and wanted to find a way to be able to see both near and far. So, smart inventor he was, he simply cut two pairs of glasses in half and placed half of each lens in a single frame. Ta da! Bifocals!

- **Urinary catheter:** Most people don't think of Franklin as being famous for inventions pertaining to the human body, but he always was fascinated by how the body worked—and how he could improve it. Take Ben's older brother, for example. He suffered from kidney stones. Franklin didn't just give him a get well card. No, he actually created a flexible urinary catheter—which may be the first produced in America. Pretty nice get-well gift!

- **Lightning rod:** You remember Franklin and his famous kite-flying story right? Well, even though he did not "invent" electricity, he did come up with the lightning rod—a pretty big deal considering how many buildings and ships it has protected from lightning damage.

- **Franklin stove:** Long ago most people warmed their tootsies at home by their fireplace. It wasn't the safest thing to do and took up a lot of wood, so Franklin wanted something better. He came up with the iron furnace stove, a safer alternative that used less wood. Franklin also happened to help create the first fire company and fire insurance company.

- **Odometer:** When Franklin was a postmaster, he had to come up with mail delivery routes. It wasn't as easy back then as it is today. He had to ride in his carriage to measure the routes—with no way to track the distance. Franklin, of course, wouldn't have that—he invented an odometer and clipped it to his buggy.

- **Long arm:** When Franklin got old, he stopped working and spent much of his time reading. But remember, he was old. It was hard for him to reach those books from his top shelves. Again, never the one to settle for less, he invented…this time a tool called a "long arm." The long wooden pole had a grasping claw at the end so he could grab his books.

GREAT THINKERS WHO DROPPED OUT

Not all great thinkers of history were academics and elites. Some actually never made it through high school. Here are their stories:

Ben Franklin

Ben Franklin accomplished many things in his lifetime. One thing he never finished, however, was school. The youngest in a family of twenty, Franklin dropped out of school at age of ten, beginning his work in printing with his father and brother.

Though he never even finished middle school, Franklin went on to become a philosopher, author, publisher, scientist, founding father, and signer of the United States Constitution.

Bill Gates

Bill Gates is the cofounder of the company Microsoft and an entrepreneurial great thinker. After reading an article in Popular Electronics about a microcomputer, Gates dropped out of Harvard University and formed the company now known as Microsoft with his friend Paul Allen. He was only a college junior at the time. Though he never finished his junior year of undergraduate college, Bill Gates consistently ranks as one of the richest men in the world.

Walt Disney

Walt Disney, Oscar-winning film producer and animation pioneer, dropped out of school when he was just sixteen years old. He had planned to join the army but was too young to enlist, so Disney joined the Red Cross illegally by forging his age on his birth certificate.

He was sent to France to drive an ambulance, which he covered in cartoon drawings—the drawings that eventually became Disney's animated characters.

At the age of fifty-eight, after winning the Presidential Medal of Freedom and founding the Walt Disney Company, he was awarded an honorary high school diploma by his alma mater.

Charles Dickens

Author of many classics, including *A Tale of Two Cities* and *A Christmas Carol*, Dickens dropped out of school at the age of twelve.

He entered the workforce at a boot-blacking company, working in a factory for ten hours per day. He later worked as a law clerk, stenographer, and journalist. He finally published his first novel, The Pickwick Papers, in 1836.

Thomas Edison

With more than 1,000 patented inventions to his name—including the lightbulb, phonograph, and the motion picture camera—Thomas Edison is one of the most famous innovative thinkers of all time. He was a recipient of the Congressional Gold Medal and a self-made multimillionaire at an early age.

Because of an illness during his youth, Edison began school late and dropped out after just three months of formal education.

Famous Words of Benjamin Franklin

- Beer is living proof that God loves us and wants us to be happy.
- A man wrapped up in himself makes a very small bundle.
- Distrust and caution are the parents of security.
- All mankind is divided into three classes: those that are immovable, those that are movable, and those that move.
- Being ignorant is not so much a shame, as being unwilling to learn.
- Anyone who trades liberty for security deserves neither liberty nor security.
- Be at war with your vices, at peace with your neighbors, and let every new year find you a better man.

Mark Twain:
Great American Novelist

Samuel Langhorne Clemens, better known by the pen name Mark Twain, is known, of course, for his novels—*Adventures of Huckleberry Finn* and *The Adventures of Tom Sawyer* among them—but also is known for his quotations and his wit. His popularity is colossal. American author William Faulkner called Twain "the father of American literature."

Twain was born in Florida, Missouri, on November 30, 1835, to a country merchant, John Marshall Clemens, and Jane Lampton Clemens. He was the sixth of seven children and one of only four to survive to childhood.

When Twain was four, his family moved to Hannibal, a port town on the Mississippi River—and Twain's inspiration for the fictional town of St. Petersburg in both *The Adventures of Tom Sawyer* and *Adventures of Huckleberry Finn*. At that time, Missouri was a slave state in the Union, and young Twain became familiar with slavery, a theme he later explored in his writings.

When Twain was eleven, his father died of pneumonia. The following year, Twain's life in printing began, first as a printer's apprentice. In 1851, he began working as a typesetter and contributor of articles and humorous sketches for the *Hannibal Journal,* a newspaper owned by his brother. When he was eighteen, he left Hannibal and worked as a printer in New York City, Philadelphia, St. Louis, and Cincinnati.

He joined the union and educated himself in public libraries in the evenings. Then, at twenty-two, Twain returned to Missouri. On a voyage to New Orleans down the Mississippi, the steamboat captain, Horace E. Bixby, encouraged Twain to pursue a career as a steamboat pilot. The money was good; wages were $250 per month, equivalent to $155,000 a year today.

Twain meticulously studied 2,000 miles of the Mississippi for more than two years before receiving his steamboat pilot license in 1859. While training, Samuel convinced his younger brother Henry to work with him. Henry was killed on June 21, 1858, when the steamboat he was working on exploded. Twain had foreseen this death in a detailed dream a month earlier, which inspired his interest in parapsychology.

Twain was guilt-stricken and blamed himself for his brother's death for the rest of his life. Still, he continued to work on the river until the American Civil War, when traffic was halted along the Mississippi.

When the war broke out, Twain joined his brother, Orion, who had been appointed secretary to the territorial governor of Nevada, and headed west. They traveled via stagecoach across the Great Plains and the Rocky Mountains, visiting the Mormon community in Salt Lake City along the way. His experiences became the basis of the book *Roughing It* and provided material for *The Celebrated Jumping Frog of Calaveras County*. Twain's journey ended in a silver-mining town, where he became a miner. Mining didn't go too well, so Twain found work at a newspaper. He continued his journalism career in San Francisco.

During this time Twain met Charles Langdon, who showed him a picture of his sister Olivia; Twain claimed to have fallen in love at first sight. They officially met in 1868, were engaged a year later, and married in February 1870 in Elmira, New York. The couple began their married life in Buffalo, New York, where Twain owned a stake in the *Buffalo Express* and worked as an editor and writer. Their son Langdon died of diphtheria at nineteen months.

In 1871, Twain moved his family to Hartford, Connecticut, where Olivia gave birth to three daughters. The couple's marriage lasted thirty-four years, until Olivia's death in 1904.

Famous Words of Mark Twain

- But who prays for Satan? Who, in eighteen centuries, has had the common humanity to pray for the one sinner that needed it most?
- Against the assault of laughter nothing can stand.
- Be careful about reading health books. You may die of a misprint.
- Anger is an acid that can do more harm to the vessel in which it is stored than to anything on which it is poured.
- "Buy land; they're not making it anymore.

CRASH COURSE
JORGE LUIS BORGES

Jorge Borges was an existential Argentine writer of moderate success until a knock on the head and eye problems changed his life and his path to fame.

Borges had many successfully published essays and poems in the 1930s. He worked for newspapers, journals, and even libraries while writing about his views on assorted subjects. They weren't always popular, but he had a following.

One of his closest allies was his father, Jorge Guillermo Borges Haslam, a frustrated writer whose death in 1938 was a great shock to Borges. Then, on Christmas Eve that year, he received a head wound from which he very nearly died of infection. And while recovering from that injury, Borges began to tinker with a new style of writing that led him to pen a story that examined the relationship between a father, a son, and the nature of writing.

During that time, he became critical of new Argentine President Juan Peron; Peron, in turn, had Borges fired from his job. Eye problems had caused him to cut back on his writing, so he couldn't support himself. He turned to public speaking, which gained him a national reputation for powerful commentary.

When Peron's government fell, Borges became the head of the National Library, and his fame grew with that prominence. His work started to be translated into English, and the power of his words soon captivated many new audiences.

The University of Texas invited him as a guest lecturer, his first exposure in the United States. In his later years he traveled the world lecturing on a variety of topics, right up until his death in 1986.

The Borges Center, which celebrates the man many consider to the most erudite writer of the twentieth century, located at the University of Iowa, celebrates his published work, his speeches, and his perspectives on life.

The Man Who Didn't Invent Peanut Butter

Although his legacies in horticultural and agricultural science are indisputable, the one contribution for which most remember George Washington Carver is false. Contrary to popular belief, the botanist and Tuskegee Institute professor did not invent peanut butter. In fact, no one knows who created the first peanut butter, although it is credited to Dr. Ambrose Straub from St. Louis, Missouri.

Carver did, however, work extensively with cultivators of the peanut, also referred to in those days as the "goober pea." Carver also concentrated his research on the black-eyed pea and yams, as well as countless other food-bearing plants. With the information he gathered from his research, Carver saved the lives of many southern farmers by teaching them ways in which to enhance their agricultural techniques.

The scientist, whose humble beginnings in the Ozarks of Missouri were that of a young slave, began his legacy as "The Peanut Man" while living with his former owners, Susan and Moses Carver. The couple, according to some accounts, was actually against slavery and made the purchase to save George's family from cruel treatment.

The Carvers adopted him shortly after his mother's death. On their farm, young George spent his days studying the various plants which grew in the Ozarks region, and meanwhile learned to appreciate the delicacy of the soil in which the indigenous plants thrived.

After years of both formal and informal education, Carver found himself in the service of Alabama's Tuskegee Institute founder Booker T. Washington. In the position of professor, Washington charged Carver with several duties, including the management of the state-funded Agricultural Experiment Station.

Carver realized early on that cotton agriculture had ruined the once-fertile southern soils, and he began impressing his theories about soil conservation on local farmers. Encouraging them to cultivate alternative crops, most notably the peanut, Carver developed a relationship with the farmers which eventually led to his representation of them in Washington D.C. The botanist's time in Washington resulted in fame for Carver, because while he was in the capital, President Theodore Roosevelt publicly acknowledged his work.

Although he didn't create peanut butter, all of his agricultural work placed George Washington Carver in the spotlight of America's greatest minds. More important than his work with the peanut, however, was his role in undermining the stereotype that blacks were intellectually inferior to the whites. Maybe one day legend will correct itself and remember the man for this incredible achievement.

George Washington Carver's Inventions

George Washington Carver invented roughly three hundred uses for peanuts and sweet potatoes.

Peanuts: All Purpose Cream, Antiseptic Soap, Baby Massage Cream, Face Bleach and Tan Remover, Face Powder, Glycerine, Hand Lotion, Peanut Oil Shampoo, Pomade for Scalp, Shampoo, Shaving Cream, Tetter and Dandruff Cure, Toilet Soap, Vanishing Cream, Caramel, Chili Sauce, Cocoa, Dry Coffee, Instant Coffee, Mayonnaise, Meat Substitutes, Milks, Oleomargarine, Pancake Flour, Peanut and Popcorn Bars, Peanut Relish, Peanut Sausage, Salad Oil, Vinegar, White Pepper, Worcestershire Sauce

Sweet Potatoes: Flour, Starch, Molasses, Ink

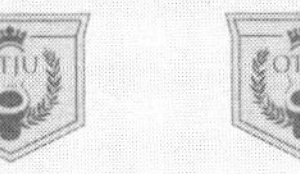 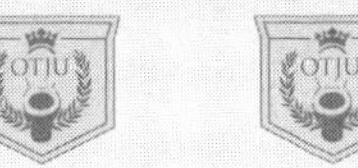    

CRASH COURSE
GEORGE WASHINGTON CARVER

1864: George Washington Carver was born in July in Diamond Grove, Missouri.

1874: He moved to Kansas.

1890: He was the first black student to attend Simpson College.

1891: Carver transferred to State Agricultural College in Ames, Iowa.

1894: Carver began teaching at Iowa State College.

1896: Carver began heading the Department of Agricultural Research at what today is Tuskegee University.

1923: Carver received a Spingarn Medal for Distinguished Service to Science.

1935: Carver was named a collaborator in the division of plant mycology in the U.S. Department of Agriculture.

1938: The movie *Life of George Washington Carver* was made.

1939: Carver received the Roosevelt Medal for Contributions to Southern Agriculture.

1939: Carver received an honorary membership into the American Inventors Society.

1941: Carver received an award of merit by Variety Clubs of America.

1942: The George Washington Carver Cabin was built at The Henry Ford.

1942: A birthplace marker for Diamond Grove was approved by the Missouri governor.

1943: George Washington Carver died in Tuskegee, Alabama. His birthplace was established as the George Washington Carver National Monument.

1948: The three-cent Carver commemorative stamp was issued.

1952: Carver was selected as one of fifty outstanding Americans by *Popular Mechanics* magazine.

1952: The *George Washington Carver* Polaris submarine was launched.

1990: Carver was inducted into the National Inventors Hall of Fame.

1998: The second Carver stamp, a 32-cent version, went on sale.

Famous Words of George Washington Carver

- When you can do the common things of life in an uncommon way, you will command the attention of the world.
- No individual has any right to come into the world and go out of it without leaving something behind.
- Education is the key to unlock the golden door of freedom.
- Since new developments are the products of a creative mind, we must therefore stimulate and encourage that type of mind in every way possible.
- How far you go in life depends on your being tender with the young, compassionate with the aged, sympathetic with the striving, and tolerant of the weak and strong. Because someday in your life you will have been all of these.
- Our creator is the same and never changes despite the names given Him by people here and in all parts of the world. Even if we gave Him no name at all, He would still be there, within us, waiting to give us good on this earth.
- Reading about nature is fine, but if a person walks in the woods and listens carefully, he can learn more than what is in books, for they speak with the voice of God.
- Where there is no vision, there is no hope.
- There is no shortcut to achievement. Life requires thorough preparation—veneer isn't worth anything.
- Fear of something is at the root of hate for others, and hate within will eventually destroy the hater.

Jean-Paul Sartre

This leading twentieth-century French philosopher won the 1964 Nobel Prize in Literature—and declined it. Why? He put it this way: "It is not the same thing if I sign Jean-Paul Sartre or if I sign Jean-Paul Sartre, Nobel Prize winner. A writer must refuse to allow himself to be transformed into an institution, even if it takes place in the most honorable form."

That was Sartre for you—the Paris native who somehow managed to make existentialism trendy and his own name a household one. His writings set the tone for intellectual life post-World War II. And his influences went on to make their way into all facets of popular culture.

The Reference Never Dies: Hell is Other People

Perhaps his most famous quote, Sartre's "Hell is other people," comes from the historically revered play *No Exit*. Published in French in 1944, the play has gone on to become one of the most quoted, most well-known Existentialist plays of all time. The famous quote can be found around the world, in television, print, and movies.

- An episode of the popular show Futurama used the title "Hell is Other Robots," as a spinoff of Sartre's famous line.
- The quote is also recited in the movie *Puccini for Beginners*, when a woman insists the main character is wrong; that hell is loneliness.
- The play has been adapted to three films:
  Huis clos, by Jacquline Audry, 1954
  No Exit, by Tad Danielewski, 1962
  No Exit, by Etienne Kallos, 2006
- An episode of the popular television series West Wing uses the quote as its title.
- Harvey Danger, in his song Diminishing Returns uses the line, "Hell is other people; some people never learn."

CLAUDE LÉVI-STRAUSS

Be clear about one thing: This is *not* the guy who started the first company to manufacture blue jeans. This guy is French and Jewish and probably wore some of those jeans. But he knows far more about anthropology than he does button flies.

Claude Lévi-Straussgrew up in Paris and studied law and philosophy. He went on a cultural tour to Brazil and spent four years there studying the tribes. When France surrendered to Germany in World War II, he fled to New York City, where he started to establish himself.

He wrote powerfully and creatively about those tribes, social function, linguistics, and many aspects of culture. He developed a thesis on myths in both hemispheres. He became a counterpart of Sartre on several theories of existentialism and was broadly published.

He most definitely did not make blue jeans. But maybe he wore them when he wrote about how different cultures create and resolve similar myths. In studying Native American myths, he compared the "trickster" of those myths to ravens or coyotes.

He believes the raven and the coyote "mediate" their foes between life and death. He also compared it to agriculture, saying that agriculture was about growing life but hunting was about death. And he extended that to a comparison between meat eaters and beasts of prey. Plant-eating animals don't catch their food.

So the two different types of animals figure out how to take care of themselves. And thus the coyote and the raven "mediate" the difference between life and death. And you had trouble figuring out where the fifth pocket was on the jeans.

194

TIMELINE
NAPOLEON BONAPARTE

1769: Napoleon Bonaparte born August 15, 1769.

1796: Napoleon marries Josephine de Beauharnias.

1796: Napoleon made commander of Army of Italy.

1798: Napoleon's Egyptian campaign.

1799: Napoleon becomes member of Consulate government.

1802: Napoleon named first consul for life.

1804: Napoleon becomes Emperor of France.

1810: Napoleon marries Marie Louise.

1812: Napoleon reaches Moscow.

1814: Napoleon forced to abdicate, exiled to Elba.

1815: Napoleon returns to France, defeated at Battle of Waterloo, exiled to St. Helena.

1821: Napoleon dies May 5, 1821.

Interesting Facts About Napoleon Bonaparte

- Napoleon—the Emperor of the French—actually was granted sovereignty over the island of Elba during his first exile.

- A genius military commander, Napoleon defeated many military forces much greater in size to his own.

- Napoleon created French satellite kingdoms in Holland, Italy, Germany, and Spain—and then placed his brothers and other relatives on their thrones.

- The army assembled by Napoleon in 1812 was the largest seen in Europe up until that time.

- Tradition had always called for the pope to crown the emperor. Napoleon, however, took the crown from Pope Pius VII's hands and placed it on his own head.

Pliny the Elder

Pliny the Elder actually was born Gaius or Caius Plinius Secundus in AD 23. He was an author—most noted for *Natural History*—and naturalist as well as a naval and military commander.

The son of a Roman equestrian, he was born in Como: a statue there on the Duomo of Como honors him as a native son.

Pliny the Elder's *History of His Times*, which he completed in thirty-one books, was set aside purposely for publication after his death. His *Natural History* was an encyclopedia—thirty-seven books completed in AD 77 and dedicated to the emperor Titus Flavius Vespasianus.

Interesting Facts About Pliny the Elder

- Pliny is a prominent character in Robert Harris's novel *Pompeii*.
- Pliny was stationed at Misenum at the time Mount Vesuvius erupted. Pliny's body was found under the ashes of the *Vesuvium*. Due to his death in the AD 79 eruption, he often is portrayed in docudramas and dramas set around that eruption, such as *Pompeii: The Last Day* (played by Tim Piggott-Smith) and *The Roman Mysteries* (played by Simon Callow).
- Pliny's quote, "True glory consists of doing what deserves to be written, in writing what deserves to be read," appears in the PC/Mac game *Civilization IV*. The quote, spoken by Leonard Nimoy, is attributed to Pliny the Elder.

Thomas A. Edison

Thomas Edison was a curious child but did not do well in school because he could not focus. The youngest of seven children, Edison (he was called Al growing up) was labeled "addled," or confused, by his teacher. Edison's mother—disagreeing profusely—yanked him out of school after just a few months of formal education and homeschooled him from then on.

When Edison turned nine, his mother gave him an elementary science book that showed him how to do home chemistry experiments. Edison thrived, soon spending every last dime on chemicals. The following year he built his first science laboratory in the family's basement. To make sure no one took his prized goods, he slapped all his chemical bottles with "poison" labels.

By about age twelve, Edison started to lose his hearing. There are various stories explaining his hearing loss. One says a train conductor walloped him in the ears after Edison started a fire in a boxcar during one of his science experiments. Edison himself explained that he was injured when the conductor picked him up by the ears onto a moving train. Others said his hearing loss was a result of scarlet fever during childhood. But the more likely option: a genetic condition. Both Edison's father and one of his brothers also suffered from hearing loss. Apparently Edison actually liked being deaf, although technically he was hard of hearing, not completely deaf. The quiet, he said, made it easier to concentrate on his experiments.

Edison was twenty-two years old when he got his first patent, for a telegraphic vote-recording machine for the legislature. The year was 1869. Each legislator would move a switch on Edison's machine that would record his vote on a particular bill. But when a business partner brought the invention to Washington D.C., Congress was not impressed. The instrument, they said, was too slow, and Edison's vote recorder was never used. But Edison went on to patent hundreds more inventions.

THOMAS A. EDISON'S INVENTIONS

Edison patented more than 1,000 inventions. Here are a few:

1869: The universal stock ticker and the unison stop.

1872: The motograph; the automatic telegraph system; the duplex, quadruplex, sextuplex, and multiplex telegraph systems; paraffin paper; and carbon rheostat.

1875: Discovered "Etheric Force," the foundation of wireless telegraphy.

1876: The electric pen (used for the first mimeographs).

1877: The carbon telephone transmitter (made telephony commercially practical and included the microphone used in radio).

1877: The phonograph.

1879: Discovered incandescent light; radically improved dynamos and generators; and discovered a system of distribution, regulation, and measurement of electric current: switches, fuses, sockets, and meters.

1880: The magnetic ore separator.

1880: Discovered the "Edison Effect," the fundamental principle of electronics.

1885: Discovered a system of wireless induction telegraph between moving trains and stations. He also patented similar systems for ship-to-shore use.

1891: The motion picture camera.

1896: The fluoroscope and the fluorescent electric lamp.

1900: The nickel-iron-alkaline storage battery.

1914: The electric safety miner's lamp; discovered the process for manufacturing synthetic carbolic acid.

1927–1931: Tested 17,000 plants for rubber content as a source of rubber in war emergencies.

Edison and the Lightbulb

Thomas Edison didn't invent the lightbulb—he just made it work. More than a dozen people were working on their versions of the lightbulb. Joseph Swan had already placed lightbulbs in homes in England. And American inventor Hiram Maxim had a bulb that would burn for 24 hours straight.

So what was the big deal for Edison? He developed a total electric system—the bulbs, the wires, the fuses—all the elements necessary to satisfy customers. He had a plan to install underground wires and light up all of lower Manhattan.

Lightbulb Trivia

- Macy's department store in New York City became the first store to use incandescent lamp lighting in 1883.

- In 1888, the Hotel Everett on Park Row in New York City became the first hotel to be illuminated by electric light. There were 101 electric lightbulbs.

- New York theaters were the first to take advantage of using lightbulbs to spell out messages on their marquees.

- The world's largest lightbulb is in Edison, New Jersey. The lamp shaped like a lightbulb stands on top of the 131-foot Edison Memorial Tower. The tower itself stands on the site of Edison's famous Menlo Park Lab.

New and Approved

Edison improved on Alexander Graham Bell's telephone by designing a carbon transmitter (mouthpiece) that improved the sound of the speaker.

WORLD LITERATURE
HOMER

No, we're not talking the Simpsons here. Think epic poems. Think the *Iliad* and the *Odyssey*. Yes, that Homer, the ancient Greek poet. At least that's what they say.

See, everything about Homer is, sort of, speculation—nothing about him is definite. But that's part of what makes "him" so intriguing.

Some say Homer is a fictitious name; some even say the two famous poems previously mentioned were created not by one poet, but by several (because of their long oral tradition). Still other scholars insist that Homer was a real guy.

So let's take a look at the two famous poems, which definitely *do* exist. The *Iliad* is commonly dated to the late eighth or ninth century BC Many scholars believe it is the oldest extant work of literature in the ancient Greek language—making it the first work of European literature. The *Iliad* concerns events during the tenth and final year in the siege of the city of Troy by the Greeks during the Trojan War.

The *Odyssey* is, in part, a sequel to the *Iliad* and mainly centers on the Greek hero Odysseus and his long journey home to Ithaca following the fall of Troy. It takes Odysseus ten years to reach Ithaca after the ten-year Trojan War. During this absence, his son and wife must deal with a group of unruly suitors to compete for Penelope's hand in marriage, since most have assumed that Odysseus has died.

EXTRA CREDIT: The movie *O Brother, Where Art Thou?* has the basic plot of *The Odyssey*; Joel and Ethan Coen admit to basing the movie loosely on the *Odyssey* (and explicitly reference it in the opening credits) but insist that they haven't read it.

The Peabody Award-winning *The Odyssey of Homer* (1981) dramatized the epic for radio in eight one-hour episodes. Syndicated in the U.S. and broadcast by the CBC, the program was later published as an audiobook.

John Calvin

If you wanted to be very precise in your language, you might say John Calvin was preordained to be a minister. At the ripe age of fourteen, John was sent off to study Latin and Catholic theology by his father, a lawyer who worked with the Catholic Church. Young John, a Frenchman who was actually named Jean Gauvin, was known to be remarkably religious.

But not even so noble a course can be navigated without interruption: Calvin's dad had a falling out with the church. The elder withdrew his son from Catholicism and sent him to law school. But what he really did was launch the career of one of history's greatest religious reformers.

Calvin got his law degree and had a transformation by God that filled him with what he called "a desire so intense" that he immediately decided to pursue theology. He was twenty-three.

Soon after, he converted to Protestantism and became a vocal leader of that reform. Calvin was banned from Paris and spent most of his life in Geneva, though he was banished from that city once, too. Many feared that he was trying to replace the Pope.

His translations and interpretations of the Bible were known for controversy. He preached to help churches find logic and systemization. He inspired their leadership and wrote how they could help grow other churches. He is known to have developed the formal structure of the Protestant church, outlining officers that remain to this day the structure of Protestant leadership: ministers, doctors, elders and deacons. Because so much of his work was controversial, he communicated many of his ideas in letters to churches under the name Charles Despeville. Nothing interfered with his passion for God and how others should reach him.

When he was forty, Calvin's health began to fail. He suffered from migraines, lung problems, gout, and kidney stones. He had to be carried to the pulpit and sometimes lectured from bed. He ate only one meal a day—an egg and a glass of wine at noon—and never stopped working, though many his friends encouraged him to rest. To which Calvin is said to have replied: "What! Would you have the Lord find me idle when he comes?"

PTOLEMY

Along with believing that the Earth is a sphere and proposing an Earth-centered universe consisting of concentric rotating spheres—it became known as the Ptolemaic system—this ancient astronomer from Egypt:

Wrote the *Almagest*, proposing his Earth-centered astronomical system. *Almagest* also contains a star catalogue of forty-eight constellations.

Compiled the eight-volume *Geography*, which charted the Greco-Roman world as it was known at the time, and included estimates of longitude, latitude and the Earth's size.

Studied the properties and behavior of light, including reflection, refraction, and color, and published his conclusions in *Optics*. This played a significant role in the beginning of the history of optics.

Published *Tetrabiblos*, attempting to establish a scientific basis for astrology.

Studied music theory and the mathematics of music, and compiled his observations in *Harmonica*. Ptolemy discussed how musical notes could be translated into mathematical equations.

The Ptolemaic system dominated astronomical thought for more than one thousand years. The heliocentric, or sun-centered, Copernican system replaced this theory in the 1500s.

Although not much is known about his personal life, it is estimated that he lived from approximately AD 90 to 170 and he worked in the library at Alexandria from 127 to 150.

ALFRED NOBEL

Alfred Nobel was not the first successful businessman to try to make up for his sins by giving to charity, and he certainly wasn't the last. But he's one of the best known, thanks to two of his biggest inventions: dynamite and the Nobel Prize.

Nobel was born in Sweden in 1833 to a father who was an inventor, engineer, and manufacturer. Alfred later studied chemistry in Paris and worked as an engineer in the United States, but eventually returned to Sweden to work with his father and brothers.

There Nobel began messing around with explosives and manufacturing nitroglycerin. The problem was that the liquid explosive was too volatile, so he started looking for a way to stabilize it for demolition work, inventing, along the way, a new type of detonator and the blasting cap.

Experimenting with unstable explosives doesn't make for the safest workplace. In 1864, Nobel's factory exploded, killing several people including his younger brother. Three years later, Nobel finally came up with a way to control nitroglycerin. By mixing the liquid with an absorbent dirt, Nobel came up with dynamite.

Dynamite was soon used by engineers worldwide to blast tunnels and canals and clear roadways. But Nobel didn't just invent things that go "boom"—his more than 350 patents included nonexplosive materials such as artificial silk and leather.

A lifelong bachelor, Nobel was often a moody loner. Always restless, he also loved literature and tried his hand at plays, poems, and novels. Still, he remained best known for his explosives. (Point in case: when Alfred's brother Ludvig died in France, the newspapers mistakenly announced it as the death of Alfred, declaring "The merchant of death is dead.")

Many believe that premature obituary may have shamed and inspired Nobel to come up with his final invention. After his actual death in 1896, the reading of the will laid out Nobel's shocking plan: to form a posthumous trust that would annually award prizes for great achievements in the arts and sciences.

The trust created the Nobel Prizes in chemistry, medicine

(physiology), physics, literature, and for peace, which were first awarded in 1901. In 1969, a sixth award, for economics, was added. (The economic prize is in Nobel's memory and, while it is not technically a "Nobel Prize," it is usually treated as one.)

The Nobel Prize

The Nobel Prize is an international award administered by the Nobel Foundation in Stockholm, Sweden. The Peace Prize was first awarded in 1901 to International Committee of Red Cross (ICRC) founder Henry Dunant. Since then, the Nobel Prize has been awarded for achievements in physics, chemistry, physiology or medicine, literature, and peace. Each prize consists of a medal, personal diploma, and a cash award. In 1968, Sveriges Riksbank established The Sveriges Riksbank Prize in Economic Sciences, in memory of Alfred Nobel, founder of the Nobel Prize.

The First World War was contradictory of what the peace activists honored by the Nobel Peace Prize had worked so hard to establish. So, the Nobel Committee, located in neutral Norway, decided to award only one prize in 1917 to the ICRC. During the war, the ICRC worked to protect the rights of prisoners of war on all sides, including their rights to contact their families.

Again, little more than 20 years later, the world was embroiled in another war. This time, Germany attacked Norway, and within two months the entire country was occupied. No Peace Prize was awarded until 1944. And it was only appropriate to award the prize again to the ICRC. In the midst of chaos, the ICRC had promoted the "fraternity between nations" that Alfred Nobel had referred to in his will when making provisions for the Noble Peace Prize.

- Since its beginning, 797 people and 20 organizations have been awarded the Nobel Prize. Some have been awarded more than once, but only 34 women have been awarded a Nobel Prize. Marie Curie received two Nobel Prizes, her husband, Pierre, daughter, Irène Joliot-Curie, and son-in-law, Frederic Joliot, also received Nobel Prizes.

- Two Nobel laureates have declined the Nobel Prize: Jean-Paul Sartre in 1964 and Le Duc Tho in 1973. On the other hand, four laureates were forced to decline the Prize. Adolf Hitler forced Richard Kuhn, Adolf Butenandt, and Gerhard Domagk to decline the prize; however they later received the Nobel Prize diploma and medal, but not the prize money. And, in 1958, Boris Pasternak was forced to decline the Nobel Prize in Literature by the Soviet Union.
- The youngest Nobel laureate is Lawrence Bragg, who was 25 years old when he received the Nobel Prize in Physics with his father in 1915.
- The oldest Nobel laureate is Leonid Hurwics, who was 90 years old when he was awarded the Nobel Prize in Economics in 2007.

Nobel Prize Trivia

- Theodor Mommsen, age 85, was the oldest person to win the Nobel Prize in Literature.
- Rudyard Kipling became the youngest when he won the price for literature at age 42.
- Mommsen was born over 134 years before the most recently born laureate, Orhan Pamuk.
- Bertrand Russell, who died at 97, lived longer than any other prizewinner.
- The oldest living laureate is Aleksandr Solzhenitsyn, who was born in 1918.
- The laureate who lived the shortest time afterward was Albert Camus, who died three years after receiving the award at age 46.
- TV and radio personality Gert Fylking began the tradition of shouting "Äntligen!" (Swedish for "At last!") when the award winner was announced.
- The first Asian laureate was Rabindranath Tagore.

Women Nobel Laureates

The Nobel Prize has been awarded to 34 women since 1901. One woman, Marie Curie, has been awarded the Nobel Prize two times, first in 1903 (Physics) and again in 1911 (Chemistry).

Physics
1903—Marie Curie
1963—Maria Goeppert-Mayer

Chemistry
1911—Marie Curie
1935—Irène Joliot-Curie
1964—Dorothy Crowfoot Hodgkin

Physiology or Medicine
1947—Gerty Cori
1977—Rosalyn Yalow
1983—Barbara McClintock
1986—Rita Levi-Montalcini
1988—Gertrude B. Elion
1995—Christiane Nüsslein-Volhard
2004—Linda B. Buck

Literature
1909—Selma Lagerlöf
1926—Grazia Deledda
1928—Sigrid Undset
1938—Pearl Buck
1945—Gabriela Mistral
1966—Nelly Sachs
1991—Nadine Gordimer
1993—Toni Morrison
1996—Wislawa Szymborska
2004—Elfriede Jelinek

Peace

1905—Bertha von Suttner
1931—Jane Addams
1946—Emily Greene Balch
1976—Betty Williams
1976—Mairead Corrigan
1979—Mother Teresa
1982—Alva Myrdal
1991—Aung San Suu Kyi
1992—Rigoberta Menchú Tum
1997—Jody Williams
2003—Shirin Ebadi
2004—Wangari Maathai

Noted American Nobel Laureates

1906	Peace, Theodore Roosevelt
1919	Peace, Woodrow Wilson
1931	Peace, Jane Addams
1936	Literature, Eugene O'Neill
1938	Literature, Pearl Buck
1948	Literature, T. S. Eliot
1949	Literature, William Faulkner
1954	Literature, Ernest Hemingway
1964	Peace, Martin Luther King Jr.
1973	Peace, Henry Kissinger
1993	Literature, Toni Morrison
2002	Peace, Jimmy Carter

DESIDERIUS ERASMUS

In the middle of Martin Luther's development of the Protestant movement—and amid all the controversy—existed a big gap: none of the Bibles available served the needs of the church.Enter Desiderius Erasmus (his first name means "desire") a man who desired to be involved in just about anything literary. In 1515, Erasmus published the first Greek translation of the New Testament. He had heard another translation effort was struggling, so he pulled together as many different manuscripts as he could and got the first, if flawed, translation into print. He even included a Latin version, too.

During the next seven years, he completed two other editions of the translation, each with its special issues—the Second Edition drops a verse from John—but broader than the prior. The whole idea that Erasmus, a man who wrote in Latin, accomplished this is unprecedented. Though he had studied in Paris and was a religious scholar, he did not know Greek. And he was broke. But he took a three-year immersion course, begging friends to send him money for food, books, and teachers. He learned well.

Erasmus was a Catholic who dedicated his Greek Testament to Pope Leo X, and Erasmus's second testament also became the foundation for Luther's translation into German. He had opened the door to new languages. Luther's reform movement took off after the New Testament was published, and Erasmus, a committed Catholic riding a literary crest, couldn't help but get into the conversation. He wrote critically about the church, recognizing the need for reform. He also respected Luther.

Luther wanted Erasmus to join his movement. He declined, saying to show partiality in this debate would inhibit his life goal of educating others. Luther basically called him a coward, and both sides thought he was sitting on the fence. He sort of was. He wanted greater reform than Luther was offering.

As with most religious upheaval, there was social upheaval, too. Wars broke out, which made Erasmus even gladder he had remained neutral. The Catholics then accused him of starting the whole mess by not taking a side.

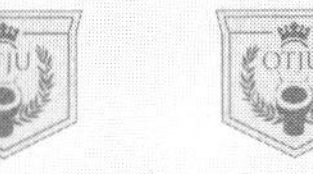

CRASH COURSE
GEORGE ORWELL

Eric Arthur Blair was an English writer and journalist well-noted as a novelist, critic, and commentator on politics and culture. You might know him better by his pen name: George Orwell. He is one of the most admired English-language essayists of the twentieth century, and most famous for two novels critical of totalitarianism in general—*1984*—and Stalinism in particular—*Animal Farm*—which he wrote and published toward the end of his life.

Orwell died in London from tuberculosis, at the age of forty-six. He was in and out of hospitals for the last three years of his life. Having requested burial in accordance with the Anglican rite, he was interred in All Saints' Churchyard in Oxfordshire with the simple epitaph: "Here lies Eric Arthur Blair, born June 25, 1903, died January 21, 1950." There is no mention on his gravestone of his more famous pen name.

Orwell's Rules For Writers

Orwell expounded on the importance of honest and clear language—and in his *Politics and the English Language* provided six rules for writers:

- Never use a metaphor, simile, or other figure of speech which you are used to seeing in print.
- Never use a long word where a short one will do.
- If it is possible to cut a word out, always cut it out.
- Never use the passive voice where you can use the active.
- Never use a foreign phrase, a scientific word, or a jargon word if you can think of an everyday English equivalent.
- Break any of these rules sooner than say anything outright barbarous.

Queen Elizabeth

- It was a pretty big deal that she survived to become Queen of England at all—her Mom was put to death for treason, adultery, and incest. She was labeled a bastard by her father, King Henry VIII.

- As Princess Elizabeth, she made it through a scandal involving herself and Thomas Seymour, the husband of her stepmother Katharine Parr.

- She survived interrogations at the Tower of London when she was imprisoned there by her half-sister Mary Tudor. She was accused of being involved with the Protestant rebellion, led by Sir Thomas Wyatt the Younger.

- Her reign witnessed widespread increase in literacy and great achievements in the arts. Great poets and playwrights emerged during the Elizabethan era, including William Shakespeare, Edmund Spenser, Christopher Marlowe, and Sir Walter Raleigh.

- Her reign also witnessed a new scientific thinking. Men such as Sir Francis Bacon and Dr. John Dee emerged during her era.

- She surrounded herself with highly intelligent and loyal advisors such as Sir William Cecil, Sir Francis Walsingham, and Sir Robert Cecil.

- The Spanish Armada of 1588 was defeated by the English fleet of thirty-four ships and 163 armed merchant vessels under Lord Howard of Effingham, Sir Francis Drake, and Sir John Hawkins.

- The English navy defeated further attempts at invasion in 1596 and 1597.

- She established Protestantism as the country's religion.

- She established the Poor Laws, achieving a new framework of support for the needy.

- She achieved recognition for England as a leading power in Europe.

Evil Genius: Saddam Hussein

Before his execution, Saddam Hussein was a thorn in George W. Bush's presidential underpants; that's common knowledge. It's a complex issue as to how the relationship between the two became so nasty, and it involves a lot of boring drivel about terrorism, sanctions, central intelligence, and one particularly hot commodity. Here are a few things you may not know about the late Iraqi dictator.

Saddam presided as the Head of State in Iraq from 1979 to 2003. Many American intelligence officials claim that the Ba'ath Party to which he belonged came to power in the 1960s with the help of... you guessed it, the United States Central Intelligence Agency.

Saddam studied law in Cairo, Egypt, for about three years before dropping out to join forces with the revolutionary pan-Arab Ba'ath Party. While living as a revolutionary, he worked as a high school teacher. Someone should have encouraged him to keep his day job.

In 1980, with financial and martial support from the United States, Iraq went to war against Iran, but neither country benefited from the event. Saddam asked for money from everybody to rebuild Iraq, including the United States. They declined.

Saddam once sent the dismembered body of a man to the fellow's widow. The man was Health Minister Riyadh Ibrahim, who unwisely suggested that Saddam "temporarily step down to promote peace negotiations."

In spite of his wish to be shot by a firing squad, Saddam was executed by hanging on December 30, 2006. The event was taped on a mobile phone.

SALLY RIDE

As America's Cold War foe, the Soviet Union assisted in turning America's eyes to the heavens. Both countries began competing fiercely after what became known as the "Sputnik Crisis," when the Soviets launched the satellite *Sputnik 1* in 1957.

The Russians outdid the United States again when it succeeded in becoming the first nation to achieve space flight with *Vostok 1* in 1961. As if developing a pattern, the United States came in second place yet again in 1963 after *Vostok 6.* On board during this momentous operation was the first woman to reach space, Valentina Tereshkova. The first American woman didn't make it to outer space for another 19 years, and her name was Sally Ride.

A physicist from California, Sally Ride began her career as a NASA astronaut in 1978. Answering a newspaper advertisement, she began training for space flight as a Capsule Communicator. In this position she was responsible for all communication between the vessel and the Mission Control Center. The responsibility rested on the belief that, of the crew, she would have the best comprehension of the situation in the spacecraft and would, therefore, be the most capable of passing information clearly and efficiently.

With the crew of the Space Shuttle *Challenger*, Ride's journey into space began on June 18, 1983. The mission, STS-7, was led by Commander Robert L. Crippen of Texas and involved the deployment of two communications satellites. The team also conducted pharmaceutical experiments and was the first to utilize a robot arm in space to retrieve a previously deployed satellite. Since STS-7, Ride has not revisited outer space. Her time has been spent teaching at the University of California, San Diego and presiding over Sally Ride Science, a company dedicated to promoting science among girls.

ART 101
CLAUDE MONET

When Claude Monet traveled to Paris to visit The Louvre, he saw other painters copying from the old masters. Monet, on the other hand, did his own thing—he plopped down by a window and painted what he saw. It worked well for Monet, who eventually became one of the founders of French Impressionist painting.

Monet's father had wanted him to go into the family grocery store business. But at a young age Monet already was selling charcoal caricatures for ten to twenty francs. Monet also took drawing lessons. One day, on the beaches of Normandy he met a fellow artist who taught him to use oil paints.

In June of 1861 Monet joined the First Regiment of African Light Cavalry in Algeria for two years of a seven-year commitment. He contracted typhoid, but fortunately, his aunt intervened to get him out of the army—under one condition: he had to agree to complete an art course at a university.

Then, after the outbreak of the Franco-Prussian War in 1870 Monet took refuge in England, where he learned even more painting techniques. The following year he returned to France and began painting some of his best-known works.

Interesting Facts About Monet

Monet and Camille Doncieux married just before the war, in 1870. She became ill in 1876. The birth of their second son in 1878 weakened her already fading health. In 1879, at the age of thirty-two, she died of tuberculosis. Monet painted her on her deathbed. Monet himself died of lung cancer in 1926 at the age of eighty-six.

In 2004, Monet's *London, the Parliament, Effects of Sun in the Fog* (1904), sold for $20.1 million. His 1873 painting of a railway bridge spanning the Seine near Paris was bought by an anonymous telephone bidder for a record $41.4 million at Christie's auction in New York on May 6, 2008.

THE WRIGHT BROTHERS

Wilbur and Orville Wright—known to the world as the Wright brothers—are generally credited with inventing and building the world's first successful airplane and making the first controlled, powered, and sustained flight. This feat took place on December 17, 1903.

During the following two years, the brothers fine-tuned their airplane, creating the first practical fixed-wing aircraft. The brothers were the first to invent aircraft controls that made fixed-wing flight possible. The pair's big breakthrough: their invention of three-axis control. This creation enabled the pilot to steer the aircraft effectively and maintain its equilibrium, a method that became standard—and remains standard—on fixed wing aircraft of all kinds.

They worked for years in their shop with printing presses, bicycles, motors, and other machinery, gaining the mechanical skills essential for their success. Their work with bicycles in particular influenced their belief that an unstable vehicle like a flying machine could be controlled and balanced with practice. Their precise wind tunnel tests produced improved aeronautical data and enabled the Wright brothers to design and build wings and propellers more effectively than any seen previously.

Ohio and North Carolina both take credit for the Wright brothers and their world-changing inventions, and perhaps rightly so. Ohio's claim: the brothers developed and built their design in Dayton. North Carolina's claim: Kitty Hawk was the site of the first flight. With a spirit of friendly rivalry, Ohio adopted the slogan "Birthplace of Aviation" (later "Birthplace of Aviation Pioneers," recognizing not only the Wrights, but also John Glenn and Neil Armstrong, both Ohio natives), while North Carolina has adopted the slogan "First In Flight." Each state features their respective phrases on state automobile license plates, and both states also included an image of a Wright Flyer on their state quarter design. The site of the first flights in North Carolina is preserved as Wright Brothers National Memorial, while the Ohio facilities are part of Dayton Aviation Heritage National Historical Park. As the positions of both states can be factually defended, and each played a significant role in the history of flight, neither state truly has an exclusive claim to the Wrights' accomplishment.

Wilbur Wright, who had never married, became ill on a trip to Boston in April 1912. After returning to Dayton, he was diagnosed with typhoid fever. He died, age forty-five, in the Wright family home on May 30.

Orville Wright, who also never married, succeeded to the presidency of the Wright company upon Wilbur's death. Orville sold the company in 1915 and made his last flight as a pilot in 1918. He retired from business and became an elder statesman of aviation, serving on various official boards and committees, including the National Advisory Committee for Aeronautics (NACA), predecessor agency to the National Aeronautics and Space Administration (NASA). On April 19, 1944, the second production Lockheed *Constellation*, piloted by Howard Hughes and TWA president Jack Frye, flew from Burbank, California, to Washington D.C. The flight lasted six hours and fifty-seven minutes. On the way back, the aircraft stopped at Wright Field so Orville could have one last airplane flight—more than forty years after his historic first flight. Orville died in 1948 after his second heart attack. The Wrights are buried in the family plot at Woodland Cemetery, Dayton.

The *Flyer I* is displayed in the National Air and Space Museum, a part of the Smithsonian Institution in Washington D.C. The *Flyer III*, the only fixed-wing aircraft designated a National Historic Landmark, was dismantled after the 1905 flights. It was reassembled with a two-man upright configuration and new control arrangement and flown at Kitty Hawk in May 1908. With the aid of Orville, the aircraft was restored back to its 1905 prone single-pilot design in the late 1940s. It is displayed in the John W. Berry Sr. Wright Brothers Aviation Center at Carillon Historical Park in Dayton. The display space for the aircraft was designed by Orville, who instructed that, upon his death, The Franklin Institute in Philadelphia should receive his collection of airfoils and devices. The Franklin Institute was the first scientific organization to give the Wright brothers credit and ranking for achieving sustained powered flight. Today, The Franklin Institute Science Museum contains the largest collection of artifacts from the Wright brothers' workshop.

POP QUIZ

1) Who wrote *Crime and Punishment?*
   a) Franz Kafka
   b) Leo Tolstoy
   c) Charles Dickens
   d) Fyodor Dostoevsky

2) What art movement did Van Gogh belong to?
   a) Impressionism
   b) Post Impressionism
   c) Surrealism
   d) Cubism

3) Which was NOT written by Sophocles?
   a) *Antigone*
   b) *Oedipus the King*
   c) *Iliad*
   d) *Trachinian Women*

4) What art movement did Pablo Picasso belong to?
   a) Impressionism
   b) Post Impressionism
   c) Surrealism
   d) Cubism

5) How old was Charles Dickens when he dropped out of school?
   a) 12
   b) 14
   c) 16
   d) 17

6) Who said, "Buy land; they're not making it anymore"?
    a) Bill Gates
    b) Karl Marx
    c) Mark Twain
    d) Franklin D. Roosevelt

7) What year did George Washington Carver begin teaching at Iowa State College?
    a) 1891
    b) 1894
    c) 1896
    d) 1923

8) Who won the 1964 Nobel Prize in Literature?
    a) Rudyard Kipling
    b) Robert Frost
    c) Leo Tolstoy
    d) Jean-Paul Sartre

9) What year was Napoleon made commander of the army of Italy?
    a) 1796
    b) 1797
    c) 1798
    d) 1799

10) What year did Edison invent the phonograph?
    a) 1876
    b) 1877
    c) 1878
    d) 1879

Answers:

1) d	6) c
2) b	7) b
3) c	8) d
4) d	9) a
5) a	10) b

Great Thinkers of History and Estimated IQ

In 1926, psychologist Catherine Morris Cox published a study of notable men and women who lived between 1450 and 1850, estimating what their IQs might have been. Her results were based largely on a measure of intelligence of each subject before they reached age seventeen.

Blaise Pascal – 195
John Stuart Mill – 200
Immanuel Kant – 175
René Descartes – 180
Charles Darwin – 165
Olof Palme – 156
Thomas Chatterton – 170
Bobby Fischer – 187
Gottfried Wilhelm von Leibniz – 205
Galileo Galilei – 185
Emanuel Swedenborg – 205
Anna Lindh – 152
Ludwig Wittgenstein – 190
Madame De Stael – 180
Linus Carl Pauling – 170
Sofia Kovalevskaya – 170
Wolfgang Amadeus Mozart – 165
George Eliot (Mary Ann Evans) – 160
Copernicus – 160
Rembrandt van Rijn – 155
George Sand (Aurore Dupin) – 150

EXTRA CREDIT: Cox also determined that different fields have varying average IQs among their leading geniuses. Her findings, on average: Philosophers – 160; Scientists – 159; Fiction writers – 152; Statesmen – 150; Musicians – 149; Artists – 153; Soldiers – 136.

Aaron Copland

Copland, who died in 1990, composed both concert and film music and played the piano—but perhaps his greatest achievement was finding a unique balance between contemporary music and American folk style.

Copland was born in Brooklyn, New York, and began digging music as a teenager. Even as a mere teen he aspired to be a composer—without any real direct exposure to the field. In 1925 he was awarded a Guggenheim Fellowship, and another again the following year.

Copland defended the Communist Party USA during the 1936 presidential election, a move that came back to haunt him. FBI investigators checked him out during the Red Scare of the 1950s, and he was blacklisted. *A Lincoln Portrait* was taken out of the 1953 inaugural concert for President Eisenhower and that same year, Copland had to testify in front of Congress. He swore he was not and never was a Communist. The investigations took years to finish and weren't officially wrapped up until 1975. No one ever proved that Copland was a Communist.

Copland often guest conducted orchestras in the U.S. and Great Britain. He also recorded much of his music, especially during the 1970s, mostly for Columbia Records.

Alzheimer's disease and respiratory failure eventually claimed Copland's life. He died in North Tarrytown, New York, which is now Sleepy Hollow.

SIGMUND FREUD

An Austrian physician from the late nineteenth and early twentieth centuries, Sigmund Freud revolutionized psychology. The founder of the psychoanalytic school of psychology, he popularized the term *libido*, and designated it as the primary motivation of human life. This, of course, is the point at which most high school students stop listening and begin giggling in class, but Freud achieved much more.

Freud suggested that solutions for mental problems could be found through discussing them, focusing great attention on human ego, super-ego and id. Listed below are some noteworthy quotations from the father of psychoanalysis. And as an aside, although most are not regarding sex directly, even the speaker would acknowledge that the doctor's libido was his principal motivation.

Famous Words of Sigmund Freud

- Illusions commend themselves to us because they save us pain and allow us to enjoy pleasure instead. We must therefore accept it without complaint when they sometimes collide with a bit of reality against which they are dashed to pieces.
- Most people do not really want freedom, because freedom involves responsibility, and most people are frightened of responsibility.
- Religion is an illusion and it derives its strength from the fact that it falls in with our instinctual desires.
- He that has eyes to see and ears to hear may convince himself that no mortal can keep a secret. If his lips are silent, he chatters with his fingertips; betrayal oozes out of him at every pore.
- I have found little that is "good" about human beings on the whole. In my experience most of them are trash, no matter whether they publicly subscribe to this or that ethical doctrine or to none at all. That is something that you cannot say aloud, or perhaps even think.

CRICK AND WATSON

Francis Crick and James Watson may not be as familiar sounding a pair as Lewis and Clark but their big discovery was as significant, if not more so, than most duos out there. At the very least they changed the course of science forever. How? By identifying the building blocks of all life on earth.

The year was 1953 when Crick and Watson discovered deoxyribonucleic acid, or DNA. Watson was a young twenty-three at the time, having graduated from the University if Chicago at nineteen and completed his doctorate at a mere twenty-two. Crick was thirty-five and still trying to finish his Ph.D. Together, the scientists were studying the structure of proteins at the Cavendish Laboratory of Cambridge University in Great Britain.

DNA technically had been discovered much earlier—in the 1860s actually—but it wasn't until the 1940s that researchers learned that chromosomes consisted of DNA and proteins. Even in the 1940s, though, no one really believed this theory. It was Crick and Watson who actually built the first DNA models. They used wire and metal plates to create the infamous double-helix structure of a DNA molecule—one that can "unzip" to make copies of itself. Watson declared they had found "the secret of life." Their work hardly went unnoticed. In 1962 they received a Nobel Prize for Physiology and Medicine.

Watson, who headed the Human Genome Project at the National Institutes of Health, eventually also was a teacher and researcher at the California Institute of Technology, Cambridge, and Harvard. He also directed the Cold Spring Harbor Laboratory, a molecular biology research center. As of 2008 he is the advisor for the recently formed Allen Institute for Brain Science, a nonprofit corporation and medical research organization in Seattle. Watson also has been awarded nearly twenty honorary degrees from colleges and universities throughout the world including Notre Dame University and Albert Einstein College of Medicine.

Crick was a researcher with the Salk Institute in California, investigating the origin of life and consciousness. He died of colon cancer in 2004, while living in San Diego.

COMPUTER SCIENCE 101
CHARLES BABBAGE

Charles Babbage has his own crater on the moon named after him, as well as a technology institute and a lecture theatre at the prestigious Cambridge University. So what did this London-born mathematician and mechanical engineer do for such recognition?

Babbage, born in 1791, is credited with inventing the first mechanical computer that eventually resulted in more intricate designs.

If you want to check out many of Babbage's uncompleted devices, you'll have to visit the London Science Museum. Take the difference engine, for example. In 1991 someone built a perfect one from Babbage's original plans—in other words, it actually worked. And nine years later, the Science Museum also completed the printer that Babbage had designed for that same engine. The printer turned out to be an amazingly complex machine for its time.

Famous Words of Charles Babbage

- At each increase of knowledge, as well as on the contrivance of every new tool, human labor becomes abridged.
- Errors using inadequate data are much less than those using no data at all.
- I am inclined to attach some importance to the new system of manufacturing; and venture to throw it out with the hope of its receiving a full discussion among those who are most interested in the subject.
- A tool is usually more simple than a machine; it is generally used with the hand, whilst a machine is frequently moved by animal or steam power.
- If we look at the fact, we shall find that the great inventions of the age are not, with us at least, always produced in universities.

MAHATMA GANDHI

Mohandas Karamchand Gandhi lived seventy-eight years, and for most of that life he lived simply, making his own clothes, eating a simple vegetarian diet, and encouraging nonviolence and truth in all situations.

Born in 1869, this political and spiritual leader was known commonly in his home country of India and around the world as Mahatma Gandhi or "Great Soul." He led India to independence and inspired civil rights movements throughout the world through his creation of *Satyagraha*, a process of resisting tyranny through mass civil disobedience, firmly founded upon total nonviolence.

In India, he was officially bestowed the honor of "Father of the Nation." October 2, his birthday, is *Gandhi Jayanti*, an annual national holiday. On June 15, 2007, the United Nations General Assembly unanimously adopted a resolution declaring October 2 the "International Day of Non-Violence" in his honor.

Gandhi first used nonviolent civil disobedience "tactics" in South Africa, in the resident Indian community's struggle for civil rights. When he returned to India, he organized poor farmers and laborers to demonstrate against harsh taxation and widespread discrimination.

When Gandhi took over the Indian National Congress, he led nationwide campaigns to alleviate poverty, liberate women, unite religious and ethnic groups, end caste discrimination, and promote economic self-sufficiency for India and the independence of India from foreign domination.

On January 30, 1948, Gandhi was shot and killed. He had been on his nightly public walk on the grounds of the Birla House in New Delhi. The assassin, Nathuram Godse, was a Hindu radical who had connections to Mahasabha, a Hindu extremist who blamed Gandhi for weakening India by insisting upon a payment to Pakistan. Godse and a coconspirator were tried, convicted and, on November 15, 1949, were executed.

Gandhi's memorial in New Delhi is inscribed with two simple words: "Oh God," which also may be the last words he spoke after being shot.

LEO TOLSTOY

One thing's for sure: this Russian novelist could write—and write, and write, and write. Most copies of his best-known work, *War and Peace*, are more than one thousand pages long. His other hit, *Anna Karenina*, wasn't too far behind. As a fiction writer, Tolstoy is widely regarded as one of the all-time greatest novelists.

Born on August 28, 1828, in Tula Province, Russia, Lev Nikolayevich Tolstoy' childhood was spent between Moscow and Yasnaya Polyana, in a family of three brothers and a sister. He lost his mother when he was two years old, and his father when he was nine. He had moved to Moscow with his family in 1836, at the age of eight, to attend school. A year later, Tolstoy's father died and the young Leo was returned to the family estate, Yasnaya Polyana, in Tula Province. His subsequent education was in the hands of his aunt, who is supposed to be the starting point of Sonya in *War and Peace.*

Tolstoy lived at the family estate until age sixteen, when he enrolled at Kazan University to study six languages: Arabic, Turkish, Latin, German, English, and French. Teachers described him as unable and unwilling to learn. He left the university in the middle of a term.

From the very beginning, his diary—which exists today—reveals a voracious appetite for rational and moral justification of life, a hunger that forever remained a dominating force in his mind. The same diary was his first experiment in creating a technique of psychological analysis to become his main literary weapon.

Tolstoy married Sofia Behrs, sixteen years his junior. Together they had twelve children—five died in their childhoods. Sophie was devoted to helping her husband in his literary work.

War and Peace includes 580 characters. The novel explores Tolstoy's theory of history, and in particular the insignificance of individuals such as Napoleon and Alexander. But more importantly, Tolstoy's imagination created a world that seems to be so believable, so real, that it is not easy to realize that most of his characters actually never existed and that Tolstoy never witnessed the epoch described in the novel.

Tolstoy became seriously ill in 1901. Still, he continued working 'til the end—his brain as sharp as ever. By 1910, Tolstoy had adopted extreme beliefs and alienated the majority of his family. In October, he set out to make a new life for himself.

However, only a month later, on November 20, 1910, Tolstoy died of pneumonia. He was buried in a simple peasant's grave in woods 500 meters from Yasnaya Polyana. Thousands of peasants lined the streets at his funeral; even more admirers mourned the loss of an accomplished author.

Interesting Facts About Leo Tolstoy

- While fighting in the Crimean War, Tolstoy was inspired to write *Sevastopol Sketches*, which was also serialized, this time in *The Contemporary* magazine.
- In 1862, at age thirty-four, Tolstoy married Sofia "Sonya" Andreyevna Behrs, with whom he had twelve children. Sonya helped her husband with the business side of writing and managing the estate. She organized his notes, copied out drafts, and handled correspondence. Sonya's help enabled him to begin writing *War and Peace*, which resulted in six volumes of commentary on the absurdity, hypocrisy, and shallowness of war and aristocratic society. The six volumes were published over a period of six years, between 1863 and 1869.
- *Anna Karenina* is considered by many scholars and popular readers to be the greatest novel ever written. In fact, Tolstoy called it his first real novel. Cleverly weaving fiction and real events, the writer created one of the earliest recorded examples of stream-of-consciousness writing.
- Tolstoy's biting commentary was not restricted to his fiction. He composed numerous nonfiction articles that criticized the government and church. His outspokenness led to his excommunication by the Russian Orthodox Church; but it only increased his popularity with the public. By the turn of the century, Tolstoy had a large following of admiring readers.

CRASH COURSE

RALPH WALDO EMERSON

Emerson was an American writer but also one of the leaders of the Transcendentalist movement in the early nineteenth century. His teachings directly influenced the growing New Thought movement of the mid 1800s. He expressed his philosophy of Transcendentalism in his 1836 essay, *Nature*—a groundbreaking work that led to speeches on the subject.

From a well-known line of ministers, Emerson was born in Boston, Massachusetts, son of Ruth Haskins and the Rev. William Emerson, a Unitarian minister. Emerson's father died in 1811, less than two weeks short of Emerson's eighth birthday. The following year, Emerson was sent to the Boston Latin School. And at just fourteen, Emerson went to Harvard College.

Emerson met his first wife, Ellen Louisa Tucker, in Concord, New Hampshire and married her when she was eighteen. She died of tuberculosis two years later. Emerson was deeply saddened by her death, visiting her grave daily and once even opening her coffin to make sure she really was dead. Despite his marriage, there is evidence that Emerson may have been bisexual. During his early years at Harvard, he found himself attracted to a young freshman, whom he wrote sexually charged poetry to.

After traveling around some, Emerson finally bought a house on the Cambridge and Concord Turnpike in Concord, Massachusetts, which today is open to the public as the Ralph Waldo Emerson House. He married his second wife, Lydia Jackson, and they had four children. Emerson is buried in Sleepy Hollow Cemetery in Concord, Massachusetts.

EXTRA CREDIT: Emerson made a living as a popular lecturer in New England and the rest of the country outside of the South. During several scheduled appearances he was not able to make, Frederick Douglass took his place. Emerson spoke on a wide variety of subjects. Many of his essays grew out of his lectures.

GEORGE FRIDERIC HANDEL

The famous "Hallelujah" chorus in the even more famous Handel's *Messiah* has been sung thousands—millions?—of times around the world. Here's the incredible thing: in the summer of 1741, Handel composed the brilliant masterpiece—in just twenty-four days.

Handel's *Messiah* is set to text from the King James Bible. The first *Messiah* was performed in New Musick Hall in Dublin on April 13, 1742, with twenty-six boys and five men from the combined choirs of St. Patrick's and Christ Church cathedrals.

In 1750, Handel arranged a performance of *Messiah* to benefit the Foundling Hospital. The performance was considered a great success and was followed by annual concerts that continued throughout his life. In recognition of his patronage, Handel was made a governor of the hospital the day after his initial concert. He bequeathed a fair copy of *Messiah* to the institution upon his death.

This German-born composer—born the same year as Bach—spent most of his adult life in England. At age seven he could already play—well—the harpsichord and pipe organ, and by age nine, he was composing music.

In August 1750, on a journey back from Germany to London, Handel was seriously injured in a carriage accident in the Netherlands. In 1751 his eyesight started to fail in one eye. The cause was unknown and progressed into his other eye as well. He died some eight years later, in 1759, in London, his last attended performance being his own *Messiah*. More than three thousand mourners attended his funeral, which was given full state honors, and he was buried in Westminster Abbey.

Handel never married, and he kept his personal life very private. Unlike many composers, he left a sizable estate at his death—worth £20,000 (an enormous amount for the day), the bulk of which he left to a niece in Germany—as well as gifts to his other relations, servants, friends, and to favorite charities.

MIDTERM

1) What was the material used for the home of controversial architect Philip Johnson?
    a) Tin cans
    b) Paper
    c) Concrete
    d) Glass

2) Zarathushtra created the world's first monotheistic religion known as _______ ?
    a) Zoroastrianism
    b) Zoology
    c) Zarathushtraianism

3) Where did famous English economist John Maynard Keynes write his famous work, *The General Theory*?
    a) In his treehouse
    b) In bed
    c) In the rain
    d) In a park

4) The world's most expensive painting, by Jackson Pollock, sold for $140 million in 2006. What was it called?
    a) Chanel no. 5
    b) Take the Fifth Train to Clarksville
    c) No. 5, 1948
    d) Five Alive

5) What did Henry Ford develop with his brother-in-law? (HINT: it's not cars)
   a) Bicycles
   b) Dynamite
   c) Charcoal briquets
   d) Rubber bands

6) Where was writer William Shakespeare born and raised?
   a) Stratford-upon-Avon
   b) Avon-is-Calling
   c) Stratfordshire

7) Niccolo Michiavelli used confrontational tactics to win over the Medici family in what book?
   a) *The King*
   b) *The Prince*
   c) *The Queen*
   d) *The Ace*

8) How many of Jane Austen's novels have been made into movies?
   a) 2
   b) 6
   c) 3
   d) 1

9) What oath is traditionally taken by physicians pertaining to the ethical practice of medicine?
   a) The Hippopotamus Promise
   b) The Hypocrite's Oath
   c) The Hippocratic Oath

10) What famous Italian scientist taught Robert Boyle, the founder of modern chemistry?
a) Figaro
b) Oleo
c) Galileo
d) O'Henry

11) Chuang Tzu's Taoist manuscript, *Zhuangzi*, encourages people to welcome what into their lives?
a) Spontaneity
b) Wealth
c) Peace
d) Neighbors

12) What career did Dutch painter Vincent van Gogh have before he began his career as an artist?
a) Missionary
b) Ear, Nose and Throat Specialist
c) Wooden Shoe Salesman
d) Astronomer

13) What did Ben Franklin invent to help his brother, who suffered from kidney stones?
a) Bifocals
b) Cranberry Juicer
c) Pain Medicine
d) Urinary Catheter

14) The Egyptian astronomer, Ptolemy, is believed to have worked at what famous institution?
a) The Library of Congress
b) The Library of Alexandria
c) The Museum of Fine Arts
d) The Mayo Clinic

15) The art form primarily used by Pablo Picasso is known as
_________ ?
   a) Cubicle design
   b) Cubit foot
   c) Cubism
   d) Cuban cigar

ANSWERS:

1) d	9) c
2) a	10) c
3) b	11) a
4) c	12) a
5) c	13) d
6) a	14) b
7) b	15) c
8) b	

W. E. B. DuBois

William Edward Burghardt DuBois was a black civil rights activist as well as a famous writer, editor, and scholar.

Born in 1868 in Massachusetts, DuBois was awarded a degree from Fisk University twenty years later. During the following summer, DuBois managed the Fisk Glee Club located at a luxury summer resort on a lake in suburban Minneapolis, Minnesota. The resort was a vacation spot for wealthy American Southerners and European royalty. Observing the drinking, rude behavior, and sexual promiscuity of the rich, white hotel guests left a lasting impression on the young DuBois.

DuBois entered Harvard College in the fall of 1888 and earned a bachelor's degree *cum laude* two years later. In 1892, he received a stipend to attend the University of Berlin. There, he traveled extensively throughout Europe while studying with some of the most prominent social scientists.

DuBois wrote many books, including three major autobiographies. Among his most significant works are *The Philadelphia Negro* (1899), *The Souls of Black Folk* (1903), *John Brown* (1909), *Black Reconstruction* (1935), and *Black Folk, Then and Now* (1939).

DuBois also was the most prominent intellectual leader and political activist on behalf of African Americans in the first half of the twentieth century. For twenty-five years, DuBois worked as editor-in-chief of the NAACP publication, *The Crisis.*

DuBois was invited to Ghana in 1961 by President Kwame Nkrumah to direct the *Encyclopedia Africana*, a government production, and a long-held dream of his. When, in 1963, he was refused a new U.S. passport, he and his wife, Shirley Graham DuBois, became citizens of Ghana.

DuBois' health had declined in 1962, and on August 27, 1963, he died in Accra, Ghana, at the age of ninety-five, one day before Martin Luther King, Jr.'s "I Have a Dream" speech. At the March on Washington, Roy Wilkins informed the hundreds of thousands of marchers and called for a moment of silence.

AMERICAN LITERATURE
T. S. ELIOT

Thomas Stearns Eliot was a poet, dramatist, and literary critic. He received the Nobel Prize in Literature in 1948. Among his notable works are: the poems *The Love Song of J. Alfred Prufrock*, *The Waste Land*, *The Hollow Men*, *Ash Wednesday*, and *Four Quartets*; the plays *Murder in the Cathedral* and *The Cocktail Party*; and the essay *Tradition and the Individual Talent*.

Eliot was born into the prominent Eliot family of St. Louis, Missouri. His father, Henry Ware Eliot, was a successful businessman, president and treasurer of the Hydraulic-Press Brick Company in St. Louis; his mother, born Charlotte Champe Stearns, wrote poems and was also a social worker. His four sisters were between eleven and nineteen years older than him; his brother was eight years older. Known to family and friends as Tom, he was the namesake of his maternal grandfather, Thomas Stearns.

Upon graduation from college, Eliot worked for a time as a schoolteacher and also at a bank working on foreign accounts. Although he was born in the United States, Eliot moved to the United Kingdom in 1914 at age twenty-five. Eventually he became director of a publishing firm, where he stayed for the remainder of his career. He became a British citizen in 1927 at the age of thirty-nine.

Eliot died of emphysema in London on January 4, 1965. For many years, he had health problems owing to the combination of London air and his heavy smoking, often being sick with bronchitis or tachycardia. His body was cremated and, according to Eliot's wishes, the ashes taken to St Michael's Church in East Coker, the village from which Eliot's ancestors emigrated to America. There, a simple plaque commemorates him. On the second anniversary of his death, a large stone placed on the floor of Poets' Corner in London's Westminster Abbey was dedicated to Eliot.

SANDRO BOTTICELLI

Sandro Botticelli was a prodigy artist of the Early Renaissance era in Florence, Italy. Chances are you are familiar with his work—his religious images are a grand part of art history—but no one really discovered his power and talent until long after he had died.

A native of Florence who studied art as a teenager and had his own studio by his mid-twenties, Botticelli made his mark in churches in the late 1400s. Around Florence, as far away as Hungary and in Rome, his frescoes adorn places of worship.

Many pieces were commissioned for specific villas and churches, and that's more or less where they remained, unnoticed as important. Some biographers think Botticelli's reputation was diminished longer than any other European artist.

It wasn't until the literary world discovered him and the first of several books was published in 1893—nearly four hundred years after his death—that his work seemed important. Between 1900 and 1920, more books were written about him than any other artist. Perhaps his biggest slight was his most famous work.

In 1482, Pope Sixtus IV called together several prominent artists from Florence, including Botticelli, to paint frescoes on the walls of the Sistine Chapel. If you've ever been to the Vatican, you've seen that intricate imagery of Biblical scenes. And though his work was incredible, when you think of the Sistine Chapel, the name that comes to mind is Michelangelo, for his ceiling fresco of man touching God.

Religion, ironically, may have hindered Botticelli's reputation and his career. He became later in life a devotee of Savonarola, a Catholic priest and leader in Florence who was seen as an early reformer before he was executed in 1498.

Savonarola was against art that he considered to be pagan, and he destroyed much of it. Botticelli was said to have tossed many of his own paintings into the famed *Bonfire of the Vanities*. And many believe Savonarola's influence stymied the artist's work for the rest of his life, costing him jobs and leaving him in obscurity at his death in 1510.

SO SAYS JOSEPH STALIN

For many in the democracies of the western hemisphere, Joseph Stalin existed as one of history's most notorious villains. As the General Secretary of the Communist Party and eventual dictator of the Soviet Union from 1928 to 1953, he symbolized the evils of communism and its threats against America. To the hearts of many Russians, however, Joseph Stalin represented a promise of change from a nation that was financially weak and struggling to a Russia of economic strength and military power. Listed below are a few quotes that exemplify his appeal to the everyday Russian of the mid-twentieth century.

- "Education is a weapon whose effects depend on who holds it in his hands and at whom it is aimed."

- "Everyone imposes his own system as far as his army can reach."

- "If the opposition disarms, well and good. If it refuses to disarm, we shall disarm it ourselves."

- "In the Soviet army it takes more courage to retreat than advance."

- "Mankind is divided into rich and poor, into property owners and exploited; and to abstract oneself from this fundamental division; and from the antagonism between poor and rich means abstracting oneself from fundamental facts."

- "One death is a tragedy; a million is a statistic."

- "When we hang the capitalists they will sell us the rope we use."

- "You cannot make a revolution with silk gloves."

- "America is like a healthy body and its resistance is threefold: its patriotism, its morality, and its spiritual life. If we can undermine these three areas, America will collapse from within."

JOAN OF ARC

With the English victory at the Battle of Agincourt in 1415, it appeared as though France was finished. Invaders from England, led by the warrior king Henry V, took control of a nation whose leaders were feeble and cowardly. A few years after the battle, however, a young girl named Joan of Arc came along and rallied the French army to liberate her beloved country.

Joan's mission began in the village of her birth in Domrémy, a small peasant town in east central France. At the age of thirteen she experienced what she believed to be a revelation from God. The revelation commanded her to drive the English from France and aid Charles the Dauphin to become the nation's king.

Joan traveled to the Dauphin's court to deliver God's message. Her appearance worried Charles, as he feared offending the Church. Realizing that he could be held responsible if the Church declared her an agent of the Devil, he had her questioned by priests at Poitiers University. After speaking with Joan, the priests reported to Charles in favor of meeting the young peasant.

Charles the Dauphin hesitantly listened to Joan as she recounted God's will. She explained that the answer to the problem was simple. Orlèans had been under attack for quite some time, and retaliation was necessary. With a confident army at her command and the Dauphin's reluctant support, Joan led a successful fight there—becoming known throughout France as the "Maid of Orlèans."

After several French victories, priests coroneted Charles at Rheims on July 16, 1429. All believed peace had been achieved. Charles believed diplomacy could be used to obtain the remaining territories from the rival family, the Burgundians. The war was not over yet, however, because Paris remained in enemy hands, making it the key to final victory. Unfortunately, Charles refused to listen to Joan's insistence that the English had to be driven by force from Paris.

The contrast in strategy between negotiation and military action resulted in a weakened army outside the walls of Paris. Joan's invasion failed, and the city was lost. More losses followed, both diplomatic and militaristic. The finale of these defeats for Joan transpired at Compiègne.

In May 1430, the Burgundians captured Joan and handed her over to the English. Charles, who now viewed the girl as an annoyance, left her to sit in prison for six months, until her trial began at Rouen. Under the decision of Bishop Cauchon, Joan was sentenced to death for heresy and witchcraft. The young hero, burned at the stake, died as a martyr for her country.

As years passed, the events of Joan's life became legendary. The French acknowledge her as a national heroine and honor her each year on June 24 with a national holiday. In 1920, the Roman Catholic Church, repentant for its own transgressions, canonized her as a saint.

EXTRA CREDIT: According to legend, when Joan went to Charles, he tested her as she came through the doors. He had dressed himself as a servant and had the servant dress like him. Joan passed the test, walking straight past the imposter and directly to the Dauphin. The servant was undoubtedly grateful, as peasants had poor hygiene.

Famous Firsts

- The first architect ever recorded in history was Imhotep, chief architect to the Egyptian Pharaoh Djoser.
- Henrietta Johnston, a portrait artist living in Charleston, South Carolina, around 1707, was the first known professional female artist in America.
- In 1809, Mary Kies became the first woman to gain a patent in the United States. She received a patent for her idea of weaving straw and silk together to make bonnets.

PHILOSOPHY 101
SØREN KIERKEGAARD

Unlike the German philosopher Hegel, Søren Aabye Kierkegaard, a Danish philosopher, strongly criticized Hegelianism philosophy—along with what he believed were the empty rules and regulations of the Danish church.

Much of Kierkegaard's writings focused on religious ideas such as faith in God, the institute of the Christian Church, Christian ethics and theology, and emotions people have when facing life's choices. Kierkegaard did not divulge everything in his works; instead, he left the duty of uncovering the meaning to the reader. You can imagine, then, the countless interpretations. Some viewed Kierkegaard as an existentialist, while others insisted he was neo-orthodoxist, postmodernist, humanist, or individualist.

Among the books dealing with religious concepts are *Fear and Trembling* (1843), *The Concept of Dread* (1844), *Purity of Heart is to Will One Thing* (1847), and *The Sickness unto Death* (1849). *The Concept of Irony* (1841) is a more direct philosophical hit and actually was his dissertation at the University of Copenhagen. The very lengthy *Concluding Unscientific Postscript* (1846) describes the potential of living by faith in a modern world.

Kierkegaard died in 1855 in a hospital. He was interred in a cemetery in Copenhagen. His nephew Henrik Lund disturbed his funeral, protesting that Kierkegaard was being buried by the official church—which made no sense since Kierkegaard throughout his life he had criticized the church. Lund was later fined.

Kierkegaard wrote more than seven thousand pages in journals. In them, he recorded and described significant events, everyday musings, thoughts about his works, and other remarks. The entire journal collection has been edited and published in thirteen volumes. Alexander Dru edited the first English edition of the journals in 1938. The journals divulge various facets of Kierkegaard to help clarify many of his ideas. The writing style in his journals is among the most graceful of all his work.

SAMUEL JOHNSON

Samuel Johnson—referred to back in the old days simply as Dr. Johnson—is among England's best-known literary figures. The single most quoted English writer after Shakespeare, Johnson has been described as being among the most outstanding figures of eighteenth-century England.

The son of a poor bookseller, Johnson was born in Staffordshire. In 1728 he enrolled in Pembroke College in Oxford. But after thirteen months, poverty forced him to leave without a degree and he returned to Lichfield. Later, just before the publication of his celebrated *Dictionary* in 1755, however, Oxford University awarded Johnson a Master of Arts degree. He was also awarded an honorary doctorate in 1765 by Trinity College Dublin and another in 1775 by Oxford University.

Johnson, who worked initially as a teacher and schoolmaster, married at age twenty-five Elizabeth "Tetty" Porter, a widow twenty-one years his elder. His first work published in 1735 was a translation from the French of Lobo's *A Voyage to Abyssinia*.

In 1736, Johnson established a private academy near Lichfield. He had only three pupils, but one of them was David Garrick, who remained his friend, while becoming the most famous actor of his day. Johnson began writing his first major work there, the historical tragedy *Irene*, which was later produced by Garrick in 1749. In 1737, a penniless Johnson left for London with Garrick. There he found employment with Edward Cave, writing for *The Gentleman's Magazine*.

For the next three decades, Johnson wrote biographies, poetry, essays, pamphlets, and parliamentary reports, continuing to live in poverty for much of this time. Between 1745 and 1755, Johnson wrote perhaps his best-known work, *A Dictionary of the English Language*.

Johnson died in 1784 and was buried at Westminster Abbey.

BERTRAND RUSSELL

- Born on May 18, 1872, in Trelleck, Wales, Bertrand Russell, along with his brother Frank, was orphaned at an early age. They lived with their grandmother who provided the boys a strict childhood and a variety of academic tutors.
- Russell enrolled in Trinity College, Cambridge, in 1890 and was elected a fellow in 1895. He married four times during his life and had three children.
- Russell, known as one of the founders of analytic philosophy, had great influence in the fields of both philosophy and mathematics.
- He believed that many of the day's propositions were unclear and oftentimes incoherent.
- Russell believed that logic and science were the most important tools of any philosopher. Early in his career he approached mathematics and philosophy using the same principles of logical thinking.
- This approach led him to create what is now known as Russell's paradox in 1901 while he was writing *The Principles of Mathematics*.

Russell's Paradox

Russell's paradox states that if a person creates two sets with one set containing all sets and the other set containing no sets, the first set is actually a member of itself. The second empty set must not be a member of itself. On the other hand, if a person has a set of all sets that do not include themselves, would this set be in itself? It is only if it is not. The same corollary is true of properties.

Other mathematicians were aware of the existing paradox, but Russell was the first to literally define it. He devoted an entire chapter of *Principles of Mathematics* to explaining the concept.

WORLD LITERATURE
JAMES JOYCE

This Irish writer is best know for his landmark novel *Ulysses* (1922) and its highly controversial successor *Finnegans Wake* (1939), as well as the short story collection *Dubliners* (1914) and the semi-autobiographical novel *A Portrait of the Artist as a Young Man* (1916).

A Portrait of the Artist as a Young Man is a nearly complete rewrite of the abandoned novel *Stephen Hero*, the original manuscript of which Joyce partially destroyed in a fit of rage during an argument with his wife, Nora, who asserted that it would never be published. It is a biographical coming-of-age novel in which Joyce depicts a gifted young man's gradual attainment of maturity and self-consciousness; the main character, Stephen Dedalus, is in many ways based upon Joyce himself. Some hints of the techniques Joyce was to frequently employ in later works—such as the use of interior monologue and references to a character's psychic reality rather than his external surroundings—are evident in this novel.

Joseph Strick directed a film of the book in 1977 starring Luke Johnston, Bosco Hogan, T.P. McKenna, and John Gielgud.

The James Joyce Ramble

Each year in Dedham, Massachusetts, literary-minded runners hold the James Joyce Ramble, a 10K Road Race with each mile dedicated to a different work by Joyce. With professional actors in period garb lining the streets and reading from his books as the athletes run by, it is billed as the only theatrical performance where the performers stand still and the audience does the moving.

Much of Joyce's legacy is protected by the Harry Ransom Center at the University of Texas, which houses thousands of Joyce's manuscripts, pieces of correspondence, drafts, proofs, notes, novel fragments, poems, song lyrics, musical scores, limericks, and translations.

One Book Called "Ulysses"

Although listed on the Radcliffe Publishing Course "Top 100 Novels of the 20th Century," and long regarded as one of the most impressive novels ever penned in English, James Joyce's Ulysses almost never made it to the United States… legally that is. Shortly after being banned by US customs in 1921, the book became one of the most commonly smuggled texts from Europe. In fact, customs agents were so accustomed to seeing contraband copies of the book that they began ignoring it entirely.

Publishing houses can get away with printing just about anything these days, but less than 80 years ago that wasn't so. A book-burning group known as the New York Society for the Suppression of Vice attempted to suppress anything they deemed immoral. In the early 20th century, the group was responsible for the prohibition of "sensualist" material, including a large selection of what has since become canonized literature. Excerpts of Ulysses, printed in The Little Review by publishers Kate Heap and Margaret Anderson, caught the attention of the New York Society for the Suppression of Vice and led to obscenity convictions for Heap and Anderson that year, as well as a nationwide banning of the novel. Joyce, ironically now an Irish national hero, had already seen his work blacklisted in Ireland. Regardlessly, the European literary audience devoured Joyce's work and didn't seem to mind the colorful language included in it. Soon it would seem as though American readers didn't mind either.

The literary public in the United States was eager to lay hands on the book, and the unauthorized copies began sliding in uncontested. It became obvious to the American publisher Bennett Cerf of Random House that something had to be done. This probably had more to do with the 1932 acquisition of the much-coveted publishing rights than an idealistic crusade, but nonetheless, a plan was set into motion in 1933. That year, Cerf and his partner, Donald Klopfer, arranged for a copy to be pasted with glowing reviews from European journals and then smuggled into the United States. The two went to the trouble to insist that this copy be seized so that the matter would be brought to trial and gain public attention.

The scheme worked well, and in August of 1933, Judge John M. Woolsey of New York presided over a case that would eventually change American publishing forever. In United States of America v. One Book Called "Ulysses," Woolsey stated that the American public has the right to legally see what an artist creates. Woolsey continued, addressing the language within Joyce's text that the New York Society for the Suppression of Vice found so inflammatory, and concluded that the book was not sensualist and that it is justifiable for a novelist to use the same language his characters would use. Because of one book called Ulysses, Woolsey made a decision that set a precedent of freedom of speech that has since become a standard in American publishing.

In an effort to combat censorship, the American Library Association publishes a list of challenged books. Lobbyists and parents contest the books for everything from "religious viewpoints" to "offensive language." Examples of challenged books include J. K. Rowling's Harry Potter series and *The Adventures of Huckleberry Finn* by Mark Twain.

JOHN MILTON

John Milton was born in 1608 in London and as a child often stayed up 'til well past midnight studying. An English poet for the Commonwealth of England, he is most famous for his epic poem *Paradise Lost*—written by a blind Milton from 1658 to 1664. The magnum opus reflects Milton's own personal despair at the failure of the Revolution, yet affirms his optimism in human potential.

Long considered the supreme English poet, Milton experienced a dip in popularity after attacks by T.S. Eliot and F. R. Leavis in the mid-twentieth century; but with multiple societies and scholarly journals devoted to his study, Milton's reputation remains as strong as ever today. Soon after his death, Milton became the subject of partisan biographies.

The John Milton Society for the Blind was founded in 1928 by Helen Keller to develop an interdenominational ministry that would bring spiritual guidance and religious literature to deaf and blind persons.

Milton died of kidney failure on November 8, 1674, and was buried in the church of St. Giles Cripplegate.

EXTRA CREDIT: In June 1642, thirty-three-year-old Milton took a mysterious trip into the countryside and returned with a sixteen-year-old bride, Mary Powell. A month later, finding life difficult with the severe Milton, Mary returned to her family. Because of the outbreak of the Civil War, she did not return until 1645; in the meantime her desertion prompted Milton, over the next three years, to publish a series of pamphlets arguing for the legality and morality of divorce. After bearing him four children, Mary died in 1652 from complications following the birth of their last daughter. In 1656, Milton remarried, this time to Katherine Woodcock. Her death on February 3, 1658, less than four months after giving birth to their daughter, Katherine, who also died, prompted one of Milton's most moving sonnets.

CRASH COURSE
PARADISE LOST

Almost everyone is familiar with the story of Adam and Eve, but John Milton tells the tale of the fall from paradise in such a unique way that the old story gains a fresh, if not slightly devilish, perspective. Milton wrote his 1667 epic poem in twelve books, giving the reader a panoramic sweep of heaven, hell, and the brief paradise in between. Surprisingly, some argue that the real hero of the book is the rebel with a (flawed) cause, Satan. Poet William Blake once said that Milton was "of the Devil's party without knowing it." Satan comes off as a Promethean hero battling against an unfair god, at least for the first half of the story where he begins as a fallen angel curious about God's latest creation. He calls a council of fellow fallen angels and they agree to send him on a fact finding mission. As we all know, he eventually tempts Eve to eat the forbidden fruit, but again, Milton takes a slightly radical approach. He portrays Eve as the more intelligent of the two humans. She deliberates and reasons and poor Adam just follows along. After the couple's expulsion from the garden, the angel, Michael, ends the story on a happy note as he assures the pair that the Son of God has already offered himself as a ransom to pay for their misdeeds.

Controversy in Literature

Harper Lee and Truman Capote

The rumor: The idea that Harper Lee's classic To Kill a Mockingbird actually came from the pen of friend and fellow novelist Truman Capote remains a question to many fans of the novel. According to conspiracy theories concerning the text, Capote either cowrote or ghost-wrote the novel.

The truth: Capote, a childhood neighbor and friend of Lee's, was the basis for one of the characters in the book. In a letter to a relative penned in 1959, Capote addresses the idea that he wrote the book, stating that "I did not see Nelle last winter, but the previous year, she showed me as much of the book as she'd written, and I liked it very much." Further information can be found in A Portrait of Harper Lee by Charles Shields.

J. K. Rowling and a Gay Headmaster

In October 2007 author, J. K. Rowling stated to a crowd at Carnegie Hall that a character from Harry Potter, Albus Dumbledore, is a homosexual. Fierce controversy surrounds the statement about the fictional character's sexuality, a fact that Rowling may have intended when making the announcement. She commented on the furor, stating that "He is my character … and I have the right to say what I say about him."

Timeline
George Berkeley

1685: Born March 12, the eldest son to William Berkeley, a customs officer, near Kilkenny in Ireland.

1700: After several years at Kilkenny College, entered Trinity College in Dublin.

1704: Graduated from Trinity and studied privately for three years.

1707: Elected a fellow at Trinity. Published two short mathematical tracts.

1709: Ordained a deacon. Published An Essay toward a New Theory of Vision.

1710: Ordained a priest. Published A Treatise concerning the Principles of Human Knowledge.

1711: Delivered Discourse on Passive Obedience.

1712: Visited England. Published On Motion.

1713: Presented to the English court by Jonathan Swift. Quickly became a court favorite.

1715: Published Three Dialogues between Hylas and Philonous. Became chaplain to Lord Peterborough.

1715–1720: Traveled as tutor to the only son of Dr. St. George Ashe.

1721: Returned to Ireland as chaplain to the Duke of Grafton. Received Doctor of Divinity. Published anonymously An Essay towards preventing the Ruin of Great Britain.

1722: Appointed Dean of Dromore.

1723: Miss Esther Vanhomrigh (Swift's "Vanessa") dies, leaving Berkeley half her property.

1724: Appointed Dean of Derry. Devised scheme to found a college in the Bermudas. Promised a 20,000-pound grant from the government.

1728: Wedded Anne Forster, the daughter of a judge. After four years of preparation for the new college, set sail for America and spent three years in Rhode Island awaiting the grant.

1732: Wrote Alciphron or the Minute Philosopher—critically exploring the various forms of freethinking in the age. Upon hearing the grant would not be forthcoming, gave books and supplies for the new college to Yale and returned to England.

1734: Appointed Bishop of Cloyne. Published The Analyst, an assault on higher mathematics as leading to freethinking.

1735: Published first part of The Querist, with part two published in 1736, and part three in 1737. Explored the reasons for the poor economic conditions in Ireland.

1744: Published Siris, beginning a discussion of the medicinal values of tar-water and expounding on the metaphysical natures of the physical and spiritual universe as well as God.

1751: Eldest son died.

1752: Retired to Oxford with his family for the sake of his son George, who was studying there.

1753: Died suddenly on January 14 while listening to his wife reading from the Bible. Buried the next Saturday in the nave at Christ Church, Oxford.

Famous Words of George Berkeley

- We have first raised a dust and then complain we cannot see
- Westward the course of empire takes its way; / The four first acts already past, / A fifth shall close the drama with the day: / Time's noblest offspring is the last.
- All the choir of heaven and furniture of earth - in a word, all those bodies which compose the frame of the world—have not any subsistence without a mind
- What is mind? No matter. What is matter? Never mind.

WOLFGANG AMADEUS MOZART

There's sometimes a subtle difference between someone we would consider a "great thinker" and a "genius." The idea of a thinker suggests work and effort—someone who toils along, keeps plugging away, asking questions, looking for answers, often heading down dead ends.

On the other hand, we think of a "genius" as someone for whom great ideas or creations seem to come naturally, emerging almost wholly formed from the brow. Of course, that's often an illusion, and what we see as effortless is still the result of lots of hard work and thought.

But for many people, the poster child (emphasis on "child") for genius is the composer Wolfgang Amadeus Mozart. The name "Mozart" has become the bar by which we now measure our own (and our children's) achievements, usually to disappointing results.

After all, young Wolfgang—who was born in Salzburg, Austria, in 1756—was playing the harpsichord when he was three and within two years was composing works. Like all good show-biz parents, father Leopold knew a performing goldmine when he saw one, and soon little Mozart was off to Munich and Vienna to perform in courts and noblemen's homes. "The miracle which God let be born in Salzburg," proclaimed Leopold, displaying both his religious devotion and his fine showmanship.

Over the next decade Wolfgang and his sister toured the great courts of Europe with their father, playing music in places such as Paris, London, Amsterdam, Switzerland, and Italy. Along the way, Mozart's musicianship and composition skills continued to evolve at a stunning rate. He was an excellent mimic of musical styles and forms and was writing Italian operas by the time he was thirteen.

The "child genius performer" gig was a good one, but as many young stars have learned, the march of time makes it a temporary one. So, as he made his way into his teens, Mozart's focus—and fame— began to shift from amazing young performer to amazing young composer.

Back in Salzburg in 1772, Wolfgang hit a productive groove, cranking out eight symphonies and numerous other works in less than a year. The pace continued as Mozart's compositions became increasingly sophisticated, and the young man began to create new types of orchestration and scale.

All the while, Leopold was trying to find Mozart a position as a court composer, often without success. Still, Wolfgang continued to write, drawing influences from time spent in musical cities such as Vienna.

One of the common themes in Mozart's creativity began to emerge: he'd plunge in and soak up the musical styles and structures of whatever scene he was in the midst of and then turn around and serve up new compositions that both pleased lovers of the familiar sounds, but also pushed and altered those sounds to meet his new creative visions.

Over the next decade, influenced by the Baroque music of Handel and Bach, Mozart churned out a steady stream of symphonies, operas, and works in just about every other form. The legend that he composed entire works in his head before putting them on paper is most likely an exaggeration, but he was stunningly prolific and well-tuned to his inner muse.

Mozart married Constanze Weber in 1782 (much to Leopold's displeasure). In the 1780s the couple spent most of their time in Vienna. This "Vienna Period" is considered to be the most productive and impressive in Mozart's career—the music landscape of Vienna was centered on the piano and so was much of Mozart's work at the time.

The money was rolling in, both for his compositions and his live performances. But, like so many geniuses, Mozart was much less adept at managing his finances then his muse. Funds were short and things got worse as the Vienna audiences, like music fans of all ages and eras, grew bored with Mozart and moved on to other musical idols. The lavish lifestyle of Wolfgang and Constanze was sucking up more money than he was making. So Mozart went looking once again for a lucrative court appointment in Vienna.

It was at this point that Antonio Salieri, court Kapellmeister to Joseph II of Austria, entered the picture. Contrary to modern belief, Mozart and the Italian Salieri were actually friends—the notion of a bitter, all-consuming (and murderous) jealousy on the part of Salieri is mostly the dramatic invention of Peter Sheffer's famous 1980 play *Amadeus* and its subsequent film adaptation.

Wolfgang performed fewer and fewer public concerts, but the presence of Salieri and his Italian musical influence on Joseph II's court did push Mozart back toward composing Italian opera. It was during this period that he created such famous operas as *The Marriage of Figaro* and *Don Giovanni.* As with his symphonies and concertos, the genius of Mozart's operas was that he took the comic Italian form and infused it with richer characterizations and emotions than were usually found in the genre.

Leopold Mozart died in Salzburg in 1787 and his passing seemed to increase Wolfgang's melancholy. *The Marriage of Figaro* had been a big hit the year before, but Mozart's fame was already fading in the vicious "what have you written for me lately?" musical landscape of Vienna.

Ironically, that year Mozart did finally get a court appointment, but by then the income was not enough to cover the debts. The post required Wolfgang to compose numerous dance pieces for court balls, but at the same time he was working on several symphonies, including what would become the classic C Major "Jupiter" Symphony.

By 1791 things were looking up for Mozart musically—he was composing steadily and he was in a good mood, despite a lingering illness. Around this time, he was commissioned to write a requiem, but as his health continued to fail, Wolfgang became increasingly convinced he was writing the requiem for himself. Wolfgang Mozart died in December of that year of a fever, the requiem unfinished. His burial in a mass grave was actually not uncommon for someone of his social standing and financial situation.

Like many geniuses, Mozart's work was not fully appreciated in his own time. Despite bursts of popularity during his lifetime, his works— especially later pieces—were often seen as too complex. Music scholars of the nineteenth century sometimes dismissed him as a very clever drawing-room composer. In fact, it wasn't really until the twentieth century that classical music lovers began to reexamine Mozart's work and see him as more than just an impressive novelty act and second fiddle to Beethoven.

AMERICAN HISTORY 101
TECUMSEH

You likely studied Tecumseh in U.S. history classes, but you probably didn't learn that this Shawnee leader was not the sort of Indian chief you saw in Saturday matinees. Tecumseh was an educated orator who led Native Americans who shared his cause, not necessarily Shawnees and not simply to destroy the White Man. He was a man with a mission.

Tecumseh took exception to the Treaty of Fort Wayne, in which tribes gave the U.S. government three million acres of land, and he challenged Indiana Governor William Henry Harrison and all the tribes on the validity of this treaty.

Said Tecumseh: "No tribe has the right to sell, even to each other, much less strangers....Sell a country! Why not sell the air, the great sea, as well the earth? Didn't the Great Spirit make them all for the use of his children?"

He united those who agreed with that mantra to fight for the land and the principle, joining forces with the British in the War of 1812. But a bad strategic concept caused Harrison's men to catch Tecumseh with the British in Toronto and to kill him in the battle.

Still, he was a respected and fabled hero. The U.S. Navy named four ships in his honor, the first in 1863, and the Canadian naval reserves have an HMCS *Tecumseh* in Calgary His bust adorns the U.S. Naval Academy. He is honored in Canada as a hero that kept the U.S. from taking over Canada in the War of 1812. Towns were named for him in six states and Canada. And Civil War General William Tecumseh Sherman was so named because his father respected the Shawnee chief.

Tecumseh in Fiction:
Tecumseh, an anthology of eight books about his life
Brave Warrior, a movie starring Jay Silverheels
The Frontiersman: A Narrative, published in 1967
Red Prophet, a two-book series

THE STRANGE AND UNTIMELY DEATHS OF GREAT MINDS

- Sir Francis Bacon died in 1626 of pneumonia. At the time, he was experimenting with a chicken, attempting to freeze it by stuffing it with snow.
- Christopher Columbus died in 1506 from a heart attack caused by reactive arthritis.
- Marie Curie died of leukemia in 1934. Her cancer was said to be caused by exposure to radiation from her chemistry research.
- Sigmund Freud died in 1939 from cancer of the jaw, tongue, and throat.
- Adolf Hitler committed suicide in 1945 with a handgun and cyanide.
- Thomas Jefferson died of dysentery in 1826, on the fiftieth anniversary of his signing of the Declaration of Independence.
- T. E. Lawrence died in a motorcycle accident, the result of swerving to avoid hitting two small boys in the road.
- Malcolm X died of fifteen gunshot wounds fired by three shooters.

EXTRA CREDIT: Edgar Allan Poe was long thought to have died of a cerebral edema caused by a drinking binge. However, a study published in the 1996 *Maryland Medical Journal* suggested that Poe had rabies. No one can be quite sure how the man actually died.

Voltaire

Voltaire's is one of those names where you go "Yeah, I've heard of him, I know he's French and an important figure in the history of thought and literature. I'm just not sure why."

At best, most of us know Voltaire as the author of *Candide*. Or maybe we're more familiar with *Candide* in the form of its 1956 operetta adaptation by Leonard Bernstein. Or maybe we just know the song "Glitter and Be Gay" from the old Dick Cavett Show. What's that? No one under forty remembers the Dick Cavett Show?

Okay, let's start over. First, Voltaire is the pen name of François Marie Arouet, born in Paris in 1694. From the start, young Arouet rebelled against authority, namely the man who claimed to be his father. (François believed his real father was an army officer and songwriter.) Instead, he preferred the company of his free-thinking godfather.

François studied at the Louis-le-Grand Jesuit college in Paris, and it was there that he nurtured his taste for the finer things: theatre, literature, and, of course, socializing. During the French Regency period of the 1710s, Arouet's reputation as a wit grew around Paris, but like many rebellious wits and satirists, he eventually made fun of the wrong person (namely the Regent) and in 1717 ended up in the Bastille for a year.

Upon his release, Arouet had a literary success with his tragic play *Oedipe*. It was also around this time that he began to publicly use the pen name Voltaire. He became known around Paris as one of its "Philosophe"—reform-minded men of letters and science.

Taking an interest in English philosophy—mainly that of John Locke—Voltaire found himself in London for two years, partly out of a desire to study. But mostly because he once again had gotten himself exiled from Paris over a fight with a nobleman.

In England, Voltaire found himself in the company of authors and thinkers such as Alexander Pope, Jonathan Swift, and George Berkeley. He was also impressed by the English freedom of thought that allowed social and natural scientists like Locke and Newton to thrive.

Back in France in 1729, Voltaire dabbled in a variety of genres, including history, philosophy, and more plays. His philosophical thoughts tended along the lines of promoting religious tolerance, embracing reason, and the need for great leaders to embrace the building of civilization rather than warfare. Voltaire felt that human happiness lay in civilization's pursuit of the arts and sciences and that political and religious systems too often repressed that pursuit of happiness.

Such ideas did not go over so well in eighteenth-century France and soon, once again, a warrant was issued for Voltaire's arrest. This time he fled not to London but to a woman, the intelligent, young Mme du Chatelet in Champagne. The two lived and traveled together for the next fifteen years. Along the way, Voltaire studied science, wrote more plays, and even carried out secret diplomatic missions to the King of Prussia.

Working his way, once again, back into favor in the court of the French King Louis XV, Voltaire wrote more successful plays, as well as *Mahomet,* which was banned after one performance for suggesting that Islam's Mohammed was a fraud. Still, Louis XV did not like Voltaire, and the author's comment to Mme du Chatelet about the cheating going on at the Queen's card table got him—again—run out of court.

In 1749, Mme du Chaletet died in childbirth, and the tragedy sent Voltaire into an emotional tailspin. His most recent plays were not meeting with success and, frustrated, he once again left Paris, this time for Berlin. More controversies followed, but Voltaire was able to finish writing his history of France which focused on the nation's arts, sciences, and social scenes.

Voltaire continued to bounce around Europe, almost always getting into intellectual (or physical) disagreements with people, always quickly moving on. This intellectual vagabond lifestyle fed into what would become his most famous work, the satiric 1758 novella *Candide.*

Primarily, *Candide* is Voltaire's ironic response to the optimistic philosophy of Gottfried Wilhelm Leibniz, who believed that this must be the best of all possible worlds because it was created for humans by a good and caring God. In the novel, the titular hero is raised by his mentor Dr. Pangloss to believe he lives in "the best of all possible worlds," but Candide's optimism is repeatedly tested and eventually cracked by one disaster or social ill after another befalling him and his friends (including the real-life Lisbon earthquake of 1755, an auto-da-fé execution of heretics, murder, illness, prostitution, and slavery). Finally Candide learns "to cultivate one's garden," that is to maintain one's own personal idealism, no matter how corrupt or corrosive the real world becomes.

Which is exactly what Voltaire himself ended up doing, living on a rural property on the French-Swiss border. (That way, if there was trouble with authorities in either country, he could simply dash over to the other.) Even in rural peace, Voltaire still managed to stir up trouble with the authorities, often in defense of village workers' rights.

By this time, Voltaire had become known as the "Innkeeper of Europe" as he played host to and kept up correspondence with all the leading thinkers of his age. Meanwhile, he continued to argue politics, reform, and science and to speak out against the intolerance of the church and the use of torture and cruel punishment by the state. Voltaire also kept writing plays and eventually, in 1778, he returned in triumph to Paris to oversee the production of one of his last works. He died in Paris that year.

Although most of his formal works, including his poetry and plays, are now considered substandard, Voltaire remains a major intellectual historical figure for his ideas on social reform, his push for clear and rational thought, and his championing of the absurd human condition.

Famous Words of Voltaire

- Judge a man by his questions rather than by his answers.
- Prejudices are what fools use for reason.
- It is dangerous to be right in matters on which the established authorities are wrong.
- Each player must accept the cards life deals him or her: but once they are in hand, he or she alone must decide how to play the cards in order to win the game.
- The best government is a benevolent tyranny tempered by an occasional assassination.

CRASH COURSE
SAMUEL CLARKE

Samuel Clarke, born in 1675 in Norwich, was between Locke and Berkeley, the most important philosopher of his generation. The Brit also was a prominent character in Sir Isaac Newton's circle after befriending him in London. His philosophical interests were mostly in theology, metaphysics, and occasionally touched in ethics.

Clarke entered Cambridge University at the mere age of sixteen. It was there that he learned Newton's *Principia mathematica* and determined to advance Newton's theories against those of René Descartes. He translated Jacques Rohault's popular physics textbook, using notes and comments to reflect Newton's ideas—and the translated textbook was used at Cambridge for several decades.

Clarke was in many ways influenced by Descartes—like Descartes he believed that the world contains two types of substances, mind and matter, and that humans consist of both. But he also shared the thoughts of Malebranche and Locke, who denied that introspection lets us reach the substance of the soul. And similar to Locke and Newton he believed that it's impossible to really know the substance of things.

On May 11, 1729, when going out to preach, Clarke was beset with a sudden illness, and he died on the following Saturday. Not too long after his death his brother, Dr. John Clarke, published from original manuscripts *An Exposition of the Church Catechism* and ten volumes of sermons. The *Exposition* consists of the lectures which Clarke read some Thursday mornings at St. James's church. In the later years of his life, he had meticulously revised them, and they were left perfectly prepared for the press.

Clarke influenced many Enlightenment philosophers such as Lord Monboddo, who referenced Clarke's writings in at least twelve different writings. Monboddo tended to agree with Clarke on religious topics and Newtonian ideas, but disagreed with Clarke in some other areas.

The Works of Samuel Clarke encompasses four volumes published between 1738 and 1742. The book was edited, with a biographical preface, by Benjamin Hoadly, Bishop of Salisbury.

EDWARD GIBBON

To many historians and those who love to read history, Edward Gibbon's *The History of the Decline and Fall of the Roman Empire* is considered to be an achievement almost on par with the Empire itself.

Gibbon was born in England in 1737, but he was a sickly child. His early schooling was erratic, and so he found himself becoming an enthusiastic reader. As a boy, he would join his father on visits to various country houses. Young Edward would usually hole up in their massive libraries, devouring everything he could. As a result of all this book learning, Gibbon developed into a very intellectually self-sufficient and somewhat solitary person.

He studied at Oxford and eventually traveled to Switzerland (where he attended parties hosted by Voltaire), and later to Paris, meeting philosophers along the way. But it was in Rome, on October 15, 1764, that Gibbon found his life's calling. While walking amongst the ruins of the Capitol he decided to write a history of Rome—later he would expand the idea to include all of the Roman Empire.

Gibbon returned to London and mingled with men of letters such as Dr. Samuel Johnson. In 1776 he published the first volume of *The History of the Decline and Fall of the Roman Empire.* The history caused somewhat of a scandal because two of its chapters displayed the author's objective skepticism toward the rise of Christianity. Gibbon was mocked by some Londoners, but he continued working on the other volumes of his Roman history, publishing volumes two and three in 1781 (taking the work up to the fall of the.Western Roman Empire), and finishing the massive work in 1787 with three more volumes. Gibbon died in 1794.

The first half of *Decline and Fall* deals with everything from the rise of the Roman Empire to the fall of the Western empire around 480. The second half focuses on the next 1,000 years, covering the Eastern Empire and its eventual fall.

Although centuries of historical research since then have shown that Gibbon had large gaps in his knowledge, his genius, accuracy, and achievement still inspire historians to this day.

THE HISTORY OF THE DECLINE AND FALL OF THE ROMAN EMPIRE:

Also commonly called *The History*, Henry Gibbon's *The History of the Decline and Fall of the Roman Empire* is known as one of the greatest literary achievements of the eighteenth century. Published in six volumes, the book endured six printings due to its popularity.

The book outlines what Henry Gibbon theorized to be the reason for the fall of the Roman Empire. Because few written records were saved from the actual time period of the Roman Empire, most of Gibbon's theories and ideas are derived from records from fourth- and fifth-century Rome.

Gibbon argued that the Roman Empire fell due to loss of civic virtue. The defense of the Empire became outsourced, and many Romans lost their patriotism and sense of civic duty to the city.

Gibbon also faulted the softening of the military, and blamed Christianity for the Romans' willingness to watch their empire fall. He argued that the belief of life after death allowed Romans to feel secure in letting their military, their city, and their government disintegrate.

Gibbon's Literary Influence

Gibbon's *The History* served as a catalyst for many other texts that argued reasons for the fall of an empire, including:

- *The Rise and Fall of the Confederate Government* by Jefferson Davis
- *The Rise and Fall of Adolf Hitler* by William Shirer
- *The Rise and Fall of British Naval Mastery* by Paul Kennedy
- *The Rise and Fall of the Great Powers* by Paul Kennedy
- *The Decline and Fall of the Roman Church* by Malachi Martin
- *The Decline and Fall of the Catholic Church* by David Carlin
- *The Rising Sun: The Decline and Fall of the Japanese Empire* by John Toland

CONSTANTINE

Constantine actually was born Flavius Valerius Aurelius Constantinus way back sometime in 272. He was the Roman emperor from 324 to 337, the year he died.

Constantine the Great, as he was called—earning the "Great" in part because of his military accomplishments—brought the Roman Empire together under one emperor and also founded the Byzantine Empire. He also:

- Was the first Roman ruler who converted to Christianity. Yet he tolerated all religions in the empire.

- Founded Constantinople, which became the capital of the Eastern Roman Empire. Today the city is Istanbul.

- Defeated Licinius, becoming the solitary ruler of the Roman world.

Defeating Licinius was a big deal. Constantine had been sole emperor in the west and Licinius had been sole emperor in the east. The two duked it out in 316, with Constantine coming out on top and winning Illyricum, Pannonia, and Greece.

Constantine beefed up his forces and in 324 they went at it again. This time Constantine won big, killing his longtime rival. Constantine then became sole ruler of all the Roman world.

That's when he chose the ancient Greek city of Byzantium for his capital and made Christianity the state religion.

Later in life, his oldest son Crispus was executed for treason. Ditto the following year, 326, for Constantine's second wife—no one knows for sure why. Here's the strange part: Constantine ordered their deaths. Crispus was poisoned, and Fausta left to die in an overheated bath.

He had planned to split the empire among his three sons, but in 340 Constantine II died in war. Constantine the Great himself died May 22, 337.

JOHANNES KEPLER

If you don't believe geometry and astronomy can sing, you need to listen to them with Johannes Kepler's ears. Kepler was the German astronomer who helped prove Copernicus's heliocentric theory that the earth orbited the sun. Even more importantly, he helped science take the first steps toward unlocking the mysteries of how the universe is structured, laying the groundwork for Newton and then Einstein.

Born in what is now Germany in 1571, Johannes Kepler studied theology at the University of Tubingen, but his interest in mathematics and especially in the previous work of Copernicus led him toward astronomy. Still, throughout his career, Kepler believed that his work was deeply religious, that he was helping uncover the secret beauty of God's cosmic creation. One of his early ideas was that the geometric sphere neatly represented the Holy Trinity of God (the center), Christ (the circumference), and the Holy Sprit (all the space within). Kepler saw nature as a reflection of God's divine ideas.

Kepler's first published work was the *Mysterium Cosmographicum* in 1596. In it he presented his theory that the layout of the six known planets followed geometric shapes and that by finding the ratios of the planets' orbital distances he had cracked the secret structure of the universe. This line of thinking also led Kepler to explore the notion that distance from the sun affected motion of the planets, a line of thinking that would make possible Newton's later laws of gravity.

In 1600, Kepler went to Prague to study with the Danish astronomer Tycho Brahe. Although Brahe died soon after, it was access to Brahe's detailed astronomical observations and data that allowed Kepler to move ahead with his own theories. His first law of planetary motion—that the planets move around the sun in elliptical orbits—was based on his discovery that Mars's orbit was not a circle, but instead an ellipse. Later, when Galileo's use of the telescope led to the discovery of moons around some of the planets, Kepler was able to show that the placement of the moons around Jupiter fit into his theories about the geometric shape of the planets' orbits.

Kepler ended up with three laws of planetary motion. The second is known as the "area law"—a law of velocity that says that the area swept by a line from the sun to a planet during a specific period of time is always equal, meaning that the further a planet is from the sun, the slower it moves in its orbit. The third is the "harmonic law"—a prediction of the relationship between the time a planet takes to orbit the sun (squared) and its distance from the sun (cubed), which when calculated gives the same number for all the planets. These were not seen by Kepler as scientific laws, but rather as "celestial harmonies," the music of the universe as it reflects God's great design. Kepler believed that when the planets moved into geometric configurations, they helped fill the human soul with their harmonic influence.

The study of stars and planets led Kepler to develop a keen interest in light and how it moves, especially when passing through the earth's atmosphere or the human eye. He also took time to publish a theory on how much wine a standard wine barrel held, showing that the general guesses made by wine merchants were inaccurate.

Personally, Kepler's life sunk into the tragic in his later years. His first wife died in 1612 and one of his sons died of smallpox. And his mother was accused of witchcraft, a charge she fought in court for six years. She was exonerated in 1621, but died a few months later. Kepler himself died nine years later.

Kepler heard the geometry of the universe as music, but more than a symphony, his astronomical work was an important bridge from Copernicus to the coming revelations of Isaac Newton.

Kepler's Laws

Kepler founded the idea of "celestial mechanics," explaining the way that planetary bodies affect one another in space, based on gravity. He created three laws that explain planetary motion:

Kepler's First Law: The orbit of a planet around the sun is an ellipse with the sun's center of mass at one focus.

Kepler's Second Law: A line joining a planet and the sun sweeps out equal areas in equal intervals of time.

Kepler's Third Law: The squares of the periods of the planets are proportional to the cubes of their semimajor axes.

KNOW YOUR NOTABLE ATHENIANS

Aeschylus: An ancient Greek playwright, often known as the founder of tragedy. Born around 524 BC, he is the earliest of the three major Greek tragedians with surviving plays. (The other two are Sophocles and Euripides.)

Pericles (from 495 BC): A prominent orator, lawyer, and general of Athens during the Golden Age.

Euripides (c. 480–406 BC): The last to survive of the three major tragedians of Athens. He is thought to have written about ninety plays, eighteen of which have survived completely.

Simonides (c. 556–468 BC): A Greek poet, belonging to the canon of nine lyric poets designated by the scholars of Hellenistic Alexandria.

Demosthenes (384–322 BC): A major orator and statesman of Athens during the fourth century BC He made his living as a professional lawyer and speech writer, and he was famous for fighting against Macedon's expansion through persuasive rhetoric.

Themistocles (c. 524–459 BC): An Athenian statesman and soldier who convinced Athens that a fleet was needed for protection against the Persian army. He was ostracized from Aparta after the Persian war, and eventually moved to Persia where he spent the rest of his life as governer of Magnesia.

Herodotus (c. 484–425 BC): Known as the "Father of History." Herodotus was the first historian to record material systematically and test it for validity. He wrote The Histories, about the origins of the Greco-Persian wars.

Nicias (c. 470–413 BC): An Athenian politician and member of aristocracy during the Peloponnesian War.

Robert Hooke

Not every thinker goes down in history for coming up with a great new idea or invention. Some of them spend their lives simply expanding and improving on existing devices or theories.

Such is the case with the British natural philosopher (aka "scientist" or "physicist") Robert Hooke. Born in 1635, Hooke attended Oxford and found himself in the middle of the British scientific revolution.

Surrounded by brilliant scientists like Isaac Newton and Robert Boyle, Hooke went to work for Boyle building the Boylean air pump. The experience got Hooke interested in the mechanics of the universe, and he would eventually come to see all of nature as one big machine.

Hooke came up with his own law of elasticity that says the more force you apply to a solid body, the more it stretches. That may seem obvious today, but scientists of Hooke's era were often laboring to prove exactly how the world around them worked.

A member of a growing scientific body, the Royal Society of London, Hooke built a new type of telescope that allowed him to sketch Mars and observe Jupiter's rotation. On the other end of the scale, he promoted the use of the microscope and studied snowflakes, fibers, and insect parts. While examining the cork, Hooke was the first person to use the term "cell" to describe the sort of microscopic, organic chambers or holes found in such materials. He also peered at tiny fossils and came to believe they had once been living things. As a result of this line of thought, Hooke became an early supporter of the general notion that some sort of biological evolution may have taken place among species.

Obviously, Hooke's interests led him all over the scientific map. He did research on gravity as it applied to pendulum and the earth and moon, and he came up with theories about the wave properties of light and the inverse square law to explain planetary motion. It was with some bitterness that Hooke later came to feel that Newton swiped much of the latter theory without fully crediting him. Robert Hooke died in 1703.

HOOKE'S ACCOMPLISHMENTS

- Robert Hooke invented the spring control of the balance wheel for watches, the compound microscope, and the wheel barometer.

- Hooke used a magnified lens to observe everything from fleas to cork to lunar craters.

- He recorded his observations in Micrographia. Published in 1664, it was his most famous publication. The book includes Hook's use of the word "cell" in a biological context, referring to cork. It was here that the word was first coined.

- Hooke's Law, which states that a spring is proportional to the weight hanging from it, came about as he studied flight and the elasticity of air.

- Hooke worked with scientist Robert Boyle to perfect the air pump. For one experiment, Hooke acted as a sealed vessel while air was gradually pumped out to gauge the pressure. As a result of the experiment, his ears and nose were both damaged.

- Throughout his career, Hooke wore many hats: he served as a land surveyor, architect, inventor, and scientist.

- In *Attempt to Prove the Motion of the Earth*, written in 1674, Hooke proposed a theory of planetary motion based on inertia and a balance between an outward centrifugal force and an inward gravitational attraction to the sun.

- Hooke also built the first reflecting telescope, observed the rotation of Mars, and noted one of the earliest examples of a double star.

EXTRA CREDIT: The universal joint on a car is also known as a Hooke's joint.

MARTIN HEIDEGGER

This German philosopher's best known book, *Being and Time*, is generally considered one of the most significant philosophical works of the twentieth century.

David Barison and Daniel Ross thought so: they produced a movie about Martin Heidegger. Actually, the 2004 film, *The Ister,* is based on a lecture course Heidegger gave in 1942 on Friedrich Hölderlin. The movie features Jean-Luc Nancy, Philippe Lacoue-Labarthe, Bernard Stiegler, and Hans-Jürgen Syberberg.

Another film director, Terrence Malick, took interest in Heidegger, translating his 1929 essay *Vom Wesen des Grundes* into English. It was published under the title *The Essence of Reasons.*

Although married, Heidegger, who was born in 1889 in southwest Germany to a Catholic family, often retreated alone to a mountain hut in a remote area at the edge of the Black Forest. He liked the secluded forest for engaging in philosophical thought. The hut also is where he wrote most of *Being and Time*, which was published in 1927. As the title suggests, the book explores the question of "being," by asking about the being for whom being is a question. It was deep stuff—and as expected it influenced many future thinkers. Heidegger had planned on writing a second half to the book, but he never got around to it.

Famous Words of Martin Heidegger

- Every man is born as many men and dies as a single one.
- Man acts as though he were the shaper and master of language, while in fact language remains the master of man.
- If I take death into my life, acknowledge it, and face it squarely, I will free myself from the anxiety of death and the pettiness of life--and only then will I be free to become myself.
- Language is the house of the truth of Being.
- Making itself intelligible is suicide for philosophy.
- Man is not the lord of beings. Man is the shepherd of Being.

BLAISE PASCAL: A THINKER OF EPIC PROPORTIONS

Before age thirteen, Blaise Pascal proved the thirty-second proposition of Euclid and Discovered an error in Descartes's geometry, which Descartes dismissed since the argument came from a child's mind.

Pascal is noted as a child prodigy for these feats.

Later, Pascal invented one of the first mechanical calculators, called the Pascaline. When he was sixteen, his father asked him to total long lists of numbers. After slaving over the totaling by hand, Pascal began thinking that there had to be a better way. The result? He began designing a calculating machine.

He finally perfected the Pascaline in 1653, but people did not immediately approve. Since it could do the work of six accountants, they believed it would create unemployment.

Pascal's Life

- In 1653 he did several experiments involving the pressure exerted by gases and liquids.
- Also during this time, he invented the arithmetical triangle and created the calculus of probabilities.
- The Pensées [Thoughts] are considered Pascal's most influential religious writings. Found as numerous scraps of paper grouped in a tentative order after his death, the full, authentic text was not published until the nineteenth century.
- Pascal also invented the barometer, the hydraulic press, and the syringe.
- Reportedly, Pascal injured his health by constant rigorous study, and at the time of his death was supposedly physically worn out. Today, scholars speculate that he suffered from stomach cancer or tuberculosis. Blaise Pascal died in Paris on August 19, 1662, at age thirty-nine.

ARISTOTLE: ANCIENT PHILOSOPHER, FOUNDER OF LOGIC

Born in 384 at Stagirus, a Greek colony and seaport on the coast of Thrace, Aristotle traveled to Athens, the intellectual center of the world, when he was just seventeen years old. He joined the Academy and studied under Plato, attending his lectures for twenty years. When Plato died, Aristotle moved to Mysia and then on to Mytilene. At Mytilene, Aristotle began tutoring the thirteen-year-old Alexander (the Great). He eventually founded his own school at the Lyceum in Athens.

- Known as the founder of logic, Aristotle practiced what is today called inductive reasoning. He conducted detailed observations and documented his findings.

- He is said to be the first to classify animals into two groups—a task that could not have been accomplished without inductive reasoning.

- Aristotle wrote his philosophies in "dialogues" for his students and composed many other philosophical treatises.

- Only fifty documents survive out of Aristotle's estimated 150 works. His writings touch on a myriad of topics including biology, politics, physics, mathematics, and more.

- When Alexander died, the government in Athens was overthrown, and Aristotle was forced to flee to Chalcis where he died in 322 BC

MUSIC APPRECIATION 101
LUDWIG VAN BEETHOVEN

The composer of nine symphonies, Ludwig van Beethoven possessed a mind singularly occupied by music. Cleanliness and clothes were, unfortunately, of little importance to the great musician:

- After becoming famous, he was arrested by a policeman who refused to believe that the "great Beethoven" would have such wild, sloppy hair and filthy clothes.

- Friends regularly replaced Beethoven's old rags with new clothes, and, according to legend, Beethoven never noticed.

- Beethoven regularly had to move, sometimes multiple times a year. Upon visiting him, Beethoven's landlords would find their property to be a complete mess, filled with rotting food and dirty laundry.

- Apart from his lack of cleanliness, Beethoven also shared a rude moodiness with the grunge rockers, making it difficult to be around him.

- If people whispered during a performance Beethoven would stop his performance and leave abruptly.

- Once while eating in a restaurant, Beethoven became angry with the waiter and dumped a plate of food on his head.

- Beethoven once wrote a piece called "Praise to the Fat One," for an obese violinist.

Sun Tzu: Author of The Art of War

There has been great debate among historians as to when Sun Tzu actually lived. One group of historians posits that Sun Tzu was born "Sun Wu" in the sixth century BC, into a family of Chinese nobles. Others propose that Sun Tzu is a fictional character, and that his work, *The Art of War*, was actually authored by a number of Chinese philosophers.

Among those who firmly believe that Sun Tzu was a noble Chinese military consultant, there is still debate about when he actually lived. References to war chariots in *The Art of War* suggest that Sun Tzu lived sometime after the fourth century BCE., when these vehicles were used.

Though there is not much biographical information available on Sun Tzu, those who believe in his existence believed he was a follower of Confucius. Both Confucius and Lao Tzu offered philosophies about the societal hardships of wartime China. Sun Tzu followed with his own philosophies, which posited that the most efficient tactic of battle was to win over an opponent without the use of force or violence. According to legend, Sun Tzu was a member of the *shi*, a group of Chinese ambassadors who had lost their land during the Spring and Autumn Period when land was consolidated.

Sun Tzu was a mercenary who acted as a military consultant, a position from which much of his writings came. One of the most cited principles Sun Tzu presents in *Art of War* is the idea that "all warfare is based on deception." This idea was so heavily influential, that upon Sun Tzu's own demise, followers believed that his death was a deception, as well.

Designed as a military handbook, the text of *The Art of War* delivers some of the most sophisticated strategies of logistics, espionage, and mental and social philosophy that can be found today.

Though many believe that *Art of War* was intended for the military elite of Sun Tzu's time, its timeless philosophies have carried through the centuries and continue to enlighten scholars of many areas of cultural study.

POP QUIZ

1) What book written by ancient Chinese philosopher Sun Tzu
   continues to be referenced today?
   a) *The Art of Art*
   b) *Warfare in the Kitchen*
   c) *The Art of War*
   d) *Life Is War*

2) French playwright Voltaire felt that happiness lay in civilization's
   pursuit of ________.

3) What was composer Wolfgang Amadeus Mozart writing by the
   time he was thirteen?
   a) Symphonies
   b) Karaoke soundtracks
   c) Commercial jingles
   d) Italian operas

4) Who revolutionized psychology?
   a) Pavlov
   b) Freud
   c) Piaget

5) Who is credited with inventing the first mechanical computer?
   a) Babbage
   b) Hooke
   c) Fermi
   d) Forest

6) Who wrote *Anna Karenina*?
   a) Dostoevsky
   b) Kierkegaard
   c) Sartre
   d) Tolstoy

7) What period of writing did Ralph Waldo Emerson belong to?
   a) Romanticism
   b) Naturalism
   c) Transcendentalism

8) Who wrote *Messiah*?
   a) Mozart
   b) Beethoven
   c) Verdi
   d) Handel

9) What does the T. S. stand for in T. S. Eliot's name?
   a) Thomas Stearns
   b) Timothy Stephen
   c) Thomas Scott
   d) Timothy Scott

10) What country was Joan of Arc from?
   a) England
   b) France
   c) Germany
   d) Ireland

ANSWERS:

1) c
2) Arts and sciences
3) d
4) b
5) a
6) d
7) c
8) d
9) a
10) b

Ivan Petrovich Pavlov

Born on September 14, 1849, in Ryazan, Russia, Ivan Petrovich Pavlov was raised attending the church school in Ryazan and later seminary school. Pavlov soon realized his interest in science and in 1875 entered the Academy of Medical Surgery.

- Pavlov studied the physiology of the pancreatic nerves and then the nervous system of the heart. He won gold medals for his work in both studies.

- He married Serafima (Sara) Vasilievna Karchevskaia in 1881; they had five children.

- In 1890, Pavlov accepted the position of director of the Department of Physiology at the Institute of Experimental Medicine, a position he would hold for forty-five years. Under his direction, the Institute became one of the most important centers of physiological research.

- He also served as professor of Pharmacology at the Military Medical Academy.

Pavlov's Theory of Conditioning

Pavlov spent much of his career studying the digestive system in mammals. However, his study of conditioned reflexes and behavior is what garnered most of his fame and remembrance. Noting the reflex regulation of the digestive system compelled him to study conditioned reflexes more closely. The discovery of the phenomenon that he called "psychic secretion" enabled scientists to study all psychic activity objectively instead of relying on customary subjective methods.

LUDWIG WITTGENSTEIN

The only book-length work Ludwig Wittgenstein ever published was the *Tractatus Logico-Philosophicus*. Still, despite the lengthy writings of other philosophers, Wittgenstein is thought to be one of the twentieth century's most important philosophers.

Works about Wittgenstein

The Jew of Linz: Kimberley Cornish puts forward the controversial thesis that Hitler's antisemitism arose from his dislike of Wittgenstein, and that Wittgenstein was a Soviet agent who recruited the "Cambridge Five."

City of God: E.L. Doctorow depicts an imaginary rivalry between Wittgenstein and Einstein, with Wittgenstein assuming the role of the narrator.

Wittgenstein: Derek Jarman produced this 1993 movie. The script and the original treatment by Terry Eagleton were published as a book by the British Film Institute.

Ludwig Wittgenstein, Architect: Paul Wijdeveld wrote this extensive account of Wittgenstein's design of the house for his sister in Vienna (1994).

The Fifth Wittgenstein: Kari Jormakka discusses the connection between Wittgenstein's architecture and his philosophy in *Datutop* (2004).

The World as I Found It: Bruce Duffy recreates the life of Wittgenstein (1987).

Wittgenstein's Poker: The Story of a Ten-Minute Argument Between Two Great Philosophers: David Edmonds and John Eidenow (2002) describe the famous ten-minute meeting between Wittgenstein and Karl Popper which occurred on October 25, 1946.

Feminist Interpretations of Ludwig Wittgenstein: Naomi Scheman and Peg O'Connor offer a look at Wittgenstein's philosophies through a feminist perspective.

Oppression and Responsibility: Peg O'Connor offers a Wittgensteinian approach to social practice and moral theory.

PHILOSOPHY 101

JEREMY BENTHAM

One of the founders of utilitarianism, Jeremy Bentham wanted nothing more than for his body to be preserved and exhibited.

His unique request started three days after his death with his body's dissection in a medical school amphitheater in London—a very illegal act at the time. The only bodies allowed to be dissected at the time were those of executed murderers. Sounding like something out of a sci-fi movie, Bentham's organs were removed, and his head was replaced with a wax one.

Since he helped found University College, Bentham is kept behind glass in a wooden cabinet in a busy hallway at the school. After some students stole the real head as a joke, it is now stored safely in the College. The body, dressed in Bentham's own clothes, still remains stuffed with hay, straw, wool, cotton, and lavender to keep moths away. He is regularly visited by scholars from throughout the world, traveled once to a beer festival in Germany, and dines annually at the Bentham Dinner.

But let's back up to his living years. Along with his philosophical achievements, Bentham also was one of the first proponents of animal rights. Animal pain is very similar to human pain, he said, arguing that the ability to suffer—not the ability to reason—should be the standard for treating other beings.

Bentham left manuscripts totaling approximately five million words. Since 1968, the Bentham Project at University College London has been working on an edition of his collected work. So far, twenty-five volumes have appeared, with many more expected to come.

Abu Musa Jabir ibn Hayyan AKA: The Father of Chemistry

- He was born in 721, in Iran, but grew up in Yemen.

- As an adult he lived in Iran and practiced alchemy, following in the footsteps of his father.

- He is also known as *Geber*, the Latin version of his name.

- Many of the chemical elements and laboratory equipment used by chemists today were discovered or invented by Geber.

- He developed hydrochloric acid and aqua regia (one of the only substances that can dissolve gold). He is also credited with the discovery of citric acid, acetic acid, and tartaric acid.

- Geber improved the way steel and other metals were made, preventing rust, and engraving gold. He developed the process of using manganese dioxide in glassmaking to avoid the green tinge caused by iron, a process that is still used today.

- As Iran was under political turmoil, in 803 Jabir was placed under house arrest where he remained for several years before his death.

Geber on the Moon

A crater on the moon is named for Geber. The lunar impact crater is located in the rugged south-central highlands of the moon.

FREDERICK DOUGLASS

Frederick Douglass, born a slave in 1818, often said, "I would unite with anybody to do right and with nobody to do wrong." The American abolitionist—one of the most prominent figures in African-American history and U.S. history—believed in the equality of everyone, no matter their gender or race or immigration status.

Nominated as the vice presidential candidate on the Equal Rights Party ticket, Douglass ran with Victoria Woodhull—the first female U.S. presidential candidate. In February 1895, Douglass received a standing ovation at a National Council of Women meeting in Washington D.C. A few weeks later, he had either a massive heart attack or stroke and died in that same city, which had become his adopted hometown, and was buried in Mount Hope Cemetery in Rochester, New York.

In 1921, members of the Alpha Phi Alpha Fraternity designated Frederick Douglass as an honorary member. Theirs was the first African-American intercollegiate fraternity. Douglass was the only man to receive an honorary membership posthumously.

EXTRA CREDIT: In popular culture, the 1989 movie *Glory* featured Frederick Douglass reviewing the new unit of Black Union Army soldiers as they prepared to go off to war. The 2004 mockumentary *C.S.A.: The Confederate States of America*, features Douglass after the Confederacy wins the Civil War. Douglass also is a major character in Harry Turtledove's alternate history novel *How Few Remain*.

Memorials to Frederick Douglass

- Frederick Douglas National Historic Site, the Washington D.C. home of Frederick Douglass.
- Frederick Douglass Gardens at Cedar Hill, Washington D.C.
- The Frederick Douglass Prize, a national book prize sponsored by the Gilder Lehrman Institute of American History in New York and the Gilder Lehrman Center for the Study of Slavery, Resistance and Abolition at Yale University.

ADAM SMITH

Adam Smith was a philosopher born in the late eighteenth century. Most famous for his timeless book, *The Wealth of Nations*, he has been one of the most influential thinkers in the fields of economics and individual liberty.

Born in a tiny village in Scotland, Smith was raised by his widowed mother until the age of fourteen when he enrolled in the University of Glasgow. After eventually graduating from Balliol College at Oxford University, Smith returned home and was appointed as a chair of logic and moral philosophy at Glasgow University because of his vast knowledge of European literature.

Smith left the academic world in the 1760s to travel across Europe. Having earned a lifetime pension by serving Henry Scott, the duke of Buccleuch, Smith was able to retire in his hometown where he began writing *The Wealth of Nations*. The book was published in 1776 and led to Smith's everlasting fame. Smith died in 1790 of illness in Edinburgh, Scotland. He donated a large amount of his wealth to charity in private, which was discovered only after his death.

EXTRA CREDIT: In 1778, Smith was appointed as a customs commissioner. The job forced Smith to have to control smuggling in customs, which contradicted his theory in *The Wealth of Nations* that smuggling was a legitimate enterprise because of poor legislation.

The Invisible Hand

Smith is most recognized for his coinage of the expression, "the invisible hand," which demonstrates his idea of self interest and its control over the economy. Smith argued that the welfare of the public is always secondary to this controlling hand of personal interest.

STEPHEN HAWKING: THEORETICAL THINKER

A famous great thinker, Stephen Hawking grew up in London during the 1940s, where his father worked at the National Institute for Medical Research as a biologist. He studied physics at Oxford, and later moved on to Trinity Hall, Cambridge, where he began his in-depth study of theoretical astronomy and cosmology.

- During his mid-twenties, Hawking began showing the symptoms of amyotrophic lateral sclerosis (also known as Lou Gehrig's disease), a neuromuscular condition.

- In 1974, Hawking became one of the youngest Fellows of the Royal Society, an exclusive group of scientists.

- He has received many other honors including Commander of the Order of the British Empire, Companion of Honour, and a member of the Board of Sponsors of The Bulletin of the Atomic Scientists.

Hawking Radiation

Hawking's principal fields of research focused on theoretical cosmology and quantum gravity. Among his many scientific investigations, he has found that black holes should thermally create and emit subatomic particles until they exhaust all of their energy and evaporate. This action is identified as "Hawking radiation." He has studied quantum cosmology, cosmic inflation, the nature of space and time, and other theories relating to the universe.

CRASH COURSE
ARISTOPHANES

When chatting up Aristophanes, you can't go too wrong, given that so many of the facts about the comic poet's life are up in the air. Even his place of birth and date of his death are shrouded in uncertainty (but the latter is estimated around 380 BC and most likely he was educated in Athens). But one thing is certain—his plays are the only surviving plays of Old Greek Comedy.

His comedies encompassed the times—the decline of the Republic, the corruption, and more—but were done in the most off-the-wall fashion. Let's just say that at the time, the laughter elicited by Aristophanes was much needed.

Humor was in the gene pool—Aristophanes' sons Araros, Philippus, and Nicostratus also were comic poets.

Aristophanes' first two comedies, *The Banqueters* and *The Babylonians* were lost. His first surviving play, *The Acharnians*, was written well into the war and was the world's first ever anti-war comedy.

The focus of his next play was Cleon, the demagogue who had replaced Pericles, and in *The Clouds*, Aristophanes turned his attention to Socrates, the great thinker of the time. In *The Wasps*, the comic returned to his favorite topic—the decline of Athens—followed by the satirization of the tragic poet Euripides.

Aristophanes left behind approximately forty plays, eleven of which survived.

EXTRA CREDIT: *Acropolis Now* is a BBC Radio sitcom—reruns still airing—set in Ancient Greece. It features Aristophanes, Socrates, and other famous Greeks. Aristophanes and his brother Heraclitus run a fish restaurant.

FREDERIC CHOPIN: VIRTUOSO

This Polish virtuoso pianist is widely regarded as the greatest Polish composer, and one of the most influential nineteenth-century piano composers.

Chopin's pieces, which almost all include the piano, are technically challenging to play, to say the least. He also created new forms of music, such as the ballade, and tweaked existing forms including the piano sonata, prelude, and waltz.

In 1926, a bronze statue of Chopin previously designed in 1907 was put up in Warsaw's Lazienki Park. The statue was supposed to have gone up in 1910, on Chopin's centennial birthday, but there were several delays thanks to arguments over its design and the start of World War I. The statue actually was ruined by the Germans during the Second World War and then reconstructed in 1958. Since the following year, free piano recitals—of Chopin's pieces, of course—have played near the statue's base on summer Sunday afternoons.

Chopin wanted to have Mozart's *Requiem* sung at his own funeral, but that was easier said than done. The *Requiem* has major female parts. The Church of the Madeleine, however, had never allowed female singers in its choir. Chopin's funeral was put off nearly two weeks until church officials caved, with one condition: the female singers had to hide behind a black curtain while they sang. Geesh.

Thousands attended Chopin's funeral in October 1849. The soloists in the *Requiem* included the bass Luigi Lablache—he sang the same piece at Beethoven's funeral. Other Chopin pieces also were played, of course.

Chopin was buried, as he had requested, at Père Lachaise Cemetery. At the graveside, the *Funeral March* from Sonata Op. 35 was played. Each year, even in the dead of winter, Chopin's grave attracts countless visitors.

CAESAR AUGUSTUS

- Alive between 63 BC and AD 14, Augustus was the very first emporer of Rome. After his great uncle, Julius Caesar, was killed in 44 BC, Augustus took over the reign of Rome and changed its republic to a monarchy, which made him the first Roman emperor of history.

- Augustus went against Caesar's beliefs that Rome should be a republic with a dictator. He instead chose to make himself leader of the monarchy, which gave him power over Rome for his lifetime.

- Originally named Gaius Octavius, he changed his name to Augustus after taking the throne. The name meant "lofty" and "serene."

- Augustus created social reform across the city of Rome, improving the welfare of the state and reconstructing buildings and streets. His statue was raised throughout the empire, and his face was featured on coins.

- Augustus created a Roman standing army to protect the state from intruders and barbarians. He extended the Roman frontier from the Rhine River all the way to the Danube.

- During his last few years of rule, military disaster riddled his reign. German armies defeated three legions of the Roman army along the Rhine, and Augustus's army was forced to retreat from German soil.

- Augustus and his wife, Julia, only had a daughter. So, Augustus had expected one of his grandsons, Gaius or Lucius, to inherit his throne. Instead, Gaius and Lucius both died before Augustus, to his dismay.

- Augustus died in AD 14, and his stepson, Tiberius, took the throne.

THE VOYAGES OF COLUMBUS

The First Voyage, 1492–1493: Christopher Columbus departed on his first voyage from southern Spain in August in charge of the *Niña*, the *Pinta* and the *Santa Maria*. The journey took Columbus to the Bahamas and Cuba. While sailing north of Cuba in November, the captain of the *Pinta* ditched the other two ships (without consent) to find an island he'd been told might have gold. Columbus, however, continued with the *Santa Maria* and *Niña* and arrived at Hispaniola in December. The *Santa Maria* grounded on a reef on Christmas Eve—not good. Columbus used the ship's remains to build a fort, calling it La Navidad (Christmas).

The smaller *Niña*, however, could not carry the rest of the crew. Columbus left behind a few dozen men at the fort and continued on. He was stunned to come across the *Pinta* in January. He was mad at the ship's captain but thrilled to have another boat to get his crew back to Spain. The two ships left Hispaniola but separated again, this time by a monster storm. By this time it was now February. Columbus arrived at Lisbon on March 4, and finally made it back home on March 15, 1493. Meanwhile, the *Pinta* had overshot home and arrived at the port of Bayona in northern Spain. After a stop to repair some damage, the *Pinta* arrived home a few hours after the *Niña*.

The Second Voyage, 1493–1496: Unlike the investigative first voyage, the second voyage was a true effort—of colonization. The journey included seventeen ships and more than a thousand crew members who brought livestock to America for the very first time. The convoy left the Canary Islands in October 1493. The first stop was Hispaniola, where Columbus had left all those men from the first trip (they would have been there eleven months by now). But back at the Navidad fort, the men were dead and the fort was burned.

Columbus then went eastward along Hispaniola to find a place to colonize. On December 8, he anchored and created the town of La Isabela, named for the Spanish queen. The next several months were spent getting the colony together and exploring the area. In April 1494, Columbus left Isabela with three ships in hopes of finding mainland China—he still thought it was close by. He reached Cuba that same month, but soon got sidetracked hearing of an island that might have some gold. Columbus anchored at Jamaica soon after. The Indians there were not too thrilled with his arrival, and he quickly returned to Cuba.

But Columbus landed in southern Cuba, and soon learned that that part of the country's shoals and small islands made exploration nearly impossible. He continued westward for several weeks, and finally gave up.

The Third Voyage, 1498–1500: This time Columbus left southern Spain in May 1498 with six ships bound for the New World. They arrived the following month at the Canary Islands. Here, the convoy split in half, with three ships sailing to Hispaniola to bring supplies to the colony and three—those led by Columbus—exploring new land south of any known islands in the Indies.

Columbus first went to the Cape Verde Islands, where he tried to get some cattle but was unsuccessful. Then he went on to the Doldrums area—where, of course, there was little wind. After they drifted for days, the winds finally picked up. By the end of July, they were running out of water. So, Columbus decided to head directly for Dominica. But that same day he spotted a new island. It had three hills, so Columbus called it Trinidad, after the Holy Trinity. The crew got water there, and while resting on the island sighted South America off in the distance. They were the first Europeans to see that continent. They then set sail again, and landed on the island of Margarita.

Columbus was getting sick at this time, so they cruised to Hispaniola, arriving in August 1498. There, in Santo Domingo, Columbus found that peeved colonists had rebelled against his rule. Columbus eventually unwillingly caved. Ferdinand and Isabela appointed Francisco de Bobadilla as royal commissioner—with higher authority than Columbus. When Bobadilla arrived in Santo Domingo, he had Columbus arrested. In October of 1500, Columbus went home to Spain in handcuffs.

The Fourth Voyage, 1502–1504: In May 1502, four ships and more than one hundred men left the port of Cadiz. The fleet included Columbus's brother Bartholomew, and Columbus's younger son

Fernando, then a mere thirteen years old. Columbus was now fifty-one, sick, and anything but embraced in his former home base of Hispaniola. But he wanted one more high seas adventure. His goal was to find a strait linking the Indies—Columbus still thought it was part of Asia—with the Indian Ocean. In reality, Columbus was looking for the Strait of Malacca—which really was near Singapore in Central America.

Columbus arrived at Santo Domingo in June 1502. He wanted harbor entrance so he could seek safety from a storm. The local governor denied his request. Columbus and his ships hunkered down in a nearby estuary. Good thing, too—a hurricane hit.

Columbus arrived at Honduras in July, and eventually traveled to what is now Panama, where the natives told about an ocean to the south. The natives also had lots of gold objects they traded with. Columbus named this valuable new region *Veragua*.

Finally, Columbus returned to western Panama in January 1503, building a garrison fort, which would be attacked by Indians. The Spanish would lose many men in the attack.

Only two ships made it to Jamaica in June 1503, and both were leaking. Diego Mendez, one of Columbus's captains, bought a canoe there and sailed it to Hispaniola. He was held by governor Ovando outside the city for several months, denied a ship to rescue the others. When Ovando finally let Mendez into the city, there were no ships around. Finally, Mendez was able to charter a small caravel, which rescued the expedition on June 29, 1504. Columbus returned to Spain in November 1504.

Famous Words of Christopher Columbus

- Gold is a treasure, and he who possesses it does all he wishes to in this world, and succeeds in helping souls into paradise.
- By prevailing over all obstacles and distractions, one may unfailingly arrive at his chosen goal or destination.
- For the execution of the voyage to the Indies, I did not make use of intelligence, mathematics, or maps.

Columbus Day

When the first-ever Columbus Day was held in 1792, New York City was partying in celebration of the 300th anniversary of Columbus's discovery of the New World. One hundred years later President Benjamin Harrison invited the United States to honor Columbus and celebrate the 400th anniversary of his landing in America. Some Italian-Americans celebrate the day in honor of their own heritage—the first such fest took place in New York City in October 1866.

Columbus Day really took off in the United States thanks to some Italians who immigrated to California searching for gold: San Francisco has the second oldest Columbus Day celebration—Italian-Americans there have honored it ever since 1869. In 1934, the Knights of Columbus asked Congress and President Franklin Delano Roosevelt to mark October 12 as a Federal Columbus Day holiday. Since 1971, the U.S. holiday has been held on the second Monday in October.

But…

- Berkeley, California, doesn't celebrate Columbus Day—technically. Instead, they rejoice in "Indigenous People's Day."

- For years in Denver, Colorado, American Indian groups have protested the Columbus Day.

- Hawaii does not officially honor Columbus Day—there, they honor "Discoverer's Day," which honors James Cook, the British guy who first recorded the coordinates of the Hawaiian Islands.

- In Nevada, Columbus Day is not a legal holiday—schools and government offices are still open—but it is still observed.

- And in South Dakota, the day officially is a state holiday called "Native American Day."

TWO FAMOUS FAILED NOVEMBER ASSASSINATIONS

Assassin: Guy Fawkes
Targets: King James I of England and the British Parliament
Date: November 5, 1605
Background: Guy Fawkes was the demolitionist hired in the Gunpowder Plot by a group of Catholic conspirators hoping to incite a rebellion and install a Catholic head of state in place of King James in a largely intolerant Protestant England.
Result: The attempt failed and had the opposite effect. Laws protecting Catholics and promoting religious tolerance were not realized for another 200 years. Many historians believe that had the plot succeeded, it would have resulted in a more severe backlash against Catholics, and the creation of a more absolute, Puritanical monarchy. Guy Fawkes Day is created to commemorate the plot, and the word "guy" is adopted, at first, in reference to an idiot, then to any person in popular slang.

Assassin: George Elser
Target: Adolf Hitler
Date: November 8, 1939
Background: Elser was a devout Protestant and Communist sympathizer and despised the Nazi party almost from its beginnings. Suspecting that Hitler's extreme views would plunge Germany into another war, he traveled to Munich where Hitler gave a speech at a local beer hall every year on November 8. Elser secretly stayed after closing every night for over a month and hollowed out a pillar behind the stage where Hitler would speak. Elser planted a bomb he built in the pillar and set the timer.
Result: The bomb exploded at exactly 9:20 P.M., thirteen minutes after Hitler had left the room. Eight people were killed and sixty were injured. Elser was captured, tortured, and executed. WWII had already begun, but the assassination would have dealt a devastating blow to the Nazi war effort.

MATHEMATICS 101
LEONARDO FIBONACCI

Born c. 1175, Leonardo Fibonacci, also named Leonardo of Pisa, was an Italian thinker considered by many over centuries as the most talented mathematician to come out of the Middle Ages.

Fibonacci is a shortened version of *filius Bonacci*, a Latin phrase that means "the son of Bonaccio." (Fibonacci's father's name was Guglielmo Bonaccio.)

Books by Fibonacci

Liber Abaci, 1202

Practica Geometriae, 1220

Flos, 1225

Liber quadratorum ("The Book of Squares"), 1225

Di minor guisa (a lost text on arithmetic)

Commentary on Book X of Euclid's Elements (another lost text)

Fibonacci Sequence

In the Fibonacci sequence (0, 1, 1, 2, 3, 5, 8, 13, ...), each term is the sum of the two previous terms (for instance, 2+3=5, 3+5=8, ...). As one goes further to the right in this sequence, the ratio of a term to the one before it grows closer to the *golden ratio*. The Fibonacci sequence is best understood when one views nature. It can be found in the center of a sunflower, the outside of a pineapple, and the spirals of a seashell. The same numerical pattern exists throughout nature, visual forms of the Fibonacci sequence.

GEORG WILHELM FRIEDRICH HEGEL

The theology-educated Georg Wilhelm Friedrich Hegel initially bounced around from job to job—a private tutor, professor, newspaper editor, and rector, then back to professorships. It wasn't until he moved to Berlin in the 1810s that he became famous.

During his time in Berlin, which included many lectures, Hegel wrote the wildly popular *Science of Logic* (1812–1816), *Encyclopedia of the Philosophical Sciences* (1817)—this outlined his whole philosophy— and *Philosophy of Right* (1821). He wrote about ethics, aesthetics, history, and religion. He lectured on philosophy, religion, aesthetics, and history—and after his death his talks were put together into eight volumes.

Hegel argued that there was a relation between nature and freedom, immanence and transcendence, and the union of these without doing away with either extreme or reducing it to the other. Hegel inspired many later philosophies including post-Hegelian idealism, the existentialism of Kierkegaard and Sartre, the socialism of Marx and Lasalle, and the instrumentalism of Dewey.

Famous Words of Hegel

- An idea is always a generalization, and generalization is a property of thinking. To generalize means to think.
- Education is the art of making man ethical.
- Genuine tragedies in the world are not conflicts between right and wrong. They are conflicts between two rights. I'm not ugly, but my beauty is a total creation.
- It is easier to discover a deficiency in individuals, in states, and in Providence, than to see their real import and value. Nothing great in the world has ever been accomplished without passion.
- Once the state has been founded, there can no longer be any heroes. They come on the scene only in uncivilized conditions.

IVAN THE GREAT AND IVAN THE TERRIBLE: A COMPARISON

Why was Ivan the Great grand? Why was Ivan the Terrible awful? Read on and see:

Ivan the Great (Ivan III) 1440–1505

- He tripled his territory by conquering ancient families from surrounding lands and by forcibly removing his brothers from their princely positions.

- During his reign, he created an autocratic government by presenting himself as "Tsar" in his interactions with foreign nations.

- He began inviting philosophers and artists to his capital in an attempt to make it a worthy successor to Constantinople, which had fallen shortly before his birth.

Ivan the Terrible (Ivan IV) 1530–1584

- Probably insane, Ivan IV went into an outrage of suspicion and executed his chosen heir, Ivan Ivanovich. As a result, he was later succeeded by his mentally retarded son Fyodor, known for traveling the country to ring the bells of churches.

- He broke the tsardom's treasury by staging a fruitless twenty-four-year war against Denmark, Lithuania, Poland, and Sweden for an area known as Greater Livonia.

- Attempted to rape his son's daughter, Irina. It is believed by many that he was poisoned with mercury by her father, Bogdan Belsky, for this offense.

GALILEO GALILEI

Galileo Galilei experimented with measuring the speed of light and sound frequency and formulated the basic principle of relativity, a concept that states that the laws of physics are the same in any system that is moving at a constant speed in a straight line, regardless of its particular speed or direction. This theory later paved the way for Newton's laws of motion and Einstein's special theory of relativity.

Galileo created sketches for a variety of ingenious ideas:

- a candle placed in front of a mirror to reflect light throughout a building
- an automatic tomato picker
- a combination of a comb and eating utensil
- a ballpoint pen

The Assayer (*Ii Saggiatore*), Galileo's first book, was published in 1623. Nine years later, he published the *Dialogue Concerning the Two Chief World Systems*, which caused him to have to stand trial on suspicion of heresy in 1633.

Found guilty, he was required to recant his ideas, was put under house arrest, and his book was banned. He was forbidden to publish anything else again.

While he was under house arrest, Galileo created one of his most famous works, *Two New Sciences*, a summary of the work he had done in the field now known as kinematics and strength of materials. As a result of this work, Galileo is often called the "father of modern physics."

Like Father, Like Son

Galileo's father, a musician, established what is known as the oldest known nonlinear relation in physics. He discovered and explained that when a string is stretched, the pitch varies by the square root of the tension, and that subdividing a string by a whole number produces a harmonious scale.

THEOLOGY 101
DIETRICH BONHOEFFER: THEOLOGIAN AND ETHICIST

Born in Breslau, Germany, in 1906, Dietrich Bonhoeffer was the son of a leading empirical psychologist of Germany. After attending Tübingen University and completing a Ph.D. in 1927, he went on to study theology at Union Theological Seminary in New York City. In 1931, he was ordained as a Lutheran pastor.

The Facts

- As head of the Confessing Church Seminary, Bonhoeffer openly called for the overthrow of the Nazi regime.

- Known for his theory on ethical behavior, Bonhoeffer drew inspiration from the teachings of both Aristotle and Jesus Christ. He believed that evil could only be combated by specific action and that people have no other option than to directly oppose evil. He believed that those who failed to act were in fact condoning evil.

- He worked on his book, *Ethics*, from 1940 until he was arrested in 1943 for his open dissent about Hitler and the Nazis. In his book, he attempted to provide a guide for those who wanted to follow the teachings of Christ but still live in the practical world.

- Bonhoeffer was executed in 1945 for his open opposition of Hitler.

Famous Works of Dietrich Bonhoeffer

Sanctorum Communio (The Communion of Saints)
Act and Being
Ethics
Letters and Papers from Prison

Ferdinand Magellan

Born in 1480 in Portugal, Ferdinand Magellan is infamous for his voyage across the Pacific Ocean, an exploration that broke new historical ground in his century.

After suffering a difficult childhood, Magellan became a page for the court in Lisbon in the early sixteenth century following the death of his parents.

He then enlisted in the Portuguese fleet and became involved in several expeditions through Africa and India.

Returning to Lisbon later in 1512, Magellan tried to reason with the king of Portugal to fund an expedition, but the king disagreed.

Magellan went to Spain and convinced the Spanish king to support an expedition to the Moluccas.

The Spanish king agreed to fund the expedition, and Magellan set out with a fleet of five ships in 1519 to cross the Atlantic Ocean.

Magellan managed to cross the Atlantic, as planned, but not without extreme difficulty. His crew was mutinous; the rough seas and weather took many lives. Scurvy, disease, and lack of food and water nearly brought the expedition to a devastating halt.

When the crew reached the southernmost point of South America, they had crossed the Atlantic entirely. This portion of land was later named after Magellan. With only three ships remaining, Magellan set out again for the Pacific Ocean, his crew dying of starvation, scurvy, and dehydration. In roughly fourteen weeks they reached land again, and sailed forth to the Philippines. It was there that Magellan was killed, in 1521, during a battle with local inhabitants.

Only one of Magellan's ships returned to Spain. In September of 1522, this last remaining ship reached port in Spain, having completed a full expedition around the globe.

Up to No Good: Really Corrupt World Leaders

Mohamed Suharto: President of Indonesia from 1967 until 1998, Suharto is thought to have embezzled somewhere close to $35 billion from his country while in power. He was eventually investigated after resigning from office and put under house arrest. Charged with corruption, he was later released due to poor health.

Slobodan Milosevic, political leader of Serbia from 1989 to 1997 and leader of Yugoslavia from 1997 to 2000, can be classified as a pretty bad dude. He was actually banned from a third term of presidency in Serbia after being blamed for many brutal military policies he enstated during wars in Croatia and Bosnia. He then went on to instill the same harsh tactics and brutal ethnic cleansing policies in Yugoslavia, leading to NATO air attacks and the deportation of many Kosovo natives. Milosevic was arrested and charged with crimes against humanity. Later, in 2001, Milosevic was rearrested with charges of corruption and was sent to the Hague. Luckily for Milosevic, he did not live to see his sentencing, as he died while still being tried for war crimes in several countries.

Mobutu Sese Seko, long reigning president of Zaire from 1930 until 1997, began his rule over the Belgian Congo when he organized a coup against the government of Patrice Lumumba. He became president after violently overthrowing the existing government, changing the name of the Congo to Zaire in 1970 and forcing all of the inhabitants to change their Christian names back to their African names. He then went on to change all names of towns, streets, and buildings in Zaire back to African names, and encouraged nationalism. Disregarding economics, he drove the nation into severe inflation and was later found to have embezzled close to five billion dollars from the country. He was expelled from his own country in 1997, and died in Morocco.

ASTRONOMY 101

EDMOND HALLEY: A THINKER OF ASTRONOMICAL PROPORTIONS

Born in 1656 in London, Edmond Halley attended Oxford University, the place where he became intrigued by the stars and planets after exposure to astronomer John Flamsteed's project cataloging the northern stars. Halley wanted to do the same project for the Southern Hemisphere. He set out for the South Atlantic island of St. Helena in 1676 and returned to England two years later with 341 stars recorded according to celestial longitudes and latitudes. He also noted a transit of Mercury's orbit across the sun.

Halley's Comet

Halley joined the scientists of the day in their quest to explain planetary motion. When Isaac Newton identified the orbit as an ellipse, Halley expanded on the work by recording the orbits of comets. He showed that three comets recorded in 1531, 1607, and 1682 were so similar that they were returns of the same object—now known as *Halley's Comet.* He correctly predicted the comet's return in 1758.

In 1716, Halley devised a method for observing transits of Venus across the disk of the sun, allowing an accurate calculation of the distance of the earth from the sun.

EXTRA CREDIT: The practice of cataloging stars came well before Flamsteed and Halley. In 134 BC, Hipparchus, a Greek astronomer, cataloged approximately 850 stars, assigning them a numerical scale of magnitude ranging from 1 as the brightest to 6 as the lightest, to indicate the star's brightness. Hipparchus's scale is still in use today although it has been modified and extended in range.

THE TWENTY-EIGHT BUDDHAS

In most Theravada countries, it is the custom for Buddhists to hold elaborate festivals to honor twenty-eight Buddhas. Their names are:

1. Tanhankara
2. Medhankara
3. Saranankara
4. Dipankara
5. Kondnna
6. Managala
7. Sumana
8. Revata
9. Sobhita
10. Anomadassi
11. Paduma
12. Narada
13. Padumuttara
14. Sumedha
15. Sujata
16. Piyadassi
17. Atthadassi
18. Dhammadassi
19. Siddhatta
20. Tissa
21. Phussa
22. Vipassi
23. Sikhi
24. Vessabhu
25. Kakusandha
26. Konagamana
27. Kassapa
28. Gautama

JULIUS CAESAR: GREAT ROMAN THINKER

Julius Caesar was born in 100 BC, the son of a politically connected Roman family. It was only natural that he would grow to become active in the Roman military and republic.

Caesar's Rule: A Series of Fortunate and Unfortunate Events

Between 61 and 60 BC, he served as governor of a Roman province in Spain, before returning to Rome to serve as a consul at home.

Later, he became a Roman governor, a rule during which he added the area of France and Belgium to the Roman Empire.
Trouble came for Caesar around 54 BC when he crossed the Rubicon River, heading through Italy, and refused to disband his army of men. Caesar defeated the forces of Pompey, the leader of the Italian Republican army, and chased him back to Egypt. It was there that Caesar began his infamous relationship with Cleopatra.

Once back in Rome, Caesar used his power and wealth to create reforms in Rome, strengthening the senate and revising the calendar. Instead of assuming his dictatorship for a fixed period, Caesar changed his dictatorship to extend for life. This angered many members of the senate, eventually leading to his famous assassination.

On the Ides of March in 44 BC (March 15), Caesar was assassinated by Cassius and Brutus, two republican senators. This act brought about a final cluster of civil wars in Rome. The Republic was dissolved, and Caesar's great nephew, Augustus, became the first emperor of the newly established monarchy of Rome.

PHILOSOPHY 101
PLATO: LOGICAL THINKER

Much of what is presumed about the life of Plato is actually approximated: the details of the great thinker's life, including even his birth date, remain unknown. Plato's exact birth date is estimated at around 428 or 427 BC, and he was most likely born in Athens, Greece. Plato is believed to have been educated in grammar and music by the top instructors of his time.

Although philosophers existed before Plato, some scholars refer to philosophy as Plato's invention, because of the way in which he revolutionized issues and influenced the world. His writing has influenced every era forward, even today.

At age forty, Plato established one of the earliest known organized schools in western civilization. The Academy, located in Athens, was closed in 529, when Justinian I of Byzantium found the school to be threatening to the rule of Christianity. Many intellectuals studied at the Academy, including Aristotle.

EXTRA CREDIT: Plato's works have influenced many contemporary thinkers, including:
Albert Einstein
Friedrich Nietzsche
Karl Popper
Leo Strauss

Platonic Love

English playwright Sir William Davenant wrote a satirical play titled *Platonick Lovers* in 1636, centered on a brief time when Platonic love was a fashionable subject at the English royal court. The play contains the first record of the phrase *Platonic love* in written English. The themes of the play come from the concept in Plato's *Symposium* of the love of the idea of good that lies at the root of all virtue and truth.

THE DIALOGUES OF PLATO

Scholars have never quite pinned down the order in which Plato wrote his dialogues. The dialogues are currently grouped into three periods with a few works that are considered transitional pieces, written in between the major periods:

Early Dialogues

Called the Socratic dialogues, each of these dialogues are considered the indirect teachings of Plato. Most of them involve Socrates discussing a subject such as friendship, piety, and so forth, with another student. Through a series of questions he explains the topic to his opponent. This period also includes several dialogues that involve the trial and execution of Socrates.

Apology
Crito
Charmides
Laches
Lysis
Euthyphro
Menexenus
Lesser Hippias
Ion

Transitional Dialogues

Gorgias
Protagoras
Meno

Middle Dialogues

Plato's own views comprise most of the middle dialogues. In these works, he features Socrates answering some of his own questions. The topics in this period include immortality, justice, truth, and beauty.

Euthydemus
Cratylus
Phaedo

Phaedrus
Symposium
Republic
Theaetetus
Parmenides

Late Dialogues
The late dialogues reveal Plato's matured thinking on many of the same issues he dealt with in his earlier writing. Scholars are still working to decipher these views. Although these later works are difficult and challenging, they are more logical than his earlier works.
Sophist
Statesman
Philebus
Timaeus
Critias
Laws

EXTRA CREDIT: Plato was not the only author to write about Socrates. Aristophanes employed him as one of the principal characters in the comedy *Clouds*, and Xenophon, a historian and military leader, wrote an account of Socrates's trial and other works in which Socrates appears as a principal speaker.

FAMOUS LOVERS: FRIDA KAHLO AND DIEGO RIVERA

Enter the young and beginning artistic heroine:

Frida Kahlo (1907–1954) was a Mexican painter strongly influenced by Surrealism. Her colorful art pictures scenes that pay tribute to the heritage of indigenous Mexican peoples. Usually her paintings display images of herself and depict her feelings, pain, or sexuality. Her paintings are on display in the Louvre Museum, and there is a museum dedicated to her housed in her former home in Mexico.

Enter the older and experienced artistic hero:

Diego Rivera (1886–1957) was also a Mexican painter. For the most part, he painted murals in vibrant colors. Much of his work reflects Mexican culture and history, focusing especially on Aztec heritage. He tended to paint simplified, flattened figures. His works are housed in many museums all over the world including the Metropolitan Museum of Art and the Museum of Modern Art.

They Meet:

The two painters met when Frida asked Diego to critique her artwork. Diego was married at the time, but that didn't stop the couple from dating. They married in 1929, when Frida was twenty-two and Diego was forty-two. They continued to inspire and discuss each other's art throughout their lives. Their marriage was a rocky one, including many infidelities by both partners, a divorce, and remarriage.

Both artists were self-proclaimed Communists. Their political connections led to their personal friendship with Leon Trotsky, a Communist political theorist who participated in the Russian Revolution. They, in fact, housed Trotsky for a short time, and Frida may have had an affair with him.

The couple stayed together until Frida died. Their lives and marriage were memorialized in the 2002 film *Frida*.

Wallace Stevens: The Unexpected Poet

During his lifetime, Wallace Stevens worked for insurance companies, graduated from law school, was the vice president of two different companies, turned down an offer for a faculty position from Harvard University, and wrote brilliant poetry

Obviously, Wallace Stevens spent much of his time focused on his professional life. The majority of his poetry writing occurred while he walked to work. He was an avid walker, using his weekends to walk sometimes ten or twenty miles in a day just for the enjoyment of walking. His couple-mile trek to work—which he walked rain, shine, or snow—gave him time to mentally compose verse which he dictated to his secretary once he got to his insurance company job. Stevens claimed the pace and regular movement of walking helped to form the rhythm of his poetry.

When he did start publishing, Stevens produced beautiful lines of paradoxically simple yet complicated poetry. His language and word choice tends to be easy to understand, but his structure and meaning are often difficult to grasp. Stevens argued this is because his poetry has no specific meaning. He said, "A poem need not have a meaning, and like most things in nature often does not have." His poetry is much more about ideas and the imagination than it is about expressing a particular meaning or message.

His poems include "The Emperor of Ice Cream," "Thirteen Ways of Looking at a Blackbird," and "Anecdote of the Jar."

Interesting Facts About Wallace Stevens

- Didn't publish anything until he was thirty-five.
- Did his best writing after he was in his fifties, and wrote into his seventies.
- Didn't quit his day job, despite his commercial success as a poet.
- Won two National Book Awards and a Pulitzer Prize.

CHARLEMAGNE

An important figure of medieval Europe, Charlemagne, also known as Charles the Great, was born circa 747, and presided as King of the Franks. He ruled as the Christian emperor of much of Western Europe, heading up the Carolingian Renaissance.

Charlemagne became the sole ruler of the Franks after his younger brother died in 771. Before, at the time of their father's death, Charlemagne and his younger sibling had taken over rule of the kingdom.

In 772, he invaded Saxony and converted the entire state to Christianity under his rule.

He then moved to conquer the entire kingdom of Lombards in Italy.

During the next twenty years, he invaded Spain, and gained control of Bohemia, northern Spain, and Danube, defeating the Moors and the Avars in the process.

At the beginning of the ninth century, Charlemagne returned to Rome to assist Pope Leo III, as a rebellion had begun against the Church.

Charlemagne and his armies defeated the rebellion, and he was crowned by the Pope on Christmas Day as emperor of the Romans.

Though Charlemagne did not remain in Rome and rule, his new title allowed him to rule over the Italian territories he had previously conquered, under the tradition of the Roman Empire.

In the many territories over which he ruled, Charlemagne made significant changes and progressive advancements. His territory, known as the Carolingian empire, was transformed with a series of administrative and social reforms. Representatives were chosen in each region, and assemblies were held annually to discuss social welfare. Charlemagne standardized the system of weights and measurements used by his people, and he improved the legal system, tax system, and religious structure.

When Charlemagne died in 814, his empire quickly followed. His successors did not maintain the rigorous vision and progressive mindset of Charlemagne, and the empire soon fell.

JOSEPH PULITZER

One of the United State's most noted journalists, Joseph Pulitzer was born in Hungary in 1847. At the age of 17, when the Austrian Army turned him down because of his health, he enlisted in the US Union Army.

He served a year in the Lincoln Cavalry along with many other Germans. He later worked his way to St. Louis, where he spent much of his free time at the city's library. Two local newspaper editors often played chess at the library, and they and Pulitzer struck up a friendship.

He was soon offered a job with the German language newspaper Westliche Post. In 1872, Pulitzer was offered a controlling interest in the paper. Within six years, he was the owner of the St. Louis Post-Dispatch and on his way to becoming a household name.

The Pulitzer Prize

Joseph Pulitzer died in 1911, leaving $2,000,000 to Columbia University for the establishment of a School of Journalism. He specified that one-fourth of the money should go to prizes or scholarships to encourage quality journalism.

In the beginning, Pulitzer specified only four awards in journalism, four in letters and drama, one for education, and four traveling scholarships. However, he left room in his instructions for growth, and today, 90 years later, there are 21 Pulitzer Prizes, including poetry, music, and photography.

The Pulitzer Prizes are the nation's most prestigious and sought-after awards for journalism, letters, and music. The prizes remain a major incentive for high-quality journalism and have focused worldwide attention on American achievements.

- Each spring for 90 years, the president of Columbia University on the recommendation of the Pulitzer Prize board has announced the awards.
- The first African-American to be awarded a Pulitzer Prize was Gwendolyn Brooks, who was awarded the 1950 Pulitzer Prize in Poetry for "Annie Allen."

- John F. Kennedy was the only US President to be awarded a Pulitzer Prize. He received the Pulitzer Prize in Biography in 1957 for his book Profiles in Courage.

Putting the Prize in Pulitzer

Of the 21 Pulitzer categories, 20 include a $10,000 cash award and a certificate. The prize for the Public Service category of the Journalism competition is awarded to a newspaper and, therefore, is a gold medal.

Some Pulitzer Prize Categories
- Public Service
- Breaking News Reporting
- Investigative Reporting
- Explanatory Reporting
- Local Reporting
- Feature Photography
- National Reporting
- Commentary
- International Reporting
- Breaking News Photography
- Feature Writing
- Criticism
- Editorial Cartooning
- Editorial Writing

ARCHIMEDES

Born in Sicily in 287 BC, Archimedes studied in Egypt and Alexandria. He is well known for his principle of the lever, quoted as saying, "Give me a place to stand, and I will move the earth." He created many inventions that proved useful to the government during wartime. He invented the compound pulley and hydraulic screw, and he came up with countless mathematical theorems.

Archimedes's famous "Eureka" moment came when he discovered the concept of buoyancy. He found that a body immersed in fluid loses weight equal to the weight of the fluid it displaces. Today, this is known as the Archimedes' principle and is explained in depth in his book *On Floating Bodies*. (According to legend, Archimedes began thinking about hydrostatics when he stepped into his bathtub and noted the rise of the water. At this point, he is rumored to have exclaimed, "Eureka!")

EXTRA CREDIT: While studying in Alexandria, Archemedes found out that some of his friends were claiming his theories and ideas as their own. To retaliate, he sent them two false theories and watched, chuckling, as they espoused them as their own work.

The Archimedes Screw

Archimedes is famous for his principle of the lever and for inventing the compound pulley, but he also invented the hydraulic screw for raising water from a lower to higher level. The screws were first used selectively to pump water out of the bilge of ships. Today, they have many uses:

- Archimedes screws are used to lift water on the Shipwreck Rapids ride at SeaWorld in San Diego, California.
- A small Archimedes screw assists a pump system used to maintain a patient's blood circulation during coronary bypass surgery.
- Farmers even use Archimedes screws in their sprinkler systems to irrigate their fields!

WORLD LITERATURE 101
OSCAR WILDE

Oscar Fingal O'Flahertie Willis Wilde was an Irish writer born in 1854. He wrote many plays, poems, short stories, and even a novel. Well known for his quick wit and his flashy appearance, he always dressed in style and wore his hair long. His most famous play, *The Importance of Being Earnest* (1895) a witty comedy with a bit of gender-bending, is based on two characters who both pretend their name is Ernest to win the love of women. His only novel, *The Picture of Dorian Gray* (1891), is a gothic horror that touches on issues of homosexuality. The novel and Wilde's personal life led to his arrest, trial, and imprisonment in 1895 for the offense of "gross indecency," meaning homosexual practices.

Famous Words of Oscar Wilde

- I can believe anything, provided it is incredible.
- Consistency is the last refuge of the unimaginative.
- If you want to tell people the truth, make them laugh, otherwise they'll kill you.
- It is absurd to divide people into good and bad. People are either charming or tedious.
- Disobedience, in the eyes of anyone who has read history, is humanity's original virtue. It is through disobedience and rebellion that progress has been made.
- Selfishness is not living as one wishes to live; it is asking others to live as one wishes to live.
- Always forgive your enemies; nothing annoys them so much.
- I have the simplest tastes. I am always satisfied with the best.
- No man is rich enough to buy back his past.

THINKERS ON THINKERS

"A friend built a modern house and he suggested that Picasso, too, should have one built. But, said Picasso, of course not, I want an old house. Imagine, he said, if Michelangelo would have been pleased if someone had given him a fine piece of Renaissance furniture, not at all." —Gertrude Stein on Pablo Picasso

"His talent was as natural as the pattern that was made by the dust on a butterfly's wings. At one time he understood it no more than the butterfly did and he did not know when it was brushed or marred. Later he became conscious of his damaged wings and of their construction, and he learned to think and could not fly any more because the love of flight was gone and he could only remember when it had been effortless." —Ernest Hemingway on F. Scott Fitzgerald

"Dickens attacked English institutions with a ferocity that has never since been approached. Yet he managed to do it without making himself hated, and, more than this, the very people he attacked have swallowed him so completely that he has become a national institution himself." —George Orwell on Charles Dickens

"Shakespeare led a life of Allegory; his works are the comments on it." —John Keats on William Shakespeare

"Mr. Aldous Huxley, who is perhaps one of those people who have to perpetrate thirty bad novels before producing a good one, has a certain natural—but little developed—aptitude for seriousness." —T.S. Eliot on Aldous Huxley

"Nikola Tesla is proof that real greatness surpasses national borders and differences." —George W. Bush on Nikola Tesla

CHARLES DARWIN

Born in Shrewsbury, Shropshire, England, in 1809, Charles Darwin was the grandson of a china manufacture, and therefore grew up in a wealthy Victorian family. His paternal grandfather was Erasmus Darwin, a top intellectual and philosopher of his time in England. Darwin's family was well connected, socially and politically.

He enrolled at Edinburgh University to study medicine, but developed an interest in natural history and began to shirk his medical studies. After two years, Darwin's father was disappointed in his lack of interest in medicine and enrolled him in Cambridge University to study theology. Again, this time at Cambridge, he ignored his studies in theology in favor of science and naturalism; however, this time he graduated—tenth in his class—with a degree in theology. He married Emma Wedgwood, a cousin, in 1839. Together, they had ten children.

Fast Facts About Darwin

- Darwin began his work on his theory of evolution in 1836.

- At first, he reflected on two important environmental observations: 1) geologist Charles Lyell's theory that fossils found in rocks were from animals that had lived thousands or millions of years ago, and 2) the discovery of the dozens of types of finches found on the Galapagos Islands.

- He then expounded on the ideas of Thomas Malthus, who explored the struggle for existence and the idea of "survival of the fittest."

- After working for twenty years on his theory, Darwin and naturalist Alfred Wallace together proposed a theory of evolution occurring by the process of natural selection in 1858. The following year, *On the Origin of Species by Means of Natural Selection* was published.

- The theory of evolution has been controversial since the beginning of its formation, because of its conclusion that humans are simply evolved animals. Contrary to many religious teachings, Darwin's theory posits that humans might have developed from apes.

Darwin's Theory of Evolution

The Theory of Evolution seeks to explain the origin biology of man by linking humans to a timeline of evolving primates. The theory describes the evolution of man as follows:

- 70 million years ago—The first primates (mice-like shrews)
- 40 million years ago—Monkeys
- 20 million years ago—Apes
- 8 million years ago—Gorillas
- 5 million years ago—Chimpanzees
- 4 million years ago—Hominids (bipeds, or animals that walk on two feet)
- 300,000 years ago—Homo erectus
- 100,000 years ago—Homo sapiens

Darwin explained that once humans evolved into Homonids and walked on two feet, they began developing neurologically, becoming more and more intelligent through generations. He described the process as a system of natural selection, where the inherited traits of a population adapt from one generation to the next based on survival and reproductive efficiency.

Works of Charles Darwin

Darwin was an avid and highly published writer. His publication list includes:

The Voyage of the Beagle

The Origin of Species

The Descent of Man, and Selection in Relation to Sex

The Expression of Emotions in Man and Animals

The Power of Movement in Plants

The Formation of Vegetable Mould Through the Action of Worms

CRASH COURSE
RENÉ DESCARTES

- After studying law, philosophy, and theology as a young academic, René Descartes joined the military in 1618 and spent ten years traveling. He referred to his extensive travels as studying "the great book of the world."

- Descartes combined his philosophical ideas with the principles of mathematics and science, adhering to the belief that every single thing in nature could be explained by science and math.

- One of Descartes's major struggles was to create a set of principles that a person could understand as true with absolutely no doubt. Using methodological skepticism, rejecting any idea that could possibly be doubted, he came up with only one principle: that thought exists. From this principle comes the famous quotation, "I think, therefore I am."

- Descartes developed what is known as the Wax Argument while studying the principles of perception and deduction. He studied a piece of wax and noted its color, shape, and smell. He noticed that each feature changed completely when the wax was exposed to heat, but that it was still a piece of wax. From this study he asserted that only deduction—use of judgment, not perception—was reliable knowledge.

- Descartes believed the human body was in constant motion. However, he said that the mind was a nonmaterial entity and lacked any motion. In considering the relationship of the mind and body, Descartes believed in a form of dualism, positing that the mind controls the body, but that the body also influences the mind. This theory, like many of Descartes's ideas, was not readily accepted during his time but was later looked upon as noteworthy.

EXTRA CREDIT: Descartes's coordinate system ultimately enabled the development of GPS (Global Positioning System) instruments.

KURT VONNEGUT JR.

Kurt Vonnegut Jr. (1922–2007) was a groundbreaking writer and the author of fourteen novels and many short stories throughout his career. He grew up in Indiana and mentions it frequently in many of his works. He attended Cornell University until he was drafted for service in World War II.

Vonnegut's experience in the infantry during the Second World War was one of the greatest influences on his life and his writing. While behind enemy lines in Germany, Vonnegut was cut off from his 106th Infantry Division along with five other scouts and wandered for days until they all were captured. While a prisoner of war, Vonnegut was one of a few American prisoners to survive the firebombing of Dresden, which leveled the entire city. He survived, in part, due to the fact he was held prisoner in an underground meat locker beneath a slaughterhouse. The prisoners named the camp "Slaughterhouse Five," after the postal address of the administration building. (Later, this was to become the title for his most famous work). Vonnegut was freed by Russian troops in May 1945. When he returned to America, he was awarded a Purple Heart, which he would later attribute to his suffering from a case of "frostbite."

Slaughterhouse-Five, published in 1969, went on to appear on *TIME* magazine's list of 100 all-time best English-language novels written since 1923. In it, like many of his novels, Vonnegut explores ideas of fate, free will, and the illogical nature of the human race.

Vonnegut was described as a humanist, atheist, deist, and socialist. He was a lifelong critic of war, politics, society, social conventions, and humanity. He wrote, "If I should ever die, God forbid, let this be my epitaph: 'The only proof he needed—for the existence of God—was music.'"

EDWIN POWELL HUBBLE

- Born in 1889, Edwin Hubble held jobs teaching high school, practicing law, and serving a tour of duty in the military before turning to astronomy as a career. After military service, he studied at the Yerkes Observatory and received a doctorate in astronomy from the University of Chicago in 1917.

- In 1919, Hubble accepted what turned into a lifetime position at the Mount Wilson Observatory in California. There, he was given the task of photographing Cepheid variables using the new reflecting Hooker telescope. His resulting photographs proved that there are other galaxies very similar to our own Milky Way, a concept that had not been previously verified. This discovery expanded our understanding of the size of the universe—and our relative size to it!

- Hubble sorted the galaxies he observed by content, distance, shape, and brightness. This led to his observation of redshifts in the emission of light from the galaxies. (A redshift occurs when the frequency of the electromagnetic radiation, or light, emitted from an object shifts downward toward the red end of the spectrum, signifying that it is losing energy.)

- Hubble could tell that the galaxies were moving away from each other at a rate equivalent to the distance between them. The formula resulting from this observation is known as Hubble's Law. Using this formula, astronomers determined the age of the universe and also proved that the universe was continuously expanding.

- Hubble's observations led to the idea that if the expansion was coming from a central point, some force or event must have caused it. This idea is known as the Big Bang Theory.

Miniaturization

While working at Texas Instruments in 1958, Jack Kilby was asked to find ways to miniaturize electronic components. His bright idea was to use a semiconductor material, such as silicon, to make tiny electrical parts. He used tiny pieces of silicon to make a circuit in which all the components were integrated. By February 1959, he had an integrated circuit that he called a microchip.

As Kilby was working on his microchip, Robert Noyce was doing the same sort of thing at Fairchild Semiconductor. He patented his planar integrated circuit five months after Kilby came out with his chip.

Noyce's integrated circuit was the first to be produced commercially; however, Kilby was the first to patent his chip, so he is known as the inventor of the microchip, and Noyce is called the coinventor.

In 1967, Kilby invented the first handheld electronic calculator, and in 2000, he was awarded the Nobel Prize for Physics. The next year, Noyce cofounded the little manufacturing company known as Intel.

EXTRA CREDIT: The forest department of Kerala, India, has put microchips in sandalwood trees to protect them from illegal logging. Reportedly, trade in contraband sandalwood is one of the most lucrative in India.

WORLD LITERATURE 101

MARY WOLLSTONECRAFT

Mary Wollstonecraft (1759–1797) was a British writer and philosopher. She is best known for her book *A Vindication of the Rights of Woman* (1792) in which she argued that women are not inferior to men and only seemed as such at the time because they lacked the education men received. This idea was revolutionary and decidedly unpopular at the time she wrote it. Her work would go on to inspire such feminist thinkers and writers as Virginia Woolf, Simone de Beauvoir, and others.

Wollstonecraft married British philosopher William Godwin. During the birth of their first child, Wollstonecraft became ill and died. The child was Mary Shelley, who later wrote *Frankenstein*. After her death, Godwin published his book *Memoirs of the Author of A Vindication of the Rights of Woman* in which he spoke of his wife's life's intimate details. He described her love affairs and illegitimate children as well as writing about Wollstonecraft's attempts at suicide. The audience of the day was shocked, and the reception led to many people discrediting Wollstonecraft's writing because of their moral issues with her lifestyle.

Besides her seminal feminist work, she wrote a travel journal, several novels, a history of the French Revolution, and children's books. Her writing was usually nontraditional. She often argued against hereditary privilege and class hierarchy. Much of her work denounces monarchy as a form of government.

Sir Isaac Newton

Born on January 4, 1643, in Woolsthorpe, Lincolnshire, England, Isaac Newton was always a sickly child, and was therefore not allowed to play with other children throughout most of his childhood. In his loneliness, he occupied himself by taking up the hobby of toy making. He created a wooden clock, a sundial, and a mouse-powered mill.

At the age of nineteen, this already great thinker enrolled in Cambridge University in 1661. While there, he studied mathematics, optics, physics, and astronomy. He said the period when the school was closed because of the plague (1664–1666) was "the prime of my age for invention." During those eighteen months, he developed theories regarding gravity, light, and calculus, sketching ideas for countless inventions.

Newton's Work in Physics

He observed the refraction of light by a glass prism and developed a series of experiments that led him to the conclusion that white light is comprised of all the colored rays found in the rainbow. He said that light consisted of streams of minute particles.

His unconventional ideas were strongly rejected, causing Newton to delay the publication of *Opticks* for twelve years, until 1704, although the book was already written.

Newton constructed the first reflecting telescope in 1668. As he observed the stars, he wondered what held them in space and kept them from falling to the earth. This curiosity led him to develop the laws of motion and theory of gravitation. He could later predict the locations of stars and planets relative to the sun.

Who Gets Credit?

A large controversy surrounded the development of differential calculus, as Newton and Leibniz both claimed to have discovered the method independently. Newton had developed the idea early in his studies, but did not publish it until after Leibniz published his own findings. Leibniz claimed to have worked independently of knowledge of Newton's work. However, documents discovered after Leibniz's death indicate that the mathematician was aware of Newton's mathematical theories.

Newton's Honors and Awards

In 1696, Sir Isaac Newton became warden of the Royal Mint, and within three years he was appointed Master of the Mint. He maintained this office until his death.

He was elected a Fellow of the Royal Society of London in 1671, and in 1703 he became President of the Royal Society, annually reelected for the rest of his life.

He was knighted in Cambridge in 1705.

Although most of his theories were highly controversial early on, Newton became the most highly esteemed natural philosopher in Europe. For thirty years, while carrying out his official duties at the Royal Mint, Newton spent time revising his earlier works, studying ancient history, and responding to critics.

Isaac Newton died on March 31, 1727, and was buried in Westminster Abbey, the first scientist to be honored in such a way.

Newton's Laws of Motion

Law of inertia: Every object persists in its state of rest or uniform motion in a straight line unless it is compelled to change that state by forces impressed upon it.

Law of acceleration: Force is equal to the change in momentum (mV) per change in time. For a constant mass, force equals mass times acceleration, F = ma.

Law of action and reaction: For every action, there is an equal and opposite reaction.

JEAN PIAGET

Born in Neuchâtel, Switzerland, on August 9, 1896, Jean Piaget was considered a child prodigy for his early accomplishments. He studied psychology and psychoanalysis after growing up with a mother who had a neurotic personality and many mental problems. Piaget published his first scientific paper at age ten.

He learned to interview mental patients while analyzing the verbal reasoning processes of children. This study led to his focus in the field of inductive and experimental psychology.

Initially trained in biology and philosophy, Piaget considered himself a "genetic epistemologist" with his main interest in how people come to know things. He believed that the ability to reason was the key to knowledge.

Piaget's Theories in Child Development

The most critical factor in a child's development, according to Piaget, was interaction with peers. He said these interactions lead to cognitive conflicts that turn into arguing and debating. The conflict leads the child to look at the other person's point of view.

He identified four stages that all children go through in the same order, although some children go through the stages faster than others:

The Sensorimotor Period, from birth to age two, children are limited to the motor reflexes.

The Pre-Operational Period, from two to age six or seven, children start to use mental imagery and language.

The Concrete Operational Stage, from age six or seven to age eleven or twelve, children understand another person's point of view and can incorporate more than one perspective simultaneously. They can also grasp seven types of conservation: the conservation of number, liquid, length, mass, weight, area, and volume.

The Formal Operational Stage, from age eleven or twelve through adulthood, people are capable of thinking logically and abstractly as well as theoretically. Piaget believed that not everyone reaches this stage of development.

Pop Quiz #3

1) What theory did Pavlov develop?
    a) Theory of conditioning
    b) Theory of relativity
    c) String theory
    d) Chaos theory

2) What new form of music was created by nineteenth century Polish composer Frederic Chopin?
    a) The ballade
    b) Disco
    c) The polka

3) Jeremy Bentham helped found ________.

4) Physicist Galileo Galilei created sketches for a variety of indigenous ideas which include:
    a) An automatic tomato picker
    b) A combination of a comb and eating utensil
    c) A ballpoint pen
    d) All of the above

5) Portuguese explorer Ferdinand Magellan was actually sponsored by what country on his expedition around the globe?
    a) Africa
    b) Spain
    c) Russia
    d) China

6) What experience was one of the greatest influences on the life and writing of writing Kurt Vonnegut Jr.?
   a) His childhood growing up in Indiana
   b) His formal education
   c) His service in the infantry during WWII
   d) Stories told by his parents about their childhood

7) Evolutionary theorist Charles Darwin received his college degree in what subject?

8) Why did physicist Sir Isaac Newton delay the publication of the completed *Opticks* for twelve years?
   a) He couldn't find an editor
   b) His unconventional ideas were strongly rejected
   c) His mother did not understand its concepts
   d) Publishers continually rejected it

9) British writer and philosopher Mary Wollstonecraft became ill and died during the birth of her child __________ .
   a) Henry Wollstonecraft, architect and gate builder
   b) Charles Darwin, evolutionary theorist
   c) Mary Shelley, author of *Frankenstein*

10) Greek astronomer Hipparchus cataloged approximately how many stars?
   a) 700
   b) 800
   c) 850
   d) 950

ANSWERS:

1) a
2) a
3) utilitarianism
4) d
5) b
6) c
7) Theology
8) b
9) c
10) c

THOMAS HOBBES

Born in Malmesbury, Wiltshire, in 1588, Thomas Hobbes was the son of a clergyman who later became one of the most dominant English philosophers of the seventeenth century. Educated at Oxford, he became a tutor and spent a vast amount of time traveling through Europe. In his travels, he met many other great philosophers and thinkers, including Galileo and Rene Descartes.

Because of his Royalist views, in 1640 Hobbes left for Paris and remained there for more than ten years, afraid that the Parliament would react negatively to his writings. In 1640, he published what is now his best-known work, *Leviathan*. Within the work, Hobbes outlined his belief that the only way for man to overcome violence is to accept a central authority, communally. He argued for the monarchy as well as a state-controlled national religion, rejecting the Roman Catholic Church. These views made Hobbes unpopular and controversial to authorities, and in 1666, *Leviathan* was investigated for being atheist. Hobbes, in response, burned much of his writing to avoid the label of a heretic.

Before his death, Hobbes published an autobiography in Latin and also translated several major titles in the last few years of his life. He died in 1679, leaving behind a set of philosophical ideas that would be studied for centuries to come.

POLITICAL SCIENCE 101
KARL MARX

Though he never lived to see his ideas become influential, Karl Marx was one of the most recognized revolutionary thinkers in political philosophy to have ever lived. Born in Trier, Germany, Marx was the son of a successful lawyer and was raised in a well-to-do family.

He started out, like many children of lawyers, studying law. But he later switched to philosophy and received his Ph.D. from the University of Jena. Afterward, he and his wife moved to Paris, which at the time was a popular place for radical thinkers such as Marx. It was there that he became a radical Communist and befriended Friedrich Engels, with whom he would later publish much work.

The Communist Manifesto and Das Kapital

After a short time in Paris, Marx was expelled from France for his outspoken and controversial political views and writings. He moved on to Brussells, where he coauthored *The Communist Manifesto* with Engels. The book outlined the most commonly known belief of Marx—that the end of class struggle would come with the rise of the proletariat, or lower classes.

Marx left Brussells for London in 1849 and spent the rest of his life there, publishing his most famous work, *Das Kapital*. From that point, Marx's health declined and he suffered slowly both physically and emotionally from the death of his wife and daughter. He died in 1883 in London, laid to rest in Highgate Cemetery.

THE NATIONAL WOMEN'S HALL OF FAME

Founded in 1969, the National Women's Hall of Fame honors the achievements of American women. Women are chosen to be included in the Hall of Fame for their contributions to society, art, athletics, business, science, education, government, and more. Many female great thinkers have been included in the National Women's Hall of Fame, including:

Abigail Adams: first lady, 1744–1818

Madeleine Korbel Albright: first female Secretary of State

Louisa May Alcott: author of Little Women and other American novels

Susan B. Anthony: major leader of the women's suffrage movement

Clara Barton: organizer of the American Red Cross

Hillary Rodham Clinton: American lawyer and political figure, Democratic senator of New York, former first lady

Dorothy Day: journalist and cofounder of the Catholic Worker Movement

Emily Dickinson: American poet

Amelia Earhart: aviator and first woman to cross the Atlantic by plane

Helen Keller: American author and leader of the blind, deaf, and dumb

Maya Lin: Chinese: American architect and sculptor

Anne Sullivan Macy: teacher and friend to Hellen Keller

Margaret Mead: writer, speaker, and anthropologist, influential in mental health

Sally Ride: astronaut and astrophysicist, the first American woman ever in space

Eleanor Roosevelt: humanitarian and first lady, 1933–1945

Sacagawea: Native American guide to Lewis and Clark

Six Degrees to Frankenstein

1. Elle Macpherson starred in the 1996 film adaptation of Charlotte Brontë's novel *Jane Eyre*. Charlotte Brontë (1816–1855) was a British, Victorian novelist. She initially wrote in secret and under a pen name to avoid the negative reception women writers received at the time. In *Jane Eyre*, she touches on issues of hierarchical class structure and patriarchy.

2. Charlotte Brontë was one of the first famous female writers concurrently with Elizabeth Barrett Browning. Barrett Browning (1806–1861) was a popular Victorian poet but was forced to write in secrecy for much of her life. Her famous poem "Aurora Leigh" broke with tradition by featuring a heroine instead of a hero.

3. Elizabeth Barrett secretly married Robert Browning (1812–1889), an English poet best known for *The Ring and the Book* (1869), a long, blank-verse tragedy based on historical events. He's one of the foremost poets of the Victorian age.

4. Robert Browning mimicked the poetic style of Percy Shelley. Shelley (1792–1822) was an English lyric poet writing during the period of Romanticism. His most famous poems include "Ozymandias," "To a Skylark," "The Masque of Anarchy," and "Ode to the West Wind." Much of his poetry is about beauty, love, and imagination and is sometimes political. He drowned (at just thirty years old!) during a boating accident.

5. Percy Shelley married Mary Shelley. Mary Shelley (1797–1851) was a British writer. She wrote *Frankenstein; or, the Modern Prometheus* (1818). It's a Gothic novel in which Shelley attempted to warn against the potential danger she saw in the progress and technological growth happening during the Industrial Revolution. Much of her writing had smart but subtle political criticism at its heart.

6. Mary Shelley created *Frankenstein*!

Dmitri Mendeleev

Born in Tobolsk, Siberia, on February 8, 1834, Dmitri Mendeleev entered the Main Pedagogical Institute in St. Petersburg in 1850. Although he was sick for the last year of his undergraduate study, he received his diploma, still ranking number one in his class, in 1854. He then moved for a short time to the Crimean Peninsula to improve his health. He returned to St. Petersburg and received his master's degree in 1856 and a Ph.D. in 1866. He married twice and had six children.

Between 1859 and 1861, he spent time studying in other countries. He observed the density of gases in Paris, and the workings of the spectroscope in Heidelberg.

Mendeleev was considered one of the greatest teachers of his time. He became professor of chemistry at the St. Petersburg Technological Institute in 1863, and in 1867, he was named Professor of Chemistry at the University of St. Petersburg. In 1868, he wrote what was called the definitive two-volume textbook of the time—*Principles of Chemistry.*

He often spent time with people of the working class, drinking tea and discussing his research as it related to agriculture or other areas of interest to them. His dedication to chemistry, and his popularity with colleagues, students, and the general public, transformed St. Petersburg into an internationally recognized center for chemistry research.

Mendeleev is most remembered for classifying chemical elements into the Periodic Table, which he called the Periodic System. Unknown to him at the time, John Newlands, Lothar Meyer, and other scientists were attempting to do the same thing. In the end, Mendeleev's table included more elements and was more practical to use.

As the story goes, Mendeleev wrote the properties of the 63 known elements on pieces of paper and tried organizing them in various ways. He suddenly realized that, by arranging the elements in order of increasing atomic weight, certain types of elements regularly occurred. He left space for new elements, three yet-to-be-discovered elements, and pointed out accepted atomic weights that were in error.

The original table has been modified and corrected several times through the years. There are now more than 100 known elements.

Things to Know

- In 1893, as director of the Bureau of Weights and Measures, Mendeleev used his knowledge of molecular weights to conclude that, to be in perfect molecular balance, vodka should have one molecule of ethyl alcohol diluted with two molecules of water, or approximately 38 percent alcohol to 62 percent water. He established by Russian law that all vodka had to be produced at 40 percent alcohol by volume.

- Mendeleev investigated the composition of oil fields and helped establish the first oil refinery in Russia.

- A lunar crater and element 101, radioactive mendeleevium, are named in honor of Mendeleev.

- Dmitri Mendeleev died from influenza in 1907 in St. Petersburg, Russia.

The Making of the Periodic Chart

As recorded history tells, Mendeleev wrote the properties of the sixty-three known elements of his time on pieces of paper and attempted to organize them in different ways. He suddenly realized that by arranging the elements in order of their atomic weight that certain types of elements regularly occurred. He left space in the chart for new elements to be added.

The original table has been modified and corrected several times through the years. It now includes more than one hundred known elements.

The Remarkable Life of Ludwig van Beethoven

Beethoven, like Bach, was from Germany, but came later—Beethoven was born two decades after Bach passed away. He was a great composer but also a famed pianist, despite a tragic hearing loss that plagued him most of his adult life. Even after going completely deaf Beethoven continued to compose and take the stage to perform his brilliant masterpieces.

His first music teacher was his own father—and a strict one at that. Eventually dear ol' dad asked a friend to help teach his son, and the training and drinking duo would sometimes arrive home after a night of boozing, deciding then was the perfect practice time. They'd pull poor Beethoven out of bed and make him hit the keys 'til morning.

But practice paid off. By age eight, Beethoven was studying not only the piano, but organ and viola. By then, his most important teacher was no longer Pops, but Christian Gottlob Neefe, the court's organist and the man who would help Beethoven publish his first composition (a collection of keyboard variations).

Beethoven's travels began in the late 1780s, with a trip to Vienna. He was excited—who wouldn't be?—to study with the prominent Wolfgang Amadeus Mozart. He might have, but he may not have (no one knows for sure), because two weeks later Beethoven's mother became sick with tuberculosis. She didn't live much longer. Beethoven was just sixteen, now motherless, with a father whose alcohol addiction was growing worse by the day. Essentially he took over as dad for his two younger brothers.

In 1792, Beethoven decided to go back to Vienna, this time for more than travels. He moved there, and began learning from Joseph Haydn (the next best thing, since Mozart had died the previous year). Beethoven quickly became a piano virtuoso and began producing his first opus pieces.

Many pre-Beethoven composers got their paychecks from a church or a noble court. Beethoven, however, opted for different career paths, living off of income or gifts from the aristocracy, concerts and lessons, and profits from his works. That didn't last, though, and soon Beethoven was in debt.

About to leave Vienna, he was offered a chapel maestro gig, this time at the court of Jerome Bonaparte, the king of Westphalia. It was 1808, and Beethoven stayed put in Vienna.

By this time, Beethoven's hearing was really waning. At the very leas, he had an annoying nonstop ringing in his ears. The cause: tinnitus. It affected him greatly—at times he'd even avoid talking to people. And sometimes, in remembering his deafness, he would become overwrought with emotion. One legend captures it well: imagine Beethoven, standing there at the end of his Ninth Symphony. There's a thunderous applause, but he cannot hear it. Someone moves him around so he can see the audience, and when he grasps what is happening, he cries.

By 1814 Beethoven had become totally deaf. He began using a special rod connected to the soundboard on a piano. He would bite down on it and the vibrations transferred from the piano to his jaw would increase his perception of the sound.

The Beethoven House Museum in Bonn houses a collection of Beethoven's hearing aids.

Because Beethoven was deaf, his unique "conversation books" are considered a priceless piece of history. His buddies wrote in these books so Beethoven could understand what they were saying. Beethoven would respond by talking, or writing in the book. So what did they "talk" about? Music, of course, but other subjects as well.

Histories usually divide Beethoven's career into three periods: early (up 'til about 1802), middle (1803–1814) and late (1815 on). During his early years, he mostly emulated Haydn, Mozart, and his other idols. His middle period began just after he started to lose his hearing and is known for larger scale, famous works that express heroism and struggle. His late romantic period is noted for more depth and intense personal expression.

Beethoven grew very sick for several years before he died in 1827. He was just fifty-six when he died, apparently of lead poisoning. He had thought about suicide, and often was edgy. His moods could have been caused by chronic abdominal pain that he suffered from beginning in his twenties—also attributed to his lead poisoning.

Beethoven apparently liked the "chase" when it came to women. He usually went after those who were married or out of his league (aristocratic). He never married.

The Custody Battle

A rather nasty side of Beethoven came out thanks to the death of his brother in 1815. Karl van Beethoven, who died of tuberculosis, left behind a nine-year-old son, Karl. Beethoven really didn't want much to do with the nephew while his brother had been alive, but suddenly he became obsessed. A lengthy custody battle ensued between Beethoven and Karl's mom, Johanna. The fight even resulted in Beethoven taking a break in composing.

A little fib having to do with his name allowed Beethoven to have his case tried in nobility court (versus the court for "commoners), and Beethoven got sole guardianship of the kid. But, oops: Beethoven slipped up in court, so the case was transferred to the "common court." On December 18, 1818, he then lost sole guardianship.

But the drama continued. Beethoven appealed, regaining custody. Johanna, in turn, appealed but lost.

And finally, in 1826, Karl got the last word, apparently sick of the whole thing—his uncle included. He tried to shoot himself in the head. He lived, and chose to move in with Mom again.

Beethoven is a 1992 funny movie about a St. Bernard dog named after the composer and owned by the Newton family. The movie, directed by Brian Levant and written by John Hughes and Amy Holden Jones, stars Charles Grodin, Bonnie Hunt, Nicholle Tom, Christopher Castile, Sarah Rose Karr and Dean Jones.

NIJINSKY

It seems Vaslav Nijinsky was destined for the stage. Both his parents were dancers, performing throughout the Russian Empire with their own dance company. And like Nijinsky, his father also was particularly famous for his enormous leaps.

Nijinsky was born in Kiev in 1890 and grew up dancing with his brother and sister, getting his first lessons from Dad. When he graduated from school in 1907, he joined the Mariinsky Theatre as a soloist. The public and critics raved over his first performances in La Source.

Just two years later, Sergey Diaghilev, former assistant to the administrator of the Imperial Theatres, was asked by the grand duke Vladimir to establish a ballet company of the members of the Mariinsky and Bolshoi theatres. Diaghilev asked Nijinsky to be principal dancer. Crowds went wild for the first performance at the Théâtre du Chatelet. Nijinsky seemed to be feather light despite his intensity and was able to perform gravity-defying leaps.

In 1912, Nijinsky began to choreograph, and created several ballets, including one, Till Eulenspiegel, that was produced in the United States.

Just seven years later, however, at the age of twenty-nine, Nijinsky was diagnosed with schizophrenia after having a nervous breakdown. Nijinsky's Diary was written during the six weeks he spent in Switzerland before being committed to an asylum. He then lived in various spots in Europe until his death in London in 1950.

EXTRA CREDIT: The race horse Nijinsky II (1967–1992), was named after the dancer.

Nijinsky's *Diary* is included in author Henry Miller's list *The Hundred Books that Influenced Me Most*.

FRIEDRICH NIETZSCHE

As a philosopher, Nietzsche was controversial for challenging the foundations of traditional morality and Christianity. He famously introduced the idea that "God is dead," and identified the difference between *master* and *slave* moralities—the former celebrating life, the latter resenting those who celebrate. This distinction is in essence "good and bad" vs. "good and evil."

A frequently recurring theme in Nietzsche's work is the "will to power," which links to his concept of *Übermensch* (translated as *superman* or *superhuman*). Nietzsche claimed the *Übermensch* as a goal that humanity can achieve for itself or that an individual can set for himself.

Nietzsche's Published Works

In 1872, Nietzsche published his first book, *The Birth of Tragedy out of the Spirit of Music*. His colleagues expressed little enthusiasm and approval over the work, and Nietzsche began to feel isolated within the academic community.

Beginning with *Human, All Too Human* in 1878, Nietzsche published nearly one book (or major section of a book) every year for the following ten years. In 1888, he completed six entire books.

The Gay Science was published in 1882, followed by *Thus Spoke Zarathustra*, which he wrote in only ten days. His writing and philosophy became even more unusual and narrowly accepted. In 1885, he printed only forty copies of the fourth part of *Zarathustra*, giving a few copies to close friends.

He self-published *Beyond Good and Evil* and revised some of his earlier works. *Twilight of the Idols* and *The Antichrist* were both written in 1888. On his forty-fourth birthday, he began the autobiography *Ecce Homo*.

Timeline

Dr. Martin Luther King Jr.

1929: The birth of Dr. King. Martin Luther King Jr. was born in Atlanta, Georgia. His mother was a teacher, his father a Baptist minister.

1948: King received a bachelor's degree from Morehouse College. His degree was in sociology, and he was only nineteen years old when he graduated.

1951: King receives another degree, this time in theology, from Crozer Theological Seminary in Pennsylvania. He goes on to enroll in a Ph.D. program

1953: Dr. King marries Coretta Scott, a student of the New England Conservatory.

1954: Dr. King becomes a Baptist minister in Montgomery, Alabama, at the Dexter Avenue Baptist Church.

1955: He organizes the Mongomery boycott of buses to fight segretation. The following year, his house is bombed. The U.S. Supreme Court rules in favor of the desegregation of buses.

1960: King moves to Atlanta to become a pastor at Ebenezer Baptist Church. He preaches alongside his father.

1963: Dr. King is thrown in jail for a segregation protest in Birmingham, Alabama. It is during this year that he delivers his famous *I Have a Dream* speech at the March on Washington. More than 200,000 protestors listen to Dr. King speak about civil rights.

1964: The Civil Rights Act of 1964 is passed. Dr. King receives a Nobel Peace Prize.

Between 1965 and 1967: Dr. King begins speaking on economics and politics, and he advances the Civil Rights Movement further north. He begins the Poor People's Campaign, publishing several essays on discrimination in the black community.

1968: Dr. Martin Luther King Jr. is assassinated during a strike in Memphis.

1969: James Earl Ray pleads guilty to the murder and receives a ninety-nine-year sentence in prison.

1986: A national holiday is created to celebrate Martin Luther King.

Left Handed Leaders

- Charlemagne – early medieval Frankish king
- Napoléon Bonaparte – first consul of the French
- Fidel Castro – Cuban political leader
- Julius Caesar – dictator of the Roman Republic
- Alexander the Great
- Joan of Arc
- King George II of England
- Tiberius – ancient Roman emperor

Economics 101
Adam Smith

It's rare to think of the economy without Adam Smith coming to mind. Known for his philosophy and writing on the economy of the West, Smith made a lasting footprint with his famous work, *The Wealth of Nations*, a text still used today to explain the trends of supply and demand.

Adam Smith's Principles of Economics

- Smith pointed out the division of labor and proposed the idea of labor expenditure's affect on the value of a material good.

- Influenced by Hume and other philosophers, Smith believed that a *laissez-faire* economy, or one run solely by the demands of the market, was the best form of economy. In other words, he believed in very limited governmental interference in economics.

- Along the line of thinking closely related to libertarianism today, Smith believed that self interest would bring about welfare to society, and that the market would regulate itself entirely.

- Though he was opposed to governmental intervention, Smith admitted that certain policies were necessary, including those that regulated trade and kept large companies from forming monopolies in certain industries to push competition down to an unfair level.

- Many of Smith's theories became void at the onset of the Industrial Revolution, but most have been revisited since; his theories on supply and demand rendered timelessly rational.

IMMANUEL KANT

Born in early 1724, Immanuel Kant was one of the most prominent metaphysicians of philosophy. A German, he became a professor of logic and philosophy and soon became well known around the globe for his writings on the subject of metaphysics.

Kant was reportedly awakened by the writings of David Hume and began to follow the belief that everything must be proven by experience, rather than assumed to be true. He believed that things could be assumed to exist without being understood, such as phenomena outside the realm of human understanding. He believed that any attempts to understand "things in themselves" would ultimately fail, that humans could only understand things within their own realm of experience.

Kant's Categorical Imperative

"Act as if the maxim from which you act were it to become through your will a universal law." (In other words, any action deemed ethical or moral must have the characteristic of being moral or ethical when universally applied.)

Kant's theories are known to have been the catalyst of the school of thought known as German idealism, a wave producing philosophers such as J. G. Fichte, F.W. Schelling, and G.W.F. Hegel.

The Copernican Revolution

One of Kant's major contributions to western philosophy was his Copernican Revolution, a philosophy that states that a representation makes an object possible, rather than vice versa. (*Huh?!*) Simply put, Kant believed that the human mind created experience rather than passively received it. All things must be processed by the mind to be "anything," proposed Kant.

WASSILY KANDINSKY

Like a lot of artists in earlier times, Wassily Kandinsky ditched law for the arts, but something made him different. He waited until he was thirty to take the plunge.

It was 1896 and he applied to an art school in Munich. Kandinsky, who is credited with painting the first modern abstract works, was not immediately granted admission in Munich and began learning art on his own.

Kandinsky taught at the Bauhaus school of art and architecture from 1922 until the Nazis shut it down in 1933. He then packed his bags and moved to France where he lived the rest of his life, becoming a French citizen in 1939 and dying there five years post-citizenship.

Sometime later in life, Kandinsky would recall being enthralled by color when he was a kid. One of the most important of his paintings from the 1900s was *The Blue Rider,* which depicts a small cloaked figure on a horse rushing through a rocky meadow. The rider's coat is a medium blue while its shadow is a darker blue. In the forefront are more formless blue shadows. The Blue Rider in the painting is prominent, but formless. The rider is more a series of colors, not specific details.

Along with painting, Kandinsky helped establish the New Artists' Association, which he headed in 1909. He later formed a new group, appropriately named The Blue Rider after his painting. The group held a couple of shows and created *The Blue Rider* Almanac, which supported abstract art.

EXTRA CREDIT: In 1921 Kandinsky was invited to teach at the Bauhaus of Weimar architecture school in Germany. When this pioneering school closed in 1933, Kandinsky left Germany and planted himself in Paris. In 1936 and 1939 Kandinsky produced his last two most important works, both painted on canvas: Composition IX and Composition X.

FAMOUS FEMALE INVENTORS

Sarah Breedlove Walker: An orphan at seven, Walker invented dozens of hair lotions, creams, and cosmetic utensils, mostly for black women. She created the Walker System, a brand of cosmetics, schools, and licensed cosmeticians. This provided employment to thousands of black women in the United States and made Walker the very first female American self-made millionaire.

Ann Moore: A Peace Corps volunteer, Moore created a baby carrier known as the SNUGLI after watching many African women carry babies on their backs using tied cloth. She observed how their hands were free to work with the baby "snugly" strapped to their backs. She later invented a system of portable oxygen tanks that improved movement for patients, as well as a line of lightweight bags and backpacks.

Bette Graham: A quite messy and inaccurate typist, Graham came up with an invention that could cover her own mistakes—Liquid Paper! She first prepared the concoction in her own kitchen, mixing it by hand. Graham and her son poured the recipe into small bottles and presented them to companies. By 1980, the Liquid Paper Corporation was sold for more than $45 million.

Gertrude B. Elion: A scientiest and 1988 Nobel laureate in the field of medicine, Elion created two of the first viable drugs to treat leukemia. She also created the drugs Imuran (which prevents the rejection of kidney transplants) and Zovirax (which acts against the herpes virus infection). She was the first woman to ever be inducted into the National Inventors Hall of Fame.

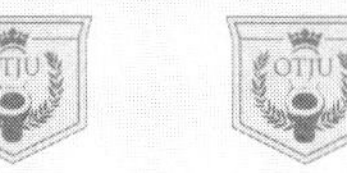

Timeline
Peter the Great

Peter the Great ruled Russia, of course, but did you know that along with his power he also was nearly six-feet-seven-inches tall? He also, as part of his attempts to turn Russia more Western Euro, imposed a tax on men who would not shave their beards. Here's a snapshot in time of the great Russian ruler's life:

1682: Born to Aleksis I, he succeeded to the throne when his half-brother, Fyodor III, died.

1682–1689: Almost immediately after he became tsar, Peter's half-sister Sofia instigated a rebellion and removed Peter from government affairs while she ruled as regent.

1689: Peter assumed leadership of Russia but left most political affairs to his mother, Natalia Naryshkin, until she died in 1694.

Early 1690s: Peter spent a lot of time in the walled foreign quarter of Moscow, learning foreign languages and details of life outside Russia.

1695: He declared war against the Ottoman Empire, and grew determined to modernize Russian forces after early defeats demonstrated Russia's military inadequacy.

1697: He toured European countries—with his Grand Embassy delegation—gathering knowledge and in a sense collecting more than 750 foreign experts from various fields, which he brought back to Russia.

1698: Peter ordered the execution of more than one thousand Russian soldiers who had plotted to overthrow him while he was gone touring.

1700: he declared the Great Northern War against Sweden and, after early defeats, modernized the Russian military.

1721: Peter defeated Sweden and gained the Baltic coastline in the Treaty of Nystad, expanding territory to the Baltic Sea and smoothing the progress of sea access to Europe.

1721: Pere was given the titles of Great and Emperor, suggesting Russia's emergence as a European power.

EXTRA CREDIT: In the 1930s, Alexey Nikolayevich Tolstoy wrote a biographical historical novel about Peter, named Petr I, which, along with its adaptations, influenced many subsequent Peter portrayals.

Linus Carl Pauling

Linus Carl Pauling is known as the father of molecular biology. Born in Portland, Oregon, on February 28, at the turn of the twentieth century, he received his Ph.D. in chemistry in 1925.

Pauling used theoretical physics—quantum theory and quantum mechanics—to study chemical bonding. Teaming with other scientists, Pauling published the structures of hundreds of inorganic substances, including topaz and mica. He then went on to make significant discoveries in genetic diseases, hematology, immunology, brain function and psychiatry, molecular evolution, nutritional therapy, diagnostic technology, statistical epidemiology, and biomedicine. *Whew!*

Pauling was gifted in explaining the most complex scientific principles in understandable language. This endeared him to the general public. He wrote a variety of articles and books for the mainstream audience including *Vitamin C and the Common Cold, Cancer and Vitamin C* (with Ewan Cameron, M.D.), and *How to Live Longer and Feel Better.* He was also a popular speaker for conferences.

Pauling is the only person to receive two unshared Nobel Prizes. He was awarded the Nobel Prize for Chemistry in 1954, and in 1962 he received the Nobel Peace Prize for his role in the signing of the Partial Test Ban Treaty, calling for the reduction of aboveground nuclear testing, which was proven to cause risk to public health.

Among his other numerous awards is the American Chemical Society Award in Pure Chemistry; Pauling became the first recipient of the award in 1931. President Harry Truman presented the Presidential Medal for Merit to Pauling in 1948, acknowledging the scientist's contributions in support of the military during World War II. And, he was named one of the twenty greatest scientists of all time by the British magazine *New Scientist.*

ACCOMPLISHMENTS OF PAULILNG

In the mid-1930s, Pauling studied the molecular structure of biological compounds known as proteins. This interest expanded to the magnetic properties of hemoglobin and the roles of antigens and antibodies in the immune response. He began experimenting with the orientation of iron atoms and the structure of crystals, developing what is called the "Pauling Rules" that govern ionic or covalent bonding.

In 1945, a physician describing sickle cell anemia sent Pauling to the drawing board—or lab bench. After three years of study, he identified the disease as molecular in origin, caused by a genetically transmitted abnormality in the hemoglobin molecule. This new concept of molecular disease launched a search for similar disorders and has become the main focus of human genome research.

Working with proteins, Pauling discovered that the polypeptide chain, formed from sequences of amino acids, would coil into a particular helical structure. He called this the alpha helix.

On top of being a famed molecular biologist, Pauling was also an inventor. During World War II, he invented a meter to monitor oxygen levels in submarines and airplanes. The device has proved invaluable in maintaining safe levels of oxygen for infants in incubators and for surgery patients under anesthesia.

The Nature of the Chemical Bond, called the most influential scientific book of the twentieth century, was first published by Pauling in 1939. The book, in its third edition, is still in publication today. It has been translated into many languages.

Linus Pauling and The Electric Car

Linus Pauling was instrumental in developing the first speed-controlled electric car. In the 1950s, Pauling proved that smog was a product of automobile emissions instead of chemical plant emissions, as was generally thought. He then teamed with engineers at Eureka Williams company to build a battery-powered car. Unfortunately, battery power was not strong enough to compete with gasoline power.

OSCAR WILDE

Mix successful playwrighting with a famous trial, throw in a couple years of prison time and lots of sexual rumors, and you get none other than Oscar Wilde, a true celebrity of his time. His masterpieces, the comic *Lady Windermere's Fan* (1892) and *The Importance of Being Earnest* (1895), were accompanied by his only novel *The Picture of Dorian Gray* (1891) and his fairy tales, especially *The Happy Prince.*

Wilde was raised in Dublin by his writer mother and eye-and-ear-doctor father, who also happened to write and was a renowned philanthropist. In college (1871 to 1874) Wilde studied classics and won the Berkeley Gold Medal—you couldn't go any higher as a classics student at Trinity College. A scholarship to Magdalen College in Oxford furthered his studies 'til 1878 and welcomed him to the Aesthetic movement.

Wilde then went back to Dublin, where he fell in love with Florence Balcombe. She did not return the favor, however, and instead became engaged to Bram Stoker—you know: the guy who wrote *Dracula.* When he heard of her other love, Wilde wrote to her, sort of threatening to leave Ireland for good. Apparently she was OK with that, because he did just that in 1878. He only returned twice, briefly. The next six years he spent in London, Paris, and the United States, where he mainly lectured.

In London he met Constance Lloyd, daughter of Queen's Counsel Horace Lloyd. Then she visited Dublin in 1884 when Oscar was there lecturing. He proposed and they married in May that same year in Paddington, London. It was a pretty sweet deal for Oscar—love and money. Constance had an allowance from her wealthy parents, which allowed the Wildes to live in the lap of luxury. The couple had two sons.

After Oscar's downfall—more on that in a bit—Constance took the surname Holland for herself and the boys. She died in 1898 following spinal surgery.

While at Magdalen College, Wilde's eccentricity really started to kick in, particularly with his appearance. He let his hair grow out, scorning so-called "manly" sports, and began decorating his rooms with peacock feathers and flowers. He called it "aesthetic values," and in

1879 back in London, Wilde started to teach this so-called aesthetic movement and actually became the leading aesthete in Britain.

Wilde worked as a reviewer for the *Pall Mall Gazette* from 1887 to 1889 and then became editor of *Woman's World.*

But back to his personal life: although living the "family life," he was often the subject of rumors, including countless affairs with young men. A few years earlier he had met Lord Alfred Douglas, an athlete and a poet, who became the love of Wilde's life—and yes, this is where the downfall part comes in.

Wilde's years of triumph ended dramatically when his association with Douglas resulted in charges of homosexuality—then illegal in Britain—and a court trial. He was sentenced to two years of hard labor for sodomy. Wilde spent time in Wandsworth prison in London, and then in Reading Gaol. During this time he wrote *De Profundis* (1905), a dramatic monologue and autobiography, which was addressed to Douglas.

After his release in 1897, Wilde wrote *The Ballad of Reading Gaol,* divulging his concern for inhumane prison conditions. He died of cerebral meningitis in November 1900, completely broke, in an unremarkable Paris hotel. He was only forty-six.

JOHN STUART MILL

John Stuart Mill, an economist and philosopher, began his journey into academia on an unlikely path. Initially he abandoned academics by dropping out of law school and becoming a salesman for the East India Trading Company. During this time, he was an avid writer and continuously published articles and met with other philosophers. He began to publish around 1843 with his work, *A System of Logic.*

Mill's work was heavily followed and influenced British thought of the period. In 1859, a year after the death of his beloved wife, Mill published his famous *On Liberty*, dedicating it to his late wife. In the decade to follow, he served in the British Parliament and published several more works.

A theme of humanitarianism began to appear in his work, combining empiricism and rationality with empathy for the human race. Many thought his work bordered on socialism.

Toward the later part of his life, Mill supported the Union in the American Civil war and spoke out adamantly in favor of labor organizations and utilitarianism. His philosophy continued to shape Western thought long after his death, in the fields of law, politics, economics, and moral philosophy.

Famous Works of John Stuart Mill

On Liberty, 1859
Utilitarianism, 1863
Auguste Comte and Positivism, 1865

LUCRETIUS

Born c. 99 BC, Titus Lucretius Carus was a famous Roman wordsmith who left little knowledge behind of his short life. He wrote, during his short forty-four year lifespan, many books that were passed to Cicero, who edited them.

Lucretius's poetry can be found in a giant collection of six books, known as *De Rerum Natura*, meaning "on the nature of things." His poetry was philosophical and driven by the ideas of both Epicurus and Democritus. Lucretius believed that man ought not fear the gods, since he felt men were in charge of their own destinies. He believed that everything, including the soul, was made of atoms, and so nature controlled all things—even the soul.

EXTRA CREDIT: During the first century BC, Lucretius created an epic poem in Latin on the subject of atomic theory. The epic poem was written in hexameters and became one of the most famous works of Western literature. Of course, during his lifetime, the work was dismissed. We know little about Lucretius, and Lucretius probably knew little about the fame that he would achieve posthumously!

Famous Words of Lucretius

- And life is given to none freehold, but it is leasehold for all.
- Constant dripping hollows out a stone.
- From the heart of the fountain of delight rises a jet of bitterness that tortures us among the very flowers.
- From the very fountain of enchantment there arises a taste of bitterness to spread anguish amongst the flowers.
- In the midst of the fountain of wit there arises something bitter, which stings in the very flowers.
- It is great wealth to a soul to live frugally with a contented mind.
- Life is one long struggle in the dark.

Vasco Núñez de Balboa

Vasco Núñez de Balboa was the Spanish explorer who crossed the Isthmus of Panama to the Pacific Ocean in 1513—the first European to see the Pacific via the New World. Balboa, born in Jerez de los Caballeros, Spain, in 1475, was a descendant of the lords of the castle of Balboa.

In 1500, Balboa had sailed from Spain to Colombia, South America, looking for pearls, gold, and other riches along the northern coast of South America. In Hispaniola he and his shipmates had to abandon ship—it was leaking. He tried to farm for a living, but that didn't work out: his plantation was deep in debt. So in 1510, Balboa and his dog stashed away on a relief boat heading to San Sebastian on the coast of Colombia.

After discovering San Sebastian burned to the ground by Native Americans, Balboa decided to travel southwest to a spot he'd seen on an earlier expedition. In 1511, he founded the first European settlement in South America, the town of Santa Maria de la Antigua del Darien. Balboa was elected governor and used diplomacy—not force—when working with the natives.

Balboa married the daughter a local Indian chief and in 1513 he sailed with hundreds of Spaniards and Indians across the Gulf of Uraba to the Darien Peninsula. Balboa left overland, leading an expedition west through dense rainforest. They fought off local Indians along the way, destroying an Indian village and killing hundreds of natiaves. Balboa, still accompanied by his trusty dog, was the first European to reach the eastern part of the Pacific Ocean.

Balboa and his men then journeyed to the ocean and claimed it and all the land that touched it for Spain. They spent about a month along the Pacific coast, stealing native gold along the way. All the excitement quickly ended, however, when Balboa was charged with treason against Spain—he was framed by a former friend who was jealous of Balboa's successes and was able to turn the king against him. Balboa was found guilty and publicly beheaded in Acla in 1519.

WORLD HISTORY 101
ALEXANDER THE GREAT

Alexander the Great was thrust into power at a mere twenty years old, when his father was assassinated, Yet he rose to become a fierce warrior and one of the greatest leaders of all time as the ruler of the Macedonians. He had no one to tell him what to do when he was left in charge of all of Macedon, a section of the northern part of Greece about the size of New York State.

Alexander's father was King Philip II and his mother was Olympias, a very spiritual woman. Olympias told Alexander that he was a descendant of Achilles and Hercules, so it is thought that from a very early age, he believed he was destined for glory and focused on becoming a great ruler.

When he was a teenager Alexander studied under the great Greek philosopher Aristotle, learning philosophy, medicine, and science. Aristotle also cultivated Alexander's interest in reading and learning.

Alexander's biggest enemy during his reign was King Darius III of Persia. In 336 BC, Darius was put on the throne for the sole purpose of defeating Alexander and the Macedonians. He spent six years on the throne trying to defeat the Macedonians. But Alexander was too much for Darius.

Alexander died in 323 BC at the age of thirty-two. Some historians believe that he died after eating salmonella typhi, a type of bacteria that leads to typhoid. Others believe he was poisoned.

Famous Words of Alexander the Great

- There is nothing impossible to him who will try.
- I would rather excel others in the knowledge of what is excellent than in the extent of my powers and dominion.
- Heaven cannot brook two suns, nor earth two masters.
- Remember upon the conduct of each depends the fate of all.
- I am indebted to my father for living, but to my teacher for living well.

Edward Jenner and the Smallpox Vaccination

- Edward Jenner began his training to become a world reknowned physician at the mere age of fourteen.

- Early in his career, he experimented with vaccination on an eight-year-old boy by injecting cells from a cowpox strand into the boy's arm.

- Jenner's experiment proved that a mild case of cowpox would prevent children from getting smallpox. The Royal Society argued that the experiment was not sound proof, so Jenner performed the same test on other children, including his eleven-month-old son.

- Jenner's discovery was later published, though the general public did not immediately accept it. The clergy, along with many others, thought the practice was repulsive and ungodly. Eventually, however, society began to understand the important protection that Jenner's vaccines provided.

- Smallpox vaccinations were being used in many countries around the world before Jenner's death in 1923.

Smallpox Be Gone!

The full annihilation took 180 years, but today, according to the World Health Organization, smallpox exists only in a controlled state in two research laboratories. The last case of smallpox occurred in 1977 in Somalia.

ISAIAH BERLIN: PHILOSPHER

Are you a fox or a hedgehog? Before you answer, let's take a quick look at the life of twentieth-century British philosopher, Isaiah Berlin.

Berlin was born in the Russian Empire (in what is now Latvia) in 1909, but his family moved to England in 1920, just before the formation of the Soviet Union. He studied at Oxford, eventually entered into the life of academia as a philosophy lecturer and fellow at Oxford, and taught at All Souls College. He would later serve as president of Oxford's Wolfson College. Berlin died in 1997.

In 1939, Berlin published *Karl Marx; His Life and Environment*, an objective biography of Marx. Berlin's focus slowly narrowed from general philosophy to political science and theory and intellectual history. He became interested in how an individual maintains his or her liberty and free will in a world becoming more and more mechanical and, in his view, totalitarian.

Berlin wrote and published many essays, but his most famous and the one for which he'll probably be remembered was "The Hedgehog and the Fox." In the essay, Berlin used a quote from the ancient Greek poet Archilochus to look at Leo Tolstoy's idea about history. The classical poet had said, "The fox knows many things, but the hedgehog knows one big thing." Berlin expanded on this basic idea and applied it to thinkers throughout history. For example, he suggested that folks like Erasmus, Moliére, and Shakespeare were "foxes" who saw the world as a mosaic of ideas and whose work could not be explained with one "big idea," but instead encompassed many ideas.

In contrast, Berlin felt that thinkers like Plato, Pascal, Nietzsche, and Dante were "hedgehogs"—they tried to fit the world into their one "big idea" that would explain everything. As for Tolstoy, Berlin admitted he was stuck at first, as the Russian writer appeared to be neither a fox nor a hedgehog. But eventually Berlin suggests that Tolstoy was himself a fox, but his writings encouraged people to be hedgehogs.

So which are you? Fox or hedgehog?

William James Durant

William James Durant was an American writer known for writing, along with his wife Ariel Durant, The Story of Civilization, a scale-tipping eleven volumes written over a forty-year period. They wrote big and won big for it. The couple was awarded the Pulitzer Prize for literature in 1967 and the Presidential Medal of Freedom ten years later. Will Durant not only wrote on many topics—he put his money where his pen was, fighting for equal wages, women's right to vote, and fairer working conditions.

In 1900, Durant learned his ABCs and then some from Jesuits in St. Peter's Preparatory School and, later, Saint Peter's College in Jersey City, New Jersey. About that time he became a Socialist. He graduated in 1907 and then the job variety came: newspaper reporter, teacher, librarian, and lecturer.

In 1917, while working on a doctorate in philosophy, Durant also wrote his first book, *Philosophy and the Social Problem.* Despite authoring a book, Durant managed to later that year receive his doctorate. *The Story of Philosophy* started out as little educational pamphlets but became so popular it was republished in 1926 by Simon & Schuster as a hardcover book. That book became a bestseller, giving the Durants the financial boost they needed to be able to travel the world over and over again and spend four decades writing *The Story of Civilization.*

The Story of Civilization is a sort of biography of a civilization—of the West, that is: its wars, politics, leaders, bad guys, culture, etc. You name it, it's probably in there—remember, it *is* eleven volumes! *The Story* is what some say put Simon and Schuster on the publishing house map.

The Durants had intended to carry the work into the twentieth century but, they ran out of time. (Is that any surprise?) As a matter of fact, the tenth volume was supposed to be the last, but they then decided on the eleventh, *The Age of Napoleon.* They also left behind notes for a twelfth volume, *The Age of Darwin,* and an outline for a thirteenth, *The Age of Einstein,* which would have taken *The Story of Civilization* through to 1945, but nothing ever came of it.

Cicero

If you've ever been seduced or stirred by a politician's stump speech, or swayed by a lawyer's closing argument, you can thank Cicero.

The Roman political leader Marcus Tullius Cicero was smack dab in the middle of the fall of the Republic and the rise of the Empire. But Cicero, or "Tully" as he was later known to the nickname-happy English, ended up best known not for what he did, but what he said. Or rather, how he said it.

Born in 106 BC, Cicero, like many politicians, started out as a lawyer. He quickly became known for his powerful, emotional closing speeches—he called it "throwing dust in the jurymen's eyes."

As a Roman senator, Cicero continued his impressive style of public speaking in his orations for and against various leaders. Using a variety of speaking styles to dazzle his audiences, Cicero also studied how a speaker's rhythm affected listeners.

Cicero believed in maintaining the Roman Republic, and so, while he supported Pompey, he ended up opposing the rise of Julius Caesar—a stance that later caused him much political grief. His speeches against Publius Clodius Pulcher also led to problems—when Clodius became tribune of the Senate, Cicero was temporarily run into exile on "profanity" charges.

Eventually Cicero found himself trapped in the middle of the fall of the Republic—he fought against Caesar's dictatorship, but was also hated by Caesar's foes. He did not participate in the assassination of Caesar, and afterward tried to use young Octavian, Caesar's heir, to oppose Marc Antony. As a result, when Octavian, Antony, and Lepidus made peace and formed their triumvirate in 44, Cicero found himself on Antony's hit list. He was killed the next year and, appropriately, his head and hands were stuck up on display on the speaker's platform in the Roman Forum.

Today not only is Cicero remembered as the best of the Roman orators, but his use of emotion to put "umph" in his speeches gave rise to what is now known and practiced as Ciceronian rhetoric.

Johannes Gutenberg: Father of Printing

Johannes Gutenberg is considered the father of printing—his moveable type invention drastically and significantly changed the history of the Western world, even though he himself only printed one project.

Born sometime around 1400 in Mainz (part of what is now Germany), Johannes Gutenberg became a metalworker and general craftsman. Run out of Mainz in the late 1420s because of a guild dispute, Gutenberg ended up in Strasbourg, France.

There he began to work on a secret project: some sort of new type of wooden press, similar to those used in paper- and wine-making. In 1450 he received a financial investment from Johann Fust. Fust, seeking a quick return on his money, wanted Gutenberg to work faster. Gutenberg, a perfectionist, preferred to take his time and get it right.

"It" was a new printing press in which a wooden screw pressed together the ink-covered type and the paper. But Gutenberg's greatest advancement was to create a mold that let him cast the type as individual letters that could be easily arranged into new texts.

Gutenberg had printed his first Bible by 1455. The forty-two-line (per page) Bible probably would have made Gutenberg and Fust plenty of money, but Fust sued Gutenberg to get his investment back. Gutenberg had to pay up, and for centuries it was assumed that this settlement led to Gutenberg's financial ruin. (However, modern studies suggest that Gutenberg may have gotten a good deal.)

As a result of the suit, Fust took over ownership of Gutenberg's Bible type and some of his printing equipment. Fust also got a Psalter that Gutenberg had been working on setting—the later printing of that Psalter was the first in Europe to have the name of the printer on the book. Fust's name, not Gutenberg's.

Gutenberg died in 1468—maybe in poverty, maybe not—but certainly not rich from his invention. Today there are only about forty-eight authentic Gutenberg Bibles in known existence out of an original printing of maybe 180.

MUSIC APPRECIATION 101
JOSEPH HAYDN

Franz Joseph Haydn gets two "fathers" for his successes: "father of symphony" and "father of the string quartet." One of the most amazing composers of the classical period and a lifelong resident of Austria, Haydn spent most of his life playing music for a well-to-do Hungarian family on their fancy estate.

Unlike other composers, Haydn wasn't immersed in music trends or exposed to the works of others until much later in life. But, as he put it, he was "forced to become original."

Fortunately for Haydn, though, his parents figured out he had some talent, and knew he had no hope to grow where he was. So, at age six he was shipped off to a relative who happened to be a teacher and choirmaster. Haydn never lived with Mom and Dad again.

Apparently life was rough in his new home. There wasn't much to eat and he got picked on for wearing dirty clothes. Still, despite the teasing and hungry belly he managed to learn to play both the harpsichord and violin. He also began to sing in the church choir in his new town of Hainburg, and eventually in Vienna, too. Then, a big break came in 1740, when he tried out for the St. Stephen's Cathedral choir, where he ended up singing for nine years.

By 1749, Haydn's voice had lowered—the high parts were out of the picture, and so was his job. He had nowhere to go. But, thanks to a friend who took him in, he could take some freelance singing jobs. Eventually he began working for an Italian composer, where he finally learned how to really compose music the "right" way.

As his actual skills got better, Haydn's reputation did, too. Soon, countesses and barons alike were asking for Haydn, and his career officially took off.

EXTRA CREDIT: Joseph Haydn's brother Michael Haydn also was a famed composer. His other bro Johann Evangelist Haydn was a tenor.

DANTE ALIGHIERI

This Italian poet from Florence was born sometime around 1265. His main piece of work, *The Divine Comedy,* is considered the greatest literary work ever composed in the Italian language as well as a masterpiece in all of world literature. Dante himself is considered by some the "father of the Italian language."

When Dante was just a lad—twelve years old—he was promised in marriage to Gemma di Manetto Donati. Such young contracted marriages were incredibly common back then, but Dante's heart was elsewhere, poor guy. He'd already fallen in love with someone else, Beatrice Portinari—everyone called her Bice for short. Years later (post-marriage to Gemma) things got complicated when he met Bice again. He'd begun writing poems, and although he wrote several to Beatrice, he never mentioned his actual wife in any of his verse.

Dante and Gemma had several children. But like straight out of the tabloids, many people have claimed to be Dante's offspring. None have been able to prove it, however. His true children: Jacopo, Pietro, Giovanni, Gabrielle Alighieri, and Antonia, who, by the way, became Sister Beatrice (a nun).

Dante dived into Tuscan poetry, and eventually Latin poetry followed. When Beatrice died in 1290, Latin literature became his latest thing. But it didn't stop there. He then explored philosophy at religious schools and became a pharmacist, something people did back then to boost their political careers. He wasn't exactly the most active politician but held various positions in a struggling city.

Like most Florentines back then, he became caught up in the Guelph-Ghibelline clashes. Dante supposedly fought with the Guelphs during the 1289 battle of Campaldino, which he referred to in the Purgatory part of *Divine Comedy.*

By 1300 the Guelphs themselves were split into the Black Guelphs and the White Guelphs. Two years later, when the Blacks took power in Florence, all Whites were banished—including Dante, who was threatened with being burned alive if he ever came back.

The *Divine Comedy* describes Dante's journey through Hell (*Inferno*), Purgatory (*Purgatorio*), and Paradise (*Paradiso*).

Diogenes

Today the definition of "cynic" is someone who thinks people act mostly out of selfishness and self preservation. But the original Greek Cynics believed that the greatest good was to live a virtuous life, free from possessions and the quest for money, fame, or power. And the ultimate Cynic was Diogenes of Sinope (not to be confused with a couple of other classical men named Diogenes, such as Diogenes of Apollonia and Diogenes of Babylon).

Diogenes of Sinope was born—you guessed it—in Sinope sometime before 400 BC He was the philosopher's philosopher and believed in teaching by simply doing—in other words, he walked the walk. Literally, according to legend—it's often said that he spent his days walking around Athens with a lamp, searching for an honest man.

In fact, much of what we know about Diogenes is the stuff of rumor, or at least exaggeration meant to illustrate his ideas. For example, it's unlikely that he actually lived in a big tub in Athens, or wandered its streets with a lamp.

He did, however, actually exist. Diogenes believed that life was best led according to a handful of ideals: self sufficiency; shamelessness (in proudly disregarding conventional rules, laws, and standards); outspokenness (in the quest to reform corruption); and a moral excellence.

In order to achieve that moral excellence, Diogenes led a life of self denial, rejecting all luxury and working to knock down conventional ideas about how to live and instead exist simply and naturally. He lived on the street, slept in public buildings, and begged food for his meals. Simple also meant no family—in fact, Diogenes's ideal community was one in which everyone lived (and slept) with everyone else and everybody cared for all the children. That's right: he was a very early hippie.

He died around 320 BC, but Diogenes would be forever immortalized in classical art as wearing a torn cloak, walking around Athens with a dog and his lantern, forever searching for that honest man.

ERIK THE RED

Erik the Red was probably pretty chilly on his big discovery—he founded the first Nordic settlement in Greenland. Although some historians have credited Erik as the founder of Greenland, it is likely that earlier Norsemen both discovered and tried to settle it before him.

Still he settled it—for the first time permanently—and that settles that. Erik, born around 950 in Norway had red hair, hence the nickname. His parents had to escape his homeland because of some killings, and settled in western Iceland. There, the rough-and-tumble Erik was sentenced to a three-year exile for several murders sometime near the year 982. The Icelanders eventually banished ol' Erik from their island, which sent him on his travels west of Iceland and led him to his discovery of Greenland.

After his banishment had expired, Erik returned to Iceland with him stories of Greenland, hoping to lure settlers—and purposely making sure Greenland sounded better than Iceland. It worked and after one more frigid winter in Iceland, Erik returned to Greenland with enough colonists to establish an eastern and western colony. Twenty-five ships made the trip, fourteen successfully. The other eleven either turned back or were lost at sea.

During the summers, when travels were made easier, men would hunt in Disko Bay above the Arctic Circle for food and other supplies. Erik eventually built himself an estate, called himself the paramount chieftain of Greenland and became both greatly respected and wealthy. The settlement grew to five thousand before a group of immigrants arrived in 1002 bringing an epidemic that ravaged the colony, killing many of its leaders, including Erik. The colony, though, survived until the Little Ice Age and other factors forced it into decline.

Erik and his Thjodhildr had a daughter and three sons, including Leif Erikson the first Viking to explore the part of North America that is now Newfoundland. Leif had invited his father on that journey but legend has it that Erik fell off his horse on his way to the ship, saw that as a bad omen, and decided not to go.

JOHANN SEBASTIAN BACH

Everyone knows Bach has something to do with music—if you don't at least know that much, you have a lot more reading to do! He is, after all, one of the greatest composers ever. But there's a lot more to Bach you might not know.

First, this German composer and organist, born in 1685, wrote more than two hundred cantatas and more than one thousand works altogether. Among his most famous pieces: the *Art of Fugue*, the *Brandenburg Concertos*, the *Cello Suites*, the *English Suites*, the *French Suites*, *Goldberg Variations*, *Mass in B Minor*, *The Musical Offering*, and *Partitas*.

In 1703, tension mounted during one of his first jobs as church organist at St. Boniface's Church in the old town of Arnstadt. The problems were twofold. First, Bach thought choir should consist of higher caliber singers. Second, Bach often missed work due to visits to stay and learn from Dieterich Buxtehude, a highly regarded organist of the time.

Three years, later, however, Bach was offered a new job, in a bigger city, with more pay and a better choir. The church was so gung-ho about Bach's arrival, it agreed to his proposal to renovate the organ and paid to publish a cantata he wrote for the inauguration of the new council. Only a year had passed, though, and Bach was climbing the next rung of the career ladder—a better job in Weimar, in the private orchestra of the ducal court.

Bach had it made when his family packed their bags and moved into an apartment right near the ducal palace. His walk to work was a sweet five minutes. There at Weimar, he learned by leaps and bounds and became smitten with the musical form called the fugue. Bach's own *The Art of Fugue* was presented to the world after he died—even though it was unfinished. The book consists of eighteen complex fugues and canons.

In 1717, Bach had his first gig as a musical director, hired by Prince Leopold of Anhalt-Cöthen. Bach worked for the prince for seven years, when he took a stint as Cantor of Thomasschule, which was located right next to St. Thomas' Lutheran Church in Leipzig. Back also was the music director of all of the main churches in the town. He would work nowhere else until he died twenty-seven years later in 1750.

In 1707 Bach had married his second cousin, Maria Barbara Bach, and together they had seven children. Only four lived to become adults. Maria died suddenly thirteen years later, and the following year, Bach married Anna Magdalena Wilcke. Anna was an exceptional soprano seventeen years younger than Bach. They had thirteen children—six lived on to become adults, and each became a talented musician.

Bach's life is sort of a big file of BWV numbers (BWV=*Bach Werke Verzeichnis*=Bach Works Catalogue). The non-chronological catalog was created by Wolfgang Schmieder and was published in 1950. Set up by theme, the first 224 numbers are the cantatas. BWV 225 through 249 consist of the large-scale choral works. The next numbers, which go up to BWV 524 are the chorales and sacred songs. BWV 525–748 are the organ works, followed by BWV 772–994, other keyboard works. All lute music is 995–1000, while all chamber music is 1001–1040. The last two groups are orchestral music (1041–1071) and the canons and fugues (1072–1126).

Bach's last hurrah was a chorale prelude for organ. He crafted it from his deathbed, How, you ask? By speaking it to his son-in-law, Johann Altnikol, who wrote it down. And there's something really cool about the dictated *Before Thy Throne I Now Appear*. Go ahead and take the notes on the three staves of the final cadence and count them and map them onto the Roman alphabet. OK, don't know how to do that? We'll spill the secret beans—you'll find the initials "JSB," for Johann Sebastian Bach. And the song, by the way, is often played after the unfinished fourteenth fugue to end performances of *The Art of Fugue*.

By about the 1740s, Bach had begun to lose his eyesight. He went ahead and had eye surgery, but died in July 1750. He was just sixty-five. Some media speculations reported that the eye-surgery-gone-bad did him in, while others speculated pneumonia brought on by stroke.

In contemporary society, Bach's style shapes everything from religious works to pop. Many of his themes—particularly *Toccata and Fugue in D Minor*—have been used in rock songs.

WORLD HISTORY 101
MARCO POLO

During the hot days of summer kids across the country jump into pools and lakes shouting, "Marco!"—"Polo!"

This most popular of swimming games owes its name to the Venetian trader and explorer of the late 1200s and early 1300s whose travels to China, India, and other parts of Asia helped to introduce the "mysterious Orient" to Western Europe. Marco Polo, born in 1254, apparently had no clue where he was going when he first set out on his travels—hence the name of the game.

Polo, together with Dad Niccolò and Uncle Maffeo, was one of the first Westerners to journey the Silk Road to China and call on Kublai Khan, grandson of Genghis Khan and then the Great Khan of the Mongol Empire.

The Polos were by no means the first Europeans to reach China over land (see, for example, Giovanni da Pian del Carpine). But Marco's book, *Il Milione* (*The Million*), made the trip the first to be most broadly known, and the best detailed due to his tremendous documentation. Polo's description of the Far East and its riches inspired Christopher Columbus's attempts to reach the same lands via a western route. A heavily noted copy of Polo's book was among Columbus's belongings.

Along with the swimming game, Marco Polo has made its way into many other areas of popular culture. Among them:

- The *Marco Polo*, a three-masted ship built in Saint John, New Brunswick, in 1851, was the fastest of her time, sailing around the world in less than six months.
- Several Italian navy ships were named *Marco Polo*.
- The airport in Venice is the Marco Polo International Airport.

GROUNDBREAKING WOMEN OF HISTORY

- In 1933, Frances Perkins was elected as Secretary of Labor, making her the first female ever appointed to a president's cabinet. (She served under Franklin D. Roosevelt.)

- In 1951, Florence Chadwick became the first woman to swim across the English Channel in both directions.

- In 1953, Elizabeth II was the first monarch to have her coronation televised.

- In 1983, astronaut and astrophysicist Sally Ride became the first American woman to ever enter space.

- Eileen Collins went to space in 1999, becoming the first woman astronaut ever to command a space shuttle mission.

- Hillary Rodham Clinton became the first First Lady ever to be elected to a US national office in 2000 when she was elected to the United States Senate.

PABLO NERUDA

From erotically charged love poems to historical epics, this Nobel Prize winner was a Chilean writer and politician—and one of the most noted poets of the twentieth century.

Neruda's Nobel Prize award—for literature—was a controversial win because he was so politically active at the time: 1971. During his lifetime, Neruda held various positions with the Chilean Communist Party, even serving for a time as a senator. So what was the big deal? Well, the Conservative Chilean president of the time had outlawed Communism. Not good for Neruda, who had a warrant issued for his arrest. Friends hid him for months in a house before he finally escaped through a mountain pass into Argentina.

But back to his writing: his father wasn't a fan of his hobby, but Neruda went off encouragement from others, including future Nobel Prize winner Gabriela Mistral. His first published work was *Enthusiasm and Perseverance,* an essay he wrote for the local daily newspaper at age thirteen. By 1920, he was publishing poetry, prose, and journalism.

Neruda briefly thought about teaching but instead latched onto poetry full time, publishing among others, *Twenty Poems of Love and a Song of Despair*, a set of controversial love poems. The hullabaloo stemmed from the poems' eroticism, especially considering Neruda wasn't very old. Still, they were praised, translated into many languages—and eventually millions of copies were sold.

Neruda was growing in popularity but also growing poor. He was desperate when, in 1927, he took an honorary consulship in Rangoon. He then worked stints in other countries, eventually landing in Java, where he met and married his first wife, a Dutch bank employee.

The next few years consisted of some diplomatic posts, a daughter—who was plagued with health problems—a failing marriage, and an older woman (i.e., twenty years older), Delia del Carril. She eventually became wife number two. His first child died in 1943.

The same year his daughter died, Neruda returned to Chile and visited Macchu Picchu—his main reason for writing *Alturas de Macchu Picchu,* a twelve-section poem which took him two years to complete. In *Alturas,* Neruda rejoiced in the triumph of Machu Picchu while disapproving of the slavery that allowed it. Also during his visit to

Macchu Picchu, he became fascinated with ancient American civilizations, something he would delve into in *Canto General.*

In 1953 Neruda won the Stalin Peace Prize. Coincidentally, Stalin died the same year. Neruda wrote an ode to the leader.

Interesting Facts About Neruda

- After escaping Chile, Neruda spent three years in exile. The famous artist Pablo Picasso was the one who helped plan his entrance into Paris, where, talk about a surprise—Neruda shocked everyone when he showed up at the World Congress of Peace Forces. Chilean officials kept insisting there was no way Neruda could have escaped. During his Nobel Prize lecture Neruda dramatically narrated his getaway from Chile.

- In 1970, Neruda was nominated as a candidate for the Chilean presidency. Neruda, though, tossed his support elsewhere—to Salvador Allende. Allende did win the election and was inaugurated that same year— the first democratically elected socialist head of state. Allende, though, returned the favor and named Neruda the Chilean ambassador to France, duties Neruda carried out for two years until 1972.

- Neruda returned to Chile when he grew ill. He died of heart failure in September 1973. He had quite the funeral—enormous police presence and mourners protesting the Pinochet regime.

- Neruda owned three houses in Chile and today, in museum form, you can visit each of them: La Chascona in Santiago, La Sebastiana in Valparaiso, and Casa de Isla Negra in Isla Negra, where he is buried.

LAO-TZU: FATHER OF TAOISM

Contrary to popular belief and best-selling self-help books, the philosophy of Taoism (pronounced "DOW-ism") was not created by Winnie the Pooh. In fact, Taoism's primary text, the *Tao-te Ching*, was probably not written by a single author. However, Taoist tradition recognizes Lao-tzu as the father of Taoism and author of the book.

Little is really known about the actual person Lao-tzu—questionable biographies of him, written later by Taoist followers, say he lived around the same time as Confucius (551–479 BC) and was an officer in the Chou dynasty's court.

Several legends exist around Lao-tzu: that he met and inspired the younger Confucius (possible, but considered unlikely), and that he spent seventy-two years in his mother's womb and then lived to be 150 years old (considerably less likely).

It is also said that Lao-tzu composed the *Tao-te Ching* at the border of China and Tibet, at the request of a guard who wanted to make sure the teacher recorded his ideas before he left the country forever. In fact, the text was no doubt written after Lao-tzu's death, but it is possible that its ideas come from his original teachings.

The word "Tao" means "the way" and refers to the general guiding idea or process of the universe. The philosophy focuses on the idea that to follow the Tao is to "do nothing," to simply follow your own nature, not interfere with the nature of other people and things, and just "be." Happiness comes when people are what they are and fulfill their destiny by setting aside worries about life and death, money, and loss.

Taoism also embraces the balance of opposites, as practiced in tai chai ("harmony of opposites") and as symbolized in the yin-yang symbol (also known as the *Taijitu*)—where the dark yin represents the passive (moon) and the white yang the active (sun). The symbol shows how the two sides flow into one another and even contain parts (the dots) of each other.

MIGUEL DE CERVANTES

His masterpiece, if bought today in paperback, is nearly 1,000 pages long. You've probably heard of it—*Don Quixote*—but may not be as familiar with its author, who also was a playwright.

Cervantes, born in 1547 near Madrid, was child number four of seven. Before making it as a bigtime writer, he was a soldier in a Spanish infantry regiment—even captured by pirates, spending five years as a slave and ransomed back to his family—a supplier for the Spanish Armada, a tax collector, and even a jail inmate.

While in uniform, Cervantes sailed on the *Marquesa*. He was sick with fever yet stubbornly refused to stay below ship, and actually begged to fight in the battle. He ended up winning his way and fought bravely. He was shot three times, twice in the chest and once in the arm. His arm had to be amputated, and he was kept in the hospital for months while he healed.

So you're probably wondering about his time as a captive. Well, Cervantes thought it was pretty interesting, too. He ended up writing about it in several of his works. He was imprisoned in Algiers and tried—unsuccessfully—four times to escape. If you read *Don Quixote*, remember the Captive's tale? That was him. And then there's the two Algiers works: *The Treaty of Algiers* and *The Baths of Algiers*, as well as episodes in a number of other writings, that include bits and pieces pertaining to his trials and tribulations of captivity.
The Exemplary Novels of Cervantes, published in 1613, includes stories of pirates and gypsies—also stimulated by Cervantes's own encounters.

In 1584, Cervantes wed the much younger Catalina de Salazar y Palacios. During the two decades following his marriage, he pretty much drifted and did his jail time, before plunking back in Madrid, where he lived out the last days of his life.

To put his writing days in a timeline perspective, Cervantes published his first major work, *La Galatea*, a romance, in 1585, and then began writing plays and dramas.

WORLD LITERATURE
DON QUIXOTE

The first part of Cervantes's *Don Quixote* appeared in 1605, and the second part didn't arrive until ten years later. The first part was a hit with the general public. If you've read it, you remember when the flock of sheep is attacked, and, of course, the incident with the barber and the shaving basin.

The second part wasn't quite so funny, but critics loved it. Why? Cervantes, they said, described his characters better and had better style.

So here's the book's gist in a nutshell: it highlights the adventures of Don Quixote (a.k.a. the man of La Mancha). Quixote is a hero with comical zest and self-deception—often without intending to be. The book, by the way, is one of *Encyclopedia Britannica's* "Great Books of the Western World" and has been translated into all major languages, appearing in seven hundred editions.

Cervantes died on April 23, 1616. He was buried—he wanted it that way, as stated in his will—in a nearby convent, one that his daughter belonged to. But apparently a few years later the nuns there moved to another convent—taking their dead with them. But whether Cervantes was included among those remains no one knows for certain.

EXTRA CREDIT: Some Euro coins made for Spain—more specifically the 0.10, 0.20, and 0.50—bear Cervantes's portrait and signature. Cervantes even has a whole "project" in his name, thanks to Texas A&M University. *The Cervantes Project* is dedicated to the study of the author's works and life. The reference and resource Web site contains a brief biographical summary, a digital library of texts, photographs, and more.

GIUSEPPE VERDI

Walk into an opera house anywhere around the world, and there's a good chance you'll hear one of Verdi's works. This Italian Romantic composer was one of the most influential composers of Italian opera in the nineteenth century.

But it all started with the help of a friend, one Antonio Barezzi. Verdi was a town music master in the town of Busseto. Barezzi was a town merchant who happened to love music, particularly Verdi's.

Verdi performed for the public for the first time at Barezzi's pad in 1830. Barezzi even invited Verdi to be his daughter Margherita's music teacher, and—you guessed it—the two soon fell for each other. They wed in 1836. They had two children, but unfortunately both died as babies. Margherita herself died just four years later. Verdi, who adored his wife and children, was crushed.

The production of his first opera, *Oberto*, was a hit. It was during the work on his second opera that Verdi lost his family. That opera was a flop, and he anguished, vowing to toss his music-writing career away. A friend, though, talked him into writing another opera, *Nabucco*. The year was 1842 and its opening performance was the one that officially put Verdi on the opera map.

He did a ton of operas after that, including *I Lombardi* in 1843 and *Ernani* the following year. But perhaps his most unique and important opera was *Macbeth*, which he wrote in 1847. Verdi went way out of the box on that one, writing an opera sans the love story.

At thirty-eight, Verdi began a love affair with Giuseppina Strepponi, a soprano also enjoying a thriving career. They lived together before getting married—pretty scandalous arrangements at the time—but in 1859 they ended the gossip and got hitched. While living in Busseto with Strepponi, Verdi in 1848 bought a grand estate near town. His parents lived there for awhile but after his mother died in 1851, he claimed "Villa Verdi" for his own until he died.

Verdi was still in his prime. He created *Rigoletto*, which premiered in Venice in 1851 and was thought by some to be his greatest masterpiece. His last opera, *Falstaff*, was based on Shakespeare's *Merry Wives of Windsor* and was an international triumph.

Sir Thomas More

There was a time when a man of principle could lose his head over a divorce. Literally.

Sir Thomas More may be recognized as the author of the philosophical novel *Utopia*, in which he described the perfect society. But in reality, More himself paid the ultimate earthly price for standing up for his beliefs.

More was born in London in 1478, the son of an upper-class lawyer. Young Thomas attended Oxford and became a well-respected London lawyer himself. However, his heart was in the church. While for four years he practiced law, Thomas also lived in a monastery. In the end, he stuck with the law, but all his life More continued to practice some monastic traits, such as fasting and wearing a hair shirt.

But he also began hobnobbing with some of the great minds of his time. In fact, Erasmus wrote his masterpiece *In Praise of Folly* while living in London with More and his wife. More himself completed *Utopia* in 1516. Taking its title from a play on the Greek phrases "ou-topos" ("no place") and "eu-topos" ("good place"), the book outlines an imaginary city-state with Communist undertones, where the government makes positive decisions for its citizens based on the ideals of reason. Reacting against the corruption and vice of medieval Europe, *Utopia* tackles the issues of education, religion, divorce, women's rights, and imprisonment, all with More's blend of humor and humanism.

The next twenty years of More's life would be spent tackling some of these issues in the real world. Professionally, he was rapidly rising in the political world, first in the city government of London (where, as undersheriff, he became known as a fair judge and friend to the poor) and then as a national politician.

More began working with the lord chancellor Thomas Wolsey to put in place some of his, Erasmus's, and the Christian humanists's reform ideas. He became a friend and advisor to young King Henry VIII and speaker of the House of Commons in 1523.

Trouble started in 1527, when Henry informed More of his decision to divorce Catherine of Aragon, not because she couldn't bear him a male heir, but because her previous marriage to Henry's late brother rendered the current marriage incestuous. More gave Henry's idea a shot, but in the end had to declare that the marriage to Catherine was legal.

But More's political career continued to rise, and when Wolsey was kicked out in 1529, Thomas became the new lord chancellor. Still, while he publicly argued on behalf of the king, More would not sign a letter supporting the divorce of Catherine and even tried to resign his post. He tried again in 1532 when the Church of England agreed that the king (or queen) would have final say in all its operation, thus making Henry the head of the Church.

The divorce of Catherine took place the next year, and More pointedly did not attend the coronation of Catherine's successor, Anne Boleyn. At this point, the writing was on the wall for More. He was hit with trumped-up bribery charges, but still refused to swear to the Act of Succession (the oath that made the divorce and remarriage official). More was tossed in the Tower of London and put on trial in 1535.

All the while, Thomas refused to publicly speak his mind about the divorce. He never spoke against Henry, the Church of England's new power structure, or the new coronation—he simply refused to acknowledge them. But once he was found guilty (on the basis of a witness's perjury), More unloaded his mind on the court and the government of Thomas Cromwell, his nemesis. He pleaded for church unity, decried the royal rule over the Church, and bemoaned the fact that Henry had used the divorce to attack (and take over) the Church.

Thomas More was beheaded five days later. Praised posthumously by Erasmus as "a man for all seasons," More was made a saint in the Catholic Church in 1935.

Famous Words of Sir Thomas More

- Ask a woman's advice, and whatever she advises, do the very reverse and you're sure to be wise.
- If I speak to thee in friendship's name, thou think'st I speak too coldly, if I mention love's devoted flame, thou say'st I speak too boldly.
- One of the greatest problems of our time is that many are schooled but few are educated.

THEATER 101
EURIPIDES

Euripides wasn't your typical tragedian, oh no. His plays were even more modern than those of his more contemporary playwrights. He took the formal structure of the traditional tragedy and shook it up—with strong women, modern clothes and conversation, and intelligent slaves (hey, we're talking BC time here). His characters were realistic. Take Medea, for example. She has recognizable emotions. He also satirized—talk about pushing the envelope—many heroes of Greek mythology.

Euripides first competed in the City Dionysia, an annual spring dramatic festival, in 455 BC, the year after the death of Aeschylus, the "father of tragedy." He took third place. He finally won first place in 442 BC, but over his lifetime, won the top spot just four times, compared to thirteen times by Aeschylus and eighteen times by the other famous tragedian, Sophocles.

But later in the fourth century BC, it was Euripides's dramas that became the most popular. His works—among his greatest were *Alcestis*, *Medea*, *Electra*, and *The Bacchae*—influenced New Comedy and Romance drama and became idolized by French classicists.

The story says this tragedian himself suffered a tragic death, in 406 BC, if the account is true. Somehow the playwright was attacked by ferocious hounds. He died at the age of seventy-five. But shortly before his death, Euripides had accepted an invitation from Archelaus, ruler of Macedon. He was treated like royalty there, and upon his death, buried with honors.

Salvador Dalí: Surrealist Painter

Dalí was born with one *really* long name—Salvador Domingo Felipe Jacinto Dalí i Domènech, so we'll call him Dalí to save room for the intriguing name-dropping facts.

Born in Catalonia, Spain, Dalí is best known for some pretty bizarre images in his surrealist work. He painted more than 1,500 pieces in his career, but that's not all. He also produced illustrations for books, lithographs, designs for theater sets and costumes, countless drawings, dozens of sculptures, and various other projects, including an animated cartoon for Disney. Production for *Destino* began in 1945, and the movie was released in 2003—after Dalí had died—receiving a short cartoon Academy Award nomination.

In 1922, Dalí began studying at the School of Fine Arts in Madrid. He stood out among the students, lean and tall, long hair and sideburns. And his eccentricity didn't end there. He was known for wearing a long coat, stockings, and knee breeches. Ever enhancing his own eccentricities, Dalí eventually would grow a long moustache.

Still, his paintings—experiments in Cubism—earned him the most attention from his classmates (there were no Cubist artists in Madrid at the time).

But Dalí was kicked out of school in 1926. Why? No one on staff was competent enough to examine him, he said. Yeah, that'll do it.

Dalí, though, didn't *really* need those exams. He'd well mastered his painting skills, as seen in the very lifelike *Basket of Bread*. And in 1926 he had the tremendous opportunity of traveling to Paris for the first time—and meeting his idol, Pablo Picasso.

In 1929, Dalí met Gala, his future wife, an older woman and Russian immigrant who was married to a poet at the time they met. Three years after their initial meeting, Dalí painted his greatest masterpiece, *The Persistence of Memory*, also sometimes called *Soft Watches* or *Melting Clocks*.

And as if his appearance wasn't flamboyant enough, Dalí did other things to attract even more attention. At a special ball thrown in his name in 1931, Dalí showed up wearing on his chest a glass case holding a bra. A few years later, at a London show he spoke wearing a deep-sea diving suit.

Dalí was presented to the United States by an art dealer in 1934. A Dalí showing in New York was a hit.

In 1940, at the onset of World War II, Dalí and his wife moved to the United States. They lived there for eight years, during which time he wrote his autobiography, *The Secret Life of Salvador Dalí.*

But by the end of his life—beginning in 1949—Dalí opted to move back to his much-adored Catalonia. It was there that he decided to branch out from painting and try out many unusual media and techniques. He was one of the first artists to use holography artistically as well as optical illusions. Dalí also loved natural science and mathematics and was particularly interested in DNA and the four-dimensional hypercube.

In 1960, Dalí put nearly all his efforts into the Dalí Theatre and Museum, located in his hometown of Figueres. He threw himself into this large project through 1974, continuing to make additions through the mid-1980s.

In 1968, Dalí filmed a television advertisement for Lanvin chocolates, and the following year designed the Chupa Chups logo. Also that year he developed the advertising aspect of the 1969 Eurovision Song Contest, and crafted a large metal sculpture for the stage at Madrid's Teatro Real.

In 1980, Dalí's health crumbled. He was seventy-six, and his hand grew weak and began to tremble. For Dalí, that meant holding a paintbrush was impossible. Two years later Dalí was titled Marquis of Pubol by King Juan Carlos of Spain. In return, Dalí gave the king his last drawing, *Head of Europa,* right after the king visited him on his deathbed.

When Dalí's wife Gala died in June 1982, Dalí went into a funk. He moved from Figueres to the castle in Púbol which he had bought for Gala (also where she died). Two years after her death, his bedroom caught fire. No one knows what happened but Dalí was rescued. He went back to Figueres where a group of his friends and artist pals made sure he was comfortable living in his Theater-Museum.

In November 1988, Dalí's heart began to fail. On January 23,

1989, at Figueres, while listening to his favorite record, *Tristan and Isolde*, he died. He was eighty-four. He is buried in the crypt of his Figueres Theater-Museum, across the street from his funeral, first communion, and baptism site, and just a few blocks from the house where he was born.

Interesting Facts About Dalí

- Dalí loved elephants and eggs. The first elephant appeared in 1944 in his long-titled *Dream Caused by the Flight of a Bee around a Pomegranate a Second Before Awakening*. And what about eggs? He linked the egg to the prenatal and intrauterine—a symbol of hope and love. The egg appears in *The Great Masturbator* and *The Metamorphosis of Narcissus*.
- Dalí painted other animals as well—ants to symbolize death, decay, and sexual desire; snails to symbolize the human head; and locusts to symbolize waste and fear.
- Between 1941 and 1970 Dalí also created eye-catching collection jewels—thirty-nine of them to be exact. Some of the intricate stones contain actual moving parts. The most famous gem, "The Royal Heart," is made of gold and is encrusted with forty-six rubies, forty-two diamonds, and four emeralds, and is crafted so that the center "beats" much like a real heart.
- Prefer to forgo the jewels and get straight to the paintings? You'll find the most paintings at the Dalí Theatre and Museum in Figueres. There also are many at the Salvador Dalí Museum in St. Petersburg, Florida, which contains the collection of A. Reynolds Morse and Eleanor R. Morse. Other great numbers of paintings can be found at the Reina Sofia Museum in Madrid, and the Salvador Dalí Gallery in Pacific Palisades, California.

GEOFFREY CHAUCER

Chaucer, a master storyteller who is sometimes called the father of English literature, was born sometime between 1340 and 1344 in London. And since we're guessing his birthday, we might as well go ahed and tell you: the facts about his life are spotty. But there are some things we do know, thanks to official records, besides the obvious fact that he wrote the legendary *The Canterbury Tales.*

For one thing, Chaucer spent a year in the army during Edward III's time. He was detained by the French and then ransomed. From 1370 to 1378 Chaucer often traveled to Italy and other countries as part of diplomatic missions. He held all sorts of official positions, from comptroller of customs on furs and hides for the port of London, to clerk of the king's works.

As far as his personal life goes, by 1366 he had married Philippa Roet, who was probably the sister of John of Gaunt's third wife; she was a lady-in-waiting to Edward III's queen.

Chaucer's writings tend to be separated into three periods. The first— his earliest through 1370—are mostly based on French models and include the *Book of the Duchess,* a sort of figurative grieving over the death of Blanche, the wife of John of Gaunt. The second period, which generally includes writings up through 1387, is considered the Italian period because the books of this time, such as *The House of Fame,* were typed mainly after Dante and Boccaccio. *The Parliament of Fowls,* about the mating of fowls on St. Valentine's Day, is thought to rejoice in the relationship of Richard II and Anne of Bohemia. Also included among his writings of this time is the poem *Legend of Good Women,* an unfinished writing about nine classical heroines which introduced the heroic couplet into English verse. He also crafted the prose *The Treatise on the Astrolabe* for his son Lewis and wrote *Troilus and Criseyde,* one of the greatest love poems—and the poem where Chaucer perfected the seven-line stanza that would become known as rhyme royal.

Chaucer wrote *The Canterbury Tales* during his final period. The unfinished 17,000-line poem starts off talking about a group of pilgrims journeying from London to a shrine at Canterbury. To help kill the boredom, they decide to tell some stories.

FELIX MENDELSSOHN

Child prodigy is an understatement. Let's see, as an adolescent, Mendelssohn often performed his works at home—but with a private orchestra for the friends of his wealthy parents.

Between the ages of twelve and fourteen, he wrote twelve string symphonies. At age fifteen he wrote his first symphony for full orchestra, and the following year he wrote his *String Octet in E Flat Major*—the first work which showed his full genius. The Octet along with his overture to Shakespeare's *A Midsummer Night's Dream*, which he wrote a year after the Octet, are the best known of his first works. His earliest works were basically ignored for more than a hundred years, but are now occasionally played in concerts.
Mendelssohn played the organ and composed for it for a *lot* of years—from the age of eleven to his death. His two prime organ pieces are the *Three Preludes and Fugues*, Op. 37 from 1837 and the *Six Sonatas*, Op. 65 from 1845.

Jakob Ludwig Felix Mendelssohn Bartholdy was born in 1809 in Hamburg, Germany. His family was a well-known Jewish one, and he was the grandson of the philosopher Moses Mendelssohn. His father Abraham was a banker; basically, he grew up around a bunch of smarties—the greatest minds of Germany often visited the family at their home in Berlin (they moved there in 1812). Another example: Mendelssohn's sister married a famous German mathematician. Abraham didn't want to have anything to do with his Jewish religion. He initially raised his children sans religion, and then later baptized them Lutheran.

Mendelssohn studied at the University of Berlin and upon graduation in 1829 traveled for the first time to Britain. There, he had fun—and success—playing in public and private concerts. In the summer he went to Edinburgh and befriended composer John Thomson. Future visits—about ten in all—brought friends in higher-up places, including Queen Victoria and Prince Albert, new fans of his tunes. Trips to nearby Scotland motivated him to write two more famous pieces, the overture *Fingal's Cave* and the *Scottish Symphony*.

In 1835 Mendelssohn began conducting the Leipzig Gewandhaus Orchestra—a really big deal for Mendelssohn. He was ready to play a significant role in his beloved country's musical life. Despite the king of Prussia trying to reel him over to Berlin, Mendelssohn stayed with Leipzig and in 1843 also founded the Leipzig Conservatory.

Interesting Facts About Mendelsshon

- Mendelssohn's personal life was pretty straightforward. He had a happy marriage (he married Cécile Jeanrenaud in 1837) and had five children.
- Mendelssohn painted, too, especially watercolors. He also was an amusing writer, both in German and English, and sometimes even included cartoons in his writings.
- Mendelssohn was very upset when his sister Fanny died in May 1847. He died later that same year after a series of strokes on November 4, 1847, in Leipzig.

GREAT THINKERS OF THE LITERARY WORLD: UNTIMELY YET FASHIONABLE DEATHS

Sherwood Anderson (1876–1941)

Sherwood Anderson died in 1941 of peritonitis after swallowing a toothpick. During a trip to the Panama Canal in the spring of 1941, the famous author of many well-known American short stories swallowed the fatal toothpick, piercing his internal organs, and leaving behind a legacy of the storytelling of smalltown America.

Rainer Maria Rilke (1875–1926)

Famous poet and essayist Rainer Maria Rilke died at the age of fifty-one from blood poisoning. He was cut by the thorn of a rose he was thought to have picked for a woman. Shortly before his death, Rilke was diagnosed with leukemia, and his heath was deteriorating. He wrote his own epitaph, and left behind over 400 poems and two very famous prose pieces, *Letters to a Young Poet*, and *The Notebooks of Malte Laurids Brigge*.

Tennessee Williams (1911–1983)

Tennessee Williams, major twentieth century playwright and Pulitzer Prize winner, died of choking on the cap of an eyedropper bottle. It is rumored that he frequently placed the cap in his mouth while leaning back to insert the eyedrops, and hence accidentally swallowed the cap. Close friends and family of Williams were suspicious of foul play and believed that he could have been murdered. The police report showed that there were many prescription drugs found in the room. Also uncovered was a large amount of alcohol, which could have contributed to Williams's inability to recover from the choking. Williams left behind famous works such as *The Glass Menagerie*, *The Rose Tattoo*, and *A Streetcar Named Desire*.

Sylvia Plath (1932–1963)

Perhaps one of the most famous literary deaths in history, Sylvia Plath died by way of gas. A famous poet, novelist, and mother of two, Plath had historically committed several suicide attempts during her early adult years. Her marriage to poet Ted Hughes caused her much pain, as Hughes had a well-known affair with Assia Wevill while Plath raised her two children. On February 11, 1963, Sylvia Plath shut herself into the kitchen of her home, sealing the doors with towels. She turned on the gas oven and stuck her head inside. Her suicide was highly controversial, and drew even more question after the suicide of Assia Wevill, Hughes's mistress.

A Nineteenth-Century Reading List

Faust by Goethe (1808)
Sense and Sensibility by Jane Austen (1811)
Pride and Prejudice by Jane Austen (1813)
Frankenstein by Mary Shelley (1818)
The Voyage of the Beagle by Charles Darwin (1839)
Oliver Twist by Charles Dickens (1837–1839)
The Count of Monte Cristo by Alexandre Dumas (1845)
Wuthering Heights by Emily Brontë (1847)
Jane Eyre by Charlotte Brontë (1847)
Moby Dick by Herman Melville (1851)
Uncle Tom's Cabin by Harriet Beecher Stowe (1852)
Madame Bovary by Gustave Flaubert (1857)
Les Misérables by Victor Hugo (1862)
A Tale of Two Cities by Charles Dickens (1859)
Alice's Adventures in Wonderland by Lewis Carroll (1865)
Crime and Punishment by Fyodor Dostoevsky (1866)
Little Women by Louisa May Alcott (1868)
War and Peace by Leo Tolstoy (1869)
The Idiot by Fyodor Dostoevsky (1869)
Twenty Thousand Leagues Under the Sea by Jules Verne (1870)
Anna Karenina by Leo Tolstoy (1877)
A Doll's House by Henrik Ibsen (1879)
The Brothers Karamazov by Fyodor Dostoevsky (1880)
Thus Spoke Zarathustra by Friedrich Nietzsche (1889)
The Awakening by Kate Chopin (1899)
Heart of Darkness by Joseph Conrad (1899)

CRASH COURSE
JANE EYRE

From orphan to lover, young Jane makes quite a journey in this romantic novel by Charlotte Brontë. Unlike typical Victorian heroines, Jane is a bit plain but really smart. She gets shipped off to boarding school where she befriends the long-suffering Helen, who dies. From there, she becomes governess to the daughter of Edward Rochester of Thornfield Hall. She falls in love with the moody Rochester, but he has a secret. The reason he is so cold to Jane is because he has a crazy wife hidden in the attic. When Jane finds out, she flees and almost marries a clergyman. Turns out, she comes into a fortune from a long lost uncle. She leaves the odious clergyman who only wanted to marry her so she could function as a servant to him during his missionary work. In a freaky, mystic way, she hears Rochester calling to her, so she returns to Thornfield only to discover that his crazy wife burned it to the ground and jumped off the roof. Rochester is blind and crippled. Jane is wealthy and free. With the power balanced out in the relationship, they happily marry.

At age eight, Charlotte Brontë was sent along with three of her sisters to the Clergy Daughters' School at Cowan Bridge in Lancashire. The deplorable conditions there traumatized the young girl, and she was convinced that they were to blame for her poor health later in life and for the death of her two sisters, Maria and Elizabeth, from tuberculosis in 1825. That terrible experience inspired Brontë to create the Lowood School, which appears in her novel Jane Eyre.

The Life of Anton Chekhov

Believe it or not, Chekhov actually stitched up wounds and set bones throughout his literary career of short stories and plays. Born in 1860 in Taganrog, Russia, he produced four classics as a playwright: *The Seagull, Uncle Vanya, Three Sisters*, and *The Cherry Orchard*—all while being called Doc.

Chekhov's mom also was a top-notch storyteller while his father's talents ran the gamut. Dad's careers included everything from store manager to choirmaster. He also was strict—a religious fanatic who regularly beat his kids.

Chekhov went to a school for Greek boys, followed by the Taganrog gymnasium, where as a teenager he bombed a Greek exam and was held back a year. Then, in 1876, Chekhov's father lost all his cash over a new house. To avoid being locked up, Daddy fled to Moscow, where his two oldest boys were attending the university. There, the family barely scraped by. Chekhov stayed behind, sold the family's belongings, and finished school.

Chekhov stayed in Taganrog for a few more years, living with a man who was just like the character Lopakhin in Chekhov's *The Cherry Orchard*—he bailed out the family for the price of their house.

In 1879, he graduated and then met up with the family in Moscow, where he started medical school. He became the main breadwinner for the family, writing mainly to pay for their lives and his tuition. In 1884, Chekhov became a physician, but unlike most doctors today, he didn't make much money. In fact, he often treated the poor for free. That same year, he began coughing up blood, apparently with tuberculosis, although he never admitted that to anyone.

He continued writing for weekly publications and eventually was able to move the family into better digs. Then in 1886 he was invited to write for *Novoye Vremya (New Times),* a primo paper in Petersburg owned by a millionaire who eventually became one of Chekhov's dear friends.

Chekhov soon was a literary smash hit. And in 1887, the prestigious Pushkin Prize came his way for his short story collection *At Dusk.*

In 1889, something great came out of something tragic. Chekhov's brother Nikolai died from tuberculosis, influencing Chekhov to write *A Dreary Story* about a man who faces the end of life understanding that his life has been purposeless. Other brother Mihail Chekhov was researching prisons at the time as part of his law studies, and Anton Chekhov—in a new quest for his own purpose in his own life—soon became obsessed with the issue of prison reform.

In 1890, Chekhov traveled by train, horse-drawn carriage, and river steamer through remote east Russia to the penal colony on Sakhalin Island, north of Japan. There, he spent three months interviewing thousands of convicts and settlers for a census.

Beatings, embezzlement of supplies, and forced prostitution of women at Sakhalin disgusted Chekhov. He was particularly touched by the dilemma of the children living in there with their parents. His eventual conclusion was that government must finance the humane treatment of those living at the colony.

The letters Chekhov produced during this journey are thought to be among the best of his writings. His social science discoveries were published in 1893 and 1894 as *The Island of Sakhalin.*

In 1892, Chekhov bought the small country estate of Melikhovo south of Moscow. There, he lived for seven years with his family, and clearly his social science passion lived on. He organized aid for victims of the famine and cholera outbreaks of 1892, helped build three schools, a fire station, and a clinic, and donated medical services to peasants for miles around.

Chekhov had a lodge built in the orchard at Melikhovo, where, in 1894, he began writing his play *The Seagull.* During his time at the estate he became quite the nature buff, tending to the orchard and a pond and planting many trees.

But three years later, Chekhov's lungs began to bleed during a trip to Moscow. Against his wishes he went to a clinic, where he was diagnosed with tuberculosis.

His father died in 1898, and thereafter Chekhov decided to buy some land near Yalta and build a villa there. He moved there with his mother and sister the following year.

In 1901 "Russia's most elusive literary bachelor" finally got married—to Olga Knipper. The pair had met during rehearsals for *The Seagull.* His marital arrangement with Olga, however, was anything but typical. He lived largely at Yalta, while she stayed in Moscow to pursue her acting dreams.

At Yalta, Chekhov wrote one of his most famous stories, *The Lady with the Dog.* The story begins with a romantic tryst between a married man and a married woman in Yalta. But the next they know, they discover themselves drawn back to each other—this time putting their family lives in jeopardy.

By May 1904, Chekhov's illness was terminal. On June 3 he took off with Olga for a German spa town in the Black Forest. There he wrote happy skippy letters to his sister, talking about how great the food was and assuring her and his mother that he was doing just fine.

Interesting Facts About Chekhov

- Chekhov's body was taken to Moscow in a refrigerated railcar filled with oysters. So his poor mourners—a few thousand of them—followed the funeral procession of a General Keller by accident.
- Chekhov did everything from sell goldfinches to draw sketches for newspapers to pay for his own education, while sending every spare penny to his family in Moscow. He also during this time tried to cheer up his family, writing them funny letters, and along the same lines wrote a comedy drama, Fatherless.

POP QUIZ

1) *The Communist Manifesto*, by German political philosopher Karl
   Marx, outlined which of these beliefs?
   a) That the rich should become richer at the expense of others
   b) That class struggle would end with the rise of the lower classes
   c) That the moon is actually made of cheese

2) Writer Oscar Wilde served as editor of what publication?
   a) *Women's World*
   b) *Writer's World*
   c) *Women's Day*
   d) *As the World Turns*

3) Roman orator Cicero used his speeches against what famous
   Roman leader?
   a) Petero
   b) Pontius Pilate
   c) Alexander the Great
   d) Julius Caesar

4) Where was Dr. Martin Luther King Jr. born?
   a) Montgomery, Alabama
   b) Memphis, Tennessee
   c) Atlanta, Georgia
   d) Birmingham, Alabama

5) What did Dmitri Mendeleev organize into the periodic table?
   a) The phases of the moon
   b) The genus and species of all animals
   c) Chemical elements

ANSWERS:

1) b
2) a
3) d
4) c
5) c

JOHANNES VERMEER

Many artists, musicians, and writers of years past moved around throughout their careers. A *lot*. Vermeer makes it easy for us. This Dutch Baroque painter spent his whole life in one spot: the town of Delft in the Netherlands.

Although today he is considered one of the great painters of the Dutch Golden Age—known for using a lot of light in his work—Vermeer unfortunately did not get to bask in any of that during his own lifetime. In fact, he left his wife and eleven children in debt when he died.

But let's cut the guy some slack. When it comes down to it, he didn't really paint all that much, so how could he have been rolling in the dough unless he had some secret side job? In 1866 an art critic said Vermeer painted just sixty-six paintings. Today, only thirty-five are attributed to him.

Vermeer was born sometime in 1632. His dad was a silk weaver and art dealer, and in 1641 the family also bought a large inn in Delft. When his father died in 1652, Vermeer not only inherited the inn but became the painting seller, too. Although he came from a Protestant family, Vermeer married a Catholic girl, Catherina Bolnes, in April 1653.

Vermeer was apprenticed as a painter, and in 1653 he joined up with a painters' trade association. The guild's records show that Vermeer could not pay the admission fee.

In 1672, bad financial times hit the Netherlands when the French invaded the country (the Franco-Dutch War, it was later called). No one could afford to buy fancy stuff, including paintings, which of course ruined Vermeer's painting and art dealing business. He had to support his family, so he had no choice but to head to the bank to borrow some cash.

When Vermeer died in 1675, his wife asked the city to claim the estate—paintings included—to pay off the debts. The following year a city councilman was appointed trustee for the estate. Nineteen of Vermeer's paintings were bequeathed to his wife and daughters. Others were sold to pay off creditors.

ARCHITECTURE 101
ANDREA PALLADIO

Along with their Washington D.C. locale, Thomas Jefferson's Monticello and John Russell Pope's National Gallery have something in common—Andrea Palladio. It's doubtful most people realize that when they gaze up at both buildings' Palladian villa formats, but that's your clue. It has to do with the architecture.

Palladio, born in 1508, was an Italian architect but also widely considered one of the most influential people in the history of Western architecture. He was born in Padova, which back then was part of the Republic of Venice.

When he was thirteen, Palladio started out as stonecutter. But apparently he quickly learned that chopping rocks in a lowly position was not his thing. After just eighteen months he broke his apprenticeship contract and fled to a nearby town. In Vicenza he got a better gig—an assistant in the leading workshop of stonecutters and masons.

But his true talents were first recognized in his early thirties by a count—really, a true count, Count Gian Giorgio Trissino. This guy gave him his first real job—a true building project. The Count also gave him his lasting name of Palladio, which refers to the Greek goddess of wisdom, Pallas Athene.

Later, some friends encouraged Palladio to study classical architecture in Rome. The Palladian style, named after him, held on to classical Roman principles. Palladio went on to design churches, villas, and palaces, especially in Venice, Vicenza, and the surrounding area.

Palladio quickly grew in powerful circles, with top people in the Venetian society choosing him for their most important architectural jobs. He was a hit not only because his work was gorgeous but because it was harmonious with the culture of the time in all three of his building types: the urban palazzo, the agricultural villa, and the church.

Pyotr Tchaikovsky: Russian Composer

A battle with stage fright didn't stop Pyotr Tchaikovsky from becoming an outstanding Russian composer of the Romantic era.

Born in 1840, Tchaikovsky began pounding the piano keyboard at age five. His parents, however, weren't too comfortable with his musical talent—common folk weren't supposed to focus on such things. So in 1850 they sent Tchaikovsky to a school for the gentry called the School of Jurisprudence in St. Petersburg to make sure he could land a job as a civil servant. So off he went, two years of boarding school, 800 miles from his family. Tchaikovsky, a "mama's boy" who lacked self-confidence, was traumatized by the absence of his mother, as he would be again a few years later.

In 1854, Tchaikovsky's mother died of cholera. It was a good thing for the music world—he reacted by delving into music. Within a month of her passing, he had composed a beautiful waltz in her memory.

Tchaikovsky graduated in 1859—his rank was titular counselor, which probably doesn't mean much to you, but back then it basically was the lowest rung on the civil service ladder. A month later he was appointed to the Ministry of Justice and eight months later—climbing slowly but surely—he became a senior assistant to his department. He rode out his three-year civil service career and then immediately bailed, finally able to do what he wanted. He began taking music theory classes through the Russian Musical Society, and again at the new St. Petersburg Conservatory. He excelled in his love of music.

Tchaikovsky was gay, but he may not have been too comfortable with that. One of Tchaikovsky's favorite students, Vladimir Shilovsky, also was gay. In 1877 Vladimir married suddenly. Tchaikovsky himself then rushed into marriage with one of his former students. Although he and Antonina Miliukova never officially divorced, they did split ways just a couple months later. And despite the rocky marriage, Tchaikovsky wrote two of his finest works during this time—the Fourth Symphony and the opera *Eugene Onegin*.

Crash Course
Eugene Onegin

What makes this Russian novel so interesting is that it is written entirely in verse. Aleksandr Pushkin portrays the life of troubled hero, Eugene. The social scene in St. Petersburg has bored poor Eugene to tears, so he heads out to a country estate where he meets Tatyana who, like many women, falls in love with him. He passes on her charms, preferring, instead, to pick a fight with the romantic poet Lensky. They duel. Eugene wins. Lensky dies. Eugene returns to the St. Petersburg social scene, not quite as bored as before. Tatyana follows him home and comes to an important realization. Browsing through his book collection, it dawns on her what a shallow putz Eugene is. She bids him farewell, goes off and marries a prince, and becomes the toast of St. Petersburg. Of course, now Eugene is interested in her, but Tatyana, though still in love with him for some odd reason, resists his affections out of duty to her husband.

In 1977, Soviet astronomer Nikolai Stepanovich Chernykh discovered a tiny new planet, which he decided to name after his favorite Russian author, Aleksandr Pushkin. There is also a crater on Mercury that is named after the famous writer.

WILLIAM WORDSWORTH

William Wordsworth was a famed English romantic poet who in 1798, along with pal Samuel Taylor Coleridge, helped launch the Romantic Age in English literature with *Lyrical Ballads*.

His solo work of genius generally is thought to be *The Prelude*, an autobiographical poem focusing on his early years. *The Prelude* actually was given a title and printed after Wordsworth died—before he passed, it simply was known as the poem "to Coleridge."

Wordsworth was a household name in England, where he was Poet Laureate, a government-appointed position which he held from 1843 to 1850, the year he died.

After graduating from St John's College, Cambridge in 1787, he traveled to France. This was during the Revolution, and he became preoccupied with the Republican movement. He also became preoccupied with Annette Vallon, a French woman and his first true love. In 1792 they had their first child, Caroline.

Wordsworth began to run out of money in France—plus there was the whole war thing—so he returned to England, solo. He never married Annette but did end up providing for both her and Caroline in later years.

In 1793 Wordsworth finally got some verses published—*An Evening Walk* and *Descriptive Sketches*. Also around that time is when he became buddies with Coleridge, becoming so close he even moved just a few miles away in Nether Stowey.

In 1802, Wordsworth married Mary Hutchinson, a friend he knew from childhood. The following year, they had their first of five children.

Wordsworth's life ended in April 1850 due to pneumonia.

EXTRA CREDIT: Wordsworth for a time also became preoccupied with walking. In 1790, he walked nearly 3,000 miles across Europe, including France, Switzerland, and Italy.

V.S. Naipaul

His full name was Sir Vidiadhar Surajprasad Naipaul but he was known, thankfully, as V.S. Naipaul for short. He was born in 1932 in Trinidad and Tobago and currently lives—at least at the time of this writing—in Wiltshire (southwest England).

Naipaul went out big in the 1990s, first being knighted by Queen Elizabeth II in 1990. He and started the 2000s in pretty good shape, too, receiving the prestigious Nobel Prize in Literature in 2001.

He is the son, older brother, uncle, and cousin of published authors; so he was pretty much destined to do something with words. Even his current wife Nadira Naipaul is a former journalist, having worked for the Pakistani newspaper, *The Nation*, for ten years before meeting Naipaul. They married in 1996, two months after Naipaul's first wife died from cancer.

In 1971, Naipaul became the first person of Indian origin to win a Booker Prize for his book *In a Free State*. His fiction writing, particularly his travel pieces, has been criticized for its indifferent depiction of the Third World. Take *The Middle Passage* and *An Area of Darkness,* for example. Both depict a very bleak India.

But inside many classrooms in the developing world, his writings have become included on mandatory reading lists.

In early 2007, Naipaul finally, after many many years, returned to Trinidad, his birthplace. He urged the people there to stop focusing on being "Indian" and "African" and instead just be "Trinidadian." He was well received by most everyone there.

POETRY 101
LI PO

Also known as Li Bai, Li Po is thought of as one of the greatest poet's in China's literary history, with approximately 1,100 of his poems remaining today. It wasn't until 1901 that the English-speaking world was introduced to Li Po's writings thanks to the *History of Chinese Literature* by a Herbert Allen Giles—and also translations of Japanese versions of his poems.

When it comes to his verse, Li Po stands out for extravagant imagination and vivid Taoist imagery. Outside of poetry, however, he was known for his love for liquor.

Li Po thought about becoming an official, but didn't want to bother with the Chinese civil service exam. So instead, at age twenty-five, he lived a carefree life, sailing on the Yangtze River and traveling around China. The year was 725. About a year later he met Xu Yushi, the retired prime minister, and married his daughter and planted his feet in Anlu, Hubei—at least for awhile. After that he pretty much spent the rest of his life wandering through his homeland.

Apparently Li Po's poems were written very quickly. He hardly had to self-edit a thing—any of today's editors would have surely loved him. His favorite verse was called the *jueju* (five- or seven-character quatrain).

Li Po has his own crater named after him. Nope, it's not on the Moon, it's on the planet Mercury.

Li Po is the narrator and guide of both versions of the Circle-Vision 360° films in the China pavilion at Epcot's World Showcase.

Li Po supposedly drowned in the Yangtze River after falling from his boat. But wait: the story gets stranger than that. Legend has it that he was trying—drunkenly, of course—to embrace the reflection of the moon. Perhaps the more realistic legends are true, those that say he committed suicide, as evidenced by his farewell poem.

Literary Feats

- The oldest complete novel in the world was written in Japan in the 11th century. The title is *The Tale of Genji.*

- The youngest author is Dorothy Straight, who wrote *How the World Began* at the ripe old age of four.

- The largest library is the Library of Congress in Washington, DC. It has more than 130 million items (including books, recordings, photographs, maps, and manuscripts) on 532 miles of shelving. It was established in 1800 as a reference library for the US Congress. When the British destroyed it during the War of 1812, Thomas Jefferson helped rebuild the library by selling his personal library.

- The longest novel is *A la recherché du temps perdu* (*Remembrance of Things Past*) by French author Marcel Proust. It contains an estimated 9,609,000 characters.

- The smallest book is a 1/25-inch square version of Old King Cole. The pages are most easily read when turned with a needle.

- The smallest reproduction of a book is the New Testament, King James Version, measuring 0.196 by 0.196 inches. It was reproduced using microlithography technology by scientists at the Massachusetts Institute of Technology in 2001.

- The most translated author is L. Ron Hubbard. His books have been translated into 65 languages.

- The oldest surviving biblical texts are from two silver amulets found under the Scottish Church in Jerusalem in 1979, bearing Numbers 6:22-27 and dated 587 BC

- The world's best-selling book ever is the Holy Bible with 6 billion copies sold in more than 2,000 languages and dialects.

- In 1945 various papyrus texts were discovered at Nag Hammadi, Egypt, including Gnostic gospels or secret books (apocryphal) ascribed to Thomas, James, John, Peter, and Paul. They were buried in AD 350, but the originals are thought to have been written in AD 120–150.

- The world's best-selling copyrighted book is the Guinness Book of World Records. Since it was first published in 1955, more than 100 million copies of the book have sold in 37 languages.
- The world's best-selling fiction author is Agatha Christie. Her characters Miss Marple and Inspector Poirot are known around the world. Christie's 78 mystery novels have been translated into 44 languages and have sold approximately 2 billion copies.

Book Trivia

- Agatha Christie wrote romance novels under the pseudonym Mary Westmacott.
- The most valuable book is John James Audubon's four-volume The Birds of America. It was sold at auction for $8,802,500.
- The first book published in America was Steven Day's Bay Psalm Book. Reportedly, there are only 11 copies of the book still in existence in the US.

HENRI MATISSE

How do you know if this artist was really good? Well, try this one on for size. Today, a Matisse painting can fetch as much as $17 million. In 2002, his *Reclining Nude I (Dawn)* sculpture sold for $9.2 million. Not too shabby.

Matisse, who grew up in Northern France, was a painter and sculptor known for his fabulous use of color. Labeled as a wild painter when he first got his start, by the 1920s he was praised for his more classical approach to French painting.

Matisse studied law—it was a bout of appendicitis and a caring mom that led him down the path to painting. The year was 1889 and his mother brought him some art supplies to keep himself busy while his abdomen healed. For Matisse, he couldn't spend enough time healing.

Like a lot of these guys who left law for the arts, his father was unhappy with him. But Matisse followed his heart, heading to Paris to study his love. His fondness for bright colors only grew, probably influenced by post-Impressionist painters such as Paul Cézanne and van Gogh.

His first solo showing was in 1904—and was a near flop. That certainly didn't shy him away from his colors, though. Instead, his colors became even brighter, especially after spending time on the French Riviera. Also around that time he met Pablo Picasso, who became a life-long friend—and bitter rival as critics loved to compare the two.

He and model Caroline Joblau had a daughter, Marguerite, born in 1894. Four years later he married Amélie Noellie Parayre and together they raised Marguerite and had two sons.
Matisse and his wife of forty-one years separated in 1939. Two years later he was diagnosed with cancer and following surgery started using a wheelchair. A Russian woman (and one of his former models), Lidia Delektorskaya, began to care for him.

In 1947 Matisse published *Jazz*, which contained prints of his colorful paper-cut collages but also was supplemented by his written thoughts. In the 1940s he also made a living as a graphic artist and crafted black-and-white illustrations for several books.

After all that, Matisse still wasn't finished. In 1951 he finished the four-year design of the Chapelle du Rosaire in Venice, including the inside, the glass windows, and all adornments.

Matisse's heart gave out in 1954 at the age of eighty-four. Matisse's son, Pierre, opened an important modern art gallery in New York City during the 1930s. The Pierre Matisse Gallery—active from 1931 until the year Pierre died, in 1989—represented and displayed many artists, often for their first time.

Matisse's grandson, Paul Matisse, is an artist and inventor who resides in Massachusetts, and Matisse's great-granddaughter Sophie also is an artist.

Famous Words of Matisse

- There are always flowers for those who want to see them.
- Creativity takes courage.
- An artist must never be a prisoner. Prisoner? An artist should never be a prisoner of himself, prisoner of style, prisoner of reputation, prisoner of success, etc.
- There is nothing more difficult for a truly creative painter than to paint a rose, because before he can do so he has first to forget all the roses that were ever painted.
- In love, the one who runs away is the winner.
- I do not literally paint that table, but the emotion it produces upon me.
- In art, truth and reality begin when one no longer understands what one is doing or what one knows, and when there remains an energy that is all the stronger for being constrained, controlled and compressed.
- He who loves, flies, runs, and rejoices; he is free and nothing holds him back.
- Drawing is putting a line [a]round an idea.
- Exactitude is not truth.

WORLD LITERATURE
GUSTAVE FLAUBERT

While some writers just let it flow and don't look back, Flaubert the perfectionist was always in search of the precise word. This French writer, generally considered one of the greatest Western novelists, is best known for his first published novel, *Madame Bovary,* which came out in 1857.

Flaubert was born in 1821 in France, the second son of a surgeon. He began writing at an early age—some say as early as eight. In 1840 he left for Paris to study law. He wasn't too fond of studying—or Paris, which was a little too unpleasant for him. In 1846, an epileptic seizure was the deciding factor for him to leave the city he never loved (and leave law as well).

Flaubert decided to move back in with Mom, and her home near the Seine became his home for the rest of his life.

Flaubert never married. For eight years, up until 1854, he had an affair with the poet Louise Colet, apparently his only serious romantic relationship.

Flaubert often griped to friends about how difficult his work was. He usually opted to work alone, agonizing in his perfectionism. Yes, sometimes it took him a whole week to finish one page—and even then he still wasn't happy.

EXTRA CREDIT: The 1870s were a difficult time for a Flaubert. Prussian soldiers seized his house during the War of 1870, and two years later his mother died. As if that wasn't bad enough—yes, break out the violins—he then went broke, followed by ill health. He died of a stroke in 1880 at the age of fifty-eight.

HENRY THE NAVIGATOR

Prince Henry, a fifteenth-century member of the Portuguese royal family, was not a navigator. Nor was he a sailor or explorer. But all the same, he's credited with helping jumpstart the great Age of Exploration.

Born in 1394, the third son to King John I, Henry probably wasn't going to get anywhere near the throne. Still, he was raised and educated in a princely manner, and in his twenties, he and his brothers led the Portuguese capture of the Moroccan city of Ceuta. As governor of Ceuta, Henry began to send out ships on short voyages. He also became grand master of the Order of the Cross and committed himself to a chaste life. Leadership of the Order motivated Henry to convert pagans to Christianity (he was especially motivated by his dislike of Muslims), but it also provided plenty of cash to finance more voyages. All of Henry's ships bore on their sails the large red cross of the Order.

At one point, Henry's older brother Prince Pedro returned from Italy with a translated copy of Marco Polo's travels for Henry. Henry began to send expeditions further and further down the Moroccan Atlantic coast to spread both Christianity and commerce. In 1434, one of his captains sailed around Cape Bojador of Morocco, a feat that dashed existing sailing superstitions. Henry's captains also sailed to the Azores and began to colonize them. One major goal became the quest for an African gold supply, but it was the spread of the Portuguese slave trade in Africa that ended up financing more of Henry's explorations and led to the founding of the first European overseas trading post on Arguin Island near Mauritania. It is believed that Henry's sailors eventually explored as far south as Sierra Leone.

Despite all the money he made, Henry poured most of it right back into more explorations, and so he died deep in debt in 1460. But for better or worse, Henry's efforts led the way to what would become the spread of European empires across Africa and, eventually, the New World.

Gabriel Garcia Márquez: Nobel Prize Winner

Known simply as Gabo in his homeland, Colombia, Márquez won the Nobel Prize in literature in 1982 and is one of Latin America's most famous writers.

Márquez has written many non-fiction works and short stories, but is best known for his novels, such as *One Hundred Years of Solitude* (1967) and *Love in the Time of Cholera*, which came out eighteen years after *Solitude*. Márquez popularized "magical realism," a style that uses magical events to describe true experiences. Some of his writings, for example, are set in a fictional town called Macondo.

On a more personal note, Márquez married Mercedes Barcha in 1958 and the following year, they had their first son. Rodrigo García is now a television and film director. In 1961 the family hopped aboard a Greyhound bus and traveled across the southern United States, eventually stopping in Mexico City. Garcia Márquez had wanted to see that part of the U.S. because he was a fan of William Faulkner.

Three years later the couple had their second son, Gonzalo, who is a graphic designer still residing in Mexico City.

In 1999, doctors told Márquez he had lymphatic cancer. Chemotherapy, which he underwent in Los Angeles, sent his cancer into remission. The illness, however, gave Márquez pause, and he started to write his memoirs. Three years later, *Living to Tell the Tale* (*Vivir para Contarla*), the first volume of a memoir trilogy was published.

EXTRA CREDIT: Márquez had retired from writing, but in May 2008 decided to write one more novel, "a novel of love," to be published by the end of the year.

Cecil B. DeMille

- The flamboyant Cecil B. DeMille had an eye for film and has a lot to show for it. From *The Ten Commandments* to *Sunset Boulevard* to Academy Awards, this American filmmaker smoked the big screen in the first half of the twentieth century.

- His passion for filmmaking was never more evident than in Egypt during the 1956 filming of *The Ten Commandments*. The then seventy-three-year-old DeMille climbed a ladder nearly 110 feet high to the top of the giant set. There, he nearly died from a heart attack. Miraculously, aided by his daughter Cecilia—but against his doctor's orders—he was back directing the movie within just a week.

- DeMille did die of heart failure three years later. He was interred, appropriately (given his love for the big H), in the Hollywood Forever Cemetery. At the time of his death, he apparently was getting ready to direct *Ben-Hur,* as well as a new space travel movie.

- The media usually wrote DeMille with a capital "D," but DeMille himself used a little "d" ("deMille"). His business address was 2010 DeMille (big "D") Drive. He preferred the little "d" for personal correspondence and the big "D" for his business work.

- DeMille's dad was Henry Churchill DeMille, an Episcopal minister and playwright from North Carolina. His mom was Matilda Beatrice Samuel. She was born to a Sephardic Jewish family in England but switched to Henry's Episcopalian faith. The family lived in Pompton (now Wayne), New Jersey. Cecil B. DeMille went to Pennsylvania Military College in Chester, Pennsylvania— he was just fifteen when he started there.

THE TRAGIC LIFE OF ACHILLE-CLAUDE DEBUSSY

Debussy disliked the term Impressionist music so it's a good thing he's long past—today this French composer is considered one of the most prominent figures working within the field of Impressionist music.

Although he had quite the acclaimed musical career, his personal life was the opposite—very turbulent. Here it is in a nutshell: Dubussy cohabited in Paris for nearly ten years with a lady named Gabrielle Dupont before ditching her to wed her friend Rosalie Texier, a fashion model. But then, see, Rosalie apparently was boring—she wasn't the brightest bulb in the bunch and didn't know enough about music, at least by Debussy's standards. So he left her for Emma Bardac—she was married to a banker at the time and was the mother of one of his students. Scandalous stuff. But in contrast to Rosalie, Emma was an accomplished singer—finally getting up to Debussy's musical standards.

A distraught Rosalie—like Gabrielle before her—tried to kill herself with a gun. The scandal was not good for Debussy and Emma—who, by the way, was now preggers—and they skedaddled to England. There, they waited for the hysteria to subside—him writing another symphony, of course. He and Emma eventually were married in 1908. The child, a daughter and his only child, was named Claude-Emma— cute, eh? She outlived her father by just under a year, one of the many victims of the 1919 diphtheria epidemic.

Debussy had survived one of the first ever colostomy operations but died from colorectal cancer a couple years later. He died in Paris during the middle of German air and artillery blasts during World War I. His poor funeral procession had to fight its way through bombarding shells from the German guns blasting into the city.

CHARLES BAUDELAIRE

Baudelaire was an influential nineteenth-century French poet who hit his peak in 1857 with his first and most famous work, *The Flowers of Evil*, which actually was a volume of poems. The verses were enjoyed by a few initially, but drew greater public attention thanks to their subject matter: sex and death, scandalous topics of the times. Baudelaire also liked to write about lesbianism and lost innocence.

He was known for using lots of imagery—smell, in particular—to stir up feelings of nostalgia and past relationships.

Despite his eventual success, Baudelaire struggled personally. He was often sick, using laudanum regularly—that's a drinkable kind of opium—and he usually was stressed out and broke. In the late 1950s, dear ol' Mom caved and agreed to let him live with her for awhile. Baudelaire at least wrote a lot during this time, including his poem *Le Voyages*.

But his financial troubles reared their ugly head again, particularly after his publisher lost all his money in 1861. Three years later Baudelaire left Paris for Belgium, hoping in part to sell the rights to his writings and start to lecture. This time he started to smoke his favorite drug, and in Brussels he began drinking too much. He suffered a big stroke in 1866 and became paralyzed. During the last two years of life he was near-paralyzed, living in both Brussels and Paris. He died in the latter in August 1867.

After his death, his mother was able to pay off his debts. Many of Baudelaire's works were published after his death and his mother glowed in the fact that her son was beginning to become famous, saying: "I see that my son, for all his faults, has his place in literature."

THE MAJOR NOVELS OF ALBERT CAMUS

The Stranger

One of the most famous works of the class of literature known as "absurdist fiction," Camus's *The Stranger* is the story of a man named Meursault who feels relatively no emotion for anything or anyone. Through the funeral of his mother, a romantic relationship, and befriending of a neighbor, Meursault continuously finds his own disregard for human emotion and meaning baffling. The story climaxes when Meursault kills a man on the beach with whom Meursault and his friend, Raymond, were previously involved in a fight. Meursault not only shoots the man, but puts four more bullets into the body. He describes his motives as being caused by the glare of the sun that afternoon. Meursault then must await his sentencing to the death penalty, subsequently becoming more and more enraged with a chaplain who insists he accept God before his capital punishment ensue.

The Fall

The Fall was Albert Camus's last piece of fiction to be published, debuting in 1956. The novel is composed in the form of monologues, with the main character, Jean Baptiste Clamence, telling a stranger the story of his life. Clamence was a wealthy lawyer whose crisis or downturn was designed, in the novel, to reflect the story of the fall of Man in the Bible. The story takes place in Amsterdam, where Clamence has taken up residence after leaving his life and professional career in Paris.

Clamence outlines several significant events that led to his "fall." The first is an incident of finding a woman on a bridge while walking home from work one evening. Clamence passed by, and then heard the woman splash into the water below. Despite her screams for help, Clamence decided to continue walking, refusing to put himself into a jeopardizing situation for the sake of the woman. The incident continued to haunt him for some time. In a second incident, an angry motorist threatens Clamence with physical violence after Clamence urges the man to move his stalled motorcycle from the roadway so that other traffic may pass. The man strikes Clamence in front of the other motorists, to which Clamence responds with nothing but walking away, humiliated. Clamence reaches the conclusion that because his life was built on being honored and revered by others, the incident has shattered the very foundation of his previous truth. Like most of Camus's novels, the absurdist quality of seemingly unrelated incidents is ever present in *The Fall* as well.

Other Famous Works by Camus

The Myth of Sisyphus, 1955
The Rebel, 1954
The Plague, 1948
The Just Assassins, 1958
The First Man, 1995 (published posthumously)

Pop Quiz #4

1) What country was Palladio from?
   a) United States
   b) France
   c) Italy
   d) Spain

2) Who wrote the book *Eugene Onegin*?
   a) Pushkin
   b) Tolstoy
   c) Dostoevsky
   d) Sartre

3) Who helped launch the Romantic Age?
   a) Emerson
   b) Thoreau
   c) Longfellow
   d) Wordsworth

4) Who is thought of as China's greatest poet?
   a) Sun Tzu
   b) Lao Tzu
   c) Li Po
   d) Confucius

5) Who is the most translated author?
   a) Dickens
   b) Twain
   c) Proust
   d) Hubbard

6) What is the only printing project that Johannes Gutenberg
   officially completed?
   a) The Bible
   b) A Psalter
   c) *War and Peace*
   d) A dictionary

7) What was significant about the funeral of Italian composer
   Giuseppe Verdi?
   a) All of the mourners brought their own musical instrument to
      play.
   b) It was held at the Coliseum.
   c) It still carries the distinction of being the largest public event in
      Italy's history.
   d) Riots had to be broken up by police.

8) Philosopher Friedrich Nietzsche introduced what concept?
   a) Animals have souls
   b) Cleanliness is next to godliness
   c) Power of positive thinking
   d) God is dead

9) Alexander the Great was told that he was a descendant of
   _________ ?
   a) Achilles and Hercules
   b) Aristotle and Plato
   c) Rocky and Bullwinkle
   d) Zeus and Medusa

10) Which of these was invented by women?
    a) Thumb tacks and Pepto-Bismol
    b) Liquid paper and drugs to treat Leukemia
    c) Cell phones and fingernail polish

ANSWERS:

1) c	6) a
2) a	7) c
3) d	8) d
4) c	9) a
5) d	10) b

The Nutcracker King

Although he spent much of his adult life in the Big Apple, George Balanchine was born Giorgi Melitonovich Balanchivadze in Saint Petersburg, Russia. At the age of nine he was dancing at the Imperial Ballet School, but that abruptly ended with the victory of the Bolsheviks in the revolution. Balanchine played the piano at cabarets and movie theatres to pay for food until the ballet school eventually reopened. As a teenager he began to choreograph, and while touring in London, was asked to join Serge Diaghilev's Ballet Russes, which not only led Balanchine to defect, but eventually to become balletmaster of the company.

In the late 1920s, Balanchine created nine ballets, and in 1933, an American with a big dream of starting a ballet company in the United States, had no trouble convincing Balanchine to pack his bags for NYC. Three months after his arrival, the doors opened at the School of American Ballet.

After some ups and downs over the years, including a brief move to Hollywood, Balanchine in 1948 created the New York City Ballet. The 1954 staging of Balanchine's version of The Nutcracker, performed every year in New York City during the Christmas season, has become a holiday tradition throughout the U.S.

In 1978 Balanchine received the Kennedy Center Honors Award, the first year the award was bestowed. That same year, he began losing his balance while dancing. As the disease progressed, his balance, eyesight and hearing deteriorated and by 1982 he was incapacitated. It wasn't until after his death in 1982 at the age of seventy-nine that he was officially diagnosed with Creutzfeldt-Jakob disease.

A Timeline of Balloon Flight

1783

- Aviation scientists Jacques and Joseph Montgolfier sent a balloon full of smoke into the air. History marks this as the first balloon flight.

- Later that same year came the first hydrogen-filled balloon to soar the sky. Introduced by Jacques A.C. Charles, the balloon reached three thousand feet into the sky and traveled sixteen miles in forty-five minutes.

- Next came the first human balloon flight, achieved by Jean Pilâtre de Rozier and Marquis François d'Arlandes. They traveled nearly 5.5 miles at an altitude of five hundred feet.

1784

- The first powered balloon, driven by a propeller, was sent into flight by Jean Baptiste Marie Meusnier, whose name alone seems enough weight to ground the balloon! The balloon flew at approximately three miles per hour.

- The first balloon navigated by a woman was airborne. Ironically, Mme. Thible, pilot of the craft, was a French opera singer.

- The first ever military use of a balloon occurred during this same balloon-filled year. Jean Marie Coutelle made two separate four hour trips in a balloon designed for the French Army.

BREAKING NEWS!

The studies were done, and the results are in…

Children + Vegetables = Great Thinkers

A 2006 Southhampton University study found that children of high IQs were more likely to become vegetarians than children of average or lower IQ scores. The data showed that those who became vegetarians by the age of thirty had, on average, scored five points higher on an IQ test at age ten.

Women + Chocolate = Great Thinkers

A 2007 US study showed that women with curvy hips and a larger hip-to-waist ration were more likely to be intelligent than women without curves. The bigger the difference between the waist and hips, the more likely a woman was to hold a higher IQ. Researchers attributed the results to the fact that most women with curvy hips had fatty omega 3 deposits around their hips, a nutrient that can improve mental ability.

Breastfeeding your Way to Einsteinhood

A 2007 study in New Zealand and Britain led researchers to discover a gene that explains why breastfed babies tend to be more intelligent than those fed bottled milk. The gene, FADS2, is found in 90 percent of people, and serves to process fatty acids in the body. Babies who were breastfed and shared the genetic variant scored higher on intelligent tests than bottle-fed babies in the study.

FAMOUS LOVERS: LEONORA CARRINGTON AND MAX ERNST

Enter the young heroine

Leonora Carrington (born 1917) is a British painter. Her painting, with its dreamy, almost magical or mythical look, is considered in the movement of surrealism. In fact, it was painter Max Ernst's painting "Deux enfants menaces par un rosignol" that was her first contact with surrealism and came to be a driving influence behind her future work. Her show at the Pierre Matisse Gallery in 1947 won her international renown. She claims to have been attracted to Max Ernst as soon as she saw his work in person in 1936, before she even met him. And speaking of him…

Enter the older hero

Max Ernst (1891–1976) was a German painter, sculptor, and poet. His work, considered both Surrealist and Dada, has grown a large fan base. His paintings are on display at such prestigious places as Musee National d'Art Moderne, in the Centre Pompidou in Paris, France and in the Metropolitan Museum of Art. In popular culture, the band Mars Volta uses his art in their albums, and the band Mission of Burma has two songs titled after him.

He met Carrington at a party in 1937 in London. The two artists found a mutual understanding in each other, and Ernst left his wife to be with Carrington. The couple lived and worked together in Paris, inspiring each other's art. When they had to flee during WWII, they were forced to go separate ways. The stress and trauma of the war and their time apart put an end to their relationship. While it lasted, it was a passionate and fruitful love affair.

CRASH COURSE

PYTHAGORAS

One of the most famous philosophers to ever live, Pythagoras was born sometime between 600 and 590 BC. The length of his life has been estimated at nearly one hundred years.

Pythagoras has been credited to have been the first man to use the word "philosopher." Before that time, wise men called themselves "sages," which was interpreted as "those who know." Pythagoras was much more modest and coined the word "philosopher," which he himself defined as "one who is attempting to find out."

He traveled the ancient world extensively and studied under a great number of sages in a variety of schools and countries. When he returned from his wanderings, he established a school in Southern Italy in the town of Crotona. He taught a small group of students the secrets that were imparted to him and instructed them in geometry, astronomy, and music, which he felt were the foundations of all arts and sciences.

He married one of his disciples when he was about sixty years old and fathered seven children with her. She was a devoted wife and was said to inspire him until his assassination and continued to spread his teachings after his death.

Pythagoras taught that friendship was the purest and closest to perfection of all relationships. He said that all bonds without friendship were shackles, and that there was nothing to be gained in their maintenance. He believed that knowledge was the fruit of the accumulation of experience. He thought that knowledge could be obtained in lots of different ways, but primarily through observation. He was a devout monotheist and taught that both the universe and man were made in the image of God (to know one was to know the other).

His school was burned, and many of his students killed, but his teachings, through a devout following, survived.

An Overview of Two Modernist Novels

Modernism was a literary movement in the first few decades of the twentieth century. Here are summaries of two important Modernist novels.

Mrs. Dalloway (1925)

This novel by Virginia Woolf is written in a third person voice, following the actions of its two main characters: Clarissa Dalloway and Septimus Warren Smith. It's written in stream of consciousness, a style that mimics an ongoing though. Often the thoughts lead into each other with no explanation or structural breaks. The entire novel takes place in a setting of one day.

It touches on issues of World War I "shell-shock," the syndrome of feeling fragmented, and depressed many soldiers reported experiencing after coming home from the war. It also comments on the state of women at the turn of the century. Women's societal role was shifting as they began working outside the home. The book also appreciates the ability of women to express themselves inside their homes.

The Sound and the Fury (1929)

William Faulkner's masterpiece novel, details events happening in the lives of the Compson family, one of the many families Faulkner created to inhabit his made up Mississippi county of Yoknapatawpha. Almost all of his novels are set in this fictitious county, and the stories and characters interrelate and pop up again and again in his books.

This book presents sections that are narrated by members of the Compson family. The plot focuses on the daughter Caddy and her out-of-marriage pregnancy. Much of the story is her brothers Benjy, Quentin, and Jason being obsessed with Caddy and her daughter Quentin.

The writing is complicated and tough to follow. It's written in several different voices, including Benjy, the mentally challenged "man-child." Faulkner gives no breaks; he requires much of his readers, but gives much back.

Six Degrees to Johnny Depp

1. Charles Darwin studied on the isolated (pirate-like) island of Galapagos. Darwin (1809–1882) was an English geologist and biologist, well-known for theories presented in his book On the Origin of Species (1859). He argued that humans, like all other species, evolve over time through a process of natural selection that favors the strongest organisms over the weaker.

2. Charles Darwin was a Utilitarian like Jeremy Bentham (1748–1832). Bentham, a British philosopher and social reformer, was a strong proponent of utilitarianism's idea that the amount of "rightness" of an action is strictly decided by how much happiness it brings in total. In other words, the more people made happy by an action, and the happier they are, the better the action. Bentham was teacher to John Mill and John Stuart Mill.

3. Jeremy Bentham's ideas were employed by Michel Foucault (1926–1984). Foucault was a French philosopher and sociologist. With his books *Madness and Civilization* (1961), *Discipline and Punish* (1975), and especially the multivolume *History of Sexuality* (1976–1984), he completely changed the face of modern philosophy. His work inspects social institutions and questions their use of power, focusing on topics such as insanity, prisons, and ideas of sexuality.

4. Foucault was the major inspiration for much of Judith Butler's (born 1956) writing. Butler is an American philosopher and feminist. In her most famous book, *Gender Trouble* (1990), she questions how "natural" the connections between sex (meaning male/female/etc), gender (masculine vs. feminine), and sexuality (sexual orientation) really are. She currently teaches at the University of California, Berkeley.

5. Judith Butler's book *Gender Trouble* is named after director John Water's film *Female Trouble* (1974).

6. John Water's film *Cry-Baby* (1990) stars Johnny Depp!

FAMOUS ASSASSINATIONS

Assassin: Marcus Junius Brutus
Target: Roman Dictator Julius Caesar
Result: Caused the Roman Civil War and indirectly lead to the fall of the Roman Republic.

Assassin: John Wilkes Booth
Target: President Abraham Lincoln
Result: Dashed hopes that the North and South could be reconcile differences and start anew after the Civil War. Many believed that only Lincoln was popular and respected enough to bridge the divide that existed after the war. What resulted was the Restoration, a period of unpopular domination of the South by the North that would contribute to cultural divisions that persists to this day.

Assassin: Gavrilo Princip
Target: Austrian Archduke Franz Ferdinand
Result: Brought down a shaky peace among European nations and led to what many consider the start of The Great War (World War I), which killed millions of people, destroyed the Austro-Hungarian Empire and the innocence of a generation.

Assassin: Sirhan Sirhan
Target: US Senator Robert F. Kennedy
Result: Robert believed that his brother John F. Kennedy's assassination was left largely unresolved and poorly investigated. RFK promised to reopen the case if elected. Robert's death ended any possibility of that happening.

Assassin: James Earl Ray (alleged)
Target: Martin Luther King
Result: Splintered a large organized movement that King, as the figurehead, helped build. Helped set back race relations in America for decades. Contributed to an overall sense of hopelessness among blacks concerning politics and reconciliation with whites.

ANTHROPOLOGY 101
CLAUDE LÉVI-STRAUSS

"The scientist is not a person who gives the right answers; he is one who asks the right questions." —*Claude Lévi-Strauss*

Lévi-Strauss (born 1908) is a French anthropologist responsible for the creation of an entire school of thought. His life long research patterns were established when he took a position as a visiting professor in Brazil. There he did fieldwork studying local, indigenous tribes like Guaycuru and the Bororo Indians. His travels in South America culminated in his book *Tristes-Tropiques* (1955), a travel journal.

All of his work focuses on understanding a subject by dissecting its underlying, formative principles or structures instead of its content. For instance, in his book *The Elementary Structures of Kinship* (1949), instead of studying the content of a common ancestor, he studied the structures that organize families (i.e. marriages, births, etc).

Again, in his masterpiece *Mythologiques* (1971), he traces a common myth that exists in many cultures around the world, but instead of discussing the contents of the myth—meaning, the story itself—he talks about the structure formed through the relationships of the elements of the story.

By employing this method of study, he created a whole school of thought called Structuralism. Structuralism is the practice of studying a subject by breaking it down into a system of interrelated parts. It suggests that one can learn a subject by starting at one part, finding a relationship with another part, learning that part, and so on until an entire network, or structure, is visible. Structuralism was the predominant method of learning for a large part of the twentieth century.

SO SAYS MARGARET THATCHER

As Conservative Party Prime Minister of the United Kingdom from 1975 to 1990, Margaret Thatcher had the longest continuous period in office since Robert Jenkinson whose service ended in 1827.

During her fifteen years in office, Thatcher created a legacy for herself as an uncompromising Cold War politician, and became known by the Soviet Media (most of whom adored her) as the "Iron Lady." By the British under her leadership she was both revered and reviled for her conservative platforms, and fought her critics tooth–and-nail throughout her tenure. Listed below are some such quotes from the Iron Lady.

- Being powerful is like being a lady. If you have to tell people you are, you aren't.

- Being prime minister is a lonely job... you cannot lead from the crowd.

- I always cheer up immensely if an attack is particularly wounding because I think, well, if they attack one personally, it means they have not a single political argument left.

- I am extraordinarily patient, provided I get my own way in the end.

- If my critics saw me walking over the Thames they would say it was because I couldn't swim.

- No one would remember the Good Samaritan if he'd only had good intentions; he had money as well.

- If you set out to be liked, you would be prepared to compromise on anything at any time, and you would achieve nothing.

- If you lead a country like Britain, a strong country, a country which has taken a lead in world affairs in good times and in bad, a country that is always reliable, then you have to have a touch of iron about you.

FRANKLIN D. ROOSEVELT

By 1931, the Great Depression was at its most awful. Many New Yorkers were unemployed. As their governor, Roosevelt formed a work program for New Yorkers in need of jobs.

In 1932, the Democratic Party nominated Roosevelt as their candidate for president. By this point, Americans were greatly disenchanted by the Great Depression. Roosevelt brought hope to voters with what he called the New Deal. He defeated President Herbert Hoover, winning the election by a landslide.

While in office, President Roosevelt managed the nation through one of the most terrible tribulations in the twentieth century. Within four months of his inauguration, Roosevelt signed multiple programs into law. He called these programs the National Recovery Act, and through them Roosevelt planned to turn the nation's economy around. His plans included the Civilian Conservation Corps (CCC), a group designed to preserve the nation's natural resources and the Works Progress Administration (WPA). The WPA created jobs for millions of Americans, constructing public buildings, bridges and dams.

President Roosevelt also signed into law the Social Security Act, which provided money to Americans incapable of finding jobs, and also to those too old for employment. The Act also provided support to people unable to afford medical care as well as people who needed help to support their children. President Roosevelt explained his New Deal plans over the radio in broadcasts referred to as "fireside chats." Although some Americans criticized Roosevelt's programs as unconstitutional, most believed he was saving the nation. His programs received enough public support for him to be reelected in 1936. In fact, the American people elected Franklin D. Roosevelt as president four times and no other U.S. president has been elected more than twice.

Please Allow Me to Think Aloud: President Franklin D. Roosevelt

Through his fireside chats and public speeches, President Franklin Roosevelt caught the confidence and trust of millions of Americans. Listed below are a few examples of his wise and comforting words.

* Be sincere; be brief; be seated.
* Art is not a treasure in the past or an importation from another land, but part of the present life of all living and creating peoples.
* I ask you to judge me by the enemies I have made.
* But while they prate of economic laws, men and women are starving. We must lay hold of the fact that economic laws are not made by nature. They are made by human beings.
* Confidence … thrives on honesty, on honor, on the sacredness of obligations, on faithful protection and on unselfish performance. Without them it cannot live.
* Competition has been shown to be useful up to a certain point and no further, but cooperation, which is the thing we must strive for today, begins where competition leaves off.
* A nation that destroys its soils destroys itself. Forests are the lungs of our land, purifying the air and giving fresh strength to our people.
* I believe that in every country the people themselves are more peaceably and liberally inclined than their governments.
* A conservative is a man with two perfectly good legs who, however, has never learned how to walk forward.
* I do not look upon these United States as a finished product. We are still in the making.

Extra Credit: President Roosevelt was the first President to appear on television. It occurred in 1939 and was filmed at the World's Fair in New York. No indication has been made as to whether or not he partook of the funnel cake.

After the Reign: President Carter's Post-Term Contributions

Former President Jimmy Carter's greatest achievements didn't occur during his presidency. Elected during a time of incredibly low morale among Americans because of a sluggish economy, energy shortages and Watergate, Carter spent his short term working with little success to correct these problems. After losing his re-election, however, he began making significant contributions to his country and the world.

President Carter began teaching at Emory University in Atlanta since being voted out of office, and he also wrote several books on politics, social welfare and foreign relations. Quite a philanthropist, Carter gave most of the money he earned to various charities, including Habitat for Humanity International (HFHI). In 1996 President Bill Clinton declared HFHI, a non-profit organization dedicated to the construction of "simple, decent, and affordable" housing, to be "the most successful continuous community service project in the history of the United States." In 2002, President Carter became the third U.S. President to receive a Nobel Peace Prize. The prize was awarded "for his decades of untiring effort to find peaceful solutions to international conflicts, to advance democracy and human rights, and to promote economic and social development."

EXTRA CREDIT: Jimmy Carter stood on the bar of Pinkie Master's Lounge in Savannah, Georgia to declare his intention to be President. Patrons of the establishment can place their beverage of choice on top of an inlaid bronze marking the spot of that historic event. There is no indication as to what he may have been drinking, but Jägermeister girls are reported to have been spotted around the corner earlier that evening.

A Revolutionary Encounter

Approximately six months prior to the Bay of Pigs Invasion, the United States unsuccessful attempt to invade Cuba and overthrow the government of Fidel Castro, a remarkable meeting took place in New York. Sometime during September 1960, the leader of the Cuban Revolution traveled to New York for the United Nations General Assembly. Among those scheduled to rendezvous with Castro was the second most influential leader of the Nation of Islam, Malcolm X.

The meeting took place at the Theresa, a hotel in New York's predominantly black neighborhood known as Harlem. As a leader of the Nation of Islam, Malcolm was a well-known constituent of a Harlem-based welcoming committee composed of black community leaders that greeted international visitors, mostly those from African countries.

During his visit, Castro's delegates had been refused accommodation by numerous hotels in the area as a result of his ever-growing reputation as an enemy of the state. Racially motivated slander followed the group, and rumors were reported that Castro's personal chef had slaughtered live chickens at another hotel in town. Although Castro refused to meet with several members of the American press while visiting New York, Malcolm X and his group of leaders offered the Hotel Theresa as lodging for the Cuban leader. Little is certain about what was discussed, as Castro spoke little English. As a result, much of the conversation was riddled with broken translation. According to some reports, however the two revolutionaries lamented the incredible power of capitalist propaganda.

Shortly after the historic meeting in autumn of 1960, the U.S. government engaged itself in a semi-secret campaign to remove Castro from power. Multiple attempts on the leader's life failed, to which Castro replied, "If surviving assassination attempts were an Olympic event, I would win the gold medal." Unfortunately for Malcolm X, the Black Nationalist did not share the luck enjoyed by Castro. On February 14, 1965, three members of the Nation of Islam rushed into a ballroom where Malcolm was speaking and shot him fifteen times.

CRASH COURSE
MARK TWAIN

Named by William Faulkner "The Father of American literature," novelist Mark Twain can be found on the bookshelves of most any southern home. Most good ol' boys and southern belles are familiar with *The Adventures of Huckleberry Finn*, but how much do they really know about Twain as he really lived? Several biographies, such as *Mark Twain: A Life* by Ron Powers, illustrate the man behind the genius.

- Twain was a vegetarian, and radically opposed to the dissection of living animals for scientific research.

- Twain, born Samuel Clemens, had several pen names. These include Thomas Jefferson Snodgrass, Rambler, Sergeant Fathom, and W. Epaminondas Adrastus Blab.

- In 1849, at age fourteen, Twain dropped out of John Dawson's school to concentrate on working for Hannibal Gazette and later the Hannibal Journal.

- Twain held three patents for inventions he funded: an automatically self-adjusting vest strap, a memory-improving history game, and a self-pasting scrapbook.

- Twain despised organized religion, and wrote posthumously published books on the matter. Among these are *Letters from the Earth* and *The Mysterious Stranger*.

- While living briefly in New Hampshire, Twain rented housecats to keep him company.

- Before publishing his first book, Twain held many jobs, including that of a steamboat pilot and a gold prospector.

- Although he briefly volunteered in the Confederate Calvary, Twain later became a staunch abolitionist.

So Says Sir Winston Churchill

While serving as prime minister of England during World War II, Winston Churchill gave grand speeches riddled with aphorisms that remain popular today. Armed with what he himself referred to as "rhetorical power," Churchill's oratory proved greatly inspirational to the embattled British. Listed below are several such quotations.

- You have enemies? Good. That means you've stood up for something, sometime in your life.

- We shall defend our island, whatever the cost may be, we shall fight on the beaches, we shall fight on the landing grounds, we shall fight in the fields and in the streets, we shall fight in the hills; we shall never surrender.

- We do not covet anything from any nation except their respect.

- Victory at all costs, victory in spite of all terror, victory however long and hard the road may be; for without victory, there is no survival.

- There is nothing more exhilarating than to be shot at without result.

- A politician needs the ability to foretell what is going to happen tomorrow, next week, next month, and next year. And to have the ability afterwards to explain why it didn't happen.

- When I am abroad, I always make it a rule never to criticize or attack the government of my own country. I make up for lost time when I come home.

- Too often the strong, silent man is silent only because he does not know what to say, and is reputed strong only because he has remained silent.

- My rule of life prescribed as an absolutely sacred rite smoking cigars and also the drinking of alcohol before, after and if need be during all meals and in the intervals between them.

- There are a terrible lot of lies going about the world, and the worst of it is that half of them are true.

Evil Genius: Pol Pot and the Khmer Rogue

The leader of the Cambodian communist movement known as Khmer Rouge, Pol Pot created a forced agrarian collectivization in the late 1970s.

The plan relocated city dwellers to Cambodia's countryside, where the government created forced-labor projects on government-owned farms. The goal of these plans was to rebuild civilization in what the authorities referred to as "Year Zero," a concept founded on the philosophy that the Khmer Rouge must destroy the culture and traditions of the previous society in order to create a new utopia. The Cambodian "Year Zero" was a direct analogy to the abolition of the French monarchy in 1792, at which point that nation created the French Revolutionary Calendar.

The results of Pol Pot's projects were genocidal, resulting in up to 1.7 million deaths. The causes of the massacre included slave labor, starvation, poor medical care, and capital punishment on a massive scale. The Khmer Rouge targeted teachers, religious figures, and intellectuals in particular in an attempt to fulfill the purging of the nation. The organization adopted the theory that a civilization's regeneration required fewer than 2 million in order to succeed, a presumption illustrated by their proverb, "To keep you is no benefit, to destroy you is no loss."

Pol Pot's role in the Cambodian genocide undeniably ranks him easily among history's greatest maniac, Adolf Hitler. The dealings of small eastern countries such as Cambodia frequently fail to capture the attention of the west, but Pol Pot's crimes horrified people throughout the world. Because his totalitarian reign was relatively short, lasting only three years, the massive scale of Pol Pot's crimes against humanity make him one of the most evil men in history.

THE AMERICAN PRESIDENT

Scores of books have been written on the assassination of Abraham Lincoln, the sixteenth President and conjectural ender of slavery in the United States. The subject has filled the pages of texts both non-fiction and otherwise, and most agree on the circumstances. As a result, most everyone knows that Lincoln's murderer was a Confederate sympathizer named John Wilkes Booth. Thanks to the abundance of documentaries on an assortment of history cable channels, the arm chair historian knows it happened in a theater. Some elite civil war buffs even discern that it happened at Ford's theater and that the President's life didn't end until the next day.

If, however, the correct response to a $1,000 *Jeopardy!* clue was "Our American Cousin," how many contestants would know? How many would look Alex Trebek dead in the eye and ask with coolness, "What was the play being performed at the time of Lincoln's assassination?"

Unfortunately for virtually unknown playwright Tom Taylor, the answer to that Daily Double is… only a handful.

The play, a farce premiering in 1858 in which an awkward American meets his aristocratic relatives from England had some impact on American culture prior to Lincoln's assassination. In modern times, however, most of the play's influences have lost their relevance. An example of a fad birthed by Taylor's production includes confused aphorisms, aptly referred to as "Dundrearyisms." This humorous twaddle experienced a brief popularity as a result of the play's character, Lord Dundreary. Dundreary, a foolish aristocrat, featured as a crowd-pleasing buffoon whose twisted clichés included such gems as "Birds of a feather gather no moss."

Ronald Reagan: What Others Say

Albeit he's not the most well-liked U.S. President of the twentieth century, Ronald Reagan was unquestionably not the most disliked of America's leaders either. From deft dealings with his public to daft dealings with Iran, his tenure as President transformed American politics forever. Listed below are a few examples of what others said about the nation's fortieth President.

- "He took an America suffering from 'malaise' … and made its citizens believe again in their destiny." —Dr. Edwin Feulner

- "A determined opponent of communism … he played an important role in bringing an end to communism and to the artificial division of Europe imposed after the Second World War." —Irish Prime Minister Bertie Ahern

- President Reagan's leadership served to define an era of sweeping geo-political change…. He helped lay the foundations for the end of the Cold War…. His wit, warmth and unique capacity to communicate helped to make him one of the most influential figures in the second half of the twentieth century." —Canadian Prime Minister Paul Martin

- "Over two terms, from 1981 to 1989, Reagan reshaped the Republican Party in his conservative image, fixed his eye on the demise of the Soviet Union and Eastern European communism and tripled the national debt to $3 trillion in his single-minded competition with the other superpower." —Associated Press

- "As the age of television progresses the Reagans will be the rule, not the exception. To be perfect for television is all a President has to be these days." —Gore Vidal

- "Someday our grandchildren will look up at us and say, 'Where were you and what were you doing, when you first realized that President Reagan was, er, not playing with a full deck?' —Barbara Ehrenreich

ELEANOR OF AQUITAINE

Eleanor of Aquitaine, born in 1122 and also known as Duchess of Aquitaine, was one of the richest and most powerful women in Europe during the High Middle Ages. She was Queen in both France, where she was married to Louis VII, and in England, where she wed Henry II, and, as a result, mother of two kings of England, Richard I and John. She also is well known for her involvement in the Second Crusade. Below is a list of her many children.

With Louis VII of France:

- Marie of France (1145–1198), married Henry I, Count of Champagne
- Alix of France (1151–1198), married Theobald V, Count of Blois

With Henry II of England:

- William, Count of Poitiers (1153–1156)
- Henry the Young King (1155–1183), married Marguerite of France
- Matilda of England (1156–1189), married Henry the Lion, Duke of Saxony
- Richard the Lionheart (1157–1199), king of England, married Berengaria of Navarre
- Geoffrey II, Duke of Brittany (1158–1186), married Constance, Duchess of Brittany
- Leonora of England (1162–1214), married Alfonso VIII of Castile
- Joan of England (1165–1199), married William II of Sicily and then Raymond VI of Toulouse
- John Lackland (1166–1216), king of England, married Isabel of Gloucester and then Isabella of Angoulême

DEMOSTHENES

Demosthenes was known for his penchant for oratory, dominating courts and discourse in ancient Greece with eloquence and tenor that commanded attention and changed society. Ironic that was, because as a boy Demosthenes had a speech impediment. He was inarticulate and stammered in his pronunciation, described as sort of a breathy tone that disrupted his sentences. And, like all kids, he was taunted by others. But he also was inspired by those taunts. He began a disciplined program to overcome these shortcomings and improve his diction. He practiced and practiced until he developed not only ability but confidence.

At age twenty, he gave what was known to be his first big speech: He went to court to persuade his guardians to give him his inheritance. The process took many arguments and numerous trials. Demosthenes believed the guardians had stolen the money his father had set aside. They left him with a house, some slaves and a small percentage of the cash. He argued for a full accounting and got it. The ending wasn't happy: He recovered only a small portion of the estate.

But in that personal and futile proceeding a brilliant career was launched. Demosthenes made his living as a speech writer and a lawyer, helping script arguments for the courts, and he soon grew interested in politics, becoming a vibrant public advocate for Athens and its needs.

He fought against kings and served as a diplomat to gain allies for the leaders of Athens. He became a powerful influence on the restoration of Athens. He was powerful and respected—though not by everyone. But, like so many politicians, Demosthenes had a scandalous private life. He was married and fathered a daughter, but many of his critics said he had homosexual encounters and even dallied with young boys. They said he kept rich young men around and made money from them. Was he an ancient pimp or an opportunist?

One writer said that Demosthenes had one young boy sleep with his wife to try to impregnate her, but another said she only slept with the boy to make Demosthenes jealous. Or maybe it was Demosthenes' opponents who were jealous.

RONALD HOEFLIN: FOUNDER OF HIGH IQ SOCIETIES

As a child growing up in St. Louis, Missouri, Ronald Hoeflin memorized pi to 200 places. He received his Ph.D. in philosophy from the New School of Social Research in New York, in addition to studying library science and receiving two bachelor's degrees and two master's degrees.

Hoeflin created the Mega and Titan intelligence tests to provide a measure for people whose IQ is higher than standard tests can evaluate. He has also established several high-IQ societies, including the Top One Percent Society, the One-in-a-Thousand Society, the Prometheus Society, the Epimetheus Society, the Mega Society, and the Omega Society.

High-IQ Societies

Sometimes people with high IQs like to get together and hang out. There are dozens of active high-IQ societies—some meeting together exclusively on the Internet and others holding regular meetings and/or annual conferences. Most of the societies require that a person achieve a certain IQ score to join. Together the organized groups of intellectuals solve problems, exchange ideas, identify and nurture human intelligence, and maintain a motivating intellectual and social environment. The most famous high-IQ societies require a score of 137 and higher.

> The Lewis M. Terman Society consists of four high-IQ Societies founded by Ronald K. Hoeflin, Ph.D. These include: Top One Percent Society (99 percent); One-in-a-Thousand Society (99.9 percent), Epimetheus Society (99.997 percent), and Omega Society (99.9999 percent).

Marilyn vos Savant: Highest IQ Ever Recorded

Born in 1946 in St. Louis, Missouri, Marilyn vos Savant attended Washington University and received an honorary doctorate from the College of New Jersey in 2003.

- She held the distinction of highest IQ from 1986 to 1989 in the Guinness Book of World Records and currently is listed in the Guinness Book of World Records Hall of Fame for highest IQ.

- She works with her husband, Robert Jarvik, assisting him with research regarding cardiovascular disease and serving as Chief Financial Officer for his company, Jarvik Heart.

- Savant has written nonfiction books on a variety of subjects including The Art of Spelling, The Power of Logical Thinking, The World's Most Famous Math Problem, and others. She writes the column Ask Marilyn for Parade magazine and has written a collection of short stories, a stage play, and two novels.

- Savant's IQ is said to be 228.

The Curvy Figures Add Up

A 2007 U.S. study showed that women with curvy hips and a larger hip-to-waist ratio were more likely to be more intelligent than women without curves. The bigger the difference between the waist and hips, the more likely a woman was to hold a higher IQ. Researchers attributed the results to the fact that most women with curvy hips had fatty omega-3 deposits around their hips, a nutrient that can improve mental ability.

FIRST AFRICAN-AMERICAN WOMAN MILLIONAIRE

C. J. Walker was born in Mississippi in 1867 and was an orphan by age seven. She made a living for herself by working first in the cotton fields then as a washerwoman. When she was 20 years old, she moved to St. Louis.

In order to treat her own hair and scalp problems, she began experimenting with various chemicals and creams. Eventually, she created fine hair care items especially for African-American women.

She employed "Walker Agents," women who would go door to door to sell the hair products. By 1910, her business had grown so much that she opened a factory in Indianapolis, and by 1915, she employed 3,000 people, making her company the largest black-owned business in the United States at the time.

According to the Guinness Book of World Records, Walker was the first self-made American woman millionaire who did not inherit her wealth or marry a man who was a millionaire.

At the time of her death, her company and the combination of her personal assets including real estate, furniture, and jewelry were valued at over $1,000,000.

First Woman to Receive a U.S. Patent

African-American Mary Dixon Kies received the first U.S. patent granted to a woman in her own name on May 5, 1809. She had developed an easy method of weaving straw with silk, making a strong fabric to use in making hats and sunbonnets. This was a popular discovery since many women wore bonnets while working in the fields. The straw and silk bonnets were cost effective and sturdy for working in the hot sun.

Kies' invention bolstered New England's hat economy, which had been faltering because of an embargo on imported European goods. Straw bonnets manufactured in Massachusetts alone in 1810 had an estimated value of more than $500,000 or over $4.7 million in today's money. Dolly Madison honored Kies for her innovation.

The first U.S. patent was given to Samuel Hopkins on July 31, 1790 by President George Washington for a method of producing pot ash and pearl ash. Since then more than 6 million patents have been granted.

SIR TIM BERNERS-LEE: INTERNET PIONEER

Born in 1955, Tim Berners-Lee grew up in London and later graduated from Oxford university in 1976 with a degree in physics. In 1980, he built a prototype, which he called "Enquire," that would allow researchers to share information using a global system of "hypertext." He presented his idea to combine hypertext with the Internet in 1989—the World Wide Web.

Berners-Lee began work at the Massachusetts Institute of Technology (MIT) in Boston and, in 1994, founded the World Wide Web Consortium at the Laboratory of Computer Science (LCS) at the university. Currently, he serves as director of the consortium and works as a senior research scientist at LCS, now known as the Computer Science and Artificial Intelligence Laboratory.

In 2001, Berners-Lee became a fellow of the Royal Society and was knighted in 2004. He has received numerous other awards and honors.

In addition to his degree from Queen's College in 1976, he has received several honorary degrees:
- Parsons School of Design, New York (D.F.A., 1995)
- Southampton University (D.Sc., 1995)
- Essex University (D.U., 1998)
- Southern Cross University (1998)
- Open University (D.U., 2000)
- Columbia University (D.Law, 2001)
- Oxford University (D.Sc., 2001)
- University of Port Elizabeth (DSc., 2002)
- Lancaster University (D.Sc., 2004)

L'il Poison: Gaming Prodigy

It doesn't take a genius to pick up an XBox controller and blow an entire day plugged-in. Fans of varying intelligence across the world have embraced the relatively new entertainment. As a result, a dedicated and loyal fan base, which began with youngsters of the late '70s and early '80s, has matured into a demographic that spends billions of dollars annually. Many concerned parents and annoyed spouses loathe the addictive and time-consuming nature of the video games that have stormed into their homes. The proud parents of Victor "L'il Poison" De Leon III of New York, however, are an exception.

L'il Poison, the youngest professional video gamer in the world, might also be the youngest breadwinner outside of Hollywood. Playing his first game of Dreamcast's NBA 2K at age two in 2000, apparently "owned," meaning he was exceptionally good. Currently grossing over six figures, the nine-year-old gamer brings new meaning to the term "young professional."

L'il Poison prepared himself for a professional career in gaming by entering his first Halo competition at age four. He dominated many of the event's competing participants, coming in fourth place overall. Major League Gaming recruited him in 2005, making him the youngest professional gamer of all time. The organization sponsored a competition which took place in Washington, D.C.

Playing against adults, he came in second place in the competition and had earned $2,000 by age seven, losing to his dad, who is aptly known by the handle Poison. The prize placed him in the 2008 Guinness Book of World Records as the youngest person to be paid to play video games.

CRASH COURSE
THE DRAKE EQUATION

Developed by Frank Drake in the 1960s, the Drake Equation is a way of estimating the number of civilizations that exist and might be transmitting radio frequencies in our galaxy. The factors of the equation include the number of sunlike stars in our galaxy and the fraction of habitable planets supporting communicating civilizations, along with several other elements of consideration. The result of multiplying these various factors is N, the number of transmitting civilizations. As you might think, many of the factors necessary for the equation are somewhat unknown; therefore, N could range from one (with our civilization being alone in the galaxy) to thousands or even millions. For this reason, the Drake Equation is related to the Fermi Paradox.

The Equation

$$N = R \times f_p \times n_e \times f_l \times f_i \times f_c \times L$$

where:

- N is the number of civilizations in our galaxy with which we might expect to be able to communicate

- R is the rate of star formation in our galaxy

- f_p is the fraction of those stars that have planets

- n_e is the average number of planets that can potentially support life per star that has planets

- f_l is the fraction of the above that actually go on to develop life

- f_i is the fraction of the above that actually go on to develop intelligent life

- f_c is the fraction of the above that are willing and able to communicate

- L is the expected lifetime of such a civilization

Robert James "Bobby" Fischer: Chess Grandmaster

Born in Chicago, Illinois, during World War II, Bobby was a high-school dropout and chess prodigy. He learned how to play at age six from the instructions in his sister's chess set. His school records indicated that he held an IQ of 187.

- At age thirteen, Fischer won the United States Junior Chess Championship. The next year, he successfully defended his junior title, and then went on to win the United States Open Chess Championship, making him the youngest U.S. champion ever.

- Fischer defeated Boris Spassky in the 1972 World Championship match—The Match of the Century. That win made him the 11th World Chess Champion and the highest-rated player in history. He appeared on the covers of Life and Sports Illustrated and on a Bob Hope television special.

- In 1992, after twenty years out of competition, Fischer challenged Boris Spassky to a "revenge match." Because of a United Nations embargo, the United States declared that it was illegal for Fischer to compete in this challenge. Following the match, a warrant was issued for his arrest.

- After denouncing his U.S. citizenship, Fischer took refuge in Iceland. Because of contemptuous political comments that he made after the 9/11 terrorist attacks on the US, Fischer's membership in the United States Chess Federation was cancelled in 2001. In 2004, Fischer was arrested in Japan for trying to use a cancelled U.S. passport.

- Fischer died in 2008.

Walt Disney: American Screenwriter and Entrepreneur

Almost everyone knows the name Walt Disney from cartoons, movies, or the popular amusement parks around the world. Born in Chicago in 1901, Disney spent much of his youth in Missouri, where he learned to draw. While attending high school in the daytime, he took night classes at the Chicago Art Institute to perfect his drawing skills.

- In his early 20s, Disney struck out for California. He teamed with his brother, Roy, to form Disney Brothers Studio, later called Walt Disney Enterprises. Their first animation project was a silent cartoon called "The Alice Comedies," based on Alice in Wonderland.

- He debuted his most famous cartoon character—Mickey Mouse—in the silent cartoon Plane Crazy and then in the 1928 cartoon Steamboat Willie. This animated film was the first ever to combine sound with motion.

- When the Mickey Mouse Club organized in 1929, children got together every Saturday afternoon to watch cartoons and play games in local theaters across the nation. There were several million members who knew a secret handshake, special greeting, code of behavior, and club song.

- In the 1930s, Mickey's animated friends came along, including Minnie Mouse, Clarabelle Cow, Horace Horsecollar, Goofy, Pluto, Donald Duck, Peg-Leg Pete, and others.

- Disney invented the multiplane camera in 1937 and changed the world of animation. This special camera increased the quality of cartoons and made full-length animated film possible. Snow White and the Seven Dwarfs was the first full-length animated film shot with the camera.

- Walt Disney was a decidedly patriotic man, and with the advent of World War II, he stopped nearly all commercial productions and concentrated on aiding the war effort by issuing training films, doing goodwill tours, and designing posters and armed forces insignia.

- For all of the cartoons through World War II, Disney himself served as the voice of Mickey. From 1946 to 1974, Jim Macdonald was Mickey's voice. Today, Mickey's voice is that of Wayne Allwine.

- Disney earned 22 Academy Awards, 8 Emmy Awards, an honorary degree from Harvard, and the Medal of Freedom, the United States' highest civilian award.

- Disney's Fantasia, starring Mickey as the sorcerer's apprentice, debuted in 1940. It used animation techniques and stereophonic sound that other studios could not match for a decade.

- In 1955, The Mickey Mouse Club became the most successful children's television show ever.

- When Disney died in 1966, 240 million people had seen at least one Disney movie, 80 million had read a Disney book, 50 million had listened to a Disney record, 100 million had watched a weekly Disney television program, and 80 million children had watched a Disney educational film.

The Woderful World of Disney

Disney comic books have been distributed in Australia, Austria, Belgium, Brazil, Bulgaria, the People's Republic of China, Colombia, Czech Republic, Denmark, Egypt, Estonia, Finland, France, Germany, Greece, Guyana, Hungary, Iceland, India, Indonesia, Israel, Italy, Latvia, Lithuania, Mexico, the Netherlands, Norway, Poland, Portugal, Romania, Russia, Saudi Arabia, Slovenia, Spain, Sweden, Thailand, Turkey, the United Kingdom, USA, and the former Yugoslavia.

PHYSICS 101
WILLIAM GILBERT

Born in 16th-century England, William Gilbert received his M.D. from Cambridge University in 1569. He set up his medical practice in London and, in 1600, became president of the Royal College of Physicians. He served as physician to Queen Elizabeth I in the last few years of her reign and then to the succeeding monarch, King James I.

- Gilbert studied magnetism and the amber effect (what we call static). He based his theories of magnetism on the magnet's polarity in relationship to the polarity of Earth.

- He believed magnetism was the soul of Earth and that a perfectly spherical lodestone, when aligned with Earth's poles, would spin on its axis, just as Earth spins on its axis.

- This theory went against traditional belief that the earth was fixed at the center of the universe. Much of Galileo's claim for the earth revolving around the sun came from his study of Gilbert's theories.

On the Magnet

Published in 1600, Gilbert's *De Magnate*, "On the Magnet," presented the time's leading theories on magnetism and electricity and was widely accepted throughout Europe.

Sir Karl Popper: Philosopher

Born in Vienna in 1902, Karl Popper attended the University of Vienna, where he received a Ph.D. in philosophy in 1928 and later taught secondary school. His first book, *Logik der Forschung*, was published in 1934 and was translated into English in 1959. Here he questioned some of the popular thought of the day and introduced his theory of falsifiability.

In 1937, Popper left Vienna to escape political oppression. He accepted a teaching position at Canterbury University College, New Zealand, lecturing in philosophy. He moved on to England in 1946 to become reader in logic and scientific method at the London School of Economics.

Popper was among the most influential philosophers of science in the twentieth century. He called his philosophy critical rationalism. He believed that positive outcomes that result from experimental testing couldn't confirm a scientific theory. His insistence that a theory should be considered scientific only if it is falsifiable led him to question psychoanalysis, quantum mechanics, and other popular theories. However, he was a proponent of Albert Einstein's theories about the universe.

Popper received many honors, including being chosen as president of the Aristotelian Society, knighted in 1965, and elected as a fellow of the Royal Society in 1976. He also received a variety of awards, including the Lippincott Award from the American Political Science Association, the Sonning Prize, and the Grand Decoration of Honour in Gold from Austria.

Karl Popper died in 1994 at the age of 92.

Daniel Bernoulli: Mathematician

Born in 1700 in the Netherlands, Daniel Bernoulli spent much of his youth in Switzerland. He learned about calculus from his father, who was a professor of mathematics first at Groningen University in the Netherlands and then at Basel University. Although his father pushed him to study medicine, Bernoulli was always more interested in mathematics.

English physician William Harvey's book On the Movement of Heat and Blood in Animals showed Bernoulli how the study of medicine and mathematics could be combined. After receiving his medical degree, Bernoulli sought a position in academics so that he could continue to study the way fluids move.

- At age twenty-three, he won first prize in a competition at the French Academy of Sciences for his design of a ship's hourglass that would produce a reliable trickle of sand even in stormy weather.

- When he was twenty-five, he was invited to become professor of mathematics at the Imperial Academy in St. Petersburg, Russia. There he took on assistant Leohnard Euler (who had been a student of Bernoulli's father), and together they developed a way to measure blood pressure by puncturing a patient's artery (it was another 170 years before the blood pressure cuff was invented).

Family Competition

In 1734, the French Academy of Sciences awarded Bernoulli and his father a joint prize. This led to his father's banning Bernoulli from his house because he could not admit that his son was an equal. Bernoulli published his work on fluids in Hydrodynamica, which reportedly his father heavily plagiarized for a work of his own. Saddened by his father's competition, Bernoulli spent the rest of his life working only in medicine and physiology. Daniel Bernoulli died in 1782, in Basel, Switzerland.

BERNOULLI'S PRINCIPLE

Bernoulli's Principle is one that can help illustrate how pressure affects velocity of liquids. The principle, in part, explains the way water moves through a pipe, the way an airplane's wings rely on pressure, and the way airflow and pressure systems relate to one another. In simple terms, the principle states that when velocity of a fluid is increased, the pressure the fluid releases is decreased.

The principle comes from Bernoulli's equation, which shows that the sum of energy of fluid flowing on an enclosed path, or streamline, is the same at any point on the path. Consider water moving through a pipe: If the diameter of the pipe decreases, the speed of the water flow must increase, and vice versa.

Bernoulli's Principle only applies to incompressible flow, such as liquids, which have constant densities and are unaffected by pressure. This is untrue of gases. Bernoulli used liquids in all of his experiments, and therefore his equation can only be applied to incompressible flow with constant density.

Bernoulli's Equation

$p + \frac{1}{2} pV^2 + pgh = \text{constant}$

where p is the pressure, p is the density, V is the velocity, h is elevation, and g is the gravitational acceleration

Many textbooks falsely attribute the cause of an airplane's lift to Bernoulli's Principle. While the principle does lay the groundwork to understanding pressure and velocity, it does not explain the airflow above and below the wings of a plane. Newton's Third Law of Motion is actually a better explanation of airplane lift, since Bernoulli's Principle is only an explanation of liquids. Newton's Third Law of Motion holds that in order for an airplane to lift, the wing must push air down.

Viktor Schauberger: Father of Implosion Technology

The forest was a fascination for young Viktor Schauberger. Born in Austria in 1885, Schauberger's family were foresters, so he grew up studying water flow and other natural phenomena related to cultivating trees.

In 1929, Schauberger began patenting inventions related to water engineering. He built a water turbine to produce hydroelectricity. His water ram pump had a spiral flow that he attributed to having learned about when visiting an Egyptian pyramid.

Implosion

Implosion is the process of destroying objects by causing them to collapse on themselves. In fluid dynamics, Schauberger's area of expertise, implosion is used to describe the process when matter flows inward rather than outward, such as it does during explosion. When matter moves inward, it moves in a spiraling path known as a vortex. Schauberger's theories are highly controversial among scientists. Today, it is classified as a pseudoscience.

During World War II, the German government forced Schauberger to continue his research into vortex (implosion) technology in order to develop a better cooling system for German airplanes. His work during this time led to a flying saucer that he called the Repulsine in 1944.

Sir Richard Arkwright: Inventor of the Modern Industrial Factory System

Born in Great Britain in 1732, Richard Arkwright was largely self-taught. At an early age he became an apprentice barber and learned to make wigs. Armed with a secret method for dyeing hair, Arkwright traveled around the country purchasing human hair for use in the manufacture of wigs.

He soon left wig making and focused his attention on making a machine to spin yarn. By 1767, a machine was used for carding cotton, and the spinning jenny spun the carded cotton into yarn. Arkwright teamed with a clockmaker, John Kay, who had been working on a mechanical spinning machine of his own. Arkwright made improvements to Kay's spinner and was able to produce a stronger yarn and use less physical labor than the spinning jenny. His new water-powered carding machine, known as a water-frame, was patented in 1775.

Arkwright established factories in Derbyshire, Staffordshire, and Lancashire and in Scotland. He was knighted in 1786.

In 1792, Sir Richard Arkwright died in Great Britain.

Arkwright constructed a horse-driven spinning mill at Preston and eventually developed mills in which the whole process of yarn manufacture was accomplished by only one machine. He often hired whole families, with the women and children working in the factory to make yarn and the men working at home to weave the yarn into cloth. This division of labor greatly improved efficiency and increased profits. Arkwright was also the first to use James Watts's steam engine to power textile machinery. With this steam engine and the water-frame, he eventually developed the power loom.

CRASH COURSE
LOUIS BRAILLE

At age three, French-born Louis Braille lost his sight due to an accident. When he was ten, he went to study at the Paris school for the blind. While there he developed a desire to read and became determined to find a way for people like himself to have access to the written word.

- In 1821, Charles Barbier showed Braille night writing, a series of dots and spaces. Barbier invented the code to help soldiers communicate with each other in the dark. This prompted Braille to came up with a system of raised dots that could be read by touch. The Braille system has been adapted to almost every known language, from Albanian to Zulu.

- The Braille Institute was founded in 1919 as the Universal Braille Press to provide services to the blind. The institute produces more than 5 million Braille pages each year.

- In 1945, the National Braille Association was established to provide continuing education for people who prepare Braille and to provide Braille materials to persons who are visually impaired.

Ada Byron Lovelace: Computing Pioneer

With a poet for a father and a mother who was terrified that her daughter would grow up to be just like her father, Ada Byron was brought up to be a mathematician and scientist. She waned to be what she called "an analyst and a metaphysician." She wanted to find a way to incorporate poetry with science. Her mathematical approach was filled with imagination and described in metaphors.

- When she was seventeen, Ada met Mary Somerville, a writer and educator. Through Somerville, Ada met Charles Babbage who was planning a new calculating engine, the analytical engine. He conjectured: what if a calculating engine could not only foresee but could act on that foresight.

- Ada herself saw foresight in Babbage's description and later suggested that Babbage write a plan for how the engine might calculate Bernoulli numbers. This plan is now regarded as the first computer program.

- Babbage worked on plans for this new engine and reported on the developments at a seminar in Turin, Italy, in the autumn of 1841. Subsequently, a summary of Babbage's talk was published in an article in French.

- Ada, married to the Earl of Lovelace and the mother of three children, translated the article and showed it to Babbage. He encouraged her to add her own notes to the translation. Her translation of the article was published in 1843 with her notes containing predictions that such a machine might be used to compose complex music and to produce graphics and might be used for both practical and scientific use.

In 1979, the US Department of Defense developed a software language named "Ada," in honor of Lady Ada Byron Lovelace.

POP QUIZ

1) Who wrote *Mrs. Dalloway*?
   a) William Faulkner
   b) J. D. Salinger
   c) Mark Twain
   d) Virginia Woolf

2) Who wrote *The Sound and the Fury*?
   a) William Faulkner
   b) J. D. Salinger
   c) Mark Twain
   d) Virginia Woolf

3) Who shot Archduke Ferdinand?
   a) John Wilkes Booth
   b) Gavrilo Princip
   c) Sirhan Sirhan
   d) Claude Strauss

4) Who served as queen of both England and France during the Middle Ages?
   a) Elizabeth
   b) Anne Boleyn
   c) Mary Boleyn
   d) Eleanor of Aquitaine

5) Who is the founder of IQ societies?
   a) Einstein
   b) Edison
   c) Hoeflin
   d) Newton

ANSWERS:

1) d
2) a
3) b
4) d
5) c

AL-RAZI:
GREAT ISLAMIC THINKER

Born in Iran in AD 865, al-Razi studied alchemy, medicine, and spiritual philosophy. He is said to be one of the greatest thinkers of the Islamic world. He composed thirty-three treatises on natural science, mathematics, and astronomy.

As chief physician and director of a hospital in Baghdad, he is said to have given patients full treatment without charging any fee, nor demanding any payment. When he was not occupied with pupils or patients, he was writing and studying.

Many medical firsts are attributed to al-Razi. He gave the first scientific description of smallpox and was the first to distinguish between smallpox and measles. He also discovered allergic asthma (also known as hay fever) and wrote articles about allergy and immunology, becoming the first physician to do so. In his study of allergies, he became the first to realize that fever is a natural defense mechanism of the body.

He is the one who developed pharmaceutical mortars, phials, flasks, and spatulas to aid in the concoction of ointments and other treatments for his patients. He also developed methods of distillation and extraction, leading to his discovery of sulfuric acid and ethanol. In his later years, al-Razi went blind, reportedly from cataracts. He died in 925.

Today al-Razi is honored by the Al-Razi Institute in Tehran and Razi University. The annual Razi Day (meaning Pharmacy Day) is observed in Iran on August 27.

Cornelius Drebbel: Inventor of the Submarine

Born in Alkmaar, Netherlands, in 1572, Cornelius Drebbel first worked as an apprentice to painter and engraver Hendrick Goltzius; however, he also worked on his own, inventing, among other things, a perpetual motion machine that told the time, date, and season.

In 1604, King James I invited Drebbel to England to demonstrate a number of his inventions. He was also invited to Prague in 1610 and again in 1619. Unfortunately, he was arrested both times that he was in Prague, but his being an inventor got him pardoned.

- Drebbel's most famous invention was the submarine. He raised the sides on a rowboat, covered it in greased leather, put a watertight hatch in the middle, and gave it a rudder and four oars. Under the seats were large pigskin bladders with pipes connecting them to the outside. At launch the bladders were tied off with rope, and then when the shipped dived, the ropes were untied and the bladders filled with water. To surface, the crew squeezed the bladder to expel the water.

- Drebbel built several submarines, the largest of which had six oars and could carry sixteen passengers. It could stay submerged for three hours at a depth of fifteen feet.

When Charles I became king of England, he hired Drebbel to make secret weapons, including an unsuccessful floating petard (bomb). Drebbel died in London in 1633.

CHEMISTRY 101

MICHAEL FARADAY

Born in 1791 in south London, Michael Faraday worked as an apprentice to a local bookbinder and spent his free time reading books on science. In 1812, at age twenty-one, Faraday attended several lectures given by the chemist Humphry Davy at the Royal Institution. This prompted him to write to Davy asking for a job as his assistant. Although Davy initially turned him down, the next year he appointed Faraday to the job of chemical assistant at the Royal Institution.

While at the Institute, Faraday published his work on electromagnetic rotation (the principle behind the electric motor), helped other researchers with their projects, and began giving lectures of his own. He also founded the Royal Institution's Friday Evening Discourses and the Christmas Lectures, both of which continue today.

In 1831, Faraday discovered electromagnetic induction, opening the door for the development of the electric transformer and generator. He coined several words including electrode, cathode, and ion.

In 1830, Faraday became professor of chemistry at the Royal Military Academy in Woolwich, where he served until 1851. In addition, he served as scientific adviser to Trinity House from 1836 to 1865.

Michael Faraday died in 1867 in England.

Lee de Forest: The Father of Radio

Born in 1873 in Council Bluffs, Iowa, Lee de Forest grew up in Alabama. His father, a minister, was president of Talladega College (Talladega, Alabama). De Forest received his Ph.D. from Yale University in 1899.

During his lifetime, de Forest received hundreds of patents. However, he may be most often remembered for his development of the vacuum tube.

In 1907, he added a grid to the Fleming valve, an element found in the lightbulb. His device, what he called the audion and today we call a triode, was in essence a three-electrode vacuum tube. It could detect radio waves and convert them into audio frequency that could be heard using headphones or amplified for a loudspeaker. He was making the first steps to creating what he called a radiotelephone.

De Forest formed his own radiotelephone company in 1907, and he eventually sent audio broadcasts of opera singers, patriotic music, and even reports of the 1916 presidential election returns.

Three years later, in 1919, he came up with the Phonofilm process, enabling synchronized sound for movie film. Phonofilm was used to record stage performances, speeches, and musical acts. He premiered eighteen short films on Phonofilm in 1923. This invention eventually earned de Forest an Academy Award and a star on the Hollywood Walk of Fame.

In reflecting on his accomplishments, de Forest said, "Why should anyone want to buy a radio … nine tenths of what one can hear is the continual drivel of second-rate jazz, sickening crooning by degenerate sax players, interrupted by blatant sales talks?"

De Forest died in Hollywood, California, in 1961.

Akira Kurosawa: Filmmaker

Born in Tokyo at the turn of the twentieth century, Akira Kurosawa was the youngest of seven children in a well-to-do family. His parents embraced Western culture and took the family to see many films that were only just beginning to appear around Japan. Even when Japanese culture began to shun Western films, Kurosawa's father continued to present films as an educational experience.

In 1923, the Great Kanto Earthquake shook Japan and demolished the city of Tokyo, killing close to 100,000 people. Kurosawa and his brother made a walking tour of the city and examined the devastation. According to him, the experience taught him to look fear in the face to defeat it. Kurosawa died of a stroke at the age of eighty-eight.

- In 1930, Kurosawa was hired as a film director's apprentice, beginning his career in films.

- He directed his first film, *Sanshiro Sugata,* and gained the attention and skepticism of the Japanese government, who heavily censored material and encouraged wartime propaganda.

- His first postwar film was quite different, however. *No Regrets for Our Youth* was highly critical of the former Japanese regime and followed the life of a political dissident's wife.

- Later, his film *Rashomon* gained Kurosawa international fame and won the Golden Lion at the Venice Film Festival and won an Academy Award for Best Foreign Film.

Rap Sheet

The films of Kurosawa have a unique look, as he experimented with telephoto lenses and multiple camera angles. He was known as a perfectionist and spent large amounts of time on particular scenes in order to achieve the effects he desired.

Major Works of Akira Kurosawa
- *Rashomon* (1950)
- *The Seven Samurai* (1954)
- *Throne of Blood* (1957)
- *Hidden Fortress* (1958)
- *Yojimbo* (1961)
- *Red Beard* (1965)
- *Ran* (1985)
- *Dreams* (1990)

Where Credit Is Due

Kurosawa's film *Yojimbo* is the basis for several western films, including *A Fistful of Dollars*, *Last Man Standing*, and *Lucky Number Slevin*.

His film *The Seven Samurai* has been remade into many versions, all of which share Kurosawa's original plot structure:
- *The Magnificent Seven*, 1960
- *Beach of the War Gods*, 1973
- *Sholay*, 1975
- *Battle Beyond the Stars*, 1980
- *World Gone Wild*, 1988

CRASH COURSE
NOAM CHOMSKY

Born in 1928 in Philadelphia, Avram Noam Chomsky was raised in a Jewish neighborhood that was divided into a Yiddish side and a Hebrew side. Yiddish was forbidden in Chomsky's household, and Catholicism was heavily discouraged.

- According to Chomsky, he identified with the politics of anarchism by age thirteen. Later, at the University of Pennsylvania, he began to study philosophy and linguistics.

- His particular interests settled in the mathematics of language structure. His political views were shaped heavily by the views of linguist and professor Zellig Harris.

- Chomsky married Carol Shatz in 1949 and received his Ph.D. in linguistics in 1955.

Chomsky has since become an instrumental figure in American leftist politics and linguistics theory, publishing many titles in both foreign policy and language theory.

Besides contributing heavily to the shaping of western linguistic theory, Chomsky was one of the leading opponents of the Vietnam War and gained both wide criticism and popularity during the late 1960s for his essays expressing American dissent.

Though he is frequently sought after for opinions and critiques of political ideas, Chomsky is also highly controversial and received many death threats because of his critique of United States foreign policy.

Stephen King: Novelist

Before producing major films and best-selling novels, Stephen King began as a short story writer. He published his first full-length novel, Carrie, in 1973 and has enjoyed a booming writing career since. Over fifty of King's stories have appeared in film today, both on the big screen and television. King has capitalized on his uncanny ability to appeal to the fears of the mass public. A genius indeed!

King's Box Office Stories

Carrie, 1976

Carrie documents the story of a young girl with an overprotective mother. Carrie gets taunted at school because of her sheltered oblivion to teenage issues and eventually breaks down from the trauma, wreaking horror and havoc on her high school prom. The story was published as a novel, made into a box-office hit, and later became a Broadway play.

The Shining, 1980

The Shining tells the story of a family snowed in at an abandoned and haunted hotel for the winter. Overcome by cabin fever, the father, Jack, loses his mind and develops hallucinations and psychotic thoughts and behavior. In the climax of the movie, Jack comes after his family with an axe, prompted by the ghosts of the hotel to murder his family. The film was directed by Stanley Kubrick and is noted as one of the best horror movies of all time on countless lists.

Christine, 1983

Due to King's popularity in the 1980s, the movie Christine was in production before he even finished writing the novel. The film is about a boy and his possessed car. The car threatens to kill anyone who gets in her way. The film and story were never regarded as King's best but still had great popularity and success in the theaters.

Children of the Corn, 1984
From a book of stories entitled Night Shift, this film chronicles the children of Gatlin, Nebraska, who become brainwashed by a preacher named Isaac. The children are called to commit murders in the town and follow diligently. A young couple tries to interfere and angers the children, causing murder and mayhem. Seven sequels of the film were released, and the film is universally well known.

Firestarter, 1984
A couple receives a dose of experimental medicine while in college, and later their offspring is infected with the chemical. The daughter, played by Drew Barrymore, instinctually starts fires with her mind, causing mass chaos around her. It is rumored that King was unhappy with the results of the original production, and the film was reproduced in 2002.

EXTRA CREDIT: Stephen King was accused of vandalism in Alice Springs, Australia, on August 15, 2007. He was secretly signing his books and managed to sign six books before a customer reported him to store manager Bev Ellis.

Ken Jennings: A Jeopardy Master

Ken Jennings, holder of the record for the longest winning streak on *Jeopardy*, won seventy-four games before he was defeated by challenger Nancy Zerg. By this point Jennings had amassed $2.52 million in winnings. During his reign, ratings for the show increased by 22 percent, according to the Nielsen TV National People Meter, as people across America tuned in to witness for themselves how deep his trivial knowledge went. In keeping with the clue spirit of the show and Jennings's wealth of useless knowledge, here's some trivial facts about the big winner:

- Jennings won the rookie division of the American Crossword Puzzle Tournament in 2006.

- He appeared twice on NPR's *Wait, Wait, Don't Tell Me* program and twice on *The Late Show with David Letterman*.

- He is currently pressing networks to help him produce a potential game show titled *Ken Jennings vs. the Rest of the World*.

- He kept a plush Totoro toy from the movie *My Neighbor Totoro* in his pocket as a good luck charm.

- During game fifty-three of his streak, Jennings was given the clue "This term for a long-handled gardening tool can also mean an immoral pleasure seeker." Jennings quickly replied, "What's a ho(e)?" Host Alex Trebek replied "No," caught the audience's laughter, and said, "Whoa, whoa, whoa, they teach you that in school in Utah, huh?" The correct response was "Rake."

- He frequently gave answers in clever ways. Examples: "What are the munchies, man?" when given a clue about midnight food cravings, and "What be Ebonics?"

John Logie Baird:
Co-Inventor of Television

Born in 1888, in Helensburgh, Scotland, John Logie Baird studied at Glasgow University, but he did not graduate because of the outbreak of World War I. The armed forces turned him down because of his poor health; however, he took the position of superintendent engineer of the Clyde Valley Electrical Power Company.

When the war ended he moved to the southern coast of England and started experimenting with making a television. By 1924, he was able to transmit a flickering image over a few feet. Then, in January 1926, he gave the world's first demonstration of his television at a meeting of fifty scientists in London. The next year his television was demonstrated over 438 miles of telephone line between London and Glasgow, and he formed the Baird Television Development Company. In 1928, he made the first transatlantic television transmission between London and New York and the first transmission to a ship in the mid-Atlantic. He also demonstrated the first color and stereoscopic televisions.

Unfortunately, he wasn't fast enough. In America, Marconi was developing an electronic system. When the British Broadcasting Company tried Baird's system alongside Marconi's system in 1935, Marconi's all-electronic television system won out. In 1937 Baird's system was dropped. Baird died in 1946, in Bexhill-on-Sea in Sussex.

- When Baird was in his twenties, he tried to make diamonds out of graphite and shorted out all the electricity in Glasgow.
- The Logie Awards, Australian television industry awards, honor John Logie Baird, who invented the first working television. The awards have been presented annually since 1959.

Wangari Maathai: Enviromentalist

The first woman in East and Central Africa to earn a doctorate degree, Kenya native Wangari Muta Maathai obtained a bachelor's degree in biological sciences from Mount St. Scholastica College in Atchison, Kansas, in 1964; a master's degree from the University of Pittsburgh in 1966; and a Ph.D. from the University of Nairobi in 1971. She taught veterinary anatomy and became chair of the Department of Veterinary Anatomy at the University of Nairobi.

Maathai joined the National Council of Women of Kenya, serving as chair from 1981 to 1987. As a part of her work with the council, she led the women in planting trees, a project that she turned into the Green Belt Movement, a broad-based, grassroots organization whose main focus is the planting of trees with women groups, in order to conserve the environment and improve their quality of life. She has helped women plant more than 20 million trees.

- Internationally noted for her devotion to the fight for democracy, human rights, and environmental conservation, Maathai has addressed the UN several times and spoken at special sessions of the General Assembly for the five-year review of the earth summit.

- She and the Green Belt Movement have received numerous awards, most notably the 2004 Nobel Peace Prize.

- In June 1997, Maathai was elected by Earth Times as one of a hundred persons in the world who have made a difference in the environmental arena.

- In December 2002, Maathai was elected to parliament and appointed Assistant Minister for Environment, Natural Resources, and Wildlife.

CRASH COURSE

ALBERT EINSTEIN

Born in 1879, in Ulm, Germany, Albert Einstein earned a Ph.D. in 1905 from the University of Zurich. As a professor of physics at universities in Zurich, Prague, and Berlin, Einstein became a well-recognized figure in the science community.

In 1916, Einstein published his theory of general relativity. Einstein had earlier theorized that distance and time are not absolute. He believed the rate that a clock ticked depended on the motion of the person looking at the clock. His theory of general relativity said that gravity and motion can affect time and space. In other words, gravity pulling in one direction is equal to acceleration in the opposite direction. This is an explanation of why a person is pushed back against the seat when a car accelerates.

In 1933, seeking to escape political oppression in Germany, Einstein immigrated to the United States. He accepted a position at the Princeton Institute of Advanced Study in New Jersey, where he taught until retirement in 1945.

During his retirement years, Einstein continued to work on his general theory of relativity.

- Einstein received the 1921 Nobel Prize in physics for his discovery of the law of the photoelectric effect and his work in the field of theoretical physics.

- He was instrumental in establishing the Hebrew University in Jerusalem.

EXTRA CREDIT: Einstein was offered the presidency of Israel in 1952. He declined.

THEORY OF RELATIVITY

The theory of relativity, proposed by Albert Einstein, explains that the speed of light is constant and an absolute boundary of motion. It states that for any objects moving near the speed of light, movement will be slower and shorter in length from the point of view of an observer on Earth. For instance, an object moving at light speed in space would appear to be moving much slower from Earth.

What is the Space-Time Continuum?

From the theory of relativity, Einstein derived the "curved space-time continuum," which shows space and time as a two-dimensional surface into which massive objects can create impressions. This explained the idea of light bending around the sun, helped predict black holes, and allowed new discoveries to be made in the Big Bang Theory.

EXTRA CREDIT: The concept of relativity was actually not introduced by Einstein, but his major contributions to the study earned him a Nobel Prize in 1921.

SIR ALEC JEFFREYS

Born in 1950, Alec Jeffreys attended Oxford University, where he studied biochemistry and received his Ph.D. in 1975. Then, after studying for two years in Amsterdam, he moved to the University of Leicester, where he became a professor of genetics in 1987.

During his early research at Leicester, Jeffreys developed techniques for DNA fingerprinting and profiling, changing the way criminals are prosecuted. This technique became the basis for the United Kingdom's National DNA Database (NDNAD), launched in Britain in 1995.

Jefferys continues to teach and do research at the University of Leicester. He became a fellow of the Royal Society in 1986, was appointed as a Royal Society research professor in 1991, and was knighted in 1994. In 1996, he was awarded the Albert Einstein World Award of Science. These are only a few of the numerous honors he continues to receive.

"Our discovery of DNA fingerprinting was of course totally accidental.... But at least we had the sense to realise what we had stumbled upon."

—Alec Jeffreys

Edgar Degas: Impressionist/Realist

Born in Paris, France, in 1834, Edgar Degas enrolled in the Lycée Louis-le-Grand, where he received a bachelor's degree in literature in 1853. At the insistence of his father, Degas enrolled at the Faculty of Law of the University of Paris, where he stayed only a few months before switching to the École des Beaux-Arts to study drawing. He moved to Italy in 1856 and studied the Renaissance artists, such as Michelangelo, Raphael, and Titian.

In 1872, Degas moved to New Orleans, Louisiana, where several of his relatives already lived. While there he painted The Cotton Exchange at New Orleans, his only work to be purchased by a museum during his lifetime.

In 1873, Degas returned to Paris and began using photography to capture action for his paintings and artwork. His paintings eventually made him financially comfortable.

Although his work is often described as impressionistic, Degas did not like the label and preferred to be called a realist. Undoubtedly he was influenced by the impressionist artists of his day; however, his early study of the old masters influenced his work so that his paintings distinctly differ from the pure impressionists of the day.

Degas mastered the techniques of oil painting as well as working in pastels. He was also an accomplished sculptor and printmaker. He spent the last years of his life nearly blind and often wandering the streets of Paris. Edgar Degas died in 1917.

- Degas served in the National Guard during the Franco-Prussian War.
- More than half of Degas' work depicts dancers.

PHOTOGRAPHY 101
WILLIAM HENRY FOX TALBOT

Born in 1800 in Melbury, Dorset, England, William Henry Fox Talbot attended Cambridge University and was elected a fellow of the Royal Astronomical Society. He was a man of varied interests, including mathematics, botany, and the Bible.

In the 1830s, people were already reproducing leaves and other objects, a process they called photograms, but Talbot wanted a machine that could actually reproduce sketches and not fade like the photograms did. He began work on this idea in 1833. He presented his "art of photogenic drawing" to the Royal Society in 1839.

During his career, Talbot developed the three elements of photography—developing, fixing, and printing. Initially, his photogenic drawings on light-sensitive paper took long exposure times; however, he accidentally discovered that there was an image after a very short exposure. He found he could chemically develop the exposure into a useful negative. He called his new, faster process calotype and patented the process in 1841. The following year Talbot was rewarded with a medal from the Royal Society for his work.

In 1844, Talbot published *The Pencil of Nature*, the first commercial book to be illustrated with photographs. Talbot's photogenic drawings were in competition with the daguerreotype process. The daguerreotypes won the popularity contest because of their quality, compared to Talbot's process, and their cost. Talbot is said to have asked too much for the rights to his patented process.

Talbot also made contributions to mathematics, astronomy, and archaeology. He died in 1877.

EXTRA CREDIT: In 1850, there were seventy-seven photographic galleries in New York.

GEORGE EASTMAN: EASTMAN KODAK COMPANY

Born in Waterville, New York, in 1854, George Eastman dropped out of high school when his father died and went to work in order to support his family. As the story goes, he was working in a bank at age twenty-four and was due for a vacation. He wanted to tour the Caribbean islands and bring back photographs, but photography equipment was too heavy and cumbersome. He decided to forgo his vacation and work on making a portable camera.

Eastman invented a dry-plate process for developing photographs, and, in 1880, established a photo development factory in Rochester, New York. Eight years later, he devised a way to make photography film out of paper and put it on a roll. He also developed a camera to use the film. In 1889, he started making film out of cellulose instead of paper.

The first Kodak camera cost $25 and took one hundred round photos, each two and a half inches in diameter. The cost of developing the film and returning the camera filled with new film was $10.

The Eastman Kodak Company, founded in 1892, was one of the first firms in America to establish a plant for large-scale production of a standardized product and to maintain a chemical laboratory. The company was also a pioneer in employee relations, creating a "progressive welfare program" including a profit-sharing plan. Within four years, 100,000 cameras had been sold.

In 1900, Eastman introduced the Brownie. The new-style camera cost only $1 and a roll of six-exposure film cost 15 cents. Color photography followed in 1928.

Suffering the pain and depression of a degenerative illness, George Eastman committed suicide in 1932.

EXTRA CREDIT: Eastman used the name Kodak because he liked the letter *K*. He tried many alphabetical combinations for the letters in the middle, but he knew the beginning and ending letters would have to be *K*.

LOUIS BROMFIELD: THE MOST FAMOUS FARMER IN AMERICA

Born in 1896, in Mansfield, Ohio, Louis Bromfield grew up with soil under his fingernails and become the most famous farmer in America.

He entered Cornell Agriculture College in 1914 and moved on to Columbia University, where he studied journalism. Upon graduation, Bromfield accepted a position with the Associated Press. During World War I, he received the Croix de la Guerre for his service as an ambulance driver for the French Army.

For thirty-one years, Bromfield wrote books and screenplays that captured the attention of critics and the public alike. In 1925, Bromfield published his first novel, *The Green Bay Tree*. The story of the struggle between farming and industry generated a great deal of attention. His next book, *Early Autumn*, received a Pulitzer Prize in 1927. Two years later he was awarded the O. Henry Short Story Award for "Scarlet Woman." His screenplays included *One Heavenly Night* and *Johnny Come Lately* starring James Cagney.

Bromfield spent the early part of his career in Paris but returned to Ohio in 1938. He purchased Malabar Farm and took on a second career as farmer and conservationist. He attained worldwide fame in the 1940s and 1950s for his soil experiments and conservation efforts while maintaining a rigorous writing schedule.

Louis Bromfield died in 1956. In the 1980s, Bromfield was posthumously elected to the Ohio Agricultural Hall of Fame.

EXTRA CREDIT: Bromfield's home, Malabar Farm, was the location of the wedding of Humphry Bogart and Lauren Bacall.

SHEL SILVERSTEIN

Known for his poetry, illustrations, plays, screenwriting, and songwriting, Shel Silverstein is somewhat of an anomaly in the international literary scene. Born in 1930 as Sheldon Allan Silverstein, the famous writer's work has been distributed to tens of millions of readers internationally, and he is often referred to as the most beloved children's author of all time.

As a G.I. in Japan and Korea during the 1950s, Silverstein began drawing his first cartoons. Never planning to write for children, he took up other hobbies such as guitar playing and songwriting. In the early '60s, Silverstein was introduced to Harper Collins editor Ursula Nordstrom, which led to Silverstein's publication of *The Giving Tree*. After selling more than five million copies, Silverstein's first book still tops bestseller lists in children's literature.

Where the *Sidewalk Ends* was published in 1974 as Silverstein's first book of poems. The book was instantly popular, and was followed by *The Light in the Attic* in 1981, which broke records on the *New York Times* bestseller list, where it stayed for 182 weeks. Silverstein continued writing songs, poems, and stories until his death in 1999.

Successful at many arts, Silverstein's talents at songwriting paid him well. His song "A Boy Named Sue" was a hit for Johnny Cash, and "I'm Checking Out", which he wrote for the film *Postcards from the Edge,* was nominated for an Academy Award in 1991. Silverstein won a Grammy in 1984 for Best Children's Album with Where the Sidewalk Ends. Silverstein wrote songs for Waylon Jennings, Mel Tillis, and Jerry Reed.

POETRY 101
E. E. CUMMINGS

Edward Estlin Cummings, born in 1894 in Cambridge, Massachusetts, was the son of a renowned political science and sociology professor at Harvard University. It is said that the "preaching voice" that Cummings adopts in many of his poems is a voice inspired by his father, who left Harvard in 1900 to become an ordained minister. Cummings attended Harvard and studied languages, particularly Greek. He was introduced to the writings of Ezra Pound who became one of his major influences.

After college, Cummings joined an ambulance corps and met William Slater Brown. Brown was arrested for writing incriminating letters and was sentenced to a concentration camp. Cummings refused to be separated from Brown, and the two were sent to the La Ferte Mace concentration camp together. They were later freed because of the political pull of Cummings' father.

After the event, Cummings wrote *The Enormous Room*, an account of his time at the concentration camp. It was published, along with many other pieces of work over the next decade, and Cummings began to focus on his writing and painting. In 1926, Cummings' father was killed suddenly in a car accident; his mother was gravely injured. Cummings wrote about the incident and moved to transform his poetry to define more serious aspects of his life, something said to be influenced heavily by his father's passing.

Cummings died in 1962 from a cerebral hemorrhage. Three volumes of his poetry were published posthumously; he left behind twenty-five books of poetry, prose, drawings, plays, and stories, all completed during his short, sixty-eight-year lifespan.

CHILD PRODIGIES

A child prodigy masters a skill or art at an unusually young age. Typically a prodigy is defined as someone who masters the fundamentals and skills of a certain field by the age of 12.

- The word Wunderkind is sometimes used as a synonym for prodigy. It can also be used when referring to adults, such as Steven Spielberg, who achieved great success very early in their careers.

- American psychologist Michael O'Boyle recently discovered through the use of an fMRI, which measures brain activity, that the mental operations of prodigies are strikingly different than those of typical humans. His research documented that the blood flow to certain parts of the brain of a prodigy calculator was nearly seven times the amount of typical blood flow in a human doing math.

- The fMRI measures activity in certain locations of the brain to gain a better understanding of how a particular brain is functioning. They are currently being tested as possible lie detectors!

A Few Famed Child Prodigies

- Kim Ung-Yong – Earned a Ph.D. in physics before turning fifteen.
- Zerah Colburn – Able to multiply six-digit numbers in his head at age nine.
- Blaise Pascal – At age eleven, worked out the first twenty-three propositions of Euclid.
- Ruth Lawrence – Youngest student to enter the University of Oxford, at age twelve.

SIR HUMPHRY DAVY: CHEMIST

Born in 1778, in Penzance, Cornwall, England, Humphry Davy first worked as an apprentice to a surgeon. Then at age 19 he moved to Bristol to study science. While there he experimented with laughing gas (nitrous oxide) and published his results in 1800. This work garnered the attention of the Royal Institution, and the following year, he was hired as an assistant lecturer in chemistry.

- He became a great success at the university, with his lectures drawing members of the fashionable London society.

- He became a fellow of the Royal Society in 1803 and was awarded its Copley Medal in 1805.

- In his further research, Davy used the newly invented battery to isolate potassium, sodium, calcium, strontium, barium, and magnesium, inventing the new field of electrochemistry.

- His exemplary work led to his being knighted in 1812.

- He invented what became known as the Davy lamp in 1815 after learning of the dangers facing miners who used candles for light in the dark mines.

Davy received many honors during his career, including a gold medal presented by Napoléon I, appointment as a baronet in 1818, and the presidency of the Royal Society of Science from 1820 to 1827. Sir Humphry Davy died in 1829 in Switzerland.

LANGSTON HUGHES: POET

Langston Hughes began writing poetry when he was a mere eighth grader. His father discouraged poetry as a career and agreed to later pay Hughes' tuition to Columbia University only if he pursued a career path in engineering. Hughes soon dropped out of the program but continued writing poetry, publishing his first piece in *Brownie's Book*, titled "The Negro Speaks of Rivers."

He later published poems, essays, and stories in many magazines. His essay titled "The Negro Artist and the Racial Mountain" appeared in the *Nation* in 1926, stirring controversy and gaining him widespread attention. The essay discussed the "false integration" of black writers or poets, arguing that many black writers wanted to write like white writers. Hughes criticized this trend.

Hughes' controversial and outspoken attitude toward race in writing gained him popularity and acclaim, leading to over sixteen books of poetry, three collections of short stories, four volumes of "documentary" fiction, twenty plays, two novels, three autobiographies, and countless musicals, children's poems, and magazine articles.

Some of his more famous collections of poetry include *The Big Sea*, *The Dream Keeper*, and *One Way Ticket*.

Langston Hughes died of cancer in the spring of 1967, leaving five plays to be posthumously published. His block of residence on East 127th Street in Harlem, New York, was renamed Langston Hughes Place in his honor.

WHEN THE BEST DIRECTORS DON'T MAKE THE BEST PICTURES

The Academy of Motion Picture Arts and Sciences (AMPAS) began acknowledging the best of Hollywood's movies in 1929 by awarding golden statuettes known as Oscars, and proclaiming them Best Picture of the Year. Since that time, the majority of directors receiving the honor of Best Picture of the Year also received Best Director of the Year, but not all of them. In a few rare moments in Academy history, the Best Director was bestowed upon someone who didn't make the best film… according to members of AMPAS anyway. Listed below are the best directors who somehow didn't make the best films, as well as the films that outdid them. We suggest that you put all of them in your renting queue.

1935: Best Director: John Ford for *The Informer*; Best Picture: *Mutiny on the Bounty* by Frank Lloyd

193: Best Director: Frank Capra for *Mr. Deeds Goes to Town*; Best Picture: *The Great Ziegfeld* by Robert Z. Leonard

1937: Best Director: Leo McCarey for *The Awful Truth*; Best Picture: *The Life of Emile Zola* by William Dieterle

1940: Best Director: John Ford for *The Grapes of Wrath*; Best Picture: *Rebecca* by Alfred Hitchcock

1948: Best Director: John Huston for *Treasure of Sierra Madre*; Best Picture: *Hamlet* directed by Laurence Olivier

1949: Best Director: Joseph L. Mankiewicz for *A Letter to Three Wives*; Best Picture: *All the King's Men* by Robert Rossen

1951: Best Director: George Stevens for *A Place in the Sun*; Best Picture: *An American in Paris* by Vincente Minnelli

1952: Best Director: John Ford for *The Quiet Man*; Best Picture: *The Greatest Show on Earth* by Cecil B. Demille

1956: Best Director: George Stevens for *Giant*; Best Picture: *Around the World in 80 Days* by Michael Anderson, Sr.

1967: Best Director: Mike Nichols for *The Graduate;* Best Picture: *In the Heat of the Night* by Norman Jewison

1972: Best Director: Bob Fosse for *Cabaret;* Best Picture: *The Godfather* by Francis Ford Coppola

1981: Best Director: Warren Beatty for *Reds;* Best Picture: *Chariots of Fire* by Hugh Hudson

1989: Best Director: Oliver Stone for *Born on the Fourth of July;* Best Picture: *Driving Miss Daisy* by Bruce Beresford

1998: Best Director: Steven Spielberg for *Saving Private Ryan;* Best Picture: *Shakespeare in Love* by John Madden

2000: Best Director: Steven Soderbergh for *Traffic;* Best Picture: *Gladiator* by Ridley Scott

2002: Best Director: Roman Polanski for *The Pianist;* Best Picture: *Chicago* by Rob Marshall

2005: Best Director: Ang Lee for *Brokeback Mountain;* Best Picture: *Crash* by Paul Haggis

STANLEY KUBRICK: VISIONARY

Born in 1928 in Manhattan as the first of two children, Stanley Kubrick grew up in the Bronx as the son of a doctor. He had a great interest in jazz music, photography, and chess.

Kubrick attended William Howard Taft High School and was a D-average student. His failures in school eliminated his chance at a college education, as soldiers returning from World War II were flooding colleges.

- After high school, Kubrick worked as a freelance photographer selling photographs to New York magazines. He registered for night school and eventually became a full-time staff photographer for *Look* magazine. He was married to his first wife, Toba Metz, in 1948 and lived with her in Greenwich Village.

- In the early 1950s, Kubrick began making his first short films. He sold his first film, *Day of the Fight*, for $100 to a distributor. His career in narrative films began in 1953 with *Fear and Desire*, a movie about a team of soldiers in a fictional war. During the making of the film, Kubrick divorced Toba and married his second wife, an Australian dancer and designer.

- In 1964, he produced the film *Dr. Strangelove, or: How I Learned to Stop Worrying and Love the Bomb*, which became a cult classic and gained a large following. It is known today as a masterpiece of dark humor. The film was based on the novel *Red Alert* but was rewritten as a satire by Kubrick, Peter George, and satirist Terry Southern.

- Five years later, Kubrick finished his next film, *2001: A Space Odyssey*. Kubrick wrote the screenplay with Sir Arthur C. Clarke, a science fiction writer. The screenplay was based on Clarke's short story "The Sentinel." The film had an enormous cultural impact, and both it and *Dr. Strangelove* brought Kubrick to the front burner in dark film.

- Two of Kubrick's most famous films, *A Clockwork Orange* and *Full Metal Jacket*, have since become cult classics.

- He also made *The Shining*, adapted from Stephen King's famous novel, and *Eyes Wide Shut*, from Arthur Schnitzler's novella *Traumnovelle*.

- Kubrick has won countless awards for his groundbreaking films.

- He is considered one of the greatest filmmakers of the twentieth century. He died on March 7, 1999. His work on the film *A.I.: Artificial Intelligence* was completed posthumously by director Stephen Spielberg.

Kubrick's Major Works

- *Paths of Glory* (1957)

- *Spartacus* (1960)

- *Lolita* (1962)

- *Dr. Strangelove: Or How I Learned to Stop Worrying and Love the Bomb* (1964)

- *2001: A Space Odyssey* (1968)

- *A Clockwork Orange* (1971)

- *Barry Lyndon* (1975)

- *The Shining* (1980)

- *Full Metal Jacket* (1987)

- *Eyes Wide Shut* (1999)

Kubrick's early film *Fear and Desire* was an embarrassment to him later in life, as it did so poorly commercially. It is rumored that Kubrick eventually bought up every copy of the film that he could find to keep others from watching it. At least one copy of the film was kept by a private collector, and eventually the movie was bootlegged on both VHS and DVD.

HAROLD EDGERTON: STOP-ACTION PHOTOGRAPHY

Born in 1903 in Fremont, Nebraska, Harold Edgerton attended the University of Nebraska and went on to get his Ph.D. at the Massachusetts Institute of Technology. He became professor of electrical engineering at MIT, where he served until his retirement.

Edgerton developed the stroboscope, which used strobe lights to isolate fast motion, allowing people to view high-speed motion that had never been seen before. Soon people could see photographs of athletes, hummingbirds, and even bullets in action.

In 1939, Edgerton began working on a way for the US Air Force to take nighttime aerial photography for reconnaissance. And using his photography techniques on the lighter side, he collaborated with MGM to produce the short film Quicker than a Wink!, for which he received an Academy Award in 1940.

In 1953, Edgerton took his photography to great depths as he teamed with Jacques Cousteau in underwater exploration. Edgerton developed sonar devices for analyzing and profiling the bottom of the sea, and in 1968, he produced the first underwater time-lapse photography.

In addition to his Academy Award, Edgerton received the Medal of Freedom for his aerial reconnaissance work during World War II and the National Medal of Science in 1973. He was named New England Inventor of the Year in 1982.

Edgerton died of a heart attack in 1990.

TIM BURTON: AMERICAN FILM DIRECTOR, WRITER, AND DESIGNER

Known for his quirky, gothic masterpieces of film, Tim Burton is an Academy Award-nominated film director from Burbank, California. A highly imaginative childhood full of isolated creativity led Burton to begin creative projects in an offbeat, horror genre.

It is rumored that at an early age, he staged an axe murder so realistic that neighbors called the police. He repeated the incident several times afterward, and spent his school days absorbed in horror films.

Burton won a Disney scholarship after graduating high school and attended the California Institute of the Arts in Valencia, California, where he studied art and animation.

He worked as a cel painter on the animated version of The Lord of the Rings and was later hired by Walt Disney Studios as an animator's apprentice. During this time at Disney, Burton wrote the poem and created the drawings that later became one of his most famous works, *The Nightmare Before Christmas.*

Burton's Major Works

* *Pee Wee's Big Adventure* (1985)
* *Beetle Juice* (1988)
* *Batman* (1989)
* *Edward Scissorhands* (1990)
* *Batman Returns* (1992)
* *The Nightmare Before Christmas* (1993)
* *Ed Wood* (1994)
* *Mars Attacks!* (1996)
* *The Melancholy Death of Oyster Boy: and Other Stories* (children's book, 1996)
* *Sleepy Hollow* (1999)
* *Planet of the Apes* (2001)

- *Big Fish* (2003)
- *Charlie and the Chocolate Factory* (2005)
- *Corpse Bride* (2005)
- *Sweeney Todd* (2007)

Tim Burton – Up Close

- Burton frequently has dinner table scenes in films he directs, notably in Beetlejuice, Edward Scissorhands, and Charlie and the Chocolate Factory.
- Often his films have gothic subtexts.
- Burton always personalizes the production logo at the beginning of each of his films.
- He is known for featuring clowns, snow, dead pets, black and white floors, butterflies, redheads, and scarecrows in his films.
- Most of his films are released close to the holiday season.
- His stop-motion films most often feature characters with long, stringy legs and small feet.

ANNA PAVLOVA

She had everything going against her—a small body, long limbs, arched feet, and constant teasing from classmates.

But Anna Pavlova's persistence along with her love of ballet turned her into one of the most famous Russian ballerinas of her time. Largely remembered for her famous dance The Dying Swan, Pavlova also was the first ballerina to travel the world to bring ballet to people who had never seen it.

Pavlova was born two months premature in February 1881 in St. Petersburg, Russia to an impoverished clothes washer. No one knows for sure who her father was. Pavlova herself claimed her father died when she was 2 years old.

Pavlova's passion for ballet was kindled when Mom took her to see The Sleeping Beauty at the Imperial Mariinsky Theatre. Then, at age 8 she tried out for the renowned Imperial Ballet School. Pavlova was too young and too gawky then but two years later she had matured to their liking. She made her first ballet stage appearance at the school as a cupid in the Maestro Petipa's A Fairy Tale.

Pavlova's years at the Imperial Ballet School were anything but easy. Technique was difficult for her, as well as the teasing from classmates. But she persevered, taking extra lessons, and during her last year at the ballet school she even had solos. She graduated in 1899 at age 18 and her debut with the Imperial Ballet received rave reviews—this time her gawkiness being euphemized—"frail femininity," the critics said.

Pavlova's enthusiasm often got away from her—once during a show in Petipa's The Pharaoh's Daughter her energetic double pique turns caused her to stumble, and she ended up plummeting into the prompter's box.

But Pavlova put those moments aside and continued to improve. She became "first ballerina" in 1906 after stunning dancing in Giselle and by the mid 1900s Pavlova had her very own company and was taking her ballet shoes around the world.

Her most famous attraction, The Dying Swan, was choreographed just for her by Michel Fokine in 1905.

While touring in The Hague, Netherlands, Pavlova was riding on a train that derailed. She was wearing only pajamas and a light scarf but decided to get out of the train to walk around and see what had happened. Three weeks later she died of pneumonia, just a few weeks shy of her 50th birthday.

There's an old ballet tradition that was followed after Pavlova died. On the day she was to have next danced, the show went on as planned, with a single spotlight circling the empty stage. Pavlova's was cremated and her urn was adorned with her ballet shoes. In 2001, after some controversy, her remains were moved to the Novodevichy Cemetery in Moscow—which is what she had wished for.

EXTRA CREDIT: Pavlova is a meringue dessert named after the Russian ballerina. Sometimes simply called 'pav,' it is crispy on the outside and light and fluffy inside.

Rudolf Nureyev

By himself Nureyev is thought of as one of the greatest male ballet dancers of the 20th century and together with Margot Fonteyn, he formed one of the most famous dance partnerships ever.

Nureyev actually came into the world aboard a train—the Trans-Siberian train—near Siberia, Soviet Union. His pregnant mother was aboard the train, heading to Vladivostok, where his Dad, a Red Army political commissar, was stationed. Nureyev did not have any brothers or sisters and was raised in a village near Ufa in Soviet republic of Bashkiria.

When his mother sneaked him and his sisters into a showing of the ballet Song of the Cranes, he was hooked on dance. But getting trained wasn't so easy at first. World War II prevented Nureyev from getting into a major ballet school. It wasn't until he was 17 that he was finally accepted into one.

It was 1955 when he began dancing with the Leningrad Choreographic School. Despite being a late bloomer of sorts, teachers quickly noticed his talents. And soon, Nureyev got a special treat: travel outside the Soviet Union.

But not long after, he got himself into trouble, and was told he would not be allowed to leave again and could only dance with tours inside the Soviet republics.

Then, in 1961 he caught a break. The Kirov Ballet's leading male dancer was injured. You guessed it—Nureyev was sort of runner up. It was a European tour and in Paris, Nureyev electrified audiences and critics alike.

The rule-breaking Nureyev, however did another no-no and mingled with foreigners. The KGB wanted to send him back to the Soviet Union immediately. So they tricked him, telling him he would not be going on to London with the tour because he had a special dance to do at the Kremlin. Nureyev was afraid that if he returned to the Soviet Union he would be locked up. Why? He thought the KGB was after him for being gay, which he was.

So on June 17, 1961 at the airport in Paris, Nureyev defected. Which certainly had no impact on his dancing career. Within just one week, he was dancing with a major ballet in The Sleeping Beauty.

While on tour in Denmark he fell in love with dancer Erik Bruhn, director of the Royal Swedish Ballet, and later the Paris Opera Ballet, both of which Nureyev then danced for.

Despite Nureyev being nearly two decades younger than Fonteyn, their pairing garnered never-before-seen international acclaim. They danced together well beyond Nureyev's departure from the Royal Ballet and their last performance together was in Baroque Pas de Trois in 1988. Fonteyn was 69 years old, Nureyev was 50.

During the 1970s, Nureyev appeared in several films and toured the United States in a revival of the Broadway musical The King and I. One of his more unusual showings was on the television series The Muppet Show—he danced with none other than Miss Piggy.

In 1982 Nureyev was appointed director of the Paris Opera Ballet. Towards the end of his life, Nureyev was sick AIDS, but worked passionately on Paris Opera Ballet shows.

Nureyev was very close with his mother. He had petitioned the Soviet government for many years to be allowed to visit her but was not allowed to until 1989. She was then dying. Mikhail Gorbachev allowed the visit.

At his last dance, a 1992 production of La Bayadère, the crowd stood and cheered. The French Culture Minister gave him the country's highest cultural award. He died in Paris a few months later, 54 years old.

His tomb at his grave at a Russian cemetery near Paris is draped in a variety of oriental Turkic-style carpet. Nureyev loved collecting beautiful carpets and old clothes.

Roman Polanski: Film Director, Writer, Actor, and Producer

Roman Polanski was born as Rajmund Roman Liebling in Paris in the early 1930s. Known for a dramatic and tumultuous life, he is one of the most celebrated arthouse filmmakers of Hollywood history.

In 1969, Polanski's wife, Sharon Tate, was murdered by the Manson Family in the famous Charles Manson mass murder. In 1979, he was arrested and pleaded guilty to having unlawful sexual intercourse with a thirteen-year-old and fled back to France to escape sentencing. He is still looked upon as a fugitive by the United States. Polanski refuses to return to the United States for fear of arrest but continues to produce films in Europe, his most recent being Oliver Twist in 2005.

Famous Works
- *Knife in the Water* (1962)
- *Rosemary's Baby* (1968)
- *Macbeth* (1971)
- *Chinatown* (1974)
- *Tess* (1979)
- *Pirates* (1986)
- *Bitter Moon* (1992)
- *The Ninth Gate* (1999)
- *The Pianist* (2002)
- *Oliver Twist* (2005)

Awards
- BAFTA Award for Best Direction, 1974, *Chinatown*
- Golden Globe Award for Best Director-Motion Picture, 1975, *Chinatown*
- César Award for Best Director, 1980, *Tess*
- Academy Award for Best Director, 2002, *The Pianist*
- BAFTA Award for Best Direction, 2002, *The Pianist*
- César Award for Best Director, 2002, *The Pianist*

Tolkien, Back to Work!

The negligence of responsibilities sometimes leads to greatness. Almost everyone has heard of *The Lord of the Rings*, even if they haven't read J. R. R. Tolkien's masterpiece of fantasy fiction. Because of the immense popularity of the film adaptation of the three-part series, Frodo has become a household name and someone who doesn't know about Gollum obviously lives in a cave. The recent sensation is a renaissance of the excitement that occurred half a century before. At the time the author published his trilogy, he also worked for *The Oxford English Dictionary*, but according to legend, he wasn't working enough.

During his tenure at Oxford, Tolkien began writing texts about a fantasyland known as Middle-earth, including *The Hobbit* and *The Lord of the Rings*. A language scholar at Pembroke College, Tolkien had duties that included etymological work on the dictionary, as well as giving lectures on Old and Middle English. The basis for the trilogy roots itself in Tolkien's infatuation with language; a point demonstrated by the presence of fictional language within the texts. During the years following the publication of Tolkien's novels, it came to Oxford's attention that for the past several years his promises of academic publications had been neglected. Upon the overwhelming success following the publication of the trilogy's final book, The Return of the King, in 1955, Oxford understood why the promises hadn't been fulfilled. Tolkien received a polite reprimand from Oxford. He responded quickly with a lecture on Celtic in the English language, which he presented on October 21, 1955, one day following the publication of the trilogy's finale.

THE BELL RINGER'S SAVIOR

A church bell ringer is a vocation no modern genius would pursue. On pleasant days in the eighteenth century, it was an honest enough career path, but heaven forbid that the sky display its powerful fury. For centuries people believed that lightning and its combustive force existed as a demonstration of God's will. With a booming cacophony, light demons filled the air, crashing into churches and homes. The method for frightening away these demons with reverent resonance came in the form of ringing church bells. Much to the dismay of the unfortunate soul whose duties included noisily distracting the devils, lightning had a taste for bell towers, regardless of reverent efforts. Many a ringer met his maker in the line of pious duty.

Not everyone thought that the sky's great crashes and illuminations represented a supernatural force. One such thinker was Benjamin Franklin. In the mid 1700s, curious minds began experimenting to discover the properties of electricity. In 1743, Franklin met a man in Boston named Dr. Archibald Spencer, whose public demonstrations were thought by many to be magic. Inspired by Spencer, Franklin began conducting his own tests of electricity. Soon, after numerous mildly shocking experiments, he began to draw several comparisons between electricity and lightning, based on their respective colors and course of movement. Much to the amusement of the esteemed Royal Society of London, Franklin sought to prove that what had long been thought to be God's wrath not only resembled electricity, but in fact was electricity.

One stormy afternoon in June 1752, Franklin's opportunity arose. Armed with a silk kite curiously crafted with a protruding metal rod, he and his son William set out to a field near their home, possibly passing a justifiably apprehensive bell ringer on their short journey. Once the kite was sailing into the darkening skies, the duo took shelter in a nearby shed to keep dry the silk string separating Franklin and a metal key tied to the cord. Franklin had experienced mild electric shocks in previous controlled experiments within his workshop. His hypothesis about lightning would be proven if he received a similar shock by touching the key, which would conduct the anticipated current.

Minutes passed and the pair noticed that the kite string had begun to fray. Because he was certain that his success was imminent, but also anxious of being electrocuted, Franklin cautiously touched his knuckle to the metal key. Upon contact he received a familiar jolt that assured him that he had been correct… lightning is electricity!

Franklin's pragmatic lightning research led to the lightning rod, a useful device designed to draw the sky's violent charges away from ships, homes, and church towers. In past experiments with electricity, Franklin had determined that electricity traveled more effectively in some materials than others, particularly metals and water. With this knowledge in mind, he assembled a long metal shaft connected to a wire. By placing the rod at the peak of a home and burying the wire, the electrical charge carried by bolts of lightning was safely rerouted. For years after, the groundbreaking invention spared buildings from flame and their inhabitants, and perhaps a few bell ringers, from electrocution and death.

Wes Anderson: American Writer, Producer, and Director

Hailing from Houston, Texas, Wes Anderson grew up the son of an advertiser and an archaeologist. He attended St. John's School, a private Houston school that he later used in his second film, Rushmore. He met actor Owen Wilson at the University of Texas. Together they produced a short-film version of the later hit Bottle Rocket and attracted the notable producer James Brooks.

Anderson is known as an auteur, as he is involved in almost all aspects of the production of his films, including writing, designing, music selection, cinematography, and direction. He notes French directors Francois Truffaut and Louis Malle as major influences in his work and approach to film.

Often, Wes Anderson features the same actors and collaborators in his movies. Some of his most prominent collaborators are Owen Wilson, Luke Wilson, Bill Murray, Anjelica Huston, Noah Baumbach, Robert Yeoman, Jason Schwartzman, and Eric Chase Anderson, his brother.

Criticism and Acclaim

- After the release of Bottle Rocket, many thought Anderson would become a major voice in American cinema.

- Filmmaker Martin Scorsese wrote raving reviews and praise about Anderson's films in an Esquire article.

- The Royal Tenenbaums garnered an Academy Award nomination and heavy praise for Anderson.

- Anderson has been criticized for his allegedly shallow and stereotypical portrayals of minority characters in his films.

Wes Anderson's Major Films
Bottle Rocket (1996)
Rushmore (1998)
The Royal Tenenbaums (2001)
The Life Aquatic with Steve Zissou (2004)
The Darjeeling Limited (2007)

Short Films
Bottle Rocket (1994)
Hotel Chevalier (2007)

> "I want to try not to repeat myself. But then I seem to do it continuously in my films. It's not something I make any effort to do. I just want to make films that are personal, but interesting to an audience. I feel I get criticized for style over substance, and for details that get in the way of the characters. But every decision I make is how to bring those characters forward."
>
> —Wes Anderson

Crash Course
Chaos Theory

Chaos theory was born in the 1960s from a desire to perfectly predict weather patterns. A meteorologist, Edward Lorenz, was working a weather prediction problem using a set of 12 equations to model weather. His system couldn't predict weather itself but did accurately suggest what the weather might be. In 1961, Lorenz wanted to look at a particular weather sequence again. He began in the middle of the sequence, instead of the beginning, and entered the numbers from his printout. When he checked his results, he found that the weather sequence had evolved in a drastically different way from the original. Eventually, he realized that he had entered the data only to three decimal points, when the original data was worked to six. From this, he derived that merely the tiniest change in a weather pattern, down to a fraction as small as a millionth, could drastically change a long-term pattern.

Today, the idea is commonly referred to as the "butterfly effect," because the variance in the starting points in the two curves of Lorenz's weather patterns were comparable to a butterfly flapping its wings.

Where Does Chaos Come In?

The name chaos theory comes from the fact that the systems the theory describes appear to be entirely disordered and unconnected. Chaos theory is really about finding the order that actually controls the apparently random data.

Six Degrees to the Indestructible Iron Man

1. Emily Brontë (1818–1848) died of tuberculosis. One of the three famous Brontë sisters, Emily wrote *Wuthering Heights* (1847) under a pen name so that people wouldn't know she was a woman. The novel is now considered a classic. She caught a cold at her brother's funeral, refused to treat it, and it became tuberculosis and her untimely death at age thirty.

2. Emily Brontë's poetry was read at Emily Dickinson's (1830–1886) funeral. Dickinson was an American poet. She spent the better part of her life in seclusion and published almost none of her work. Only after her death was her poetry discovered. Her poetry is crafted and intentionally technical but still easy to read.

3. Ted Hughes (1930–1998) edited a book of Dickinson's poetry. Hughes was an English poet and children's writer. He served as Poet Laureate for the United Kingdom from 1984 until his death. One of his children's stories, *The Iron Man*, was the basis for the animated film *The Iron Giant*.

4. Ted Hughes was married to Sylvia Plath (1932–1963). Plath was an American poet and novelist. Her deeply personal poetry is full of elegant metaphors. She wrote the novel *The Bell Jar* (1963), a semi-autobiographical work that describes the ever worsening mental illness of a young girl. Plath's own mental illness ended with her taking her own life just one month after the book was published.

5. Actor Gwyneth Paltrow plays the role of Sylvia Plath in the 2003 film *Sylvia*, which documents Plath's adult life.

6. Gwyneth Paltrow plays the role of Pepper Potts in the 2008 film *Iron Man*.

The Amazing Chinese Card Shuffler

When there is gambling to be done, there are millions of dollars to be made. Time is money and talk is cheap, but slow shuffling is not. Casinos hire dealers based on many qualities, one of which is quick and efficient shuffling. Over the last several years the nature of many games, not to mention the reasonable suspicion of casino managers, has led to the use of shuffling machines. For this reason, the card-slinger is slowly going the way of the buffalo. Nonetheless, the ability to shuffle a deck of cards in a flash is a sight to behold, and spectators love it when someone publicly performs the card-shuffling task at record-breaking speed, as did Zheng Taishun of China.

At a *Guinness Book of World Records* event on June 10, 2006, in Fuzhou City, China, Taishun displayed his superior card-shuffling prowess to the amazement of an eager audience. In fact, he did it so fast that several of the onlookers probably missed his display of skill. In only 39.28 seconds, Taishun placed a randomly shuffled deck of cards in order for all suits: Ace - King - Queen - Jack - 10 - 9 - 8 - 7- 6 - 5 - 4 - 3 - 2. The astonishing achievement landed him a position in the 2008 Guinness Book of World Records over the previous champion, Kunihiko Terada of Japan, whose 2004 record was 40.3 seconds.

The accomplishment has granted Taishun some international acclaim, particularly among those who strive to usurp the man his position as the record holder. Little else is known about Taishun, but although his current occupation is not public information, it wouldn't be implausible to discover that in consequence of his extraordinary demonstration he scored a new career and relocated to the gambling hotspot of Macau shortly thereafter.

THE ONE, THE ONLY

- Abraham Lincoln was the only president of the United States to ever be granted a patent. He was the inventor of a hydraulic machine that lifted ships over shoals.

- Gerald Ford was the only president of the United States who was never elected either president or Vice President.

- James Parks is the only person buried in Arlington Cemetery who was also born on the Arlington Cemetery property. He was a former slave of Arlington Estate.

- Nicholas Breakspear was the only Englishman to become Pope. He was Adrian IV, reigning from 1154 to 1159.

- The only sculpture that Michelangelo ever signed was "The Pietà," which he completed in 1500.

- Franklin D. Roosevelt was the only United States President to be elected to the presidency four times.

- James Buchanan was the only United States President who was never married.

Famous Firsts

- In the year 1797, André-Jacques Garnerin was the first person to parachute. He jumped from a balloon over Monceau Park in Paris.
- Sir John Alexander McDonald became the first Prime Minister of Canada in 1867.
- In 1903, Maurice Garin was the first person in history to win the Tour de France.

SIR EDWARD APPLETON: 1947 NOBEL PRIZE FOR PHYSICS

Born in 1892, in Bradford, West Yorkshire, England, Edward Victor Appleton attended Cambridge University, where he studied natural science. During World War I, he served in the Royal Engineers. Then he returned to Cambridge to research atmospheric physics, mainly using radio waves. In 1924, he accepted a position as professor of physics at London University, and he returned to Cambridge in 1936 as professor of natural philosophy.

Appleton's research into the strength of the radio signals indicated a signal during the daytime was constant but varied at night, rising and falling in an almost regular manner. He believed that, at night, his radio received two waves, one traveling directly and the other being reflected by the atmosphere.

Appleton was knighted in 1941 and received the Nobel Prize for physics in 1947. Two years later, he become principal and vice chancellor to the University of Edinburgh, a position he held until his death in 1965.

As he conducted more experiments to prove his theory, Appleton discovered a third atmospheric layer that reflected back shorter wavelengths in daytime as well as at night. They were reflected back with greater strength than the initial layer. Appleton realized that this was the atmospheric layer responsible for reflecting short-wave radio around the world. His findings led Robert Watson-Watt and his colleagues to develop radar, a crucial weapon in war.

FAMOUS LOVERS: CHARLES DICKENS AND MARIA BEADNELL

Biographies lament on behalf of the great novelist Charles Dickens that he experienced a severe heartbreak at an early age when his beloved, and wealthy, Maria Beadnell discovered the truth about him. The young man, not yet as great a writer as he is known today, was hard working but penniless, was ambitious but altogether without heritage. Upon her realization about Dickens's background, she rejected him and left him with his heart in his hand.

The years went by, and the man began to write novels, eventually becoming one of the most famous men in Europe and the Americas. He also married, but the biographies proclaim that the marriage was not a happy one. Although it is difficult to prove, a cynical yet bitterly satisfying legend exists concerning Beadnell's return. According to legend, the lost love turned gold digger, upon connecting the admirer of her youth with the now internationally renowned writer, decided to pay him a visit. While the years gone by had affected Dickens profitably, as his wealth exploded and his celebrity grew to international acclaim, his old crush experienced growth of a different sort.

Over the years, Maria Beadnell had gained considerable weight. So much weight, in fact, that Dickens didn't recognize her when she graced his doorstep one afternoon. Legend has it that the two enjoyed their visit together, and that Dickens found Beadnell just as charming as he had in his youth.

LITERARY SCANDALS

Lewis Carroll and Queen Victoria

The story: It has been long rumored that British writer Lewis Carroll once presented Britain's Queen Victoria with a mathematics text as a jest. Queen Victoria was tremendously impressed with Alice in Wonderland and Through the Looking-Glass, written by Lewis Carroll, the pseudonym of the mathematician Charles Dodgson. According to a well-known myth, the queen requested a copy of his next work, and he responded mischievously by delivering a copy of An Elementary Treatise on Determinants.

The truth: Dodgson held utmost respect for the British court. He undoubtedly felt honored by the queen's appreciation for his work, and when confronted 30 years later with the rumor of the prank, he stated that it was a "silly story," and that "it is utterly false in every particular: nothing even resembling it has occurred." By this point of course, the story was legend.

Virginia Woolf and the Dreadnought Hoax

Academia often lumps notable writers from distinct eras together into periods, but sometimes the grouping of like-minded artists spontaneously occurs because of similar locations and philosophies. In the early twentieth century, one such group developed that included Virginia Woolf, the author of A Room of One's Own. Controversy surrounded the Bloomsbury Group, a collective of artists and writers, because of their hedonistic lifestyle and the antiwar sentiments they expressed during both world wars. While they spent much of their time engrossed in cultural endeavors, they also occasionally gained attention with high-profile pranks. One such incident occurred in 1910 and involved a few well-designed costumes, the newspapers, and a British naval vessel.

On February 10, 1910, the British navy received a telegram announcing the imminent arrival of a group of dignitaries who wished to tour a warship. Shortly thereafter, a group of well-dressed dignitaries from Abyssinia approached Britain's most secret warship, the HMS Dreadnought. After being introduced as princes of Abyssinia, the assembly embarked on an incredibly exclusive tour of the ship. In actuality, the gathering consisted of Woolf and other members of Bloomsbury dressed in fine costumes and phony beards. Woolf and her gang spoke in a mixture of Swahili and Latin, and managed to succeed in their ruse without attracting any unwanted attention from their tour guides. The pranksters immortalized their trick by having a photograph printed in the Daily Mirror. The picture embarrassed the navy, resulting in the caning of one of the participants and national attention for the group.

Useless Trivia

If marrying your thirteen-year-old cousin isn't enough of a red flag to prove you are nuts, then running around the streets of Baltimore in a panic attack—while wearing another man's clothes—should be. Edgar Allan Poe did both. On October 3, 1849, he was found wandering, delirious, and incoherent. He spent the next several days in and out of consciousness at Washington College Hospital and never got the chance to explain the episode before he died four days later. Unfortunately, Poe's physicians and acquaintances never agreed on a cause of death. Some said he had gotten miserably drunk, while others argued that they never smelled liquor on his breath. Every possible condition was considered, but the true tale of his demise may never be known.

John James Audubon: Wildlife Artist

Born in Saint Domingue (now called Haiti), in 1785, John James Audubon grew up in Nantes, France. At age 18, he moved to Pennsylvania, where he studied native birds, drawing them and conducting the first known bird-banding experiment in North America. He and his wife later moved to Kentucky, where Audubon ran a dry-goods store and spent his spare time drawing birds. In the early 1820s, he took a tour following the Mississippi River, drawing birds and taking notes. Even before he left on his tour, he had created an impressive portfolio.

In 1826, Audubon took his art collection to England where his paintings and descriptions of the birds of America made him quite successful. He soon became known as America's foremost wildlife artist. Before the end of his career, Audubon traveled the country several more times, searching for and documenting native birds. John James Audubon died in 1851, at age 66.

The Audubon Society was named in honor of the nation's most famous birder. George Bird Grinnell, one of the founders of the Audubon Society, wanted a name that would draw inspiration for the organization's work of protecting birds and their habitats.

EXTRA CREDIT: John James Audubon painted 435 watercolors of birds during his lifetime. In 1819, he was jailed for bankruptcy.

Interesting Facts About a Few Famous Minds

The lives of geniuses, artistic or otherwise, are sometimes envied by many who aspire to live a life of grandeur. It might be interesting to find out that they weren't always so glamorous. Below are some of the once-held day jobs of notable musicians, authors, actors, and more:

- E.B. White was once a salesman of roach powder.
- Bette Midler worked in a factory chunking pineapple.
- Billie Holiday was a prostitute at one time.
- Madonna worked as a coat check girl in her younger years.
- Christo scrubbed away at a garage car wash.
- Cyndi Lauper cleaned kennels at a veterinary office.
- Warren Beatty sprayed for pests as an exterminator.
- William Shakespeare sold real estate.
- Jack London worked making burlap in a jute mill for $1 per day and at an electrical company shoveling coal.
- Boris Pasternak worked at a chemical factory during World War I.
- Agatha Christie was a pharmacist during World War I.
- At 17, Ernest Hemingway was a reporter for the Kansas City Star.

C. S. LEWIS

Born in Belfast, Ireland, Clive Staples Lewis grew up writing and illustrating adventurous stories about animals. With his brother, Warnie, Lewis created a mythical world called Boxen, which was ruled by animals. As a teenager, he began to write operas and epic poetry and developed a serious interest in Norse mythology, which later influenced his most famous work, The Chronicles of Narnia. Lewis is well known for the Christian parallels in his works and is widely studied by scholars of literature and Christian symbolism.

C. S. Lewis was a close acquaintance of J. R. R. Tolkien, the author of The Lord of the Rings. They taught together at Oxford University and led a literary group called the Inklings. During his friendship with Tolkien, Lewis converted to Christianity. He began doing radio broadcasts about Christianity and gained a wide following of listeners. He had been an atheist from age 13 to age 31, as during those years he viewed religion as a chore. His interests drifted toward the occult and pagan ideas. During his years at Oxford with Tolkien, however, Lewis was reunited with Christianity. In 1931, he joined the Church of England, although Tolkien was a devout Catholic and had encouraged Lewis toward Catholicism. Lewis died in November 1963 and was buried in the churchyard of Holy Trinity Church in Oxford.

November 22, 1963, marked the deaths of three notable men of history. On the same day that C. S. Lewis suffered a fatal collapse, Aldous Huxley died of cancer, and John F. Kennedy was assassinated.

THE CHRONICLES OF NARNIA

Written by C. S. Lewis, *The Chronicles of Narnia* is a seven-novel series of children's books. With over 100 million copies sold in over 40 languages, it is Lewis' most well-known work. Though there are many Christian parallels in the Narnia series, it was not originally intended to be a biblical allegory. The stories instead have a literal meaning, chronicling the lives of a group of children who influence the history of a fictional land. While the stories are full of adventure and vivid ideas, they also present traditional Christian ideas in a way that is accessible to young readers. Also evident in the series is the influence of Greek and Roman mythology and British fairy tales.

The books feature children from the human world who magically find their way to Narnia, where they are summoned to help a lion named Aslan restore the well-being of Narnia. In *The Lion, the Witch and the Wardrobe,* the children join forces with other creatures to defeat the White Witch who has controlled Narnia for a century. This book is perhaps the most famous and has been made into several films and animations.

Certain Christian organizations have criticized the books for suspected pagan themes and supposed heretical depictions of Christ as a lion. Also, many argue that Lewis portrays mythological creatures in a positive light, suggesting the promotion of paganism. Dissenters argue that the stories are not intended to be a biblical allegory but only loosely borrow many images and concepts from mythology, the Bible, and fairy tales.

Notable Young Achievers

Temba Tsheri

At the age of 16, Temba Tsheri, a boy from Nepal, reached the top of Mt. Everest with a hiking group from France. He was the youngest person to ever climb Mt. Everest, which stands at 29,035 feet and claims several climbers' lives per year.

Ruth Elke Lawrence

At the age of 11, Ruth Lawrence passed an entrance exam and was admitted to Oxford to study mathematics. She was the youngest person ever to attend the prestigious college and had to be accompanied to class by her father. Then, she graduated the program in just two years, while most students take three. Lawrence currently teaches at Hebrew University in Jerusalem.

Tatum O'Neal

In 1974, ten-year-old actor Tatum O'Neal won an Academy Award for her roll in the film Paper Moon, making her the youngest actor to ever win an Oscar. After such early success, her career turned to focus mainly on television.

Balamurali Ambati

Born in 1977, Balamurali Ambati graduated from NYU at the age of 13. He then went on to Mount Sinai's School of Medicine, from which he graduated four years later, becoming the youngest doctor in the world in the year 1995. Currently teaching and researching in the field of ophthalmology, Ambati has won countless awards and received many honors for his medical achievements.

CRASH COURSE
STRING THEORY

String theory is a class of thinking in which everything in the universe can be explained by the relative tension on strings. Like musical notes that come from plucking the strings of a guitar, particles are said to be affected by the tension on a string. Unlike a guitar, though, the strings of the universe are not attached to anything, but floating. They are, instead, acted on by the tension of gravity.

String theory is, in essence, a microscopic theory of the way gravity works. Instead of viewing a particle as a point, it is viewed as a loop on a string. Take an electron for example—a string theorist would view an electron as a loop on a string that oscillates in different directions. When viewed under a microscope, at a particular oscillation of the string, the viewer might see an electron. But if the string were to oscillate in a different way, the viewer might actually see a quark, or a photon. In reality, the particle is not a photon, quark, or electron, but actually a string. String theory holds that the universe is actually just…strings!

While there is no empirical proof that string theory is correct, many scientists believe that the theory actually represents a feasible explanation of how the universe works.

EXTRA CREDIT: String theory is sometimes called the Theory of Everything, as it attempts to explain that everything in the entire universe can be viewed as one thing.

FINAL EXAM

1) What famous operas were written by Italian composer Giacomo Puccini?
   - a) La Boheme and Madama Butterfly
   - b) The Barber of Seville and Carmen
   - c) The Marriage of Figaro and Don Giovanni

2) Which celestial bodies did Christopher Wren write about?
   - a) Earth and Sun
   - b) Moon and Venus
   - c) Bo Derek and Angelina Jolie
   - d) Mercury and Pluto

3) Name the first major work by American poet Walt Whitman.
   - a) A Tree's Leaves
   - b) A Picnic in the Grass
   - c) Grass Fire
   - d) Leaves of Grass

4) What is physicist J. Robert Oppenheimer known for creating in the Manhattan Project?
   - a) Catapult
   - b) Bazooka
   - c) Atom bomb
   - d) Subway

5) Artist Paul Cezanne's father wanted him to go into what field?
   - a) Law
   - b) Architecture
   - c) Mathematics
   - d) Medicine

6) Pythagoras developed the Pythagoream theorem as a rule for what subject?
   a) Economics
   b) History
   c) Geometry
   d) Greek

7) How long did it take for famous Italian artist Michelangelo to complete painting the ceiling of the Sistine Chapel?
   a) Forty years
   b) Four years
   c) Four months
   d) Four hours

8) Albert Einstein received the 1921 Nobel Prize in what?
   a) Physics
   b) Astronomy
   c) Relativity
   d) Gravity

9) What is the subject of some of Dutch painter Rembrandt's most moving works?
   a) Himself
   b) Fruit
   c) Landscapes
   d) His wife

10) What peanut-based product did George Washington Carver NOT invent?
   a) Hand lotion
   b) Peanut butter
   c) Mayonnaise
   d) Shaving cream

11) According to legend, what was Greek philosopher Diogenes searching for while walking around Athens with a lamp?
   a) His glasses
   b) A wife
   c) An honest man
   d) A good restaurant

12) John Calvin's translations and interpretations of the Bible were known for what?
   a) Controversy
   b) Readability
   c) Glossy illustrations
   d) Inaccuracy

13) Who did Napoleon place on the thrones of Holland, Italy, Germany, and Spain?
   a) Catholic priests
   b) His brothers and other relatives
   c) His children
   d) French generals

14) Besides the Nobel Prize, what was Alfred Nobel's best known contribution?
   a) Dynamite
   b) Toothbrushes
   c) Paper clips
   d) High-heeled shoes

15) Sally Ride and her team of NASA astronauts she flew with conducted what type of experiments on their space mission?
   a) Anti-gravity
   b) Geological
   c) Pharmaceutical
   d) Exercise

16) What area of the great composer Ludwig van Beethoven's life suffered because he was completely focused on his music?»
    a) His love life
    b) Cleanliness
    c) His social life
    d) Education

17) What was the title of Thomas More's book about a perfect, imaginary city state?
    a) Perfecto
    b) Dream World
    c) Moresland
    d) Utopia

18) Henry the Navigator was actually a Prince of what country?
    a) Portugal
    b) Spain
    c) England
    d) Russia

19) What style of architecture is named for Italian architect Andrea Palladio?
    a) Georgian
    b) Palladian
    c) Modern
    d) Italiano

20) Besides the bizarre images in artist Salvador Dali's surrealist work, what was bizarre about him?
    a) He traveled with an entourage of cats.
    b) He wore only green and shades of purple.
    c) He wore attention-getting clothing such as knee breeches and a deep sea diving suit.
    d) He would never sleep inside the house.

21) Scientific thinker Stephen Hawking is famous for his book titled

_______ .

    a) A Brief History of Time
    b) Time in a Black Hole
    c) Universal Radiation
    d) Hawking Time

22) Visual forms of the numerical Fibonacci sequence can be best seen when one views _______ .
    a) Traffic patterns
    b) Body language
    c) Mob mentality
    d) Nature

23) What did astronomer Edmond Halley correctly predict about the comet named after him?
    a) Its size
    b) Its return
    c) Its color
    d) Its origin

24) Philosopher Lao-tzu is known as the father of what?
    a) Poohism
    b) Schism
    c) Taoism
    d) Monotheism

ANSWERS:

1) a	13) b
2) b	14) a
3) d	15) c
4) c	16) b
5) a	17) d
6) c	18) a
7) a	19) b
8) a	20) c
9) d	21) a
10) b	22) d
11) c	23) b
12) a	24) c